# A DESPERATE DESIRE

"Why *did* you come here?"

"Damned if I know. Maybe 'cause I wanted to see you again, say something that would be an explanation, but I don't have one. Maybe that's what I want to say, after all. I just don't have an explanation, Maggie."

"For not coming here, or for wanting to come here?"

Devon looked startled. "I don't know that, either," he said slowly. "Both, I guess. I know better. If I show up here too much, everybody in town will have us sleeping together, you know that."

"They do anyway."

He looked away with a grimace. "I guess I should have come back and thanked you for helping me, but—"

"I don't want your blasted gratitude!" Her anger took him back, and she was gratified by the wary look in his eyes.

"Then what the hell do you want?"

She stared at him, unable to answer. She didn't know what she wanted. Or maybe she did, because when he reached out to jerk her to him, she fell into his embrace with a muffled cry.

"I know what you want," he muttered in a low, savage tone that sent a shiver down her spine. "Even if you don't."

He tangled his hand in her hair, loosening the knot at her nape so that it spilled down her back. He held her head still, kissing her roughly. His mouth moved from her lips to her throat, then back. She knew she should protest, but her mind wouldn't cooperate with the rest of her. The only thing that seemed to be working properly was the part of her that responded to Devon's touch . . .

# WILDEST HEART

# WILDEST HEART

## VIRGINIA BROWN

ZEBRA BOOKS
KENSINGTON PUBLISHING GROUP

ZEBRA BOOKS are published by

Kensington Publishing Corp.
475 Park Avenue South
New York, NY 10016

Zebra the Z logo are trademarks of Kensington
Publishing Corp.

First Printing: February, 1994

Printed in the United States of America

*To my cousin Jim McKinney and his wife Lydia, who first took me to Belle Plain. Thanks for your patience, and for hiking through the tall weeds and cactus of a ghost town with me. I will always admire your fortitude!*

*And a special thanks to David Bates, who graciously allowed me to use him as the model for Devon, and tried not to be too embarrassed about it.*

# Prologue

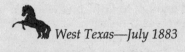 *West Texas—July 1883*

"Cimarrón."

The name hung in the abruptly still air like a sword. Devon Conrad glanced up. His own image was hazily reflected in the mirror over the bar—a blur of pale hair and dark features. Behind him, the distorted face of a stranger waited tensely for his reaction.

Devon turned slowly. One hand stayed close to the pistol tied low on his left thigh. "Yeah?"

"I came to kill you, Cimarrón."

Devon stared at him coldly. He didn't recognize the face, though there was something all too familiar about the stance, the expectant tension that emanated from the stocky man standing with one hand hovering near the pistol he wore high around his waist.

"Do I know you?" Devon asked finally. He didn't want this. All he wanted was a drink, a bath, and sleep. He didn't want to face some man with vengeance or glory on his mind. He was tired. Too tired.

"You knew my brother," the man said, his words a hoarse whisper. "Will Jenkins."

Will Jenkins. Devon thought a moment, then a face flashed in his memory, a blur, just like all the other faces that had confronted him across a dusty street or crowded saloon. He nodded slowly.

"I remember. He braced me down in Tucson."

1

"That's a lie. Will wasn't stupid. Hell, he was only twenty-four years old. Just a kid."

Devon almost laughed. A kid? Not at twenty-four. He was four years older than Will Jenkins, and he'd learned to shoot to kill when he was still in his teens. He'd had to if he wanted to survive. And he survived, though he was damned if he knew why he bothered.

"Your brother was old enough to draw on me in the middle of the street," Devon said wearily. "If a man's old enough to act the fool, he's old enough to die."

"Damn you, Cimarrón, you're a cold-hearted bastard."

"Tell me something I don't know." Devon straightened in a slow, languid motion, recognizing that Jenkins wasn't about to let this go. He'd call him out, and one of them would die. Devon wondered if he cared which one it was, and knew that when the time came, his body would act of its own accord. It always did. When his mind said, *"Forget it,"* his reflexes kept him alive another day. Waste of time, as far as he was concerned. He'd died over three years before, and just hadn't lain down yet.

"Step outside," Jenkins said, and Devon glanced around the now-quiet saloon.

Avid witnesses stood still and silent, afraid to miss something, afraid they might not be able to recount later what Cimarrón said or did. Cimarrón. Another lie in his life. He wasn't that man. But he wasn't Devon Conrad anymore, either, and it had ceased to matter what name he was called.

He looked at Jenkins and was suddenly sick of it all. He decided to try one more time. "What if I don't want to step outside?"

Jenkins stared at him. "You scared?"

"Tired, Jenkins. Drop it. I didn't want to draw on your brother. He forced me into it, and living has been kind of a bad habit of mine. Go home."

"Not until you pay for killing my brother."

Devon took a step away from the bar. His spurs rattled loudly in the hushed room as he deliberately turned his back on Jenkins. "No. I don't want to kill you."

Jenkins stood quivering with outrage in the middle of the floor. "You coward!"

Devon shrugged, but the hand that curled around his glass of whiskey was white-knuckled. Was it that obvious? Could everyone see that he was afraid? Not of dying. No, never that. He was afraid of living forever, lost in his own personal hell.

Jenkins shifted on the sawdust floor, and someone coughed. Devon kept his gaze on his glass of whiskey until he felt the change in the room. He glanced up, saw his own reflection in the gilt-framed mirror over the bar, saw the moment Jenkins made his decision. There was no time for regret, no time for anything.

He turned, hand flashing down, and then his pistol cracked loudly. Jenkins stared at him stupidly, his face beginning to sag into an expression identical to those Devon could see even when he closed his eyes at night. Slowly Jenkins toppled to the floor of the saloon and lay still, his unfired pistol still in his hand.

Devon looked down at the sprawling body. The familiar weight of his heavy Colt fit his hand as if welded there, and he wondered if any of those watching knew how sick at heart he was. He doubted it. No one seemed to care that a man had just died, only that they'd witnessed it.

Murmurs of excitement raced through the room like a prairie fire, growing in intensity as Devon straightened from his half-crouch and holstered his pistol. He dug into his vest pocket, took out a coin, and flipped it to the surface of the bar.

"If the sheriff wants to talk to me, he'll find me over at the hotel," he said to the bartender. The bartender glanced down at the coin, then shoved it back across the bar. Devon looked at it, then up at the bartender.

"Your drinks here are free, Cimarrón."

Devon's eyes narrowed. Ignoring the coin, he turned on his heel and walked out of the saloon. Kill a man and they gave you free drinks. *God*, he wanted to hide from what he'd become. He just didn't know where or how.

## Chapter 1

Maggie Malone stared out the window of the stage as it rocked over rutted roads. Everything looked the same. Texas hadn't changed in her absence, but she had. She wondered if Johnny was as changed as she, then smiled.

No, her brother would never change. He would be as hardheaded as ever, and as lovable. In a crusty sort of way, she amended with a smile. John Clark Malone may not win any prizes for a sweet personality, but he could be charming enough when he wanted to be.

As the miles rolled past, Maggie hoped that Johnny would choose to be charming when she told him her plans for the future. She never knew about him, and what might be acceptable one day would be beyond understanding the next. He was as changeable as the blue northers that roared through Texas every winter.

The stagecoach rocked heavily as it hit a rut in the road, and Maggie had to grab hold of the strap hanging from the side to keep from tumbling to the floor.

"Rough ride," commented the man sitting across from her, and she nodded.

"As usual. Hank Whitten has always managed to hit every rut on this road in the past. I don't suppose he'll start missing them now."

"You from here?"

"Yes." Maggie freed her hand from the strap and looked out the window again.

"You don't talk like you're from west Texas," the man said, and she stifled a resigned sigh.

5

She'd avoided personal conversation since boarding the stage, but now it seemed as if she would have to reply or be rude.

"I've spent the last four years in New York. At school."

"School?" His eyebrows rose as if amazed that a woman would need an education.

"Yes, college." Maggie smothered the impulse to add insult to injury and point out that she had a degree in medicine. Not many men wanted to believe a woman capable of such feats, much less accept a female physician.

"And now you've come home." He cleared his throat, then ran a hand across his jaw, gazing at her for a long moment that seemed to draw out forever. "My name is David Brawley. I'm headed to Belle Plain to meet my partner."

"I hope you enjoy your stay," Maggie said politely. She turned her gaze out the window. She knew better than to ask many questions and give him the opportunity to tell her his life story. She'd much rather watch for the occasional tree relieving the rolling landscape, and look into the distance toward the flat hills which rose stark and familiar against the horizon.

"Maybe you could tell me a little bit about the area," Brawley suggested, and Maggie turned to look at him. He seemed nice enough; brown hair cut neatly, a three-piece suit with string tie and high, starched collars, rather dusty shoes, and a face that she supposed some women she knew would call handsome. His were regular features, with white, even teeth that showed in a pleasant smile.

"What would you like to know?" she asked. If only they would arrive in Belle Plain before this man got too friendly. She wasn't looking for male companionship. Men would only complicate her life. Except for Johnny, of course.

Shrugging, David Brawley said, "Oh, just little things, I guess. Things my partner wouldn't think to tell me."

Maggie laughed. "There's not much to tell. Belle Plain was going to be the county seat, and was for a while, until the railroad bypassed us on its way to Abilene. Now people are moving out, sort of drifting toward Baird, where the railroad is selling its own lots and making money. The cattlemen have made Abilene a shipping point, and since it's so close to Baird, the locals can ship merchandise from our county seat. Prices are cheaper." She surveyed him for a moment. "What's your business?"

"Hotels."

Maggie was startled. "I had no idea that Belle Plain had grown enough to lure such businesses."

"It was my understanding the cattlemen persuaded the railroad to build a spur to include Belle Plain. If so, the increased business will more than support a new hotel."

"I wonder why Johnny didn't tell me about that?" Maggie mused aloud.

"Johnny?"

"My brother. We—he—owns the Double M." That still hurt, that their parents had left the ranch entirely to her brother, though she knew in her heart that she would never have wanted it. She'd been left furniture and a comfortable amount of money instead.

"The Double M? A ranch, I presume."

Maggie smiled. "Yes. It's the prettiest spread in Callahan County, though not as big as the 74 Ranch. But the Double M is doing well enough. I can't take any credit for its success, however, as my brother runs it."

"Then he is doubly blessed," David Brawley said with a smile that Maggie recognized. She knew what was coming when he finished, "For he has not only a successful ranch, but a very beautiful sister."

"I'm sure he would argue the point with you, sir."
When Brawley opened his mouth—to offer another
flowery compliment, she was afraid—she added
quickly, "There is Belle Plain just ahead."

It wasn't that she was falsely modest about her
looks, for she knew she was attractive to men, but she
found it the height of irritation to field easy compliments. If she agreed, she sounded vain; if she disagreed, she sounded as if she were fishing for a more
elaborate description of her "exotic beauty." The last
was a recent depiction she'd found particularly hard to
swallow and had made the mistake of bursting into
laughter, thus angering the earnest young man voicing
such sentiments.

When the stage rolled to a halt in front of Merchant's
General Store on Callahan Street, Maggie wrenched
open the door and stepped down before David Brawley could offer to help. She caught a brief glimpse of
his outstretched hand, but ignored it in her eagerness
to see her brother again.

"I'm sure I'll see you again soon, Mr. Brawley," she
called with a wave of one hand, and saw him pause
uncertainly by the stage. Too bad. He'd have to accept
disinterest gracefully.

With her skirts lifted just above her ankles, Maggie
navigated the ruts in the dirt road and reached the
wooden walkway in front of the store. She stepped up
and into the shade, half-blinded by the transition from
hot glare to diffused light.

Still holding her skirts in her left hand, she reached
for the door with her right. A loud yelp sounded from
just under her feet, and she jumped back, startled as a
small dog bolted off the porch. Too late, she realized
that someone was right behind her as she bumped into
him. She heard a masculine *whoof!* and tried to regain
her balance as she began to fall.

A low, rough oath sounded in her ear, but there was

no time to be offended by language she'd heard from her brother on more than one occasion. She reached blindly for something to stop her fall. Strong hands grasped her upper arms, and Maggie was shoved upright.

She was turning to thank her rescuer when he growled, "There not enough room on that porch for you, ma'am?"

Maggie's temper flared, and she shot back, "There is when I don't have to share it with a dog and a cowboy at the same time."

Half-embarrassed, half-angry, she wrenched free of the man's steadying hand and looked up at him, shoving her hat back out of her eyes so she could see. The feather bobbed, and she felt the satin ribbons holding her hat give way, so that she had to grab the bonnet before it slipped from her head.

Her rescuer stared back at her coolly, and Maggie had the startling thought that she'd never seen eyes so blue. Or so cold. They regarded her from beneath a fan of thick, lush lashes that should belong to a woman if Mother Nature had any generosity at all, and were set in a dark face that was tanned even darker by the sun. It was obvious this man had Moorish ancestors in his family somewhere, because few men with hair that blond would be so dark.

Speech momentarily failed her, and Maggie stood like a tongue-tied schoolgirl while the handsome cowboy regarded her with growing amusement.

"Did you step on your tongue, ma'am?" he drawled.

Maggie swallowed. "No, but I think I dropped my manners. Thank you for catching me."

"I always try to catch beautiful women before they knock me into the street."

"Judging by the dust on your clothes, you must not be very good at it," she said, and could cheerfully have

bitten her tongue the moment the words were out. "I
. . . I mean—"

"No, I guess I do have a few inches of trail dust on
me." The blue eyes softened slightly, making her think
of the noonday sky, bright and painful at the same
time. "Nice of you to remind me."

Maggie felt a dull, hot flush creeping up her neck to
her face. She'd rarely been so rude on so short an ac-
quaintance. She gripped her bonnet tightly and cleared
her throat.

"Really, I apologize for being rude. I shouldn't have.
I've frequently been told that I speak out of turn."

"Have you?" A faint smile curved his hard mouth,
easing the harshness of his features. He flicked a
glance up and past her, then looked down. His smile
widened. "Do you always shred your hats?"

"Pardon?"

His hand was warm, not as rough as she would have
thought it would be when he reached down and took
the hat from her hand. He held it up, and Maggie
blinked as she looked at the shredded feather. What
had been a thick, curved ostrich feather now looked as
if it belonged to a scrawny chicken.

"I only shred feathers when I feel particularly embarrassed," she said frankly, and he grinned. She
barely had time to think what a nice, engaging smile he
had when she heard her brother's familiar bellow coming from across the street.

"Maggie! Maggie, what in Sam Hill are you doin'?"

She lifted a brow and saw the cowboy tense. "That's
just my brother," she explained. "He's more holler
than harm."

"I know you won't mind if I don't take your word
for it."

Maggie could understand. Johnny Malone could
look mean as a yard dog when he chose, and she knew
that he chose to more often than not. Kept trouble at

bay, he'd once said, if he looked like he could skin a live panther with his teeth. But this man wouldn't know that, and she could understand if he felt intimidated by Johnny.

When she turned to explain the situation to Johnny, she saw that he looked as worried as he did mad, and wondered why.

"Johnny," she began when he drew near, but her brother cut her off.

"Get out of the way, Maggie."

Slightly startled by his brusque order, she hesitated. He reached out and jerked her to him, and she stumbled.

"What is the matter with you, Johnny Malone?" she demanded angrily. "Have you taken leave of your senses?"

He flashed her a baffled look. "Have you? What do you mean, standin' here chattin' cozily with a man like him?"

"I'm not 'chatting cozily,' as you put it. I'm apologizing for being rude."

Johnny's square jaw thrust out. "Rude? You? Did this man insult you, Maggie?"

"No, you buffalo-eared lunatic, I almost knocked him into the street, and he saved us both from falling. What is the matter with you?"

Dark eyes darted from Maggie to the man's carefully blank face, and Johnny snapped, "Don't you know who this is?"

"No, we haven't been properly introduced." Irritated, and more than a little mystified by her brother's behavior, Maggie glanced at the stranger again.

His lean frame was posed in a stance of masculine aggressiveness that said much more than her brother's sharp words. Even his body conveyed a clear message that he would not tolerate insults lightly. Before

Johnny explained, she knew what he must be, if not
who he was.

"Cimarrón," Johnny growled, as if that would explain everything. Maggie shrugged.

"Cimarrón. I don't know who that is."

"He's a gunny. Killed Mort Baxter last month in El
Paso. Killed a man named Jenkins yesterday down in
Ed Murphy's saloon." Johnny glared at Cimarrón.
"Man like that don't need to be talkin' to decent
women."

"I'm afraid he didn't have much choice," Maggie cut
in when it looked as if her brother might say something else as insulting as the last. "After I almost
knocked him into the street, he had to speak."

A nervous shiver washed through her when she
glanced at the man called Cimarrón and saw his cold
gaze directed at her brother. Didn't Johnny have any
sense at all? If this man was what he said, then he'd be
quite capable of drawing on her brother for insulting
him.

She turned to him, but Cimarrón's attention was
trained on Johnny. He hadn't spoken or moved, but
there was something so predatory about him, so dangerous, that her voice came out shakily.

"Sir, I appreciate your courtesy. If there has been
any misunderstanding, I'm sorry."

He flicked her a glance at last, a quick, ice blue slice
of his eyes that made her pulses leap. "No need to
apologize, ma'am. Quick tempers seem to run in your
family." He touched one finger to the brim of his hat
and moved past them. The door creaked as he opened
it.

"What did he mean by that?" Johnny demanded
when Cimarrón stepped into the store. He glared
down at Maggie, and she didn't know whether to sag
with relief or tell him what an idiot she thought him
for provoking a man he knew to be dangerous. Of

course, Johnny wouldn't think of it that way. He backed down for no man.

"He probably meant just what he said—we both have evil tempers." Maggie tucked a hand into the crook of his arm. "I guess this is your way of telling me you're glad I'm home?"

Johnny grinned suddenly, and Maggie saw the reason most of the females in Belle Plain threw themselves at him. He was a handsome charmer with dark hair like hers and eyes so dark gray they were almost black.

"Yeah, kinda. Actually, I wanted to surprise you with flowers, but all I could find was some bluethorn. That good enough?"

"From you, yes," she retorted with a smile. "I wouldn't expect anything different."

"Where's your stuff?" Johnny asked as he escorted her across the porch and out into the sunlight again. Heat struck her, and dust rose in a choking cloud as a wagon rolled slowly down the street.

"If I know Hank Whitten, it's still on top of the stage."

"Likely." Johnny hugged her, one arm draped casually over her shoulders. "Glad you're home. Now things can get back to normal."

"I shudder to think what that might be."

"Yeah. There's been a bit of trouble lately, but nothing I can't handle."

"Trouble?"

"Somebody's runnin' a maverick factory. We just got to find out who and where."

"Rustlers?"

"Made off with cattle from every ranch in these parts. I hear Zeke Rogan's hired some fast guns to help him find 'em, but I don't know if I want to go that far." His eyes darkened to a stormy gray. "Brings in men like Cimarrón, and we don't need that."

"Is that why he's here?"

"Hell, I don't know. But if I have my way, he'll be ridin' out again quick like."

"Don't let your temper get you killed, John Malone," Maggie said sharply, and saw her brother's eyes light with that stubborn gleam she knew well.

"Did I say I was gonna do anything? That's up to Ben."

"If you mean Ben Whittaker, all of Callahan County could fill up with gunslingers and bank robbers, and he wouldn't do anything." She flashed him an impatient glance. "The only man more worthless than Whittaker is six feet under, as far as I'm concerned."

"Aw, Maggie, you've still got a tongue that can skin a mule," Johnny grumbled. "Didn't that fancy school teach you anything useful?"

"Useful enough." Maggie had no intention of telling her brother about her plans. There was time enough for that argument later. Now she just wanted a hot bath and a good meal. "Let's have Hank bring my trunks to the hotel. I'm dying for something cool to drink and fresh clothes."

"Go on then, sugar. I'll take care of your stuff."

"Be careful," Maggie said. "Some of those trunks have very breakable things in them."

"Sure thing, sugar. I'll catch up to you."

Maggie picked her way across the rutted street, waving at former acquaintances. Belle Plain hadn't seemed to change that much at all. It was still a sleepy little town in the middle of the vast Texas prairie, sunbaked and serene in the noonday sun. Nothing ever happened in Belle Plain.

## CHAPTER 2

"Heard you killed two of Bart Starkey's men in Dodge last year."

Devon didn't reply. He just stared at Zeke Rogan until the other man shifted and glanced toward the open saloon doors and deep night shadows outside.

"Yeah, well," Rogan muttered, turning back to him. "After yesterday, I guess you're quick enough. Frank says you got Jenkins before he cleared leather."

"You want a recital, Rogan, or you want me to catch your damn rustlers?" Devon asked impatiently. "If you're having second thoughts, I can give you back your money and ride on. It doesn't matter a damn to me."

"No, no second thoughts, Cimarrón."

"Don't call me that."

"Cimarrón?" Rogan's fleshy face creased in surprise. "Isn't that your name?"

Devon shrugged. "Yeah. Forget it. What do you want me to do?"

"Like I told you, I need men to catch rustlers. I've lost too many cattle, and it's costing me money. Maybe you could ride herd—"

"I'm not a cowpuncher."

"Hell, I know that. I've got plenty of those. I need a man who's quick with a gun to ride along, see what he can find out, then take care of it."

"Thought the law handled that sort of thing."

"Normally they do. Texas is too damn big and the

15

law round here is too damn slow. Sheriff Whittaker's all right at shootin' stray dogs, but I'm losing money, and I don't want to sit around and wait for a tin star to show up and decide he can't handle it either."

Devon nodded. "Fine. When do you want me to ride out?"

"Tomorrow's soon enough. Frank here will show you around the Bar Z." Zeke Rogan's chest swelled. "It's so damn big you can't ride it all in a week."

Devon watched the beefy rancher as he began to brag. He wasn't at all certain he wanted to take this job. Catching rustlers wasn't new to him, but he disliked being tied down to one spot too long. Folks got to wondering about him when he did, asking questions, thinking that maybe he wasn't as fast as they'd heard, that they might make a name for themselves as the man who'd killed Cimarrón. It could be a damn nuisance, and he might have moved on if he didn't have another reason for being in Belle Plain. This job would save a lot of unnecessary questions being asked.

He stood up abruptly, interrupting Zeke Rogan's monologue of success. Devon tossed a coin to the table to pay for his drink and ignored Rogan's look of surprise.

"I'll meet you at the livery stable in the morning."

"Sure, sure, Cimarrón," Rogan said, glancing at his hired hand. "Frank can be there at daybreak."

"Eight's soon enough."

Rogan looked confounded, but recovered quickly. "Sure. I guess eight's fine."

Devon felt their stares, as well as most of the others in the saloon as he strode to the swinging doors and pushed them open. It always made him edgy to have men at his back. He'd been shot at from behind too many times to trust them.

He was glad to feel the wash of cool air on his face and breathed deeply. Belle Plain was a quiet little town. It boasted two saloons, a few stores, a blacksmith's, one hotel, and a livery stable. Other than that, the neat stone buildings belonged to the citizens. It had been laid out in a perfect square by the founding fathers, but the railroad's fickleness might doom the town. Too bad.

Devon stepped off the sidewalk and into the street. Off in the distance, a coyote howled. A dog barked an answer, and the wind blew softly. He crossed to the hotel and paused before going in.

Habit made him look up and down the street, and when he caught a glimpse of movement, he turned swiftly, his hand dropping to the gun on his thigh.

"Wait!" a feminine voice said. "I'm harmless."

"That's a matter of opinion," Devon said when Maggie Malone stepped into a pool of light streaming through one of the hotel windows. "Your brother almost shot me today just for talking to you."

"You're a big boy. I think you can handle my brother."

Her saucy reply made him smile. He remembered how she'd looked at him earlier, her big gray eyes wide and assessing beneath a curtain of lashes. He'd liked it. And he liked the way she took up for him, even though it had irritated him at the time. Maggie Malone was a potent female, and he knew better than to get involved. His entanglements with women were usually swift and painless. No fuss, no bother, no trying to hang on. That's the way he wanted it.

Maybe that's why he was surprised to hear himself say, "Maybe I can handle your brother, but I'm not so sure about handling you."

"What makes you think I can be handled?"

"Quick and to the point, aren't you?" Devon drawled.

"It saves time."

"And what do you do with all that time you've saved, Maggie Malone?"

Her dark head tilted to one side, and he spared a moment's admiration for her before she said, "Insult cowboys who try to help me."

"I'm not a cowboy."

"And you weren't helping me. You were just trying to keep from being knocked into the street."

Amused, Devon leaned back against a wooden porch post and reached into his vest pocket for his cigarette makings. "So where's your watchdog?"

"Johnny? If I know my brother, he's showing one of the prettiest girls in Belle Plain the stars."

"Not a bad idea."

"It's our main attraction. Besides coyotes and cactus, that is."

Devon struck a match, held it to his cigarette, watched her over the curl of smoke that drifted up. "So why did you come back to Belle Plain?" he asked when it was lit.

"How'd you know I was gone? Been asking questions about me?"

"No." He pinched the match out. "I saw your brother helping unload your trunks. No one hauls around that many trunks unless they've been gone a while."

"You're very observant." She walked to the edge of the porch and looked out over the street. He could smell a faintly familiar fragrance, and it took him a moment to recognize it.

*Roses.*

His belly knotted, and his eyes closed with pain he'd hoped to put behind him. The sweet scent of roses always hit him hard, made him think of things he wanted to avoid. When he opened his eyes, she was looking at him curiously.

"Are you all right?"

His voice was harsh. "I'm fine. Why are you out here talking to me? Aren't you afraid your brother will get mad?"

"Aren't you?" she countered.

"I'm used to angry men."

"So I hear."

Devon felt a spurt of irritation. "Got an answer for everything, don't you?"

She wet her lips with her tongue in a female gesture that made him ache suddenly. Her voice was a soft whisper. "No, I don't. I've got lots of questions without answers."

He shifted restlessly. "Yeah. So do I."

A silence fell between them. It wasn't uncomfortable, nor awkward. He was surprised by that. It should have been. The few decent women he'd had contact with in the past years had been uneasy in his presence, and he'd grown used to it. Saloon girls were more his style, and those were taken only to satisfy a basic physical need.

Maggie Malone was definitely not a saloon girl. Though she was no longer wearing the fancy dress with too many yards of material that hid a woman's best curves, she was still every inch a lady. Her outfit showed off her small waist and tempting curves without making a man feel like he'd be hugging horsehair and crinoline instead of warm female. It was a tempting thought.

"Have you ever looked through a telescope?" she asked, and he gave her a startled glance.

"No."

"You ought to. There are more stars than I ever dreamed existed, and if you're using a powerful lens, you can see almost into infinity." She turned and looked at him, and he noticed how dreamy her eyes were, soft, luminous, light-tricked in the pale glow of a lamp. His heart lurched oddly, and it took him a moment to decipher her next words.

"I have a telescope I brought back home with me. Would you like to look at the stars?"

Before he realized it, Devon said yes, and Maggie smiled at him.

"Good. Come on."

He hesitated. "Where is it?"

"In my room upstairs. We can take it up to the roof. The town lights sometimes diffuse things."

"I don't know," he began, but she was already walking to the hotel doors, obviously expecting him to follow. For some reason, Devon did.

The lobby was almost deserted. A man stood behind the desk, and looked up and frowned when he saw them come in together.

"Miss Malone, are you having any problems?"

"No, of course not. Is the door to the roof unlocked?"

The man looked startled, and Devon almost sympathized with him.

"Unlocked?" he repeated, flashing Devon a tight glance. "Why—"

"I want to go onto the roof, Mr. Brawley." Maggie paused and turned around. "That should be obvious. Would you mind unlocking it if it's fastened? I won't be but a moment."

Devon's amusement grew at the baffled rage on the man's face when Maggie turned away, obviously expecting Brawley to grant her request. As he followed Maggie's slender figure up the stairs to her room, he could imagine the thoughts running through Brawley's mind. He'd be wondering, too, if it was him.

Maggie stopped, fished a room key out of her pocket and held it out to Devon. It took him a noticeable instant before he realized he was supposed to be gentlemanly and unlock her door, and he hoped he wasn't flushing like a kid.

"I'll wait out here," he said when he'd swung it open for her. At her laughing glance, he added wryly, "I'm not in the mood for fighting big brothers tonight."

"Excellent thinking. I won't be but a moment."

Maggie Malone, Devon discovered a few minutes later, was a complete surprise. After their first introduction, he hadn't expected to see her again, much less be invited to view stars through a telescope. Yet, here he was, up on a roof in Belle Plain, Texas, looking at stars through a clumsy apparatus that resembled a thick lead pipe on legs.

"Do you see anything?" Maggie asked, absorbed in fiddling with knobs and dials on the telescope.

"A blur." Devon squinted. "Ah. Now I see something."

"What?"

"It looks like . . . a pink cigar."

"That's my finger, silly. Look again."

Laughing, he did, and saw a flash of brilliant white. He recoiled, then squinted again.

"Damn," he breathed, fascinated. "It looks like white fire."

"That's what it is. Some of them are in colors. Let's see if we can find a planet. Those don't twinkle."

"What—do you have a map of the sky or something?"

"Or something."

She stepped close, and he caught a whiff of fragrance again, sweet and pleasant. Maggie Malone smelled good, damn good, and it made his belly knot.

When she edged in front of him and adjusted the telescope to her height, he stayed where he was, enjoying the feel of her so close. Her shirtwaist dress was feminine without frills, and her silky black hair was braided into a sensible coil on her neck. But to Devon, she was the most alluring woman he'd seen in a long time.

He felt a pang of betrayal and stepped back.

This wasn't supposed to happen. Physical need was one thing; actually *liking* a woman was another thing entirely.

As if she felt his withdrawal, Maggie turned around and surveyed him for a long moment. "You don't have to look at the stars, you know."

"I know." He looked away from her, gazing out over the rooftops, then looked back. "What are you doing up here with me, Maggie Malone? Don't you know what people will say? What your brother will say?"

"No. What will they say?"

His voice was rough. "They'll say you must be crazy to come up here with a man like me."

"What kind of man are you?"

"Didn't you listen to your brother?"

"Johnny blows steam like a boiling tea kettle. What was I supposed to hear?"

"I've killed men, Miss Malone."

Starlight illuminated her face, and she gazed up at him with serious gray eyes. "Yes, I know that."

Devon stared back at her in exasperation. "Don't you care?"

"Not as much as you do, I'm willing to bet."

When Devon couldn't reply, thunderstruck, she smiled faintly. "You don't seem like the kind of man who kills for the pleasure of it. If you were, you wouldn't have listened to my brother's insults today."

"The way he was shouting them, it would have been hard not to listen," Devon muttered.

"You know what I mean. Your reputation as a mad-dog killer is slightly in error, I believe, Mr. Cimarrón."

Devon raked a hand through his hair and sucked in a deep breath. "My name's not Cimarrón."

"What is it?"

"Devon Conrad."

She repeated it softly and smiled. "I much prefer that to the other. Do you mind if I call you Mr. Conrad?"

"Devon suits me better."

"Devon then." She glanced away from him, and he thought she had the purest profile he'd ever seen. When she looked back at him and said, "I think Venus is visible now," he felt like agreeing. She was beautiful. And she expected him to stare up at the sky. He obliged.

"I'll never look at the stars the same way," he said, peering through the telescope.

"Neither will I."

He turned and looked at her, and felt an odd loosening in his chest. He knew, then, that this girl was going to matter to him, and he didn't want that. He looked away, focusing on stars that were as distant and unattainable as the hopes he'd once held so dearly.

# CHAPTER 3

"What in the blue hell do you mean—a doctor?"

Maggie gazed calmly at her infuriated brother. Sunlight slanted through the open window of the parlor and onto the neat, planked floor of the house where she'd been born. It was already hot, but she couldn't suppress a shiver at the anger mirrored in Johnny's dark gray eyes, anger mixed with disbelief.

"I mean just what it sounds like, Johnny. A physician, you know, one trained in the healing arts, a surgeon, dentist, or even a veterinarian. A person who holds a degree of medicine from a university or—"

"I know the goddamn definition," he snarled. One fist balled into his open palm, and he stared at her in growing frustration. "I thought Mrs. Blackwell's was some sort of school for refined young ladies."

"It is. It's a medical college for refined young ladies who want to be more than empty-headed puppets."

"But a *doctor*." He said the word as if it soured his tongue. "Dammit all, Maggie, what got into you? I thought you went East to learn how to be a lady, not poke your nose into something you don't have any business knowing."

Rage clouded her vision for a moment, but she struggled to remain calm, telling herself that if she lost her temper, she would lose the argument.

"Can't I be a lady and a doctor? Must I choose between the two?"

24

"Ain't no woman around who can be a lady when she's digging buckshot out of a man's ass, as far as I'm concerned."

"If the man concerned wants the buckshot out badly enough, he won't care who's digging it out." Maggie met his furious gaze with the same calm dignity that she strove to retain each time they had a confrontation. This time, she wondered if she had not misjudged Johnny's reaction. He looked more angry than she'd ever seen him.

"I won't have it." His brows lowered angrily. "I ain't havin' folks sayin' you got more interest in strange backsides than you do settlin' down and gettin' married like a woman should do."

"What on earth is this preoccupation you seem to have with backsides? And besides, I've never been one of those females who would 'get married and settle down' as you say. I think I have more to offer than a baby every nine months and a hot meal three times a day."

"Well dammit, Maggie, a man needs those things more than he needs a doctor."

"Tell that to a man with a ruptured appendix. Or a child with scarlet fever. I bet you'll get a completely different opinion from someone who needs a doctor more than a hot meal or buttons on their shirt."

Johnny raked a hand through his dark hair and stalked to the sideboard against one wall. There was the brittle clink of glass as he poured himself a drink from a decanter.

Maggie could see his face in the mirror over the sideboard and almost felt guilty at the distress she was causing him. She'd known he'd be horrified at the idea of his sister becoming a physician, but she'd worked hard for it. She straightened with determination.

"I've already rented a small house just outside town to use as my office and residence. My bags are in my room, and when I've finished packing, I'll be moving out." Maggie sucked in a deep breath when Johnny remained stiff and silent. "I should have told you before, I know, but we haven't seen each other in so long, and I wanted to spend time with you without this coming between us. This past week has been good, and—"

"You lied to me these past three years." Johnny turned to look at her, and Maggie winced at his flat, dull tone.

"Yes."

"Damn."

That one soft word made her feel even worse about the situation. Though she had, indeed, attended the finishing school he'd wanted, she'd also enrolled in Elizabeth Blackwell's Medical College for Women in New York. At first, it hadn't seemed quite so—well, deceiving—but now, seeing Johnny's face and hearing the disillusion in his tone, she realized she'd been deceiving herself as well. Johnny had done without to pay her tuition from his own funds, not touching hers. He wanted to make a lady of her, make folks in Texas "sit up and take notice," he'd often said. Well, they'd notice her now, but not as he'd envisioned. Another pang of guilt made her sigh silently. She hated being made to feel guilty for pursuing her dream.

"I wish you could understand my reasons, Johnny."

"So do I." He tossed back the last of his drink and set the glass down with deliberate care. His dark eyes burned with a sullen fire. "But I can't, Maggie. I can't understand why you'd do this when you know how I hate it. Don't you care what folks will think?"

"And since when have you cared so blasted much about what folks think?" Maggie held his gaze. "I can't remember a time when it mattered to you before."

"That was for me. Not you. I care a whole hell of a lot what folks think of you, and you'd know that if you'd just stop and think about it a minute." Johnny's mouth twisted in a grimace. "It's different for a woman than it is for a man, and you can't change that. It's always been that way, always will be. I won't have folks sayin' you ain't a decent woman. And you know that's what they'll say."

"Coward." When Johnny's eyes narrowed angrily, Maggie added quickly, "I never knew you to be afraid of people's opinions before, not when it was something important. I remember you telling me after Mother died that it didn't matter a bit what folks said about me going off to school to try and better myself, that the Malones had always been brave enough to challenge new territories. Well, that's what I did, Johnny, even if it's not the way you thought it would be. Isn't curing the sick or easing the dying better than sewing a fine seam or serving afternoon tea correctly? It was all right for me to learn Greek and Latin, but not something that might make a difference? Why are you so dead set on me being socially correct in a small town like Belle Plain anyway?"

"Because, dammit, I intend to make the Double M the most important spread in Texas, and you should set the style for more than just a small town. I'd like to see you marry a senator, maybe become the governor's wife, and then—"

"For heaven's sake!" Maggie stared at him in amazement and saw the color mount in his high cheekbones. "You have high aspirations for me as long as I'm riding some man's coattails, John Clark Malone. What of yourself? Why not be a senator or even a governor?"

"I don't have the schoolin', and you know it."

Maggie suddenly understood. He wanted for her what he'd wanted for himself, only felt that he could never achieve. He had been thrust into a role of responsibility at a young age when their parents died. It was doubly hard for her to refuse him, knowing that, but his dreams were not hers.

"Johnny, listen to me. That's not what I want. When I marry, it will not be to attain a goal, but to spend the rest of my life with a decent man I can love and respect. If he happens to be a senator or politician, fine. But if the man I choose to wed one far-off day is a shop-keeper, that's fine, too. It won't matter *what* he is, but *who* he is. Do you understand that at all?"

"Do I look like an idiot? Of course I understand that. I may not agree with it, but I understand it."

"Then I don't understand the problem here."

When Johnny's brows pulled down in a scowl and his mouth flattened, Maggie recalled that look as one of his most stubborn. "You should understand it," he said shortly. "I've said it often enough. Being a doctor isn't—well dammit, it ain't genteel, Maggie."

"Genteel." She stared at him. Frustration battled with amusement. "Is that what this is about? Your re-luctance is because you don't think a female physician can be *genteel?*"

"You know that's not all of it. It's just one small part of it."

"Excuse me, but I fail to see that as an important enough reason. Perhaps I should wear white cotton gloves while performing surgery, and a hat with rib-bon and feathers. Would that be genteel enough for you?"

"Maggie—"

"Or maybe I can chat about genteel subjects while I operate on a ruptured spleen, discuss something like lace tatting or the correct way to pour tea or the latest Paris fashions—"

Johnny crossed to her swiftly, cutting her off in mid-sentence when he grabbed her arm. Her head tilted back, and she stared up at him defiantly when he gave her a slight shake, his voice rough.

"Enough. I get your point. And I see that what I wanted for you doesn't matter to you a damn." He released her arm, and the bleak light in his eyes almost made her reach out to touch his clenched jaw, but she didn't. She couldn't. She'd gone too far to yield even an inch now, though it cost her dearly to see his distress.

Johnny expelled a long breath. "Looks like you're gonna do what you want anyway, Maggie. Hell, you've already done it. You'll be back here quick enough, I bet. Once you see that no one around here cottons to a female doctor, you'll come home where you belong."

"Don't bet on it."

Her cool reply seemed to take him back, and he stared at her for a moment before shaking his dark head. "You sound pretty sure of yourself. How do you intend to meet expenses without money?"

"I do have my small portion of inheritance left, don't I?"

Johnny's eyes narrowed slightly. "Yeah, but it's in my name, remember. I haven't touched it these past three years, but the way it was set up in Pa's will, I'm the executor."

"Then you're saying you won't give me my money unless I do what you want, is that right?" Maggie's throat grew tight when Johnny didn't reply for a moment. She hadn't expected this. Anger, yes, disappointment, but not this obdurate refusal to bend at all.

Finally he growled, "You can have your money, what there is of it. I won't help you, though, do you understand that? When it's gone, if you're still so blamed bullheaded, you'll have to figure out how to meet your bills or come back home. That's all I'll do. I won't help you make this mistake."

"I didn't expect you to help me."

He shot her a bleak glance. "I just hope it's worth it to you, Maggie."

Her throat ached with suppressed emotion. She wanted to reassure him that it was all right, that things would be right between them again, but the expression on his face—like a wounded animal, baffled at the source of his pain—kept her from it.

"It will be worth it to both of us," she managed to say softly. Johnny looked away from her with a shrug, his mouth tight with bitterness. She saw the way his hand clenched and unclenched at his side, and the tension in his lean, hard frame. His voice was rough and raspy.

"I'm goin' down to the barn. If you need help loadin' your things in the buckboard, ask Hank. I've got to tend to a mare in foal." He didn't look at her as he headed for the door, and Maggie didn't try to stop him.

He'd get over his anger after a while. They'd never been able to stay angry with one another for too long, not since their parents had died and they'd found solace in each other's grief. It had brought them closer together, and in some ways, her older brother was parent, friend, and confidante all rolled into one. In others, his way of thinking was so different as to be alien to her. She didn't understand how two people who loved each other so much could hurt each other so much, but that seemed to be the way it was.

Maggie slumped against the upright piano and heard the muted *plink* of a key strike in the sunny haze of the parlor. The sound made her suddenly recall her mother and how Ann Malone had enjoyed sitting at the piano and playing for her family in the evenings. Life had seemed serene then, though if she let herself recall the times her parents had worried about Comanches and drought and cattle disease, she knew that it had not been as idyllic as she remembered. Time erased the worst of the memories, and one day, time would ease her brother's anger and her own pain. It was the way of life.

Johnny shoved roughly at the corral gate, getting a splinter in his palm for his efforts. It only made him swear more roughly. Damn. What was she thinking of, going off East like that to be a doctor? Women got strange notions, he knew that well enough, but for Maggie—who had always been the most level-headed female he knew—to study medicine and come back with a degree was beyond understanding.

Next thing he'd know, she'd get some idea in her head like Lindsay had done, running off to a big city where there were lots of shops and fancy parties. "Life," Lindsay had said when he'd asked why, "I want to enjoy life." *Lindsay.*

That particular memory only made the bile rise in the back of his throat, and he resolutely shoved it aside. No point in thinking about what was done and over with. He'd put thoughts of Hank's daughter behind him.

Now Maggie had done something just as incomprehensible, and he felt as lost as a day-old calf in a snowstorm. It didn't make sense. Why would she want to saddle herself with long hours and little pay for people who wouldn't thank her in the end? There was no future in it for her, not like there would be if she'd come back all fancied up in pretty new clothes and with the kind of manners Lindsay had always insisted upon.

"Women like beautiful things, Johnny," Lindsay had said. "Not dust and cactus and the stink of cattle. Beautiful music and clothes and the laughter of people around them—that's what women like. No woman wants misery all her life."

Apparently Lindsay did not speak for Maggie. It was as confusing as it was enraging. Johnny wished for what must have been the hundredth time that day that he understood women and what they wanted. There were times he thought that women themselves didn't even know.

Except for Lindsay. She knew what she wanted, and he guessed she'd found it.

Sunlight blazed overhead, and Devon swept off his hat to wipe the sweat from his face with one sleeve.

"Hot as hell, ain't it?" Frank Jackson commented, and Devon shrugged.

"Hot enough, anyway." He could feel Jackson looking at him curiously, with a trace of animosity in his gaze, and he knew the reason. It had to be galling that Zeke Rogan had called in another man to take care of what Jackson should have been able to handle. The gunman was bound to resent Devon's presence.

"You don't commit to much of nothin', do you, Cimarrón?"

Devon didn't reply. He tugged his hat back on his head to shade his face and took up his reins. His gelding took off at a swift trot when he gave it a nudge in the ribs, and he heard Jackson follow. They rode silently for a time over ground dotted with cactus and bluethorn. Tall grass waved in the wind. Small clumps of mesquite trees were staggered over the flat-topped ridges and slopes.

"Is this the area where the last batch of cattle disappeared?" Devon reined in and indicated a grassy area crossed by a barbed wire fence that had been cut to hang loosely. A flattopped ridge edged one side, and the other sloped down to a thin stream trickling through raw red earth that had eroded into gullies in places. Beyond that, he could see the hard-baked rut of a road that snaked westward.

"Yeah. Over a hundred head at one time. Mostly steers." Jackson shot him a quick glance. "Any ideas?"

Devon didn't answer. He rode through the sagging line of barbed wire, carefully avoiding the sharp barbs as his gelding picked its way over the sandy soil. Tracks were cut into the ground in places, too blurred to distinguish in others. It was easy to tell hoofprints from cow tracks, and his gaze lingered on one particular set of prints. His mouth tightened. He knew those tracks. There was a crescent-shaped notch cut into one edge of a hoof. Anger coiled inside him, and he had the thought that coincidence could be amazing.

When he rejoined Jackson, the gunman asked again, "Any ideas?"

"Yeah. I'm going back to the bunkhouse."

Jackson stared at him, eyes incredulous beneath the brim of his hat. "Going back?"

"Yeah. Got a problem with that?"

"But you ain't—"

"There's nothing I can do here. I've seen what I came to see. It's getting late and I'm hungry, and I don't intend to argue with you." Devon could feel Jackson glaring at him when he turned his mount around and nudged it into a lope. As always, he was careful to keep the man within sight to monitor his movements. Too many men had tried to put a bullet in his back for him to be trusting, and he could feel Frank Jackson's animosity as if it were tangible.

Not that he blamed him that much for feeling like a bobtailed nag in a swarm of horseflies. He'd be angry and frustrated, too, if he was Jackson. Rogan had made it plain enough that none of his men were effective at catching the rustlers. The others he'd met at the bunkhouse were as sullen and suspicious as Jackson, and clearly resented him.

Devon didn't care in the least. He got serious about few things now. He didn't feel the need to prove himself a man by engaging in gunfights he didn't want or taking on jobs he didn't want. Nothing mattered that much anymore, not even women.

Not even Maggie Malone.

He'd been drawn to her despite his resistance, an immediate attraction that he hadn't been able to control. It had come so swiftly and inexplicably, it had shocked him, and he'd thought himself beyond being shocked by anything or anyone.

But there was an indefinable quality about the self-assured young woman that intrigued him at the same time as it set off all the warning signals he could muster. She was a threat to him in a way, a definite threat to his usual indifference, and he didn't like that.

The evening spent looking at stars and inhaling that sweet scent of roses had stayed in his memory as if burned there with a hot iron. He couldn't get it out of his mind no matter how hard he tried. Maggie, of the soft white skin and ebony hair, those soft gray eyes like clear rain drawing him in and making him forget things he should remember. Outspoken, confident, beautiful. God, he had to be careful, or he'd find himself in the kind of trouble he hadn't encountered in well over three years.

Women like Maggie Malone weren't for men like him. They belonged with men who had a life; men who had a future. His life wasn't his own, only the death that was sure to be swift and early. It was inevitable, like the seasons of the sun.

And he'd already been responsible for more deaths than he wanted to think about. *Molly.* Just her name made him ache with remembered pain, and he resolutely turned his attention back to the present instead of lingering in old memories.

When they arrived at the bunkhouse sprawled behind a cluster of corrals and pens, Devon dismounted and unsaddled Pardo with swift efficiency. Several of Rogan's men lounged nearby, watching. The hair on the back of his neck prickled at their scrutiny, but Devon continued tending his horse as if he didn't notice them.

Gene Tully, one of the older hands, spoke at last, his voice a lazy drawl. "Heard tell that Cimarrón killed an unarmed man down in San Antone last year. Any of you boys hear that?"

"Plugged him in the back, the way I heard it," someone answered, and Devon recognized Frank Jackson's voice.

He still didn't turn. He was familiar with this game, knew what they expected and what he'd have to do. It wasn't long in coming.

"Mebbe that's why he's said to be so fast," Butch Cady said with a short, ugly laugh. "Bein' a backshooter don't leave any room for mistakes."

"Reckon he's not as fast as we heard, Tully?" Jackson took a step forward; Devon heard his boots scuff dirt clods and straw. "How 'bout it, Cimarrón? You a backshootin' gunny like they say?"

For the space of several heartbeats, Devon acted as if he had not heard the question. He dragged the curry brush over Pardo's damp, gleaming hide in a long, smooth motion from withers to croup, then let the brush slide from his hand to the ground as he turned.

Jackson's reflexes weren't as swift as Devon's. A fraction slow in drawing, his move clumsy, Jackson stood with his mouth open and his pistol barrel pointed toward the ground as Devon beat him to the draw, thumbing back the hammer on his Colt.

"Anyone ever tell you that a big mouth can be a dangerous thing, Jackson?" Devon asked softly. "It can get you killed if you're not careful."

He waited, then let the hammer down easy and slid the Colt back into his holster when Jackson let his pistol fall to the ground. None of the others spoke. They stood silently as Devon led the dun to the corral and turned it loose, then they began to drift away.

It was usually like that wherever he went, Devon thought wearily. Someone had to test him, had to provoke him. It usually took a killing to make them wary of him. At least this time all were able to walk away. He hated it when he was forced to shoot because some man was too dumb or too embarrassed to admit he was outdrawn. Some men just didn't know when to quit. Apparently Frank Jackson was smart enough to admit defeat, even at the cost of his pride. Devon was grateful for that, though he knew Jackson would not forgive him the humiliation.

As he'd known would happen, none of the men bothered him again in the following days. They kept their distance, which suited Devon. He wouldn't be here long, and he didn't care to make friends with any of the men he'd seen. The other gunmen were an unpredictable, volatile breed that he detested, either full of conceit about their ability to draw quick and shoot straight, or so unsure of their ability they felt the constant need to prove themselves. Either type of man only caused trouble, and Devon didn't consider them professional gunmen.

He'd met the true professional and, though hating the fact that he was lumped in with them, had found those men to be more bearable. A true gunman prided himself on his ability to shoot with accuracy and did not allow himself to be drawn into unnecessary killings. While most he'd met had seemed to have no conscience, they did have a certain code of honor and justice. No professional shot an unarmed man, nor did he shoot a man in the back, nor did he harm a lady in any way. Those acts were beneath him, and he chose his jobs carefully.

Devon also chose his jobs carefully, preferring those that were on the right side of the law. He'd spent too many years as a youthful outlaw not to remember how it felt. Odd, that he was more of a renegade now than he'd been then, but there were no posters on him anymore.

There didn't need to be. Just the name Cimarrón was warning enough. Maybe that Mexican drover had done him a favor, after all, when he'd hung that name on him. Cimarrón—wild, untamed, as savage as the wilderness where he'd earned the title by shooting his way out of an ambush of almost twenty men. Cimarrón wasn't just a name to him—it was a way of life.

## CHAPTER 4

"Where do you want this hung, Miss Maggie?"

Maggie took a step back and gazed up at the overhang in front of her office. Hank Mills waited patiently, her shingle still in his broad, work-roughened hands.

*Dr. Margaret Anne Malone, M.D.*

"Hang it from the porch, Hank," she directed. "I want it highly visible from the street."

"Won't matter none," Hank muttered as he moved to the small ladder on the planked porch. "Folks who know you're here won't come, and folks who read your sign will pass it by."

"Thank you for your vote of confidence. I suppose you have been listening to my brother again."

"Don't need to." Hank stepped up onto the ladder. "But you should."

"If I listened to Johnny, I'd be spending the rest of my days pouring tea and munching on cakes instead of being a worthwhile individual."

Hank grunted, which Maggie took to mean that he disagreed with her. She gave him a brief glare, then stepped into her new office to bask in the glow of fresh paint and a framed certificate that proclaimed her to have completed her medical education with honors. Several benches were lined against the walls of the waiting room, and a table and magazines gave it a comfortable look. She'd even purchased a pot of zinnias that sat in the light of the large front window.

Shelves bore a host of curatives for sale. Hostetter's Stomach Bitters nudged against bottles of vegetable-based worm destroyer, and there was an ample selection of herbs such as mandrake root and squaw vine.

All in all, Maggie thought, it was a very satisfactory place to begin her new life. Her examination room was large and airy, with a high wooden table for examinations and a cot in one corner. The surgery held a pristine row of the latest medical supplies. Gleaming surgical instruments were placed neatly by rows of brown bottles containing everything from arsenic oxide to sulfuric acid. Scalpels and knives were carefully wrapped in cotton batting in a closed wooden case, waiting to be cleaned and sanitized.

Behind the waiting room were her private quarters, two bedrooms and a kitchen. Maggie wandered into the kitchen to admire her sturdy table, chairs, small cast-iron stove, and brand-new icebox ordered from a catalog and delivered only the day before. Charlie Wiggins had already delivered a huge block of ice and the icebox was quite cool.

A covered plate of cakes on the cloth-draped table smelled warm and spicy. Those cakes were the only housewarming gift she was liable to get, Maggie thought ruefully. Betsy Puckett, the minister's wife, had brought them earlier in the day. Though she hadn't voiced an opinion, it had been obvious that she, too, disapproved of Maggie's desire to be a physician.

The hammering outside stopped, and Maggie opened the icebox to retrieve a pitcher of lemonade she'd made to go with the cakes. Might as well feed Hank before allowing him to return to the ranch.

She went to the door and shaded her eyes with one hand as a shaft of late afternoon sunlight blinded her. "Hank? I have some fresh lemonade made if you'd like a glass."

A muffled grunt was followed by, "Like that fine."

Maggie smiled to herself. Another man of few words, like that laconic gunslinger she'd met her first day back in Belle Plain. Maggie put out two clean glasses and chipped some ice from the huge block cooling the icebox. She was pouring the lemonade when Hank stepped into the kitchen, his hat in his hands.

"Here," she said, and thrust a glass toward him. "You look hot."

He took the glass and drained it in several thirsty gulps, and Maggie refilled it for him. This time, he managed a faint grin.

"Tastes good."

"Glad you like it, Hank." She set the pitcher on the table and sipped at her lemonade for a moment. "There are some sugared cakes there on the plate under that napkin. With compliments from Betsy Puckett. She's the only one to welcome me back without making some kind of sarcastic comment about my new profession."

Hank didn't seem inclined to discuss that, but did justice to the sugared cakes with a hunger that betrayed the fact no woman lived on the ranch to cook for them.

"I understand that the cattlemen in our area presented a proposal to the railroad to build a spur here," she said after a moment, and Hank looked surprised.

"First I heard about it."

Maggie frowned. "Oh? How odd. The man on the stage said that . . . well, perhaps he had the wrong information. Guess he's found that out by now."

"Who told you that?"

"David Brawley. He's part-owner of the hotel."

Hank grunted. "Never heard nothin' about that. Last I knew, Murphy still owned it by hisself."

"Maybe he's taken in a partner. I did see Mr. Brawley working at the hotel."

"Mebbe. Don't seem likely though. Who'd want to invest their money in a town that's dyin'?"

Her brow lifted. "Is that a hint that I've made a mistake by putting my money into this house, Hank? Don't be shy. Tell me straight out."

A faint flush burned his cheeks, and Hank gave her one of his most stubborn stares. "Ain't none of my business what you do with your money, Miss Maggie. That's between you and Johnny."

"My brother seems to think I have no opinion in the matter, however."

"That's between you and him," he repeated stubbornly.

Maggie sighed. It was obvious Hank would be little help in encouraging her. She switched subjects, unwilling to offend him. "Have you heard from Lindsay?"

Hank nodded. "Got a letter last month."

"And?" Maggie prompted with a trace of exasperation for his scant conversation. "Is she coming back soon?"

"Nope."

"Hank Mills, I know you're a man of few words, but will you be kind enough to tell me about your daughter? After all, we did grow up together and are practically sisters."

Hank chewed the last of a cake and swallowed, then said, "She's still in Atlanta with her mother's kin. Likes it well enough."

Maggie suppressed an irritated sigh. "Good. We exchanged letters for a while, but then lost touch. You know, I always thought Lindsay and Johnny might get married one day. Does he ever mention her?"

A dull flush stained Hank's face, and he shook his head. "Nope."

Maggie threw up her hands and laughed. "I can see I'm not going to get any information out of you. Guess I'll write to Lindsay myself one day soon. Maybe she'll come back for a visit. I imagine you'd like that well enough."

A wistful expression touched the burly foreman's face for a moment, and he nodded slowly. "I'd like that right fine."

"So would Johnny, I imagine, even though he's probably too stubborn to admit it." Maggie poured Hank another glass of lemonade and saw the way he avoided her gaze. Something odd must have happened, and she wondered what it could be.

Lindsay Mills had come to them along with Hank, a poor motherless child terrified of her own shadow and crying nightly for her dead mother. It had been Ann Malone who had comforted her most, taking the child into her home and her heart. Lindsay had grown up with Maggie and Johnny as a sibling and had been as grief-stricken as them when Jack and Ann Malone had died. Not long after, Lindsay had gone back to visit her mother's family for a time but had never returned.

Something had happened before she'd gone, something that Maggie had never been able to discover. There had been an inexplicable strain between them that had not been there before, as if Lindsay knew something Maggie didn't and did not want to tell her. It had been Lindsay who had cut off the correspondence, not Maggie. She still didn't know why.

"Well," Maggie said after Hank had finished his third glass of lemonade and declined another, "give Johnny my love."

Hank said nothing, but tugged on his hat and ducked a brass pan hanging from an overhead hook. He shifted from one foot to another, then stepped to the back door.

"Goodbye, Miss Maggie."

"Bye, Hank. Thank you again for being such a big help. I don't know how I would have gotten it done without you."

Hank paused in the open door and looked back at her. A faint smile touched the hard lines of his mouth. "You'd have done it. You always manage."

"You're probably right. It just would have been a lot harder without you."

On impulse, Maggie went to him and stood on tiptoe, brushing his grizzled cheek with her lips. He flushed, but his smile was pleased as he touched the brim of his hat with two fingers in farewell. With Hank gone, Maggie was truly on her own.

As dusk fell that evening, she went to sit in the rocker on her front porch. She unbuttoned the top two buttons of her blouse and pushed up her sleeves, hoping for a cooler night. The sign Hank had hung swung slowly in the soft evening breeze. It creaked gently in rhythm with Maggie's rocker.

The house was on the edge of town, far enough away to give her privacy, close enough in to be convenient. A small patch of land surrounded the stone and wood house, bearing ragged tufts of grass that trembled in the breeze. Jagged spears of bluethorn waged a winning battle with a cluster of bright purple wildflowers along the dirt road in front of the house.

Maggie looked toward Belle Plain, watching idly as an occasional horseman rode past into town. Then her gaze sharpened as she recognized a rider, and her heart inexplicably leaped. The man looked like Cimarrón, riding a line-back dun with easy grace. When he glanced toward the house, Maggie was certain of it and impulsively waved. Her pulses skipped a beat when he reined in and turned back.

He walked the dun to the edge of the porch, and Maggie drew in a soft breath. What was there about this man that she found so potent? His lean frame radiated confidence and a predatory wariness that was as intriguing as it was alarming, and Maggie was startled to find that she considered it so. She'd always detested the gunmen who'd passed through Belle Plain and considered them vultures. It was vaguely disquieting to discover that she felt an attraction to this Devon Conrad and had from the first. Certainly he was good-looking in a rough, dangerous sort of way, but she'd never been drawn to men like that before. Indeed, she'd rarely felt an attraction to any man, much less one that carried himself with all the deadly grace of a lethal weapon. There was nothing remarkable about him that she could immediately pick out, but the combination of lean, hard body and erotic features made her breath shorten and her pulses quicken.

That confusing blend of reaction was only heightened by the slight smile curling his mouth, deepening the grooves that cut down each side of his face. His half-grown beard was thicker since the last time she'd seen him. It was much darker than his hair and gave him a piratical appearance that belied his obvious amusement.

"So *you're* the new lady doctor in town?" Devon Conrad looked slightly astonished as well as amused.

"I am. I take it *you're* the new Rogan gunman in town?"

His grin was as white and blinding as a flash of summer lightning. "You don't mince words, Miss Maggie Malone."

"Not usually. Unless I have a reason to do so. Care to have a seat and enjoy a cool breeze?"

Now why had she said that? Maggie wondered crossly. She certainly didn't need to invite trouble, not with everyone in town just waiting for her to make a mistake.

He seemed to hesitate, then shook his head. "Better not. Don't want folks to think I'd let you compromise me."

Despite an instant's perverse irritation that he'd refused her, Maggie couldn't help a soft laugh. "No, we wouldn't want to tarnish your spotless reputation with the ladies, would we?''

Saddle leather creaked loudly as Devon shifted, and she could feel his gaze burning into her from beneath the brim of his hat. His voice was low, husky with that familiar rasp that she'd found so attractive before.

"I heard the new doctor was from around here, but no one thought to mention it was you."

"I'm not surprised. 'Local girl makes good' would not be in their vocabulary when it's a profession for a man. I'm afraid I've become a pariah of sorts."

"There's worse things."

"Ah, tell that to my brother. He'd give you a good argument, I think."

Amusement curled his mouth. "I reckon he would at that. He struck me as a man who'd be a bit narrow-minded about some things."

"Narrow-minded? Nearer to close-minded in this instance. Johnny's normally wonderful and has never stood in my way over anything I thought important, but this time is different."

She hadn't realized how wistful she sounded until Devon said softly, "He'll come around."

"Maybe. I hope so, but I've no intention of sitting down and moping until then."

"You're not the type to sit around and mope about anything."

"No?" Maggie smiled up at him, glad he'd pushed his hat back on his tawny head so she could see his eyes. They were so blue, bright and burning and reflecting the late afternoon sun in their depths. She felt another peculiar tingle when his eyes narrowed slightly, the brush of his lashes lowering in a lazy drift. Ignoring the odd, breathless anticipation he sparked in her, she said, "What type am I, may I ask?"

"The type to get things done, not wait for others to

do them." Devon shrugged. "I'd bet a gold dollar that you don't have the patience of a gnat, either."

"You'd win." Maggie stood up and moved to the edge of the porch. She leaned against the smooth wooden post and tilted her head back to gaze up at the new sign swinging above. Emotion battled reticence, and her voice was soft and resigned. "I expected to have my first patient by now. After all, my sign has been up all afternoon."

"Before long they'll be lining the walls of your waiting room like cattle at feeding time."

"You're teasing, but I'm serious. I suppose I may have underestimated the good people of Belle Plain."

"Or overestimated them." Devon glanced toward the busy streets of the town where wagons and carriages slowed down for pedestrians. "Anything new takes some getting used to. I guess it's the same here as everywhere else."

"Probably. I have to admit I'm surprised at the attitude of some of the people I once thought of as my friends, however. Some of us went to school together over in Comanche County. We played as children, went to the same local dances when we got older, then drifted apart. Yet I never thought I would be made to feel unwelcome in the land where I was born. Few people seem to believe that a woman can do the same job as well as a man. In *most* instances," she added, laughing when Devon lifted his brows with a grin. "I'm not foolish enough to think I can match you arm-wrestling, but I can certainly meet you on an intellectual level."

"Reckon you'd pass me there. I never finished school."

"That has nothing to do with intellect. Intellect is defined as the ability to think, reason, and learn."

Devon looked surprised. "That right?"

"That's right. So you see, we're almost equals."

"Almost?"

"Well, I must admit that I probably have an edge, being a woman and all."

Devon's grin flashed again. "I'd have to agree with that, Miss Malone. You're definitely a woman."

His husky words sparked a slow fire in her, a gentle burning that warmed her inside more than the Texas heat warmed her outside. She found herself smiling at him and felt slightly foolish for it. She'd always felt a sort of superiority over any woman credulous enough to gaze at a man with calf eyes as she was certain she was now doing.

"Yes." She cleared her throat, embarrassed at the thick sound of it. "Well, I'm a woman with a medical degree, and I think that should count for something."

"So do I."

She tilted her head to one side. "Do you? It's unusual for a man to have such an opinion, and even more unusual for him to admit to it."

"I can understand that. You females have enough potent weapons as it is to use against us poor males. Let a woman know you think she's smart or pretty, and it's a lost cause."

"You sound very familiar with lost causes," Maggie said with a teasing laugh. She was startled to see Devon's smile abruptly vanish.

He straightened with a jerk, and the blue eyes that had been filled with humor and light, darkened as he stared at her. He looked away, then back. His voice was rough.

"I'm too familiar with lost causes. And I should know when I see another one coming."

As he reined his dun around, Maggie blurted, "I guess I shouldn't take that personally."

Devon didn't glance back. "Take it anyway you want," he said as he nudged his mount into a brisk trot.

Dust rose up in hazy clouds that drifted on the breeze, stinging her eyes. Maggie stared after him, not quite certain why her teasing remark had wiped the smile from his face so quickly. Did he think she couldn't succeed as a doctor? That she was a lost cause? Why did everyone seem to think she couldn't accomplish anything more complicated than baking bread?

Anger flashed through her, and Maggie's jaw tightened with determination. She'd show them. She'd show them all. If someone would just give her a chance, she'd show them what she'd learned, and that she could be a doctor and a woman without losing any of her femininity. Or her skill.

"I will show every one of you," Maggie whispered aloud, her eyes raking over the town. "Especially Devon Conrad."

# CHAPTER 5

"Saw you talkin' to Maggie Malone," Rogan commented. He took a sip of his beer, watching Devon over the rim. It was noisy in the saloon with men laughing and the piano pounding out a lively tune.

Devon didn't take his gaze from the smoky glass of the giltframed mirror hanging over the bar and reflecting rows of whiskey bottles. "Didn't know it was any of your business who I talk to, Rogan."

"It ain't. Just makin' small talk, Cimarrón, that's all." Rogan took another sip. A frown etched his mouth downward. "Just some friendly advice—her brother's ornery as a hungry bobcat. And he don't like anybody messin' round with his sister. He's kinda partic'lar 'bout who she talks to, way I hear it."

"That sounds more like a warning than advice, Rogan."

Rogan shrugged. "Maybe it is. Malone's a dead shot, and he's got a hair-trigger temper. If you're lookin' for a woman, there's—"

"I'm not looking for a woman," Devon cut in, and saw Rogan's eyes widen slightly at his tone. "And if I was, I know which pasture to graze. I'm a big boy, Rogan. I don't need your advice."

Rogan cleared his throat and looked away, his frown deepening. "Yeah. So I see. Look, Cimarrón, some of the boys are complainin' that you're right surly to work with."

"I don't work with them."

49

"Yeah, that's right. You work alone. But just the same, it'd be a mite easier around the place if you'd—"

Devon turned to face Rogan. "I didn't hire on to be sociable. I hired on to catch your rustlers. That doesn't give you a right to interfere in my personal life, and if you think it does, I'll take the pay I've earned and ride on right now."

"Jesus, don't get your hackles raised on my account, Cimarrón. Told you I didn't mean nothin' by it."

Devon dug into his vest pocket for a coin and flipped it to the surface of the bar. "I'm riding out tonight and won't be back for a few days."

Rogan looked startled. "You quittin' me?"

"No. Not unless you want me to."

"I hired you to stop the damn rustlers, Cimarrón. I ain't likely to fire you 'cause you got a yen for our lady doc." When Devon just stared at him coldly, Rogan shrugged. "Where you goin'?"

"Looking around. I don't expect the men who're stealing your cattle to be too obvious since you've hired so much firepower. They're probably lying back and waiting to see what we're going to do."

"And you think you'll find them?"

"I think I'll find sign of them." Devon swallowed the last of his beer and set down the mug, then turned and left the saloon with Zeke Rogan staring after him.

He wasn't in the best of moods. He should never have yielded to the temptation to linger near Maggie Malone. It was stupid. And useless. There was no time in his life for a woman like her, and he should have stuck to just admiring her from a distance, as he would a beautiful horse that belonged to someone else.

And she *was* beautiful. There was something about her, a certain grace, or the luster of her silky black hair and the shining honesty of her gray eyes—aw hell, he shouldn't be thinking of that. Shouldn't be remembering how tempting and feminine she'd looked sitting in that rocker with her top two buttons undone, her creamy skin misted from the heat and her hair in loose, dark tendrils around her face. He didn't know if it was her eyes that got to him most or the ripe promise of her mouth, those lips that looked to be made for kissing. Maggie Malone wasn't meant for a man like him.

Besides, she reminded him too much of Kate, with her fiery independence and bluntness. If Kate wasn't his sister, he could never have endured her prickly nature. Maggie Malone would be the same way. Too much time in her company, and he'd be tempted to set her on her backside. No, it was best he stay away from her and not let the old yearnings tempt him into making another mistake. The last mistake had been too costly.

"*¿A mí qué?*"

A gust of wind caught the edge of the wide-brimmed sombrero and flattened it, revealing the fear in the man's eyes at Devon's curt question. With a placating shrug and half-smile, he mumbled, "*¡No importa!*"

Devon switched to English. "You must have some reason for telling me that, amigo. *¿Qué haces?*"

The abrupt change from Spanish to English and back seemed to unnerve the man even more. He'd obviously not thought the blond American spoke or comprehended his language, and so had conversed freely in front of him. Now, he must have realized his mistake and was frightened.

"Señor," he began nervously, "I only meant that the men you seek have not been here in some time. That is all, I swear it."

"But that's not what you said earlier. I heard you. I am not deaf, and I speak your language quite well. You told your amigo that they were here only last week." Devon let that sink in for a moment before adding softly, "Now, I want to know when they will come again."

"You will not tell where you heard this?"

"*Según y conforme.*"

Beads of sweat formed on the Mexican's upper lip. "It depends on what, señor?"

"On whether or not you tell me the truth."

"I will tell you the truth. I swear it by the Blessed Virgin and all the saints."

"For your sake, I hope so."

Devon's softly drawled words held a distinct threat, as he had meant them to. The Mexican *bandolero* looked shaken, glancing from left to right as if for help. But no one was close by as they stood in the hot sun and blowing wind, only a sleeping dog and a horse dozing at a sagging hitching rail. All were inside seeking refuge from the noonday heat, taking siestas or sitting in the closest cantina sipping cool drinks.

"The men you seek will be here tonight, señor. After dark."

"Where?"

"At Por Ventura, on the edge of town. Ask for Rosa if you do not know them by sight. Give her a few pesos and she will point them out to you."

"That's not necessary." Devon took out a coin and tucked it into the man's unwilling hand before gazing down the wide, rutted street where dust blew up in thick swirls. "I know them by sight."

Night had fallen thickly on the flat expanse of prairie and scrub before several horsemen dismounted in front of Por Ventura. They moved warily toward the open doors of the small cantina, easing one at a time into the crowded room filled with smoke.

Devon watched from his vantage point in the rear of the room where shadows were deep. His hat was tilted low over his face. His booted feet were propped on the table near a half-full bottle of rye and an empty glass. He sipped slowly from a dingy glass in his right hand. His left hand rested on his thigh not far from his holstered gun.

It didn't surprise him at all when the woman he figured was Rosa sauntered past the men, nor did it surprise him when she whispered *"Rubio hombre"* as she passed. It would have been more surprising if there had been no effort made to warn them that he was waiting.

Devon sensed the tall leader's glance in his direction, saw the way the others fanned out behind him. One of the men brought up his rifle as if in warning, but the leader was already walking toward him.

He moved through the crowd gracefully, like a dancer, while men silently parted to make way for him. Bandoliers crossed his chest, and he wore a double-gun belt that bristled with cartridges and various knives. Tall and lean, with long black hair that brushed against his shoulders, he looked every inch a vicious bandido when he came to a stop at Devon's table.

Devon hadn't moved, but watched his progress through the crowd. The cantina had fallen quiet. A hushed silence lay as thickly as the stinging wisps of smoke.

*"¿Quién es?"*

Slowly Devon pushed back the brim of his hat and saw a light of recognition in the man's black eyes. For a moment neither spoke, then the leader turned to the others with a dismissive wave of one arm.

*"Zarco,"* he said, then shrugged. "You should have told me he was blue-eyed. I would have known at once then. No man has the blond hair and cold blue eyes of Cimarrón. May I, compadre?" He indicated the empty chair across from Devon.

In answer, Devon swung his legs down from the

table and pointed to the empty glass and bottle of rye. "I've been waiting on you, Danza. You're late."

"Late, amigo?" Danza pulled out the chair and eased into it, then reached for the bottle and glass. His dark gaze never left Devon's face. "Why do you say so?"

"I expected you here yesterday."

"And you have not enjoyed waiting?" An eloquent shrug lifted his shoulders. "You should have sampled Rosa's charms. She would have made the time pass quite pleasantly."

"If I survived."

Danza's mouth curled in a faint smile. "I would wager on you, I think."

Devon leaned forward. Danza's eyes narrowed slightly when he asked softly, "Who rides a horse that leaves a quarter-moon cut in the track?"

"Why do you think I would know, amigo?"

"Because you make it your business to know every track in Texas."

Danza shrugged. "Ah, if I did that, I would be a very busy man."

"You are."

"*Sí*, at times I am very busy." Danza sipped his drink before saying slowly, "This track is important to you, Cimarrón?"

"It's important." Devon held his gaze. "The man who rides that horse killed a friend of mine a while back."

"Someone I know?"

Devon looked away. His voice was rough when he replied. "No. His name was Ralph Pace and he was just a green kid not much more than seventeen. He was bushwhacked for two dollars and his horse. That horse made quarter-moon tracks, and Ralph's killer is riding it. A little grulla gelding. I want to know who's riding it, because whoever it is, I've tracked him to Callahan County." He paused and ran a hand over his beard, frowning. "Looks like he's running a maverick factory and putting wet brands on any brush-popper he can find. Took over a hundred head from Zeke Rogan a while back, and Rogan hired me to catch him."

Danza frowned. "I know of Zeke Rogan. I do not like him."

"Neither do I, but this has gotten personal all of a sudden."

"And the man who rides the horse that leaves this print—you are sure he's the same one who killed your friend?"

"That I won't know until I find him." Devon sat quietly as Danza mulled over his decision. He knew the Apache would not normally betray another man unless it was for personal reasons. Danza didn't get involved in other men's business, and he expected the same courtesy. On more than one occasion Devon had witnessed Danza's ruthless reaction to anyone incautious enough to provoke him.

After Danza poured another shot of rye into his glass, he said, "When we rode together, Cimarrón, you were always a fair man, despite what others said of you. You do not meddle where you should not. I respect your judgment." He tossed down the whiskey and met Devon's intent gaze. "Ash Oliver rides a grulla gelding that leaves that mark."

"Ash Oliver." Devon's mouth tightened. "I know of him."

"There are not many who do not. He leaves a wide trail of death behind him. I heard he was in Abilene not long ago. Though he is known to rob and kill at the slightest whim, I have never known him to rustle cattle before. It would not seem to be something he would want to do as it involves too much work."

"His tracks were there. I saw them."

"Coincidence?"

"Maybe." Devon rose to his feet, and Danza stood also. "I don't think so, though." He held out his hand. *"Mil gracias, amigo."* Danza clasped his hand firmly.

*"De nada.* I do not see how I have helped you that much, Cimarrón. Why do you not stay a while and we can talk over old times?" A sudden grin lightened his dark features, and Danza seemed much younger. "Do you recall the pretty sisters in San Antonio that took us home with them?"

Devon groaned. "Too well. I thought we were going to end up buried when their daddy came round the corner with that shotgun."

"Who would have thought that two saloon girls would have an angry papa? I think perhaps he was more, eh?"

"I've had that thought myself." Devon shook his head at the memory. "I'll have another drink with you, but then I need to ride on."

"For Abilene?"

Devon nodded. "Yes."


Maggie had been asleep for several hours when something woke her. She lay quietly for a moment, drifting in that halfworld between awareness and slumber. Her bedroom window was open to allow in cooling breezes, and the curtains fluttered gently.

When it remained quiet, she closed her eyes again and relaxed back into her feather pillow. Noise from town was a distant, muted murmur that she'd grown accustomed to in the past weeks, but occasionally there was an uproar that was easily discernible. Something must have happened and been quickly quieted.

She was almost asleep again when she heard the sound of breaking glass. It jerked her to a sitting position. Her heart began to pound furiously when she realized the noise had come from her office at the front of the house.

Maggie had grown up in Texas, and she'd been taught at an early age how to shoot a rifle and a pistol. Now she reached for the single-action revolver that always lay on the small table beside her bed. It was handy for shooting villains and varmints, Johnny had told her a long time ago when he'd given it to her. It had been a while since she'd even handled it except to clean it, and she hoped she could still hit the side of a house with the heavy pistol.

Another crash and tinkle of breaking glass warned her that something—or someone—was definitely in her office and creating havoc. Anger began to replace fear, and she checked the gun chamber before creeping to her door and easing into the dark hall. The hem of her white nightgown floated around her ankles, brushing against her skin in an irritating whisk that was unnerving. The planked floor was cold under her bare feet, and she curled her toes against the wood as she tiptoed down the hallway to her office door.

A thin thread of light flickered then grew steady under the closed door, and Maggie tensed. There was no doubt that the animal in her office was human, and therefore infinitely more dangerous and unpredictable. The reason for the intrusion didn't matter, only that whoever it was be run off before destroying her precious equipment.

Maggie sucked in a deep breath and eased back the hammer of the pistol as she reached for the doorknob. It swung open easily enough, and she saw the dark shadow of a man across the room. Apparently he'd lit the lantern that sat on her desk. A huge pool of light wavered erratically, leaving the intruder in shadow but illuminating the shattered window where he'd gained entrance. Broken glass lay on the examining table and the floor, and the man seemed to be looking for something particular on the shelves behind her desk.

He had his back to her, and she could hear his heavy breathing while she stood trembling in the doorway with the leveled pistol. It took her a moment to summon enough courage to confront the intruder, but finally she said loudly, "Put your hands up!"

Her words jerked him around, and she saw the glassy gleam of a medicine bottle in his hand. Her finger tightened on the trigger of her revolver in a reflexive action before she caught herself. And at the same instant, she saw the bottle drop to the floor as Devon Conrad slowly went to his knees.

His eyes focused on her, and his voice was a painful, grating sound. "Sorry . . . 'bout the . . . mess, Maggie."

Then he keeled over.

# CHAPTER 6

Maggie stood there for a heartbeat, staring down at him in shock. Then she carefully lowered the hammer on the pistol and set it down as she gingerly sidestepped the broken glass on the floor. She knelt beside him, frowning.

"Devon?"

There was no answer, no sound but the slight hiss of the lamp and his harsh breathing. He was bareheaded, and the light gleamed in his thick, tawny hair like trapped sunbeams. She put out a hand to touch his forehead and felt the moist heat of a fever. He was sick. Dear God, and she'd almost shot him.

"Devon," she said, and put a hand on his shoulder to try to rouse him. "Devon, can you get up?" She shook him and he groaned, and she felt a wave of frustration. She'd have to try and get him to the examining table by herself, but she had no idea how. He was a big man, and she wasn't that strong.

"All right," she muttered, "I'll have to drag you." Broken glass still lay on the floor, and she made her way around it to fetch the broom from the kitchen. By the time she had it swept up reasonably well, Devon seemed to be regaining consciousness. She knelt beside him again, and he opened his eyes.

They were feverishly bright and unfocused, and Maggie put a hand on his cheek. The rough scrape of his beard bristled against her palm. "Devon? Can you help me? I have to get you up on the table to examine you."

59

His eyes focused on her, suddenly clear, though tinged with pain. "I'll try."

The words were hoarse and guttural, indicating how sick he was. Then, with a grunt of pain, he rose to his knees, swaying. Maggie caught him by the arm when he lurched sideways, and felt a warm stickiness smear her hand.

"You're hurt!"

He made a noise in the back of his throat that she took to mean agreement. She reached for the lamp and moved it closer to the edge of the table so that it fell across him. He didn't protest when she lifted his leather vest away from his side, but grimaced when she gasped. Blood soaked his entire left side. A ragged hole punctured his shirt, and now she caught the sickly sweet stench of infection.

"When did this happen? Oh Devon, you should have come here sooner."

"Came as . . . quick . . . as I . . . could."

His words were forced and breathless, and she immediately concentrated on a cure instead of the cause. "You've got to get up on this table. Hold my arm, and I'll do my best to lift you."

"Do it . . . myself." He stubbornly avoided her effort to lift him, and Maggie held her breath as he lurched to his feet and staggered toward the table.

When he half-fell across it, she snapped, "No more heroics, please. If you came to me for help, then you should let me help!"

"Didn' come . . . to you . . . for help. Too dang'rous." His eyes closed. "Get bullet . . . out quick. Got . . . to go."

"Don't be an ass." Maggie began unbuttoning his shirt. "If you didn't come to me for help, why are you here?"

His eyes opened. "Medicine."

She suddenly understood. He'd come to take medicine, intending to doctor himself. "It's a good thing you're not a quiet thief," she said tartly as she pulled open his shirt. "Otherwise, you'd be dead by morning. Any man who doctors himself has a corpse for a patient before long."

"Tact-ful," he got out with another grunt of pain when she stripped his shirt completely off.

"There's no time for tact now. Unbutton your pants, please." She met his faintly startled glance. "The bullet entered low but came out high in the back, it seems. At least I won't have to probe for it, but your pants are in the way. If you can't get them unbuttoned—"

He pushed her hand away from his belt buckle. "I'll do . . . it."

Maggie felt another sweep of frustration that he was so uncooperative, but took the opportunity to make her preparations. She moved briskly, setting a kettle on the stove to boil water and getting out clean cloths and the long, needle forceps from her cabinet. Then she scrubbed her hands with strong lye soap before fetching the metal tray where she kept her other surgical instruments. She placed it at the end of the table where Devon sat watching her.

He'd unbuckled his gunbelt, and she noticed his pistol gleaming dully in the holster that lay near his hand. His pants were open, and the waistband was soaked red with his blood. It looked bright and fresh, which was a good sign, though the odor of infection was strong.

"When did this happen?" she asked as she lit another lamp and placed it near.

"Day . . . or two . . . ago."

"You're lucky to be alive. No major organs must have been hit. It seems to have gone through the fleshy part just below your ribs without doing too much damage, though why you waited this long to find a doctor is beyond me."

"Trust you. No one . . . else."

Maggie glanced up at him in surprise. A tiny thrum of satisfaction beat inside for a moment before she turned her attention back to the wound. "Well, now that you're here, let's get this thing taken care of."

Devon clenched his teeth when she placed a steaming hot cloth soaked in herbs on the wound, and his muscles went rigid. It took a while to soften the dried blood and draw out as much poison as she could, but finally Maggie was satisfied that most of the infection had been drained. The wounds looked raw and puckered, and Devon's face was a chalky white.

"Here," she said, handing him a glass, "drink this."

He stared at it suspiciously. "What is . . . it?"

"Something to stop the bleeding and ease the pain."

"I don't . . . need . . . anything for . . . pain."

"Oh no, I can see you don't. You're as thick-skinned as an ox, and you must have the same constitution, or you would have died before now. Drink it. It won't kill you if a bullet didn't."

Devon didn't take the glass. "No. I have . . . to leave."

"If you do, you'll be dead before sunrise." Maggie turned away and began tossing bloodstained instruments into a pan to soak. "I suppose you don't want me to finish cleaning your wound, either."

"I didn't . . . say . . . that."

Maggie turned to look at him. He sounded weaker. There was a new quiver in his voice that hadn't been there before. She frowned. Damn him, he had to be sensible or he would die.

"Fine," she said. "I'll get you a glass of whiskey for the pain and wash the wounds with tea. Will that do?"

"You're . . . the doctor."

"I'm not the one who seems to have forgotten that."

Maggie went to the kitchen for the whiskey she kept in a cabinet, and returned with a liberal amount. Devon drank it without hesitation, tossing it down in a long swallow. She watched silently.

Though she'd seen her share of half-clothed men in the examining room at the medical college, she wasn't quite prepared for the effect Devon Conrad had on her. His chest and stomach were roped with bands of tight muscle that gleamed in the soft lamplight with a golden sheen. A thick mat of hair covered his chest, arrowing down to his open waistband. Despite his injury, he exuded a masculinity that made her all too aware of her brief attraction to him. It was disconcerting, to say the least.

Maggie looked away and felt an awkward heat stain her face. This was ridiculous. She was a doctor, and Devon had come to her as a patient. He was wounded, and she should be focusing on the task at hand instead of—other things.

When Devon handed her the empty glass, she set it down without comment. After washing her hands again, she picked up her clean instruments and turned back to him.

"This will hurt."

"I know."

Maggie lapsed into silence. Devon's eyes were an excellent indicator of his mood and thoughts, and now they were a dark blue that was smoky with pain.

"I'll try to be gentle," she said softly around the sudden lump in her throat.

"Just . . . be quick."

Devon lay on his side as she motioned, and didn't make a sound while she worked. The thin tweezers pulled out tiny bits of shirt and slivers of lead as well as a bone fragment. The bullet must have nicked one of his ribs. When she'd removed all she could see, Maggie applied pressure around the wound to force out any remaining foreign bits. Her hands trembled with strain; beneath the dark hue of his skin, Devon had bleached to a pasty white that didn't look good. She swallowed a surge of nervous fear and tried to hurry before the pain became too much for him.

Devon tensed under her efforts, and she began to talk in a soothing tone, saying whatever came to mind to distract him from the pain she was inflicting.

"I used to help my father tend some of the ranch hands when I was a child. Maybe that's what sparked my interest in the medical field." A stream of dark blood and infection oozed from the exit wound as she pressed harder, and she felt his muscles quiver with strain. Perspiration beaded on her forehead.

"Ever . . . tend a . . . bullet wound before?" Devon asked in a labored tone.

"Yes. But not since I left medical school. You're my first."

"Great."

His mutter made her smile. "Don't worry. None of my live patients have ever died." She felt the quick flick of his eyes as he glanced over his shoulder.

"Live?"

"We used to study on cadavers. You know— corpses."

"*Jesus!*"

"Be still." Maggie smeared a thick ointment on both wounds, then bandaged them, winding clean strips of cotton around his torso. Devon sat up again, and she glanced up at his face. His eyes were half-closed, the thick fan of his lashes drifting lower. A faint smile touched her lips.

He must have seen it, because his hand closed

around her wrist with surprising strength. "Wha' was in tha' whiskey?" he slurred.

"You need rest," she began, and his fingers tightened like a steel vise, making her gasp.

"Damn . . . you." He released her suddenly, uttering another hoarse curse.

"It was just a little laudanum, Devon."

He slid from the table to his feet, weaving slightly. Maggie held her breath as he fumbled for his gunbelt and tried to pull it around him. His opened pants slipped a bit lower, baring his lower abdomen and the dark vee of hair. To her chagrin, she flushed hotly and jerked her gaze away.

"Just go on," she said harshly. "But when you get back on your horse, your wounds may reopen and you'll bleed to death. If you don't fall asleep and fall off and break your neck first."

"Y'don' unnerstand," he muttered thickly, still trying to buckle his gunbelt around his waist. "Dang'rous to stay here."

"Dangerous?"

His gaze lifted to her face, fevered and determined. "I didn' kill him. If he fin's me here . . ." His voice trailed away, and Maggie felt a spurt of alarm when the unbuckled gunbelt slid from his waist and dangled loosely in one hand.

She took a step forward, but he lifted his hand palm outward. "No. Lemme go."

"I don't think you can," she said softly, and saw the frustration in his eyes as he realized she was right. When he tried to take a step, his legs went out from under him. Maggie leaped forward but barely broke his fall, and his heavy weight took her to the floor with him half-atop her.

Breathless from the bruising fall, Maggie glared up at Devon angrily and panted, "I hope you're satisfied!"

His blue eyes locked with hers, and she saw the subtle shift from frustrated panic to angry determination. "Not yet," he said jerkily.

Before she could read his intentions, he bent his head and set his mouth over hers in a bruising kiss. Maggie was as surprised at his strength as she was at her response. By all rights, Devon Conrad should have passed out a half-hour before, but instead he was pinning her to the floor with his weight and kissing her until she felt as if *she* was the one about to pass out.

Afraid to struggle for fear of opening his wounds, she found herself stroking her hands up the curved muscle of his arms to his shoulders to hold him lightly. His skin was hot and damp, and she felt the heated press of his body through her thin cotton gown. The nightrail was all that separated her body from his from groin to throat, and Maggie shivered when he shoved her thighs apart with his knees and rocked his hips against her.

Before she had time to protest, he'd lifted his head and was staring down at her. "Damn," he husked. "Of all . . . the times . . . to pass out. . . ."

The sudden lowering weight of his body on hers left her staring up at the ceiling of her office and holding him in her arms, and she didn't know whether to laugh or cry.

Devon woke slowly. He blinked against the bright press of sun against his aching eyes and peered through his lashes in pounding confusion. Where was he? His memory was sketchy, and he could recall only vague impressions.

Dust and heat and horses and bullets . . . searing pain and a jolting ride. Then the sound of breaking glass and a soft, worried voice.

*Maggie.* That's right. He'd come to Belle Plain to get some medicine from Maggie. And she'd found him.

He grunted with pain when he tried to sit up, and fell back to the pillows. Damn. It all came back to him now, how he'd gone to Abilene to find Ash Oliver. He had. And they'd faced one another across a wide expanse of street.

This wasn't the first time he'd been shot, but it was the first time in recent memory that he hadn't killed his opponent. Ash Oliver, he remembered, had gone down but not stayed down. Now Oliver would be looking for him, and he certainly didn't need to be found here at Maggie's. It would endanger her as well, and he didn't want that.

"Where do you think you're going?" a crisp feminine voice demanded when Devon managed to sit up on the edge of the bed.

Painfully he turned his head toward the door. She stood framed in the open doorway, her hair a dark cloud piled atop her head, her hands on her hips in righteous indignation. She wore a prim blouse and skirt. He grunted sourly.

"Liked your other dress better."

"You would. It was my nightgown."

"Ah."

Maggie sailed toward him and, to his dismay, easily pushed him back on the bed. "Lie down. You're too weak. Besides, you're naked under that sheet."

Startled, he lifted the sheet and glanced down. It was true. He looked back up at her. "Where are my clothes?"

"Clean and safely tucked away." She grasped his wrist with competent efficiency, lips moving as she counted the beats of his pulse. Apparently satisfied, she released his arm and tucked the sheet back up around his chest. "There's a carafe of fresh water on the bedside table. Drink it. If you think you can eat a bit, I'll—"

"How long have I been asleep?"

"Two days."

"Two—!" Devon shoved the sheet down as if to get up, but she caught his arm.

"Do you have to fall on me again before you admit that you're too weak from loss of blood?"

Her words jarred another memory, and he had a flash of her lying beneath him in her thin gown, her thighs cradling his almost naked body. He'd kissed her, too, and he saw that she was remembering the same thing as a faint flush stained her cheeks a rosy pink. He grinned.

"Well, falling does have its compensations, it seems."

She took a step back. "Yes, such as opening your wounds so that I had to stitch them up to stop the bleeding. That was a definite compensation, I imagine, but you were lucky enough to sleep through it."

"Too bad. From the way you're glaring at me, you would have preferred me awake."

"You're surprisingly astute, Mr. Conrad."

Devon plucked at the sheet, suddenly too weary to hold his eyes open. It was galling to admit that she was right, and it was even more galling to be so weak.

"I'm hungry," he muttered, more to avoid her sharp eyes than because it was true.

"I happen to have some beef broth simmering on the stove in case you lived through your stupidity." Her tart tone jerked his gaze back to her, and he felt a wave of remorse.

"Guess I'm a lot of trouble. You just don't understand why I—"

"I understand perfectly. Do you think Oliver will find you here?" She smiled at him. "Your fever had you raving."

"Raving." He spat the word out and saw her brows lift.

"Yes, raving. Out of your head. Babbling like a moonstruck girl. Just think how convenient that would have been somewhere out on the trail. And from what you said, it sounds as if this Oliver was wounded as well. Of course, if he's more sensible, he's well on the road to recovery by now."

"Thanks for cheering me up."

"Anytime, Mr. Conrad."

Devon eyed her silently for a moment. "I'd rather you called me Cimarrón than say 'Mr. Conrad' in that tone."

"I'll keep that in mind." She moved to the door, then turned to look back at him. "No one knows you're here yet, though I sent a message to Zeke Rogan that you'd be delayed. I signed your name."

"Why did you do that?"

"Because if you didn't return, Rogan might have sent men out looking for you. This way, Rogan thinks you've gone somewhere else, and if Oliver checks, so does he."

"No, more than likely they both think I've crawled up into the hills to die."

"Either way, they shouldn't be looking here for you."

Devon glanced around the small neat room. It was obviously feminine, with white cotton curtains fluttering at the window and a bright quilt flung over the bed. Silver-backed hairbrushes stood on the dresser, and a pitcher of wildflowers were slowly wilting on a small table next to the washstand. His gaze moved back to Maggie. She was watching him closely, and he wished he knew what she was thinking.

"This is your room," he said softly, and she nodded.

"Yes. It was the closest, and the bed in the spare

room is comfortable enough. It's unlikely anyone will stumble over you in my private quarters. Or even on the cot in my examining room, for that matter."

He didn't miss the faint sarcasm in her tone. "Are you very busy?"

"If you mean, do I have any patients yet, you're the only one. Except for three skinned knees on two boys who got into a fight at the school, and a cat that'd gotten its tail caught in a door." She smiled suddenly. "At least the children believe in me enough to bring their skinned knees and pets. I guess that's a start."

"Maybe they'll recommend you."

Maggie nodded. "But will you?"

"Hey, I was alive when I came to you. That's an improvement over your former patients."

Maggie laughed. "You *would* remember that. Now rest, and I'll bring you some hot broth and bread."

"How about a steak?"

"Not yet. Maybe next week."

"By next week, I intend to be back on Oliver's trail."

The smile vanished from Maggie's face and was replaced by white-hot anger. "Wonderful. I patch you up so you can go out and get yourself killed. Why did I bother?"

Before he could remind her that he hadn't asked her to tend him, she'd slammed the door behind her. He heard her quick, angry footsteps fade down the hallway.

"Most prickly woman I've ever met," he muttered, and sagged back into the comfortable feather pillows. It didn't help in the least to know that he also found her to be the most intriguing woman he'd ever met. His hands clenched into fists atop the sheets, and he closed his eyes in frustrated helplessness. He hadn't wanted this, and he was as weak as a day-old kitten and couldn't do anything but lie in the bed and think. And sleep. And think some more.

Devon groaned aloud, not with pain, but with a sense of futility.

# CHAPTER 7

"I've been thinking." '

Maggie shot Devon a quick glance. His color still wasn't that good, and she was afraid to hear what he'd been thinking. She continued changing his bandage, and her tone was sharp.

"How comforting to know that you can think."

"Sarcasm don't suit you, hellcat."

"I resent that term, Cimarrón."

"Ouch!" Devon looked at her reproachfully as she pulled the bandage more tightly. "Don't know what hurts worse—your mouth or your hands."

"If you don't listen to me, you'll discover that it won't matter anymore. I've asked you to drink more water. You cannot take the chance of dehydration, and you still do not urinate freely."

"Damnable discussion to have with a woman." Devon's mouth tightened when she thrust the water jug into his hand. "Mix some whiskey in it and I'll drink it."

"Drink it, or I may end up taking drastic measures to force you to urinate."

To Maggie's amusement, Devon actually blushed. She saw the flush of red creep up his neck to stain his face and was glad that it was him who was uncomfortable for a change. She'd done nothing but blush since meeting him, and it was a most disconcerting reaction for a woman her age who'd seen and done the things she'd experienced.

72

"You were a lot nicer when I first met you," Devon said irritably, but he lifted the water jug to his mouth. When it was empty and she was satisfied, he set it down on the table beside the bed and looked at her. "Happy now?"

"I will be when there's no sign of blood in your urine. Until then, I reserve comment."

"Hell. A man has no privacy around you."

"No, not when he's very sick. That's what you haven't admitted yet—that you could have easily died from your injuries."

"I've been lying in this damn bed nearly a week, and I'm about as weak today as I was the day I got here."

"Yes." Maggie met his angry gaze. "And I told you why. The infection you had was serious. It poisoned your entire system. You're very lucky to be alive. It could easily have turned out differently."

For a moment, Devon didn't reply. Then he said softly, "I'm leaving here tomorrow, well or not. I can't risk staying any longer than that."

"No one knows you're here." Maggie ignored the surge of dismay his words provoked, unable to understand why she kept trying. He obviously didn't want to stay, and in one way she understood why, but any mention of his leaving threw her into turmoil.

"I want to keep it that way," Devon said. "If no one knows I'm here, that keeps you safe as well as me." He paused to stare out the open window where the distant flat ridges edged the horizon. "You said Oliver's bullet went in low and came out higher."

"Yes."

"That means he was down when he fired."

Puzzled, Maggie stared at him. "So?"

Devon's gaze shifted back to her, icy and pale. "So, that means that he was on the ground when he fired because I hit him first. He was fast, but not quite fast enough."

"Ah. I suppose you intend to try this again, then."

"Yes."

"Damn you, Devon Conrad! Just let it go, can't you? Do you have to go out and get yourself killed just because of your stupid pride? I'll never understand why men feel they must be the fastest and the best, or what they're trying to prove except that they're dumber than most wild animals."

He looked at her silently, his eyes going opaque and unreadable, and Maggie whirled away in frustration. Her throat ached, and she wished wildly that she'd never met him and that he'd never sought her out again. The past days of caring for him had only intensified her attraction to him, and she couldn't imagine why. Their conversation usually consisted of teasing remarks or barbed comments, certainly nothing that could be misconstrued as sexual banter. Yet, beneath their casual talk lay the memory of how he'd held her under him and kissed her, and she couldn't forget it.

"Maggie."

She turned away from the door. Devon was sitting up in bed, his bare chest dark against the white sheets, bronze skin gleaming in the soft sunlight that streamed through the windows. Her throat tightened at the sheer male beauty of him. His sun-kissed hair tumbled into his face, and the lucid blue of his eyes were a brilliant counterpoint in his dark, bearded face. There was something very disturbing about the way he was looking at her. She cleared her throat. "Yes?"

"I'll leave tonight when it's dark."

Her heart fell. "No, that's not necessary."

"I think it is."

"Devon—try to understand my position. It's very difficult for me to comprehend the fact that I worked so hard to help you, and you're willing to risk your life again as soon as you get on your feet. It doesn't make sense to someone who has dedicated themselves to *saving* lives to watch while one is thrown carelessly away."

"I have my reasons."

"No doubt. And you probably think they're very good, but I can't agree. There just can't be a reason good enough to risk your life to go out and take another life. I'll never understand that way of thinking."

"Then it's a waste of my time to try and explain." He wadded a fist of sheet in one hand, his mouth thinning. "If you'll bring my clothes, I'll get out of your way."

Tears blurred her vision, and she fumbled with the door and shut it behind her. She leaned back against the wall just outside his door, trying to understand why she was so miserable. She should just say good riddance, but somehow she couldn't. It was a mystery to her why not.

"Cimarrón. Where the hell you been?"

"Around." Devon eased closer to the bar. His side hurt like the devil, and it had damn near killed him to ride a horse. If his dun wasn't so easy-gaited, he'd probably have fallen off like Maggie predicted he would. Fortunately her house was less than half a mile from the saloon on Callahan Street where he'd hoped to find Rogan.

Frank Jackson stared at him narrowly. "You look like hell."

"Where's Rogan?"

"Out at the ranch." Jackson took a step back, eyeing Devon for a long moment. "You get hurt?"

"Why do you ask?"

" 'Cause I heard that you had a run-in with Ash Oliver in Abilene last week."

"Did you." Devon kept his eyes and tone noncommittal.

"Yeah. Oliver didn't come out so good, but they said that you walked away."

"I did." Devon stared back at Jackson. "And you can see that I'm still standing upright."

"Yeah. Guess you are at that." Jackson rubbed a hand over his jaw. "Oliver holed up at a doctor's office, but he rode out of Abilene a day or so ago."

"Why this sudden interest in Ash Oliver, Jackson?" Devon sipped at his beer, watching Frank Jackson's face. The other man glanced away and shifted his feet; his voice was a low mutter.

"Ain't much else to talk about lately. And you sure as hell don't say much."

"When I have something to say, I'll say it." His beer tasted flat. He set down the mug and eased away from the bar with a slow, deliberate motion.

"You ain't leavin' yet are ya, Cimarrón?"

Devon tossed a coin to the bar to pay for his beer and walked away without replying. Jackson got on his nerves. And it was a long way out to the Bar Z ranch. He hoped he would make it without falling off again, but the damnable weakness made him feel light-headed.

It didn't help his temper any to suspect that Maggie had been right.

"Put him over there." Maggie held the door wider for the two men carrying a sagging burden. Her mouth went dry when she recognized Devon's lean form hanging between them like a sack of dry meal. A nauseating smell emanated from him, and she saw the blossoming dark stain on his shirt.

"Be careful," she said sharply when the men slung Devon heavily to the cot in her office. "You might injure him."

One of the men made a harsh sound in the back of his throat. "Don't reckon it'll make much difference to him right now. He don't seem to be awake."

"I can see that, but you may have worsened his condition by treating him so roughly. Where did you find him?"

"Side of the road 'bout two miles outta town. Hadn't of been for his horse standin' there, we wouldn't have seen him at all."

The other man had been watching Maggie silently. Now he stepped into the pool of lamplight while she began unbuttoning Devon's shirt. "Ma'am, you seen this fella before?"

Maggie shot him a quick glance, her hands busy. "You're standing in my light. Why do you ask me that?"

" 'Cause he said your name a time or two. Me and Tully brought him to you 'cause we thought maybe you'd been helpin' him."

"You did the right thing. I appreciate it. I *am* a doctor, you know."

There was a short pause before the man added, "Ma'am, don't you know who this is? Cimarrón. You ever heard of him?"

"Yes," Maggie said calmly, "I certainly have. And if he is injured and needs my help, then I'll help him."

"Just wanted you to know who you're helpin', that's all."

Maggie was well-aware of the man's steady, knowing gaze and had the uncomfortable feeling that he knew Devon had been to her before. And why. It was as if he waited for her to confirm or deny it. She evaded the issue instead.

"I understand that Cimarrón works for Zeke Rogan. Is that true?"

"Yes, ma'am. We both do."

"Then perhaps you should inform Mr. Rogan of his employee's condition as soon as possible. I will do what I can for him, and Mr. Rogan can do what he thinks best."

Still the man hesitated, and impatient now with the

need to tend Devon, Maggie snapped, "Do leave! Unless you want to help me?" She'd opened Devon's shirt, and her hands were smeared with the blood and pus that had seeped through his bandages.

The man took a step back, gagging at the stench. Then he exchanged a glance with the man he'd called Tully. "No. I'll tell Rogan. Hope this don't cause you no trouble, ma'am."

"No more than usual with a patient who is suffering, I imagine."

"That ain't quite what I meant."

Maggie flashed him a quick glare and went back to her work. "I can handle Cimarrón's injuries much more efficiently if you will get out."

After a moment, she heard the scrape of their boots across the floor, then the shutting of the door. She immediately turned her attention back to Devon.

"Stubborn, mule-headed idiot," she muttered more to herself than for his benefit, and was startled to see his lashes lift. The bright, fevered glitter of his eyes peered through the inky brush, and his mouth turned down.

"Nice to . . . see you . . . too."

Unexpected tears stung her eyes, and Maggie fought them back. "Playing possum, were we? Don't blame you. Those men looked fairly rough, and not at all pleased with you."

Devon grunted with pain as she pulled away the last of his bandage. She'd already guessed from the foul odor what had happened, but the sight of the dark, ropy blood and yellow infection still took her aback. It was worse than she'd thought.

Her hands trembled as she dropped the fouled bandage in a metal pail. Had she failed to remove something? Missed a piece of lead, or bone, perhaps? It was obvious that something had caused the infection, and if Devon hadn't opened the wound, it would have eventually poisoned his entire system.

But at least, she told herself, the infection was not spreading inside him now. The fall had done him a favor by releasing it.

Maggie administered Devon a dose of laudanum, and to her vague surprise, he didn't protest. He must be in severe pain not to offer his usual stubborn resistance, she thought as she swiftly gathered her equipment.

By the time she'd finished, Maggie had no idea how much time had passed. Her back ached, and her eyes burned. She'd cleaned out every trace of infection she could find, drained the rest of the abscess, and stitched him up. Then she removed the rest of Devon's clothes and managed to replace the dirtied linens with clean, rolling him to one side as she slid fresh sheets under him, then the other.

His skin was hot and dry to the touch, and she washed him down with tepid water, dragging a cloth over the hard, sculpted lines of his body with first anxiety, then a growing appreciation. Devon's body was a marvel. He had the strong, clean lines of a young Apollo, with smoothly flowing muscles and bronze skin bearing faint marks of former mishaps. The thick pelt of hair on his chest barely covered some of his old scars, and she resisted touching them. It was unsettling to discover that she could not regard him dispassionately. She should be able to.

But somehow, her medical training had never touched on the possibility of being too emotionally involved with her patient. A physician rarely treated family for that reason, but Devon Conrad was not family.

Maggie forced herself to finish bathing him, then tucked the sheet around his sturdy frame and left him sleeping quietly. She went into her small kitchen and put a kettle on to boil water for tea, musing over her inability to regard Devon Conrad with the necessary objectivity.

Something had ignited at their first meeting, some small spark that she'd banked with the ashes of indifference, not noticing how strong it was until recently. After a week in his company, she had to acknowledge to herself that she was helpless against her growing attraction to him.

"Damn," she said softly. The kettle began to shriek and rattle, and she poured boiling water into a cup and stirred in tea. Why couldn't medical science define and cure the alchemy between a man and woman? It would be much handier, and probably save a lot of heartache if they could. Falling in love with the wrong person had certainly caused more pain and death than even the lure of greed and power could do. The annals of history proved that in many ways. So why did she have to be so blamed attracted to the man they called Cimarrón?

It just didn't seem fair.

Especially since he didn't seem to share the same depth of attraction.

Maggie took the cooling tea back to her office and sank down into a chair not far from Devon's cot. The rise and fall of his chest was reassuring, though he muttered with pain on occasion. She watched him and, from time to time, rose from her chair to sponge him down with cool water in an effort to lower his fever.

She was still in her chair when the morning sun rose.

Devon opened his eyes and glanced over at her. His head pounded, and he had to squint to focus his gaze on Maggie. She slumped in a chair, her head and one arm resting on the edge of the examining table not far from his cot. He could see the lines of weariness in her face, saw the way her dark hair straggled from its neat coil to tangle over her back and shoulders. Maggie. All contradiction, sweet femininity, and prickly temper formed into an alluring shape that made him balance between irritation and interest. Damn. Too bad he hadn't made it to the Bar Z before falling. Being back with her would only complicate his life even more, and he didn't need that.

He was still watching her when he saw her jerk awake suddenly, sitting bolt upright in the chair while her eyes flew to him.

"You're awake," she said, her voice slightly husky with sleep.

"Seems that way."

"It's about time. You're the laziest man I've ever met, always lying around in bed."

She rose from the chair and smoothed her skirts as she approached, a feminine gesture that belied the professional way in which she lifted his arm to check his pulse.

"Am I alive?"

"In spite of yourself." Her eyes briefly met his, and her fingers tightened slightly around his wrist. "But I'm certain you'll find a way to rectify that before long. No, stay still. I'm getting tired of repatching you."

"Then why do you keep doing it?"

"Maybe I feel sorry for you. Or maybe I'm a glutton for punishment. I lean toward the latter theory myself."

Devon didn't comment. Talking was too wearying, especially the quick banter with Maggie. She was hard on a well man; an injured man didn't have the chance of an icicle in hell.

Maggie released his wrist and checked his bandages, then asked, "Do you have any family you want me to notify?"

"Am I dyin'?"

"Not yet. It's just customary to let a patient's family know of their condition so arrangements can be made."

"You make it sound like funeral arrangements."

"Take off before you're well again, and it will be." Her cool tone was uncompromising. Devon's mouth thinned.

"No. No family."

"No family, or you don't want them notified?"

"The only family I have is too far away to do either one of us any good. If I don't bother her when I'm all right, I sure as hell don't intend to bother her when I've got bullet holes in me."

"Your mother?"

"No. My mother died a long time ago."

"I see."

Devon glanced up and saw the quick flutter of some emotion in her eyes, then it was gone. Her voice was flat again, her manner brisk and remote.

"Then if you are stupid enough to take unnecessary risks again, I'll just see that they put you in the local cemetery without notifying anyone."

"Good." He closed his eyes, exhausted. "Where's Pardo?"

"Pardo?"

"My horse."

"Good heavens. I never thought of your horse."

He opened his eyes at the sound of her footsteps crossing the floor. "Maggie."

She turned. "Yes?"

"I guess I'm a sorry bastard."

For a moment he thought she didn't intend to reply, then she shrugged. "At this moment, I agree with you."

The door closed behind her, and he smiled. Prickly

all right, as prickly as a clump of cholla cactus. And about as inviting when she gave him that cold stare that could freeze a man to the bones.

So why did he want her so damn bad?

## CHAPTER 8

Sunlight flooded the kitchen with yellow heat despite the door and windows left open to allow in cooling breezes. Maggie blinked at the bright glare and her brother. "Excuse me?"

"I can't understand you." Johnny's eyes narrowed with hot anger, and Maggie fought a wave of anger just as hot.

"Did I ask you to understand me? For that matter, did I ask you to interfere in my business?"

"Dammit, Maggie! The whole gawdammed town is talkin' about you lettin' Cimarrón stay here."

"Keep your voice down. You'll disturb my patient." Her cold tone and clipped words did not appease her brother's fury in the slightest. He took a step closer, narrowing the distance between them. Maggie could almost feel his frustrated fury, and noted the way his hands were clenched into fists at his sides. A muscle leaped in his jaw as he ground his teeth together.

"He's not a patient, Maggie. He's a killer. Haven't you got that yet? A killer. Why the hell did you bother patchin' up a cold-blooded killer?"

She folded her arms over her chest to keep from betraying the trembling of her hands. "Because he was an injured man—a human being—and I took an oath to do my best to save human life whenever and wherever I can."

"I suppose you'd patch up a rattler."

"That's not the same thing, and you know it."

"Sounds like the same thing to me. Hell, he's been here for almost two weeks. People are sayin'—"

"People are saying what?" she demanded when he jerked to an abrupt halt.

Johnny's dark eyes flicked away from her, then back, and she saw misery as well as anger in his gaze. "They're sayin' that you and Cimarrón are doin' a lot more than playin' doctor and patient, that's what they're sayin'."

"Do you believe that?"

"Would it matter if I did?"

"Probably not." Her honest reply made his mouth thin into a harsh slit. Maggie sighed. "Look, Johnny, he's my patient. Old Mrs. Lamb is staying in the spare room as a combination assistant and chaperon. If there are some people who choose to make it sound tawdry, there's nothing I can do about that. People are always going to find something to talk about, and you know as well as I do that it doesn't make a nickel's worth of difference if there's any truth to it. Why are you letting this bother you?"

"Because you're my sister and I'm responsible for you, dammit. Why do you think? When folks look at me and ask about you, or mention Cimarrón stayin' here, I feel like hittin' something. It ain't right, Maggie." His tone altered subtly, becoming more pleading instead of angry. "Please think about what you're doin' to yourself by lettin' him stay here. I guess I understand that you want to help him and all, but send him out to Rogan. Let him stay at the Bar Z instead of here."

"He couldn't get adequate care there. Johnny, he could have died from his wounds. There was an infection, and—"

"It'd be better for everyone round here if he did die. Why do you think you have to save him?"

She stared at him with a rising feeling of helpless-

ness choking off any reply. It was useless. Johnny
would not listen or understand, and it was simply a
waste of breath to try and explain her reasons to him.

"Maggie, sugar, listen to me. Cimarrón is a killer. He
went after Ash Oliver like a damn crazy Comanche or
somethin'. I'm worried about you bein' here alone
with him like this. He's capable of doin' anything."

Maggie stood stiffly. "He wouldn't hurt me, if that's
what you're implying."

Johnny raked an impatient hand through his hair
and gave her a doubtful glance. "Just what do you
know about him? Nothin'. Nothin' except his reputation as a killer. He gunned down that man in the saloon, and he tried to gun down Ash Oliver."

"When did you become such a defender of Ash Oliver? I seem to recall you once referring to him as lower
than a snake's belly at the bottom of hell."

A faint flush colored his face, but Johnny stubbornly
refused to give up. "I don't particularly care about Oliver, but I don't trust any man who's gunned down as
many men as Cimarrón has."

"Weren't any of the men he gunned down provoking it? Did he always just shoot first? The way I heard
it, that man in the saloon wouldn't leave him alone and
even went for his gun first."

"I don't know where you heard that, but David
Brawley was there and he said Cimarrón just shot Jenkins down in cold blood, slicker than cat spit."

"I heard it from Ira Howell, and he was there, too. I
don't know Mr. Brawley that well, but I've known Ira
most of my life."

"Ira Howell's blind as a cockeyed mole, and you
know it. He couldn't see his hand in front of him without those bottle-thick spectacles he wears, and those
stay fogged up most of the time."

Maggie turned away irritably and pulled open the
door to the icebox. "Care for some lemonade?"

"You're changin' the subject. Reckon I know why."

Still kneeling in front of the icebox, she turned on the balls of her feet to glare up at him. "You don't know a blessed thing. You're the one who's blind, blind to reason. I intend to do exactly what I'm doing whether you like it or not, and whether the entire town likes it or not. I'm not breaking any rules or committing any sin, so you can just go on back to the ranch and leave me alone."

Several moments crawled past before Johnny said grimly, "I've tried to get you to see reason. You're a hardheaded woman, Margaret Anne Malone, and I hope you don't regret this, but I know you will."

"Thank you for your vote of confidence in me."

"It ain't you I don't trust, dammit—it's Cimarrón."

"You make him sound like a mad-dog killer. Your only reasons are gossip and unfounded rumors. Do you really expect me to believe everything I hear?"

Johnny lapsed into bristling silence, then said slowly, "If I can get you proof he's what I say, will you listen to me then?"

"Proof. I can't imagine what you intend to get as proof, but you're welcome to try. By the time you can find out anything, he'll be well and gone, so go ahead." She slammed a pitcher of lemonade to the kitchen table. "Until then, I intend to go on exactly as I am."

"Promise me you won't be careless."

His soft plea made her throat ache with suppressed emotion, and Maggie nodded wordlessly. Johnny studied her a moment, then picked his hat up off the table and set it on his head, adjusting it.

"Well. Reckon I'll go on. Keep your .45 loaded and close. If you go into town, don't be surprised when folks look at you funny."

She made an impatient sound, and he shrugged, then moved past her out the open door. His boots sounded loud on the porch, and she heard the jangle of bit chains and his spurs as Johnny swung into his saddle and nudged his horse into a brisk trot toward Belle Plain.

"Damn," she said softly, staring after him.

It was a sentiment her brother echoed fervently. What was the matter with Maggie? Couldn't she see the danger? Did she always have to be so blamed pigheaded? Well, he didn't intend to let her be hurt, in spite of her stubborn sense of loyalty. Maybe he shouldn't have said all those things about her being a doctor and all, but dadgum it, she just didn't realize how people looked at a woman who did those kind of things. He did, only too well.

When he dismounted in front of the telegraph office in Belle Plain, Johnny saw David Brawley just leaving.

"Malone," Brawley said easily, pausing in the shade of the roof overhang. He tucked a sheet of paper into the inner vest pocket of his tailored three-piece serge suit, then put out his hand. "How are you doing today?"

Johnny shook his hand. "Well enough."

"Good to see you in town again. You don't get in very often."

"No. It takes a lot of time to run a ranch if you want to make anything of it." Johnny shifted restlessly from one foot to the other. "How's the hotel business?"

"Better than expected. I'm hoping that the railroad makes its decision soon. It will mean a lot to Belle Plain to have a depot here, you know. More businesses will open, and more people will come."

Johnny snorted. "That ain't exactly my idea of doin' good. Don't need more people out here squattin' on the land. Too many people means more trouble and less cattle."

"What a novel way of viewing it." Brawley's mouth curled with amusement. "I suppose you're right, but to men in my business, that way of thinking doesn't seem very profitable."

"Maybe not."

When Johnny nodded and started to move past, Brawley asked, "How's your lovely sister?"

He stopped and turned, eyes narrowing slightly. "Fine."

"I tried to call on her yesterday, but she said she was too busy to visit."

"Then she was probably too busy to visit."

"Do you think it's wise for that gunslinger to be staying there with her?"

"Ain't what I think that matters," Johnny said gruffly. "It's what Maggie thinks. She wouldn't do nothin' wrong."

"That may be, but Cimarrón is not known for his finer character traits."

Johnny glared at him. "Think I don't know that? If I could talk her into throwin' him out, I'd do the honors, but she won't. Keeps talkin' about her duty as a physician."

"She's a woman first, and I can assure you that Cimarrón is well-aware of that fact."

"Just what the hell are you sayin', Brawley?"

"Now, now, Malone, don't get upset. I'm only saying what everyone in town is saying."

"Which is?"

David Brawley eyed Johnny for a moment, a flicker of disquiet in his hazel eyes. "Only that your sister is asking to be talked about if she allows Cimarrón to stay. He's a known killer, an outlaw since he was a kid robbing trains up in Colorado."

"How do you know that?"

"I have a long memory, and I spent some time in Leadville a few years back. That was when Cimarrón was riding with an outlaw known as Colorado Kate."

Johnny stared at Brawley. Apparently he knew a lot about Cimarrón. "Can you prove any of that?"

Brawley looked startled. "Prove it?"

"I mean, can you give me enough details where I can check it out to tell Maggie? If she knew the truth, I don't think she'd be taking chances with Cimarrón."

"Sure, I can tell you everything I know. If you ask me, though, the best way to help your sister is to round up a few good riflemen and go drag Cimarrón out to the nearest big tree for a rope party."

"Yeah, that'd be the quickest way, but I don't know about the best. Maggie can get mad quicker than any woman I know, and besides that, she's just liable to try and defend him. I'd hate to have to try and take a gun away from her."

Brawley smiled. "Perhaps you're right. She's not only a beautiful woman, but a dedicated one."

Johnny drew in a deep breath and glanced up the street. "Come on, Brawley. I'll buy you a beer while you tell me what you know about Cimarrón."

"You don't need to defend me, you know." Devon leaned against the doorframe and watched Maggie whirl around to face him. Shadows darkened her clear gray eyes to smoke.

"I don't know what you mean."

"I'm weak, not deaf."

Her face colored, and he watched with interest. It had not bothered him in the least to hear the things Johnny Malone had said about him; what had bothered him was the way Maggie came to his defense. He wondered why. It wasn't as if he was that nice to her. Most of the time, he resented the way she made him feel, and showed it.

Yet she had defended him to her brother.

"How much did you hear?"

Devon smiled slightly. "Enough to know he'd like nothing better than to use me for target practice."

Maggie smoothed her skirts. She was wearing a plain pink cotton gown with short sleeves and a scooped neck, and an apron over that, and he wondered how she managed to make it look so damnably attractive. The heat had put a rosy glow on her face, and a sheen misted her skin. Loops of dark hair were clustered at the crown of her head, half-falling in some places, damp tendrils curling toward her face and straggling down the back of her neck.

"Johnny's always had a short temper. He's usually fairly harmless."

Devon snorted. "Right. If he'd had a rope handy, I'd be riding it through a field of cactus right now."

"Scared?" Her lips twitched, and he recognized the glint of amusement in her eyes.

"Yep. He looks mean as a grizzly to me. I'm not as brave as you are."

Maggie grinned. "I'm not brave, just more ornery than he is."

"Then maybe it's you I should be afraid of."

"True." She moved the glass pitcher on the table. "I made more lemonade. Sit down and I'll pour you some."

Devon dragged out a chair and seated himself slowly. It amazed him how long it had taken to get his strength back. Only in the past few days had he been able to walk from the house to the convenience in the rear without getting weak.

While Maggie chipped ice from a block and put it into glasses, he watched, enjoying the graceful feminine motions she made. There was something soothing about being around a woman; even the most slatternly female had a certain sense of femininity that comforted a man. It had nothing to do with sex, and everything to do with serenity.

With a shock, Devon realized that he'd miss Maggie

Malone when he rode away. The realization was quickly followed by a burning sense of guilt. He couldn't allow himself the luxury of caring for a woman. That had ended when Molly died in his arms. He'd been responsible for her death, and he had no intention of being responsible for the death of another woman who cared about him.

And he knew that Maggie cared. It was obvious in the way she watched him, her eyes soft and full, her hands gentle and personal when they tended him. No, he wasn't going to let it happen again.

When Maggie handed him his glass of lemonade and sat across from him, he looked up at her, mindful of the way they'd sat at this table for the past three nights as if they were married. She'd served him dinner, and they'd talked about anything that came to mind. She was an uncomplicated, secure woman, confident in her own ability and not reluctant to show it. It was one of the things about her that attracted him most.

"I'm leaving tomorrow," he said abruptly, and felt her gaze shift to his face.

"It's too soon."

"No, it's probably too late, Maggie." He held her eyes with his and ignored the rising dismay in them. "I can't stay any longer. Your brother's right. My being here has hurt you."

"Ordinarily that may be true, but there's some fundamental part of me that detests being bullied. And that's what this town is trying to do, Devon—bully me into being something other than what I am. It's not as if we set up housekeeping together. And old Mrs. Lamb is a decent chaperon."

"She's half-blind and deaf to boot, and you know it. I could toss your skirts over your head and make love to you three feet from her and she'd probably doze off."

He saw from the way Maggie's pupils dilated and the way her lips parted that he'd shocked her, and managed a smile that felt more like a grimace. "You know what I mean."

"Yes." She cleared her throat when the word came out a husky rasp. "Yes, I suppose I do."

A strange sort of current flowed between them, charged with as much intensity as a bolt of lightning. Devon felt it tighten around him, binding him to her in some inexplicable way that he couldn't explain and didn't want to acknowledge.

His tone was involuntarily savage when he muttered, "If I don't leave soon, Maggie Malone, I may do exactly that."

"Do—?"

He stood up, blood boiling in his veins as if heated. The memory of her soft skin was a temptation that he did his best to resist. "You know what I mean, dammit."

"No. I don't think I do. Devon . . . what are you—?"

Without pausing to think, he reached out to pull her to him, one hand around her wrist and the other hand moving to the small of her back. Maggie seemed to melt into him, her body boneless, soft breasts pressing against his chest as he pulled her close.

His mouth found hers, and he kissed her with a fierce urgency that grew hotter and higher when she made a small noise in the back of her throat. Ah God, she was so sweet and fine, so damn fine. He couldn't help himself. He knew better than to touch her, better than to kiss her. He knew he wouldn't want to stop at kisses, and Maggie deserved to be treated with more respect.

So why wasn't he stopping?

"Dev—Devon." Her voice was a thick whisper, her breath fluttering against his lips.

"Open your mouth for me," he said, and felt her

quiver. He stroked her cheek with one hand, then gently clasped her chin between his thumb and finger. "Come on, open for me."

Slowly her lips parted, and he slid his tongue inside in a velvety smooth motion that sent jolts of response into every fiber of his body. Maggie was shivering despite the heavy press of heat in the house, and he felt as if he was on fire with need. Her fingers dug into his biceps. His tongue stroked in a simulation of sex that soon had him to the breaking point, and he tore his mouth from hers, his chest heaving with the effort to catch his breath.

"Sweet Jesus," he muttered hoarsely.

Maggie was clinging to him as if drowning. He could feel the rapid rise and fall of her breasts, knew she was as breathless as he was. His blood was thundering through his veins, drowning out his common sense. He wanted her. He wanted to carry her into the next room and take off her clothes and make love to her until neither one of them could move.

He closed his eyes and buried his face in her hair, inhaling deeply. The gentle fragrance of roses wafted up, and his throat tightened. He was raw with pain and need.

"Maggie, look at me."

Obediently she tilted back her head. Her eyes were glazed, almost confused, as if she didn't know what had happened. Devon felt his gut clench.

"Now do you see why I have to leave?"

She stared at him. God, she was looking at him as if he'd slapped her. He quickly smothered a twinge of conscience when her hands fell away and she took a step back. He watched her gather her poise around her like a cloak, and she held his eyes with a steady gaze.

"If you're leaving because you're afraid I'll throw myself at you, that's not necessary."

Her cool reply was like a dash of icy water. Devon

stared at her. "I'm leaving, dammit, because if I don't, I'm liable to forget my good intentions and put myself inside you until we're both too weak to walk. Do you understand what I'm saying?"

"I believe you've made it perfectly clear." She took a side step, and her hand trembled when she reached for her half-empty glass of lemonade.

Frustration welled in him. Before he realized it, he was reaching for her again, not knowing why, only knowing that he needed to touch her, to make certain she understood why he couldn't stay.

"Maggie—"

"Touch my sister, and I swear I'll blow your head off."

The terse words whipped him around, and he damned himself for being so lost in Maggie that he hadn't heard Johnny Malone come up onto the back porch. Malone stood in the doorway, face dark with fury. Devon thought of the pistol he'd tucked into his belt at his back and knew he couldn't draw on her brother.

Maggie dropped her glass with a shattering crash, and lemonade splashed across the table in a sticky pool. "Johnny, what do you think you're doing?"

"Keepin' that bastard from touchin' you, that's what." His eyes narrowed beneath the brim of his hat. "Or maybe that's what you want. Is it?"

Devon's tone was harsh. "Back off, Malone."

Johnny's eyes shot to him. "You feelin' frisky enough to try and make me?"

"No!" Maggie screamed, startling both men with the intensity of her cry. Her face was white, eyes like huge charcoal pools.

"Stay outta this, Maggie," Malone said shortly. "This is between me and Cimarrón."

"You're in my house, Johnny." When Malone shot

her a fierce glance, she added more calmly, "You have
no right to say who comes and goes here."

"Dammit, Maggie, I heard what this bastard said to
you. Are you dumb enough to think he's in love with
you? 'Cause that sure as hell ain't what I heard him
say."

Maggie's face colored, and Devon felt an aching
emptiness inside him. Malone was right. It just
sounded so harsh and cold, coming from him. Maybe
he should say something to soften it, something that
would erase that stricken, hurt expression from Maggie's face, but he couldn't. The words wouldn't come.

After a moment of charged silence, Maggie sucked
in a deep breath and said calmly, "Both of you leave.
Just go."

When she turned to look at him, Devon had the
thought that he'd never felt quite as ashamed of himself as he did at that moment.

# CHAPTER 9

"Have you heard from that nice young man, dear?"

Maggie looked up at Mrs. Lamb with a faint frown. "Who do you mean?"

"Why, the young gentleman who was injured so badly. Devon."

*Devon.* Maggie winced.

"No. No, I haven't, Mrs. Lamb. Why do you ask?"

Mrs. Lamb's brown eyes twinkled softly. "Because I had the distinct impression that he was quite taken with you, that's why. I thought perhaps he might have come back for a visit since getting well."

Yes. One would think Devon would at least let her know if he was still alive, as a courtesy if nothing else. But he hadn't. There had been no word from him in the month since he and Johnny had stood like two bristling tomcats in her kitchen. Maggie sighed.

"I understand that he's busy. Rustlers have been worse than ever lately, and from what I hear, Rogan and some of the other ranchers have joined forces and men."

"Yes, so I heard." Mrs. Lamb bustled about the kitchen with an energy that never ceased to amaze Maggie. Widowed for almost fifteen years, Amelia Lamb was one of those women who did not let life get her down. She'd borne nine children and lost four of them, and the remaining five had long since left Texas and their mother behind. Though rarely without a letter in her apron pocket, Mrs. Lamb was alone in the world. Maggie frequently wondered if she could be as cheerful, given the same circumstances.

"Do you think they'll catch them?" Mrs. Lamb asked as she removed a pan of cookies from the oven. Maggie leaned over to pluck one from the pan, laughingly avoiding Mrs. Lamb's admonishing tap with a spatula.

"Sooner or later, I suppose. Mmm, this cookie is good. I miss my mother's sugar cookies."

Mrs. Lamb's face was flushed from the heat of the oven as she turned with a smile. "I miss baking cookies. I'm glad that you asked me to help you out."

"I need you."

"Poppycock. You could do all this yourself. My coming in twice a week doesn't change things that much. Don't think I don't know what you're doing. But I'm grateful for it. I get lonely in that house by myself." A wistful smile touched her lips for a moment, and her eyes grew damp. "Since my Charlie was killed, it's been too lonely."

"There aren't many Comanches around here anymore."

"That doesn't mean they're gone. The Army just has them run off for the moment."

Maggie nodded silently. The Comanches had once freely roamed the area around Belle Plain, and then white settlers had begun staking claims and running cattle on their hunting grounds. The frequent raids had been fierce and deadly, and it had been in one of those that Charlie Lamb had died.

"Too bad the Army doesn't help with the rustlers," Maggie said after a moment. "The Double M has been hit pretty hard lately. Johnny is fit to be tied about it. One of his prize bulls was taken, as well as some of the other stock. He's out for blood, and I'm afraid for him."

"He's not the only one, dear. All the ranchers are up in arms about it." She pushed at a strand of white hair in her eyes, frowning. "I was told that one of Zeke Rogan's hired gunman brought in three of the rustlers. They're in the jail now."

Maggie snorted derisively. "Ben Whittaker is useless as a sheriff. I hope someone is watching him watch the prisoners. Otherwise, they're liable to be broken out of that shabby jail by their comrades."

"Some of the townsmen are taking turns at being deputies. It seems to me that the cavalry at Fort Griffin should be helping with this. They're close enough."

"They've got troubles of their own, with all those gun-happy cowboys, buffalo hunters, and outlaws. Hardly a week goes by that there's not a gunfight in the street."

Mrs. Lamb gave her a shrewd glance. "Rumor has it that your nice young man is the gunfighter who brought in those three rustlers."

Maggie's throat tightened, and she swallowed the last bite of cookie before replying. "He's said to be. And he's not *my* young man."

"Humph. Couldn't tell that by me. The way he looked at you—"

"Mrs. Lamb, he looked at me with gratitude for saving his life. That's all." She cleared her throat. "Besides, I think he's married."

"Married?"

Maggie nodded slowly, forcing the words out. "Yes. From what little he has said while conscious, there's some woman he doesn't want to worry. And when he was unconscious . . . he said the name 'Kate.' "

Silence fell. Then Mrs. Lamb nodded. "Have another sugar cookie, dear, before more patients arrive."

Maggie shook her head. "I'd better get the examination room ready. Yesterday was quite busy at times."

"Yes, people are beginning to realize what a local treasure you are. About time, I say."

"Some of them still refuse to see me, preferring to ride all the way into Abilene or Baird rather than let a woman doctor them."

"That's their problem. You're good, and the people who do come to you agree with me."

"Thank you." Maggie silently forgave Mrs. Lamb her meddling. "I have to ride out tomorrow to check on Mary MacTavish. She had a difficult delivery, and I want to be certain she hasn't hemorrhaged."

"Is the baby well?"

"The baby is perfect. Another boy. That makes four." Maggie laughed, shaking her head. "I'll never understand it. After hours of pain, Mary held her baby and said that the next one would be a girl. Why on earth would she want to put herself through that again?"

"It's a joy, bringing life into the world, dear."

"Not for me. I'm too selfish. A child would only complicate my life, and I'm sensible enough to recognize that."

"Perhaps, but one day you won't think that way. When the right man comes along, you'll want to have his children."

"*If* the right man ever comes along, I may want him, but he'll have to do without the children." Maggie shrugged. "I don't even want the responsibility of having a pet. I certainly won't want a child. Being a doctor is a full-time job, and I don't intend to let anything interfere with it. No, I'll never have children."

"In my experience, those folks who say 'never' usually end up doing that very thing." Mrs. Lamb laughed when Maggie made a horrified sound. "You'll see, dear. You'll see."

* * *

It was nearing dusk when Maggie finished with the last of her patients, a young boy who'd fallen into a clump of cactus.

"There," she said with a final dab of ointment, "that should help ease the pain and prevent infection."

It was obvious he was trying not to cry, and Maggie bit back a smile when he said glumly, "It'll hurt worse when my pa finds out that a horse got loose."

"I'm certain your father will be glad to know you weren't seriously hurt, Mark. He won't mind about the horse."

Mark gave her a doleful glance. "He'll mind, all right. It weren't our horse. Belonged to a customer. Dang mean-broke hoss, dragged me half a mile before I lost him in that clump of cactus. 'Most as mean as his owner."

Maggie put some ointment into a cone-shaped paper and gave it to him. "Use this whenever you need it. And stay away from mean horses."

"Huh. Wish I could. 'Specially this hoss." Mark slid from the table. He pushed a long strand of brown hair from his eyes, his expression lightening a bit. "Only good thing is knowin' that when Cimarrón finds out Ash Oliver's in town there'll be a fight fer sure."

Her heart lurched. "Ash Oliver?"

Mark nodded. "Yep. He left his hoss at our livery is how I know he's here. Bold as brass, ain't he? Comin' inta a town where there's a gunslick like Cimarrón waitin' round to brace him. Pa's says I'm ta stay out of it, but you can betcha I'm gonna be watchin' when Cimarrón gits into town."

"How . . . how do you know he'll be here?"

"The whole town knows. Everybody's talkin' about it. I peeked in the doors of the Brass Lady, and anybody who can walk is sittin' at the bar waitin' to see it. A couple of men rode out to the Bar Z to let Cimarrón and Rogan know that Oliver is here and waitin'."

"But that's stupid!"

Mark just stared at her blankly, and Maggie realized with a surge of frustration that few people would agree with her. It was exciting, the promise of a gunfight between two well-known gunmen, and would draw curious townsfolk.

"Uh, is it all right if my pa sends over the money?" Mark asked hesitantly. He stepped to the door, obviously eager to be gone.

"That's fine. And Mark—be sensible. Stay at home and out of harm's way."

"Uh-huh. I don't intend to be dragged through no more cactus."

"That's not what I mean. If Ash Oliver and Cimarrón meet, it will be dangerous."

Maggie saw the obstinate light in the boy's eyes and sighed. He wouldn't listen. He'd be like most of the other males in town, avidly waiting and watching.

When Mark had gone, Maggie shut the front door behind him and leaned against it, frowning. If Ash Oliver was there for Cimarrón and there was another fight, Devon could be killed. Or at the very least, he might be wounded, and in his weakened condition it could be the end of him.

She put a hand over her eyes. Maybe she should try to get to Devon first, get him to listen to reason.

"Cimarrón."

Devon glanced up, his .45 balanced in his hand. "Yeah?"

Tully made a nervous motion with one hand. "Put that away. I just came to give ya a message."

"What?"

"Ash Oliver's in Belle Plain."

Devon rose slowly from where he'd been sitting at the table in the bunkhouse, cleaning his rifle. "You see him?"

"No, but Jackson did. He gave Frank a message for ya." Tully glanced at the others in the bunkhouse, apparently pleased to have witnesses.

"And what would that be?"

Tully cleared his throat. "That he'll be sittin' in the Brass Lady tonight if ya still want to see him."

With slow, unhurried movements, Devon snapped his rifle closed and worked the newly oiled lever. It moved with a smooth, snicking sound, and he replaced it on the table and shoved his .45 back into his holster. Out of long habit, he never took apart and cleaned but one weapon at a time, preferring to have something within easy reach. He saw Tully's glance at the table and smiled to himself. It looked like a small arsenal, from knives to boot pistols, and he could almost read the other man's mind.

"I like to be prepared for any varmint that might come sneaking up on me, Tully."

Tully's face turned an ugly shade of red and his mouth tightened. "Yeah, well you better do some sneakin' of your own if you want to beat Oliver. Don't know what you boys got between you, but Jackson said he's mad as a pissed-on snake. Reckon that's got anything to do with the fight in Abilene?"

"I reckon you're too damn nosy for your own health, Tully, is what I reckon." Devon eyed him coolly as he picked up his weapons.

Tully backed away. "You think you're so damn fast, Cimarrón, but Oliver managed to plug you a good one, don't forget."

"I haven't. Don't you forget that I'm faster than you are, Tully. And not nearly as nosy."

One of the men guffawed, and Tully's hand closed into a fist that lightly grazed the holster on his thigh. For a moment they eyed one another, then Tully pivoted on his heel and stalked from the bunkhouse. No one spoke as Devon crossed to his bunk and pulled his saddlebags from beneath the hard cot.

He'd been expecting Oliver since he'd surprised some of the rustlers up in a grassy gully at the far edge of the Bar Z. Though alone at the time, he'd given them the chance to surrender. They had chosen to fight instead. Two of them lay dead when the shooting stopped, and three had been taken into Belle Plain and the sheriff. Rogan had been surprised, then had begun bragging that his gunman had been the one to shoot them.

Since then, most of the Bar Z gunmen and riders had viewed Cimarrón with wary respect, steering clear of him. He'd overheard one of them mutter that it wasn't natural for a man to take risks like that, that Cimarrón must not care if he got killed.

For some reason, that had rankled. And he didn't know why. The reckless indifference had been with him for so long that he'd grown accustomed to it, almost attached, as if to a favorite horse. To lose it would be dangerous. A gunman who was afraid to die didn't live very long. One of the things that had kept him alive so long was that he didn't care.

Or did he?

"Put him over there." Maggie pointed toward the cot in her examining room, hands trembling with nerves.

Puffing and panting, three men heaved the inert form toward the cot, dropping him onto the mattress. "I don't think he's gonna make it," one of them grumbled. "Damn gunman plugged him good."

"Yeah," another man muttered, "and Oliver got away quick as scat, too. Took off when he saw Whittaker comin'."

Maggie cleared her throat, already examining the man on the cot. "Were there any other woundings?"

"Not fixable ones. It was rigged, an ambush from the start. Ain't never seen a man move as fast as Cimarrón did, though. He's everythang they say he is—cat-quick reflexes and sure as shi—shootin'. Shot one of the men with Oliver before he'd even cleared leather, right between the eyes. Looked like he was on wheels, by God, spinnin' around and shootin'—lead flyin' everywhere."

Maggie glanced up at the wounded man's face. She knew him from somewhere, though she couldn't recall where.

"Who is this man?"

"Gene Tully. Rides for the Bar Z. He was behind Cimarrón when they rode in. One of Oliver's men got him."

"And Cimarrón?"

There was a brief silence. Maggie glanced up, saw the quick look exchanged, and knew the reason. Apparently, to her chagrin, Johnny was right. Most of the citizens of Belle Plain believed her to be intimately involved with Devon.

"Not a scratch, ma'am. Uh—Doc. Cool as ice, he is. Hot lead buzzin' around his head like a swarm of bees, and he took his time and his shots. Too bad Oliver got away. That there is one man I wouldn't mind seein' dance at the end of a rope. Ain't got no use for a bushwhacker."

"No doubt." Maggie stood up, gazing down at the man on the cot. "There's nothing I can do for this man, gentlemen. He's dead."

"Kinda thought that when we brought him here, but Cimarrón said if anybody could help him, you could." Another embarrassed silence fell, and Maggie squared her shoulders.

"He was shot in the heart. He was probably dead before you got him here. I'm sorry."

"Ain't nothin' to me," one of the men grumbled.

"It's what he gets for ridin' with Cim—" He jerked to a halt as the door swung open and Devon filled the opening.

An appalled silence shrouded the room, and Maggie could almost hear the erratic thump of her heartbeat when Devon leaned lazily against the doorframe and crossed his arms over his chest. A mocking grin gleamed white in his bearded face.

"Ordinarily I'd agree with you, Thompson, but Tully wasn't riding with me. He was on his own. I ride alone."

"Yeah, right, Cimarrón. Didn't mean nothin' by it." Thompson couldn't meet his gaze, but stared at a spot on the floor.

Tension rippled through the men, and Maggie's eyes locked with Devon's. Her throat tightened, and she fought an inexplicable urge to fling herself into his arms despite the gazes of the others. It was crazy, this needy feeling that swept through her like a Texas wildfire, hot and burning and making her feel as if her soul was aflame.

Had it been a month since she'd seen him? It felt as if it had been a year. An eternity since she'd felt the sizzling heat that he sparked in her, the breathless singing of her pulses and kindling excitement that made her stomach churn and her heart leap.

Someone spoke, and it took her a moment to register the fact that the men were wrapping Gene Tully in a blanket and lifting him from the cot. Devon watched silently, face as impassive as a stone statue's, his eyes remote and unreadable.

"Reckon we'll take Tully on over to Wiggins Ice House till we can git him buried," Thompson said gruffly. "Who's gonna tell Rogan?"

"I will." Devon stepped aside as the men carried Tully from the room.

Thompson cleared his throat. "Fine. Guess we'll be

goin' on then." He avoided Devon's gaze and flicked Maggie a quick glance as he scurried from the room with the others.

Maggie heard the front door shut behind them, leaving her alone with Devon. A clock on the mantel ticked loudly, sounding almost too loud in the suddenly quiet room. After a moment, Maggie moved jerkily toward the blood-soaked sheets on the cot, aware of Devon watching her.

"Need some help?" he asked, and she turned.

"No. Mrs. Lamb comes in two days a week or whenever I need her."

"She coming tomorrow?"

"No. She came today."

Devon moved toward her and reached out to take the sheet from her hand. "Then you need help with this."

Sudden tears burned her eyes. "I think I can manage a few soiled sheets, Devon."

He made an inarticulate noise, and she looked up at his face. "Maybe I just need to be with you right now, Maggie."

"Why?"

"Hell, I don't know. I wish I did. You—you're like the calm after a storm."

"Apparently your life has been storm-free until today." When his eyes narrowed fractionally, she said, "I haven't seen or heard from you."

"Thought your brother made it pretty plain that I wasn't wanted here. And so did you."

"Devon, what was I supposed to say, with you two glaring at each other like two dogs quarreling over a bone? And I asked you both to leave."

"Ah, that makes me feel better. I wasn't the only one thrown out."

He sounded cynical, his voice a mocking drawl that

brought a hot flush to her face. "It wasn't like that at all and you know it."

"If I knew it, Maggie, I wouldn't have stayed away."

She drew back to look at him. "Wouldn't you? I think you were glad to be rescued. You had the look of a man who has had a narrow escape and is grateful for a way out. I merely made it easy for you to leave without having to say anything that might commit you."

Devon's mouth tightened, and a cold glitter chilled his eyes. It changed him, made him seem less accessible and more dangerous, and she shivered.

"Dammit," he growled, "what do you expect? Your brother is right. I won't fall in love with you. And I won't stay. I want you, but that's all."

"How charming. Do you declare your sentiments so sweetly to all women?"

"No. I don't usually have to do more than take them to a room over the saloon."

His blunt reply took her by surprise. She didn't know what she'd been expecting; an explanation, perhaps, or at least an attempt at one. Apparently Devon had no intention of justifying his actions. Her chin lifted with hurt pride.

"I see. Is that what you want to do with me?"

"I already told you what I want to do with you."

"Yes, you did. Aren't there enough women at the Brass Lady to satisfy you?"

"No. Not when I want you."

She made an awkward motion with her hands, heart pounding at his rough, snarling reply. He looked angry and frustrated, and she wondered if he felt as raw and on edge as she did.

"I wish I could believe that."

His gaze burned into her. "Believe it. I don't like it any better than you do."

"Devon . . ." She closed her eyes, battling her churning emotions. He was more than likely married. She had to remember that, had to remember that he wanted nothing more from her than he wanted from any saloon whore. But it was so hard remembering those things when he was standing so close, when just his proximity made her entire body quiver with uncertainty.

"Who's Kate?"

"Kate?" She could hear the surprise in his echo. "My sister. Why?"

Maggie opened her eyes. "She's not your wife?" She wasn't prepared for the bitter pain she saw in his eyes, in the quick twist of his mouth.

"No. My wife is dead."

"Devon—I'm sorry."

"So am I."

She looked down at her hands twisting in her skirts, ashamed of the fleeting wave of relief she'd felt at his reply. She shouldn't feel that way. It was wicked to feel that way, and she knew it, but she couldn't help it. It was so confusing, feeling gratitude that he wasn't married. She knew herself well enough to realize that she was content with her life as it was, that a man would only complicate it, yet she had this consuming attraction to Devon that she didn't understand.

Maggie felt wretched and looked back up at him with a sigh. "Devon, I don't know what I want. I only know that you make me feel strange inside, different to myself. Do you understand what I'm trying to say?"

"No. But that's all right. I knew better than to come here." His jaw clenched, and she saw his throat cord as if he was holding back.

"Why *did* you come here?"

"Damned if I know. Maybe 'cause I wanted to see you again, say something that would be an explanation, but I don't have one. Maybe that's what I want to say, after all. I just don't have an explanation, Maggie."

"For not coming here or for wanting to come here?"

He looked startled. "I don't know that, either," he said slowly. "Both, I guess. I know better. If I show up here too much, everybody in town will have us sleeping together, you know that."

"They do anyway."

He looked away with a grimace. "I guess I should have come back and thanked you for helping me, but—"

"I don't want your blasted gratitude!" Her anger took him back, and she was gratified by the wary look in his eyes.

"Then what the hell do you want?"

She stared at him, unable to answer. She didn't know what she wanted. Or maybe she did, because when he reached out to jerk her to him, she fell into his embrace with a muffled cry.

"I know what you want," he muttered in a low, savage tone that sent a shiver down her spine. "Even if you don't."

He tangled his hand in her hair, loosening the knot at her nape so that it spilled down her back. He held her head still, kissing her roughly. His mouth moved from her lips to her throat, then back. She knew she should protest, but her mind wouldn't cooperate with the rest of her. The only thing that seemed to be working properly was the part of her that responded to Devon's touch.

Despite any rhyme or reason, her mouth opened under his coaxing tongue. A moan caught in the back of her throat, and her legs quivered with a weak, fragile crumbling. Devon was touching his tongue to hers, and his free hand cupped her breast. That sparked a reaction she hadn't expected, and she cried out softly, the sound mingling with the harsh rasp of his breathing and hers.

Devon only deepened his kiss as his fingers teased her taut, aching nipple into a hard knot, sending currents of hot fire arching from her breast to her stomach. Nothing had ever prepared her for this tingling, breathless need, the raging inferno inside that he ignited with his mouth and hands.

She couldn't think; she could only feel, only respond to what Devon was doing to her. It was vaguely dismaying that while she was raging inside, he seemed coolly deliberate. He wanted her, yes, but there was none of the wild, mindless passion that she'd sensed beneath his surface, only this calculated passion. Her sense of dismay was quickly drowned out by the overwhelming tide of desire that washed over her at his caress.

"Put your arms around my neck," he said hoarsely when his mouth left hers, and she obeyed without thinking.

Then he was scooping her into his arms and carrying her from the examining room down the narrow, shadowed hallway, and she knew where he was going. Her cheek pressed against his chest, and she could feel the strong thud of his heart beating. He smelled of wind and leather and tobacco, and though it should have been unpleasant, it was a clean masculine scent that she found comfortingly familiar. All her young life had been associated with those smells. She heard him slam the door with his foot, his spurs jangling in the quiet house. Maggie did not loosen her grip until Devon laid her on her bed and gently disengaged her arms from around his neck.

Then he straightened, staring down at her in the gloom of her bedroom, where shadows lay thickly beyond the glow of lamplight. She saw the pale glistening of his eyes, heard the rasp in his voice.

"I want you, Maggie. And you want me. But I won't lie to you and say it's forever. This is your decision to make. If you say no, I'll leave."

She knew that. He hadn't had to tell her. And God help her, she wanted him anyway, wanted him with a ferocity that was so intense it was frightening. Whatever it was he would do, however it made her feel later, she knew that she had to be as close to him as she could get or die.

Wordlessly she lifted her arms, and Devon came to her on the bed, the mattress dipping with his weight. He kissed her for a long time until she could barely breathe and the air was hot and steamy between them. Somehow, her dress was unbuttoned, and his mouth was tracing hot, damp kisses over her skin. The thin chemise and pantalettes were all she wore beneath her gown. Stays were too confining for the weather and work, and she heard Devon's mutter of satisfaction at the feel of nothing but female beneath his hands. His hands were gentle but moved over her body with an urgency that was arousing. She was on fire everywhere he touched, burning for him, twisting restlessly beneath him.

Devon kissed her throat, her lips, then her throat again, moving steadily downward until Maggie was trembling and almost whimpering, his name a faint whisper on her lips. When his mouth closed around the aching peak of her breast, she arched upward with a wordless cry, fingers tangling in the silky strands of his hair. His mouth ignited a fire all the way to her center, then the flames focused between her thighs in a sweet aching that made her moan.

"Sweet Maggie," Devon murmured against the cushion of her breast. He sucked gently on the linen-covered peak, then more strongly, wetting the material. Maggie stirred, needing him closer, needing the thin barrier between her skin and his mouth removed. She plucked at the chemise with a fretful sound, and he pulled it slowly down, sighing as he circled the rose-tipped nipple with his wet tongue. It was all she could do to keep from crying out, and her hands tightened in his hair to hold his head still. Devon's other hand moved to caress and tease her breast until she couldn't think, couldn't do anything but seek an end to the yearning that grew hotter and higher until she could barely breathe.

"Devon . . . Devon, please . . ."

"Do you want me, Maggie? Tell me how much. I need to hear that you want me as badly as I'm wantin' you . . ."

A half-sob broke from her lips and raveled into a sigh when he paused, and she heard herself telling him that she wanted him, that she needed him, her words a frayed litany. It was sheer torture when he pulled away from her, but when he began to peel away her clothes with the same impatience she felt, she was fiercely glad. She wanted nothing between them, nothing but this insane heat that threatened to consume her.

"Jesus," Devon said with a groan, sitting back to stare down at her with hot, glazed eyes. "You're beautiful. I knew you would be."

Maggie flushed. For some reason, for Devon to tell her she was beautiful meant more than all the other flowery compliments she'd ever received. She held the words to her heart, cherishing them. And suddenly she wanted him as naked as she was, wanted to see his muscled, golden body.

"Devon . . . let me help you take off your shirt," she said, not quite able to bring herself to say exactly what she meant. He seemed to understand, and his fingers moved with hers to unbutton his shirt, then his pants.

He groaned when her hand brushed against the hard ridge of his arousal, and his stomach muscles clenched. The sleek movement of those muscles told her how affected he was by her touch, but when he stood up by the bed to flick open the last metal button and shove down his pants, she felt a sudden heat clench her throat and stomach. She froze, staring at him.

Maggie had seen the male body before, but not like this. Her experience had been limited to children and the patients at the medical clinic, and she was aware of all the bodily functions of a normal male. This, however, was not at all the same.

She'd seen Devon's body, bathed him, tended him, and knowing how sex worked, she'd expected mild discomfort at best. That hope died a swift death at the evidence of his arousal. He was strong and healthy, his body a lean, powerful promise. Fully aroused, Devon took away her breath.

Heat moved from her stomach to blossom between her thighs, to flush her face with a fire she knew he could see. "Maggie." He took her hand and pulled it toward him, holding it against his stomach. His breathing was ragged, and she could feel the quick, indrawn breaths rattle his frame as he pulled her hand slowly downward. The dark curls that arrowed downward from his navel to his groin felt soft and wiry and cool beneath her palm. The contrast between that and the hard heat of his erection was shocking. He shuddered when her hand closed convulsively around him, and his fingers tightened over hers. "Don't move yet."

It didn't sound like Devon's voice. It was so low and thick, guttural, that it was as if it had been torn from him. She held him silently, feeling him throb and pulse in her palm, the hot, slick satin of him a marvel she couldn't deny. When he finally opened his fingers, she slid her hand upward again, caressing him, exploring the heat and strength of his body with appreciation and not a little apprehension. She stroked him until he groaned loudly and grabbed her hand again, holding it still.

"No . . . more. God, no more."

In a swift, lithe motion, he'd shoved his pants all the way off and shucked his boots, then he was moving toward the bed again. The bed creaked as he returned to her, stretched out beside her, and took her into his arms. It was a warm night, with a slight breeze filtering through the curtains over the window, yet Maggie was trembling.

Devon kissed her for a long time until she began to relax in his arms again. She didn't expect pleasure, not this first time; she just wanted to be held close to him, to feel one with him. He kissed her again, lingering on her lips, then moving slowly down to her breasts, pausing to nip lightly at whatever interested him on the way. When his mouth closed over a tight, beaded nipple, Maggie gave a sigh of relief, arching upward. He drew her into him, made her shudder with rising need, and she began to ache in the very center of her, a throbbing pulse that grew higher and hotter with everything he did.

It was sweet torment, and when his hand moved between her thighs, they parted willingly, seeking his touch. He explored gently, fingers easing into her in a scorching slide that took away her breath. His hand met her fragile virgin barrier and grew still. Maggie heard him mutter something in a language she didn't understand. Then he lifted his head to stare down at her with searching eyes.

"You sure this is what you want, Maggie?"

"Sure—? Yes." She couldn't think. Her body was on fire with need for him, and he was trying to talk to her. She reached for his hand again, wanting him to stroke her, to kiss her, to take her with him into that swirl of sensation where she didn't have to think. Yet he still hesitated, his dark brows drawing down in a frown.

"Devon ... what ... ?" She twisted with frustration, and he gave another sigh.

"Easy, sweetheart, easy." His mouth moved over hers, claiming her lips, kissing her and caressing her until she was reduced to incoherent moans and awkward movements. She wanted an end to it, an end to the rising tension that coiled tighter and tighter until she felt as if she would shatter with it. He seemed to know that, and with a swift, annihilating move of his hand between her thighs, took her over the edge into a blinding whirlpool of scalding release.

Maggie thought she cried out, but she wasn't certain. She wasn't certain of anything but Devon, holding her in his arms, his voice a low, comforting murmur against her cheek, his hand stroking back damp tendrils of hair from her face as she lay panting in his arms.

Then he began the courtship of senses again, a slow dance of rising tension that he ignited with his mouth and hands. His breathing was harsh, his chest damp and hot against her breasts when he moved over her, nudging her thighs apart with his knees. His arms slid beneath her to cup her hips in his palms.

"Hold me," he said hoarsely, and she did, her arms curling around his neck as he slid into her with a groan. Before she had time to tense, he thrust deeply, wrenching a startled cry from her. Shocked, she shoved hard at him with the heels of her hands, but he caught her arms, held them gently to her sides, then lay still, panting. His breath feathered over her cheek as he rested his forehead against hers. He was buried deeply inside her, an invasion that burned as hot as the fire of her need.

Devon lifted his head. "Maggie, honey—are you all right?"

She nodded mutely. Maggie was well-aware that a woman's first time might be uncomfortable, but she still hadn't been prepared for the reality. He was full and heavy and hard, stretching her almost unbearably. Though she knew he hadn't meant to hurt her, she couldn't help twisting in an effort to ease away from him.

"Be still," he groaned, his arms tightening around her. He lay that way for a long moment, seeming to gather himself before he began to move again, a slow penetration that gradually grew less painful. The friction of his body was incredible, sending tremors up through her all the way to her fingertips as he increased his pace.

The aching, breathless feeling grew until she felt him tense, felt the driving movements increase with a fierce pressure, then he went still, his lean body tightening as he erupted inside her. He shook with the force of his release; a wordless groan tore from his throat.

Devon was breathing heavily, sounding as if he'd run twenty miles as he shifted his weight to his elbows to keep from crushing her. Maggie nuzzled his neck, her tongue flicking out to taste his salty skin. She felt warm, weightless, and closed her eyes.

"Next time will be better," Devon murmured finally, his breath warm against her cooling skin. "For you, anyway. I don't think it could get much better for me."

Emotion swelled her throat. Nothing mattered but

that she was close to Devon, as close to him as a woman could get to a man. She loved him. Whatever else happened, she knew she loved the man they called Cimarrón.

# CHAPTER 10

Hank Mills eyed Johnny warily. "Ask me, that's buyin' trouble."

"Didn't ask you." Johnny thrust out his jaw with a belligerence that he didn't usually feel toward Hank. "This has gone on too long. If Whittaker ain't gonna hang those damn rustlers, we will."

Hank slowly shook his head. "Don't count me in on that. I ain't got no hankering to be part of a lynch mob."

"You sayin' they should go free?"

"No. I'm sayin' you shouldn't go off half-cocked and primed for murder."

"Murder! They're rustlers, Hank. *Rustlers.*"

"Then let the law handle them."

"Wouldn't mind that, but Whittaker don't plan on doin' nothin' but whinin' about how much money it takes to feed 'em until the district judge gets here."

"Johnny, I know. But a man can't take the law into his own hands without losin' something."

Frustrated, Johnny balled his hands into fists and struck them against the table top, making the flatware dance noisily. Several ranch hands stood awkwardly to one side, waiting on their meal but too wary to approach the table. He made a resigned motion with one hand.

"Come eat. We're through talkin'."

When he stalked outside to cool off, Hank joined him beneath the spreading branches of a cottonwood.

They stood quietly for several minutes, watching cattle graze on the rolling hills. Finally Hank cleared his throat.

"Your pa was a man who liked action. But he had enough sense to know when to act and when not to."

Johnny grimaced. "Guess that's your tactful way of telling me I ain't got no sense."

"You got sense. You just get too blamed mad and don't stop to think."

A faint smile flickered unwillingly on his mouth as he turned to face the older man. "Reckon that's the same thing, don't you, Hank?"

"Sometimes."

"Ouch. Maybe I shouldn't have expected you to disagree with me."

"Not if you want the truth."

Johnny leaned against the rough bark of the tree trunk and dug into his vest pocket for his tobacco pouch. Nothing had gone right in so long. First the rustlers, then Maggie being so damn defiant and stubborn about ruining her life, then Cimarrón showing up and causing trouble.

He built a cigarette, and propping the sole of his boot against the trunk, he smoked silently. It had all started with Lindsay leaving. He could almost pinpoint the exact minute when his life had started to go wrong. *Lindsay.* Damn her, anyway, with her cool blond beauty and hot eyes, and that condemning gaze whenever she looked at him. It still haunted him, how she looked at him like that, accusing him without speaking a word. He closed his eyes, but the image didn't disappear.

Hank cleared his throat, and he opened his eyes.

"Got a letter from Lindsay," the foreman said, and Johnny's gut twisted into a knot.

Were his thoughts that evident? Had Hank somehow known he was thinking of her? Impossible.

"How's she doin'?"

"Well enough."

*Did she ask about me? Did she mention what a bastard I was to her?*

Johnny nodded. "That's good. Guess she's settled down in Georgia forever."

"No, she's comin' back."

An icy stillness blanketed him, and Johnny stood there immobile and tried to absorb the implications. "Comin' back?" he finally croaked, and felt Hank's curious gaze.

"Yep. Said she missed me." Hank paused, shifted from one foot to the other, then added softly, "She plans on gettin' married and wants me to come to the weddin'. She's comin' to talk me into goin' back with her."

The world tilted and fell sharply away, and Johnny waited until it righted again to risk a question. "Are you goin'?"

"Naw. I ain't got no business in Georgia. But I'll be glad to see her. She probably knows I won't go and just wants to see me before she gets married."

"She bringing her husband-to-be with her?" Johnny asked carefully.

"Didn't mention it."

*Good.*

"Too bad. I'd like to meet him."

Hank eyed him silently, then shrugged. "Reckon you could tell Miss Maggie that she's comin'? She's asked about her a few times."

"Sure. I'm ridin' into town in a day or two. I'll tell her. Maybe Lindsay can talk some sense into Maggie, get her to forget that doctor nonsense and come back home."

Hank gave a noncommittal grunt, and after a moment he walked back into the house. Johnny finished his cigarette and tried to remember just why he'd gone

so wrong with Lindsay. He knew what had come between them; he just couldn't think why it had mattered
so much at the time.

The first rays of dawn filtered through a crack in the
curtains and slanted across the bed. Devon studied
Maggie in the hazy, pale light. Silky black hair curled
in a fan across the pillow, framing the sweet luster of
her ivory face. He watched, fascinated, as the dark
sweep of her lashes fluttered against her cheeks and
her parted lips quivered ever so slightly. What was
there about this woman that drew him despite his better judgment? It wasn't just sex, though his body was
ready for her again.

There was something else that drew him, kept him
perilously near the brink of losing control. It made him
almost desperate to realize that Maggie Malone was
the closest he'd come to a woman since Molly. Others
had been just a physical release. Maggie was different.
Maggie was dangerous.

She shifted restlessly, and he turned his attention to
coaxing her awake. His mouth found the soft pulse in
the hollow of her throat, and he teased her with gentle
kisses. It had been so long since he'd lain in the early
dawn hours with a woman, and he felt awkward and
damnably shy when Maggie opened her eyes and
looked at him.

"Mornin', sleepyhead," he rasped, chagrined that
his voice betrayed his uncertainty.

"Morning yourself." She smiled and reached up to
touch his cheek. "You talk wide-awake, but you look
sleepy."

"Do I?"

"Um-hmm." She stretched like a languid cat, arms
ending up around his neck. Her nose nuzzled into the
bend of his neck and shoulder, and she nipped lightly.
"Thought you said you had to leave early."

"Changed my mind." His arms tightened around her. "Do you mind?"

"Oh no, Devon Conrad. I don't mind at all." She snuggled closer. "In fact, I'm glad."

"Maggie—" He paused, not knowing what he wanted to say to her, what he could say that wouldn't sound inane or silly after the night. Her head tilted back, and he could feel her eyes on him.

"I know," she said softly. "I'm not sure what to say, either."

He grinned. "Is it that obvious?"

"As obvious as a camel in a sheep pen."

Devon muffled his laughter in the wealth of her hair, breathing deeply. "You smell like roses."

"I bought a year's supply of soap and shampoo when I was in New York. It's cheaper there."

When he rolled to lay half over her, looking down into her soft gray eyes, he murmured, "It'd be worth whatever you had to pay." He toyed with her hair, curling a long strand around his fingertip, frowning slightly. He felt her shift beneath him, her gaze questioning. A faint smile curved his mouth when she traced his lips with her fingertip. "I hurt you last night," he said against her palm.

"Yes."

"I wanted it to be good for you."

"According to most reports, it rarely is for a woman the first time, Devon. Don't look so distressed. I know you didn't want to hurt me." She smiled suddenly, and a dimple flashed in her right cheek. "And it wasn't *all* pain. What you did at first . . . was wonderful."

He took her face between his palms and kissed her lingeringly. "Give me some time, and it will all be wonderful."

"Not modest are you?"

Laughter thickened his voice. "Should I be?"

"Oh no. You should be proud of yourself, all right.

It's just a woman's duty to keep men humble, that's all."

"Thanks for the warning." Devon kissed her again, unable to resist her sweet mouth. Or her adorable chin. Or the small spot beneath her ear. Or the dimple in her cheek. He kissed them all thoroughly, and when he had finished, he moved lower to the crazily beating pulse in the hollow of her throat. Her collarbones looked so fragile, her skin as smooth and soft as warm butter, yielding beneath his hands and mouth with a sweet resilience.

When his mouth found her breast, he heard her gasp and felt her arch toward him, her hands going to his shoulders. "Devon . . . Devon, wait."

He lifted his head and saw the bright color staining her face. Then he understood when she said, not looking at him, "I need some ointment first."

She was sore, and he should have thought of that. He nodded. "Where is it?"

"In my office. It's in a green jar labeled slippery elm. It will . . . help."

He kissed her again, then rose from the bed and went down the hallway to her office. It was quiet, the house still and gloomy in the early morning shadows. He found the jar and returned to the bedroom, and saw Maggie wrapped up in the sheets again, a flush still staining her cheeks.

"Don't be embarrassed, Maggie." He sat on the edge of the bed, watching her. His throat closed with emotion, and he didn't know what to say or do. It wasn't as if this were *his* first time, yet he felt as shy and awkward as if it was. Maybe it was because it was Maggie, and he wanted it to be something she would remember fondly.

"Well," she said with a shaky little laugh, "I'm not really embarrassed, but this is rather awkward for me.

After all, the last man to see me without my drawers was the doctor who delivered me, I think."

He grinned. "Then I'm honored."

"You should be." She took the jar of ointment he held out, then hesitated.

"No." He reached for the jar and took it back. "Let me. This is something I can do for you, for a change."

"Devon . . ."

Despite her protests, he drew away the sheet and gently parted her thighs. He applied the ointment with soft strokes of his hand, watching her face for the slightest sign of discomfort. When she flinched, he paused.

She managed a smile and said, "No, go ahead. You're being very gentle."

"I don't want to hurt you, Maggie."

"I can see that. As a physician, I know that sometimes it's not possible to keep from hurting a patient. This time, you're the doctor."

When he'd finished, he put up the ointment and brought back a cloth and basin of warm water. He washed her, half-embarrassed, half-pleased at her gratitude. The evidence of her virginity humbled him, and he wondered if she could see it in his face. She'd given him such a special gift, and it occurred to him that he wasn't worthy of it. He'd wanted her, yes, but he didn't deserve her. It had just seemed like the only thing that would get her out of his mind, ease the need he felt to be with her. He'd used her body to purge her from his mind, thinking that to satisfy his sexual need for her would end it, but it hadn't worked.

The knowledge left him with a bitter taste in his mouth and an ache in his chest.

"All done," he said finally, and stood up. She lay looking up at him, her creamy skin flushed a faint pink and her eyes wide. He looked away, wishing his body didn't respond so readily to her.

"Devon."

He forced himself to look back at her, saw her arms come up, and he moved into them as if drawn by invisible cords. He couldn't stop himself from taking the comfort she offered him, though he damned himself bitterly for being so weak.

"I'll just hold you for now," he said against her skin. "It's too soon and you're too sore."

"Too bad."

Her sighing murmur wrenched a chuckle from him. "You are an insatiable wench, Maggie Malone."

"Only for you, Devon Conrad."

He lifted his head, saw the light shining in her eyes, and felt something break loose inside him, leaving him open and raw. God. It was too soon, too much, and he'd forgotten his basic rule for survival—not caring enough to be hurt. He needed to leave before it was too late, before Maggie's sweet body and sweeter nature lulled him into dangerous complacence.

"You'll change your mind about that soon enough," he said roughly, and saw the sudden hurt in her eyes at his words. He looked away, throat closing. "One of these days, some man will come along who'll make you forget all about me."

Her fingers stilled in his hair, and he felt her tense beneath his arm. "Do you really think so, Devon?"

"Sure."

"Then you don't really know me."

It was said quietly, softly, but sounded as loud as if shot from a cannon. Devon couldn't look at her. He should tell her that he was leaving, that he wouldn't be back, but he knew he'd be lying. He knew that he wasn't strong enough to stay away from her yet.

His eyes found hers, locked with them. "You don't know me, either, Maggie. Remember that. I'm not—"

"Hush." Her fingers touched his lips gently. "I know. I didn't ask for anything from you and I don't expect anything. You may not have noticed, but I'm content with my life as it is. You're a part of my world, but you're not the center of it.''

That should have comforted him, made it easier for him to accept what she offered, but somehow it didn't. Somehow, knowing that he wasn't the most important facet of her life rankled.

"That's a hell of a thing to say after what we've done," he growled, and saw her faint smile.

"You sound like a wronged lover."

"Well hell, Maggie. You make it sound as if none of this matters to you."

"It matters." She paused, then added, "Oh, it matters a lot to me. But so does my profession."

Nonplussed, he stared at her, unable to understand just what he wanted. Hell, hadn't he wanted a woman who wouldn't cling, would give and not expect more than he could give? Yes, but for Maggie to state so bluntly that he was only a part of her world was faintly galling. No, he didn't understand what he wanted at all.

Johnny's eyes narrowed, and Maggie sighed. "I told you before that you have no right to command what I do in this house. I resent your interference."

"But dammit, Maggie, you're lettin' that outlaw come and go like he has a right to be here. Like he's staked a claim on you."

Maggie met her brother's angry gaze steadily. "The trial for those rustlers is next week. Devon is—"

"Devon. What do you mean—Devon?"

"Cimarrón. His real name is Devon."

Johnny stared at her. "So you know about that. Do you know all of it?"

"What are you talking about?"

"I'm talkin' about Devon Conrad. Cimarrón. Leader of the Lost Canyon Gang." Johnny tossed a large packet on the kitchen table. "There's enough old posters in there to say more than I can. Your friend Devon rode with a cutthroat band of outlaws a few years ago, and one of them was Colorado Kate. She was his lover, the way I heard it. And he had a wife as well. He managed to get one of them killed in a crossfire up in their mountain hideout. Is that what you're wanting for yourself? To end up full of lead because you were dumb enough to believe in some fast-talkin' outlaw?"

"It's not as you claim." Maggie's hand shook slightly as she grasped the back of a kitchen chair.

"No? Then maybe you can tell me just how it is."

"Well, I don't—"

"I thought so. He ain't told you nothin', has he? And he won't. He knows if he does, you'll toss him out on his ass."

"Maybe he hasn't felt the need to defend himself against unfounded rumors," Maggie snapped back, irritated and afraid at the same time. Why hadn't Devon told her? Why didn't he explain what had happened to his wife? Any of her attempts to discover his past were met with stony silence or steamy kisses that quickly made her forget what she'd asked. The past week had flown by in a haze of long nights filled with passion instead of questions.

Yet despite his passion, she knew that Devon had not fully committed himself to her in any way. He was still wary, still careful, and only came after dark and was gone before first light. He was trying to protect her from gossip, and while part of her was grateful, part of her wanted to abandon the pretense.

Though she enjoyed their lovemaking and Devon was attentive and loving, she recognized that his emotions were not involved, and that marred it for her. The nights she spent with him left her feeling empty and aching for what should have been.

Now Johnny was bringing up her deeply buried worries.

He snorted rudely at her silence. "No, guess he doesn't have to defend himself when he's got you to make up excuses for him. Hell, Maggie, I never thought my sister would be the lightskirt of an outlaw."

Before she thought about it, Maggie brought up her hand and slapped Johnny. Her palm made a loud crack against his cheek and snapped his head back, but he didn't move for a long moment. He stood there, black eyes burning into her, the imprint of her hand slowly whitening against his brown skin.

Appalled at what she'd done, Maggie stared back at him without speaking. She'd never struck her brother in anger, not since they were small children quarreling over silly, trivial matters.

"So," he said finally. "It's come down to a choice. Never thought you'd choose so wrong."

"Johnny." She stopped, her throat aching when he shot her a bitter glance as he picked his hat up off the kitchen table.

"Forget it. Reckon I know when to stop beatin' a dead horse." He paused in the doorway and half-turned, not quite looking at her. "By the way, Lindsay's comin' back."

"Lindsay? To Belle Plain?"

"To the Double M. But only for a visit. If you want to see her, I'll tell her where you're stayin'."

Maggie stared at him. "Are you saying you don't want me to come to—"

"Yes. If you're so dead set on havin' your outlaw, you can do it here. I don't want you out at the ranch. I don't think I can stomach seein' you and knowin' what you're doin' nights." He twisted his hat, frowning down at it. "If you ever come to your senses and stop actin' loco, I'll take care of Cimarrón for you. You

won't have to do nothin' except send me word that
you want to see me. Understand?''

Her stomach tightened with cold fury. "Perfectly. If
I decide I'm tired of my current lover, I just tell my
brother so he can shoot him and rid me of an unpleasant, tiresome burden. How charming. Did anyone ever
tell you that you are a bigoted, thickheaded jackass?''

Johnny glared at her and slammed his hat on his
head. "Not since Lindsay left town.''

When the door banged shut behind him, Maggie
sagged into a kitchen chair. She was shaking. Johnny
had made her so mad she'd wanted to scream at him
and throw every kitchen utensil she had at his head. It
was a wonder she hadn't. How could he be so wrong?
Why wouldn't he at least listen to her about Devon?
And who the devil was giving him all this information?

Her gaze moved reluctantly to the package on the
table. It was thick. The envelope seemed to be
crammed with enough paper to set the town afire. Her
hand trembled as she reached out and pulled it closer,
and her fingers shook so badly when she unfolded the
flap that she wondered if she'd be able to open it at all.

But once open, the posters spilled across the table in
a flood of paper. She recognized a crudely drawn
image of a man with a bandanna over his face, and another of a woman. All that could be seen were the eyes,
but it was evident that the artist had faced Devon at
one time or the other. No man could have looked into
that chilling gaze and not remembered it vividly, and
it was depicted to the last eyelash.

Posters listed his crimes from train robbery to murder to kidnapping and rape. Colorado Kate was said to
be as dangerous as her cohorts, and the leader of the
gang. A frown knit her brow as Maggie studied the
posters carefully. She knew Kate was supposed to be
his sister. Was the girl he was accused of kidnapping

and raping his wife? Her name was Molly McGowan, aged seventeen, the niece of a judge in Leadville, Colorado.

Newspaper clippings had fluttered from the envelope, and she lifted them slowly, not quite certain she wanted to read what they'd say. Local Colorado papers had obviously delighted in detailing the events surrounding the escape of one Devon Conrad, alias Mark Kittering, from a Leadville cell just as a lynch mob stormed the jail. It reported that he'd kidnapped Judge Murphy Monroe's niece as a hostage, and U.S. marshals had been called in to assist in the capture of the dangerous outlaws.

Maggie thumbed through more clippings, some of them obviously exaggerated, others reporting tersely that the Lost Canyon Gang had increased robberies and branched out to the Texas and Pacific line as well. Then a headline caught her eye, and she lifted a yellowed clipping to read,

## OUTLAWS CAPTURED IN SPECTACULAR SHOOTOUT!

The following story told how G.K. Durant, the owner of the rail line shipping silver from a local mine, had ambushed and killed several of the members of the Lost Canyon Gang in their mountain hideout before being killed by Devon Conrad, one of the leaders of the gang. U.S. Marshal Roger Hartman identified Durant as George King, wanted in several states for various crimes, and declared that the charges be dropped against Devon Conrad and Caitlin Conrad, known as Colorado Kate. Lawman Jake Lassiter had participated in the final arrests and testified on the behalf of the two Conrads, as well as certain surviving members of the gang. Regrettably, Molly McGowan, the niece of Judge Monroe, did not survive the ambush by Durant.

Maggie lowered the clipping. Was Molly Devon's wife? Was that the reason he'd sounded so bitter? Had he, as Johnny claimed, been responsible for her death?

She smoothed out another folded scrap of news clipping and saw that it had been written just a year before. It spoke of the phenomenal success of the Lucky Eight mine in Colorado, owned by Jake and Caitlin Lassiter. Though many mines in the area had since played out, a placer vein in the Lucky Eight promised to be the richest found in recent history. Near the end of the short article detailing ore loads and market values was a short sentence:

> *Devon Conrad, silent partner of the Lucky Eight, is said to be in seclusion somewhere in Europe.*

Obviously this reporter had not connected Devon Conrad with Cimarrón, she thought grimly. So. Devon was wealthy. Somehow that made his choice of careers even more appalling, though she could understand why he'd felt compelled to leave Colorado after so much personal tragedy. Other articles ranged from wildly improbable to uncannily close to fact. The overriding question in her mind was *why?*

"Looks like interesting reading," a husky voice drawled, and Maggie jerked around to find Devon leaning against the doorframe watching her. He pushed away in a smooth, lazy motion and approached the table. She didn't say anything when he lifted one of the clippings, then tossed it to the table. "Where'd you get this?"

"Johnny."

"That figures."

"Devon—are these true?"

"Haven't read them all, so I can't say. Probably."
His eyes met hers, cold and hostile, and she flinched.

She sucked in a deep breath and asked before she
lost her nerve, "Was Molly your wife?"

"Yes."

"She was only . . . only seventeen." The full force of
his icy blue eyes hit her like the slam of a hammer.

"I know."

Maggie looked down, tears blurring her vision.
Devon couldn't hide the bitter pain in his tone, and she
knew he still suffered for the girl who had been his
wife. Dead, Molly McGowan stood between them
more firmly than if she had been alive and breathing.

"I don't know what to say, Devon," she murmured
after a moment. "What a terrible thing to happen."

"Yeah. Well, if you wouldn't pry into something
that's not any of your business, maybe you wouldn't
find out things that upset you."

Her head jerked up. "I wasn't prying. Johnny seems
to have made it his personal mission to keep me in-
formed as to what you have done as well as what you
intend to do."

"If he keeps that up, I might just go lookin' for him."

Devon's flat, emotionless comment took her breath
away. She rose shakily to her feet. "No, you can't mean
that. It would be the end of us, Devon, if you and
Johnny fought, no matter the outcome."

Something flickered in his eyes but was gone so
quickly she couldn't interpret it. "There's some things
a man can't forgive, Maggie."

"My brother seems to feel the same way."

His brows lowered over his eyes, chilling the vibrant
blue to a pale, almost colorless opacity. Deep grooves
cut down each side of his mouth, and he muttered,
"Reckon I can understand his reasons well enough."

"I think you can. Surely there were times when you
were at odds with your sister over something each of

you thought was important. It's the same with me and Johnny."

Devon turned away and stepped back to the door, leaning against it again to stare out into the night. After a moment he said softly, "Ash Oliver is holed up in Buffalo Gap. I'm going after him."

Her heart plummeted to her toes, and she rose blindly from her chair and went to him. "Devon, please don't go."

He turned on her, anger creasing his face. "Don't ask anything of me, Maggie Malone. You knew about me when I came here, so don't expect me to change what I am."

She didn't quail from his angry gaze but stood her ground. "Yes, I knew what circumstances made you, but that doesn't mean that's the way you have to be. Let it go. Don't go after Oliver just to prove who's the best."

He expelled a furious breath and snatched her to him when she took an involuntary step back. "I've said what I intend to do. If you want me to stop by here on my way back through, I will. If not, say so now."

Matching anger shot through her. The weeks of uncertainty and frustration, of not knowing if he cared, made her reckless.

"You can go to hell for all I care, Devon Conrad. I won't be a convenience for you like any saloon whore that you can take upstairs for the price of a few drinks. I have to admit, I haven't seen too much to recommend sex anyway."

She saw his reaction in the sudden starburst of light in his eyes, but still wasn't prepared for the frightening speed with which he moved. There wasn't time to step back or protest before he'd grabbed her arm and jerked her into a hard, bruising collision with his iron-muscled chest. His mouth came down over hers in a searing heat, his teeth raking over her parted lips as his tongue ravaged her mouth.

Shakily Maggie realized that Devon had lost his tight hold on self-control, that finally he was reacting to her with something other than cool deliberation. Her insult had provoked a reaction that was as exhilarating as it was frightening.

When she kissed him back, she felt him shudder, then he picked her up and took two steps to the table. With a shock, she realized what he meant to do, and shivered with reaction. She'd wanted honest emotion, honest reaction, but had never expected that Devon would be so fiercely primitive.

He slid her back on the table, bending over her, his hands tearing the buttons of her blouse as he unfastened them. Dazed, she didn't move when he shoved up her skirts and tore aside the open crotch of her cotton drawers, then moved between her open thighs. She heard the rending sound of tearing material and didn't care. He kissed her again, his tongue a heated invasion. There was the metallic clink as he unbuckled his gunbelt, then he began unbuttoning his pants.

His mouth moved to her breast, lips closing around it and making her gasp as she arched upward, her hands tangling in his wheat gold hair to hold him. When he lifted his head to look at her, she caught her breath at the fierce, wild light in his eyes, the unguarded need that shimmered like an inferno.

Devon reached under her, curving his hands over her shoulders to hold her, his penetration of her body hard and fast as he thrust forward. Every muscle in her body shuddered at the exquisite impact, and she made a soft whimpering sound in the back of her throat. His fierce urgency was contagious, and a surging rise of need made her arch toward him with a gasp. Her nails scraped over his shoulders and down his back, ripping at the thin material of his shirt.

It was what she'd wanted—the abandoning of his tight grip on control—and she responded with as fierce a passion as his own. When he pounded into her, she lifted her hips to meet him, taking all she could of him as if there would never be another time for either of them. Her legs lifted to wrap around his waist as he hammered into her, and before she knew what was happening, a shattering wave carried her to a breathtaking crest and beyond. She cried out, and he absorbed her cry with his mouth.

Then he shifted her beneath him to pull her even closer when she'd thought she could get no closer, pulling her up and higher so that he moved even deeper inside her. She was half-sobbing, shuddering, clinging to him, and he began to move faster and faster until she felt the tremors begin inside her again, sending her whirling into mindless release. This time, she felt him shudder, saw the fierce tautness of his features sharpen, heard his hoarse mutter as he stiffened with his head thrown back.

For a heartbeat, he was suspended motionless, then he slowly relaxed across her, holding her in his embrace. Maggie was still breathless, still stunned by the force of her response and his. She held him quietly, and neither of them spoke.

When she turned and kissed him gently, Devon groaned, and began the sensual lulling of her senses with his mouth and hands, luring her into a passion that was no less urgent than the one just passed. Satisfaction came slower, but was just as hot and wild, and when it was over and they lay panting for breath, he muttered, "We don't have a lick of sense to be doing this on the kitchen table."

"No," she agreed dreamily. "This isn't the sturdiest piece of furniture I have."

"Or the most comfortable." His head lifted. Slow, hot lights burned in his blue eyes. "Let's go to bed."

"Yes. Let's."

It was after midnight before they lay exhausted, and Maggie had the thought that she'd never felt so content in her life. Was this what it was supposed to be like? She wished she had something to compare it to, some other man who had been important in her life, so she would know if it was the kind of love that would last. With Devon, she wasn't certain.

She'd managed to break through part of the wall he'd built around himself, but she wasn't foolish enough to think that a few hours of unbridled passion would mean as much to him as it did to her. In some ways, he still grieved for his dead wife, still carried a burden that he refused to share with anyone. If she wanted him, she had to find a way around that wall to show him he could share anything with her and she'd love him.

Finally Devon stirred, stretching his lithe, lean body in a graceful glide like a tomcat. The lamp on the far table cast only a hazy light, and it was guttering as the wick burned lower. He propped himself on one elbow and gazed down at her, stroking her damp skin with his palm.

"You're a distraction, Maggie Malone."

"Complaining?"

"Not me. I'm no fool." He bent to kiss her, his mouth moving gently from her lips to her cheek, then to her chin before he lifted his head again. She felt the tightening of his muscles, his rising tension, and suspected what he was about to say. "I have to go."

Her throat tightened. There was no point in arguing with him. His mind was made up to go after Ash Oliver and there was nothing she could do to change it.

Tears burned her eyes, but she blinked them back as she disengaged herself from his embrace. "I'll be here when you make it back."

Devon stared at her. It was obvious he hadn't ex-

pected her to say that. Some of the tension drained
from him, and with a muttered curse, he drew her
gently against him and held her pressed against his
chest, stroking her hair with one hand.

"Maggie, I don't know why you'd ever want to see
me again."

"Neither do I," came her muffled response, and she
felt his amusement. He loosened his tight clasp and
smiled down at her.

"Guess I figured you wouldn't want to see me after
reading all that stuff the papers must have said."

"Guess you figured wrong."

He sighed. "Guess I did." He cupped her chin in his
palm and bent his head to kiss her, lightly at first, then
with an increasing pressure that bordered on violence.

She accepted his kiss, understanding the reason for
his ferocity, feeling some of the same turmoil herself. It
was beyond her comprehension why she allowed herself to be dragged through the emotional morass she'd
experienced since meeting him, but it was unthinkable
to be without him. Devon Conrad, with his blue eyes
that could flash like summer lightning and sear her to
the soul with only a glance, had become much too important to her. He had become a necessity, as essential
as oxygen to her survival.

## CHAPTER 11

 "Danza."

The Apache turned, long hair flowing like silk over his bare shoulders. "You came."

"You knew I would."

"*Sí.* I knew you would come for Ash Oliver."

Devon looked beyond Danza to the cluster of wood and adobe buildings that was Buffalo Gap. "Where is he?"

Black eyes glittered slightly as Danza pointed, and Devon frowned. "In jail?"

"*Sí.*"

The two-story brick jail sat serenely in the sun, and Devon felt a wave of frustration. "Hell, how am I supposed to get to him in that fortress?"

Danza shrugged. "Perhaps he will come out."

Devon shot him a glance of disbelief. "I've seen the inside of that jail, amigo. Metal doors. Bars. Guards. The only way out is down the pee hole."

"Or to be set free."

"What are the charges?"

"Murder. But there will be witnesses who will swear that it was self-defense."

Devon grunted irritably. "His own men, no doubt."

"No." Danza leaned against a log wall. "Mine."

"Yours?"

Dark eyes shifted to Devon. "You want him free, do you not?"

"Yeah, but—"

"So he will be free. Do not ask questions, amigo."

"I always work alone. You know that."

"*Sí.* But this time, you were not here. I have only made it possible for you to do what must be done."

That sounded fine to Devon. He shrugged. "When is the trial?"

"Tomorrow. Judge Carnahan."

That explained a lot. Carnahan was an old associate of Oliver's. He'd have been set free even without the convenient testimony of whoever Danza had chosen. At least this way, Devon might be able to get to him before he got away.

"Another thing," Danza said when Devon had bought the first round of drinks at a cantina, "I have learned some interesting information about Zeke Rogan."

"Such as?"

"He and Ash Oliver knew each other a long time ago, up in Kansas."

"How well?"

Danza leaned back in his chair, exchanging a cool glance with a frowning cowboy at the next table. The cowboy turned away finally, and Danza said, "Very well. They did some gunrunning during the war. For a while they worked with the Comancheros, then Rogan found a way to make his ranch profitable."

"That sounds convenient."

"*Sí.* Very convenient. It takes a lot of money to buy cattle and fencing and hire men. Rogan seems to have made a lot."

"So you think there's still a connection between Rogan and Oliver?" Devon frowned, dragging his glass through the wet rings on the table top. "That doesn't make sense. Why would Rogan let Oliver rustle his cattle?"

"Who has lost the most cattle, amigo? I think it is not Rogan. A few, maybe, mixed in with others. But not enough to hurt him. Enough to give him back some profit if sold with the others, maybe, heh?"

When Devon stared at Danza for a long moment, the Apache's mouth curled in a slight smile and he shrugged. "It makes as much sense as anything else I have heard, Cimarrón."

"You don't usually get involved." Devon stretched out his long legs and hooked a chair, then propped his feet up. "Why have you gotten involved this time?"

Shrugging, Danza said, "You and I rode together. I do not like men who—how do you say it?—*acecho?*"

"Ambush. I should have seen it coming. I rode right into it."

"Oliver does not like it when another man is faster, and if what I heard is true, your bullet was faster."

"But not fatal." Devon's mouth twisted. "He managed to get off a shot of his own."

Danza studied him a moment. "You are recovered?"

"I had a good doctor."

"Ah." Danza's brows lifted. "So I heard. The pretty lady doctor in Belle Plain."

"Where the hell do you get your information?" Devon muttered.

"I have many ways. Very thorough."

Devon glared at him, but Danza was unperturbed by those icy eyes that could make other men take several steps back. He tossed back his drink, returning Devon's stare calmly. It was irritating.

"Sometimes I don't know about you, Danza."

"Do not know what, amigo?"

"Why you say one thing and do another."

A flash of amusement lit Danza's eyes, but he said nothing in answer, and Devon gave it up. He knew by now that if Danza wanted to tell him his reasons for helping, he would. If he didn't, nothing could get it out of him. He was the same way himself, so while it was annoying, it was understandable.

"I assume you have an idea what will happen after the trial. What have you planned?"

Danza nodded slowly. "*Sí.* I have a very good idea what will happen after." He leaned forward, his voice lowering. "I think you will be able to meet Oliver more fairly this time, amigo. In fact, I have seen to it."

Grim satisfaction made Devon smile, and he wondered what was in his eyes that made Danza recoil slightly.

The courtroom was on the first floor of the Buffalo Gap jail. It was filled with spectators who'd heard about Ash Oliver, as well as those who had a personal interest in him. Devon leaned against a back wall, hat pulled low over his face.

It went just as he expected. In less than an hour, the proceedings were over and Ash Oliver was released. He walked nonchalantly from the crowded courtroom, and several of his men followed close behind. Devon waited, shoulders pressed back against the wall, watching Oliver make his way through the crowd.

When the courtroom was almost emptied, Devon pushed away from the wall and stepped outside. People stood in small clusters, staggered along the road and close to log and brick buildings. The sky was a peculiar color, a haze of yellowish light that seemed thick and waiting. A cooler wind blew down the street, seeming to sift down through the flat-topped ridges with a strength he hadn't expected.

A storm was coming, and it only served to make him more edgy and impatient to get it over with. A low bank of black clouds hung threateningly on the horizon, rolling over the table of land in a slow sweep.

Devon stepped out when he saw some of Danza's men come around a corner. One of them stumbled, falling against the man next to Oliver. With a muttered curse, Heck Raines shoved Danza's man back and away.

"Damn 'breed! Why don't 'cha watch where you're goin'?"

Roe Frayser, whom Devon had known almost as long as he'd known Danza, turned in a peculiarly graceful glide that took Raines by surprise. A knife glittered in Roe's hand, and his jade green eyes sparked with the same deadly light.

"Care to show me where you want me to walk, Raines?"

It was a carefully orchestrated fight, with Frayser and Raines luring the spectators' attention while Devon began to cut Oliver from the crowd by cautious manipulation. A few men pushed through, with Danza and the others managing to squeeze through the crowd with precision. Ash Oliver stood at the fringes, his face creased in disgust at the delay.

"Oliver," Devon said softly, and saw the gunman turn. "We got some unfinished business."

He saw the brief surprise in Oliver's face, then the sneering acceptance. "Yeah, I think we do, Cimarrón. Let's go out back where it ain't quite so crowded."

It was what Devon had expected, and he nodded. Oliver was wearing his gun again, and when they had walked behind a nearby building, he bent to tie the thong around his thigh. Devon waited silently. He knew better than to trust Ash Oliver for an instant, that the gunman was capable of shooting him in the back or without warning, as capable of murder now as he'd been when he shot Ralph Pace down in cold blood.

Oliver straightened and backed away several steps, letting his hands hang loosely at his sides. "Before I kill you, Cimarrón, why don't you tell me what burr you got under your saddle? Why'd you brace me in Abilene?"

Devon studied him silently for a minute. Oliver was

wearing a black frock coat and embroidered vest, with a high-starched collar around his neck and a string tie. He looked dapper. And deadly. The flat-crowned black hat atop his head bore a satin ribbon hatband with a small cocky feather jutting up.

"It won't mean anything to you, Oliver," he said shortly. "Just one more shooting in a never-ending line of them."

"Maybe. And maybe I'm interested in hearing what got you on my trail."

"What got you into rustling?"

Oliver looked amused, his mouth stretching into a wide smile. "I don't usually get involved in something that's hot and dusty work, but I had an offer I couldn't pass up."

"That offer have anything to do with Zeke Rogan?"

Devon was rewarded with a brief flicker of surprise on Oliver's face, but it was quickly replaced with open amusement. "Why would I need to take an offer from Rogan? I can get all his cattle I need by taking 'em."

"Maybe." A strong wind blew eddies of dust into the air, swirling it in small funnels around them. Oliver's black frock coat flapped loudly. The sky darkened, and the sound of rushing wind grew louder. "And maybe there's another reason you and Rogan might want to talk."

"Y'know, Cimarrón, you're getting to be a nuisance. You killed two of my best men, took three more to jail. Maybe I underestimated you."

"That's possible."

Oliver spat in the dust, but the wind carried it away before it hit the dirt. He shifted position slightly, edging to his left. Devon let him go without comment, but his body gravitated as if tracking Oliver's movements, subtly altering position by the merest shifting on the balls of his feet.

"Yep," Oliver muttered, "a damn nuisance. Best to get rid of you quick."

Oliver took a step back, and Devon tensed. He saw from the sudden, fierce concentration on Oliver's face that he'd decided to stop talking.

A sudden, loud cracking split the air, followed by a blur of objects whipping past. Dust peppered the air, stinging unprotected skin, and over the roar growing louder and steadier by the moment, he could hear the frightened bawl of animals and screams of women.

"Tornado!" someone shouted, and Devon saw the telltale funnel skimming over the flat land beyond Buffalo Gap. It was coming closer, generating high winds and sending debris through the air. He saw Ash Oliver barely avoid a wooden shingle; he himself just managed to dodge what looked like a tree branch. It felt as if all the air was being sucked into that gigantic funnel-cloud, and the roaring was as loud as a freight train bearing down on them.

Mentally cursing the luck that had separated him from Oliver, Devon saw the gunman sprinting toward a sturdy log building. He started to follow, but Danza came toward him, shaking his head.

"No, amigo! Not safe . . . devil-wind!"

Devon could barely hear him over the roar of the storm. Instinct made him follow Danza, and they barely managed to leap into the hard-baked ruts of a ravine as the funnel cloud howled over them. It felt as if it were raining boards and tree limbs. Devon put his arms over his head to protect it, and realized that his hat was gone. Something hit him in the back, and the air was so thick he could barely drag in enough to fill his lungs.

Then it was over, and the noise decreased, leaving his ears ringing. He lifted his head, and rain began to fall.

Danza nodded in satisfaction. "When it rains, the devil-wind has gone."

Devon stood up, heedless of the rain. "Looks like a few buildings are gone, too."

Danza followed his gaze. The building where Ash Oliver had taken shelter was a pile of rubble, and men were slowly beginning to climb out from underneath broken logs that looked like kindling.

But when everyone was removed from beneath the rubble, Ash Oliver was not among the dead or surviving. He'd gotten away again.

Maggie saw Devon ride in and put his horse into the lean-to, and was waiting anxiously in the kitchen. He washed up on the porch, then stepped inside, glancing at her.

"What's the matter, Maggie?"

"Is it that obvious?"

Devon smiled faintly. "Obvious enough."

"Where have you been?"

His brow quirked upward, and there was a distinct cooling in his eyes that made her impatient. "Don't look at me like that, Devon. I have a good reason for asking."

"Mind telling me what it is?"

"Not at all," she snapped, and tossed a newspaper to the kitchen table. He picked it up and scanned it, then dropped it back to the table and shrugged.

"This isn't the first time I got the blame for someone else's killing. That's one reason I don't read the papers."

"But Devon—"

"Look, Maggie, I wasn't even in Abilene. I was in Buffalo Gap. That's south."

"But the paper says that you killed two men, one of them unarmed, by shooting them in the back. There was a witness."

"And you believe that?"

She saw the opaque waiting in his eyes and his abrupt stillness, and shook her head. "No, of course not."

"Then don't worry about it. I didn't do it. I was in Buffalo Gap at a very quick trial for Ash Oliver."

Startled, she stared at him. "Trial?"

"Murder. That he did but got away with."

"They freed him?"

Devon raked a hand through the thick, tawny strands of his hair and sighed wearily. "Yes. He was acquitted. And then acquitted by a tornado before I could get to him."

"So you didn't kill him."

Devon shot her a sour glance and eased gingerly into a kitchen chair. Evening shadows darkened the corners of the kitchen, and a lamp glowed overhead, picking out the weary lines in his face. "Don't remind me."

"Why are you moving so stiffly? Are you hurt? Did he shoot you again?"

"No, and you don't need to remind me of the last time, either. I just got hit with a few boards."

"A few—!"

"The tornado. I got caught in the open. That's how Oliver got away." He shook his head disgustedly. "Have you got something stronger to drink than lemonade?"

Without a word, Maggie went to the cupboard and pulled out the bottle of whiskey. She set it on the table and gave him a glass, watching silently as he poured himself a drink.

He looked awful. His eyes were red, and his beard had grown straggly. Deep lines cut into his face, and his pale blond hair was streaked with mud in places. It was longer than she'd seen it before, curling down over his collar in the back and covering his ears.

"You look disreputable," she commented to hide her concern, and saw his blue eyes narrow slightly.

"Thanks."

"If you came here looking for compliments, I passed them all out earlier."

"Your patients must have been more numerous than one."

She grimaced. "Much. I ran out of flowery phrases long before the fourth patient."

A faint smile touched the edges of his mouth. "Looks like the folks in Belle Plain have come round."

"Not really. They're just desperate." She carved several hunks of beef off a roast, then sliced some bread, eyeing him with a professional survey while she did so. Though he looked weary and disgusted, he didn't seem to be suffering any ill effects, and she felt a wave of relief.

"Got a tub?" Devon asked when he'd devoured most of the roast beef, half a loaf of bread, and leftover apple pie. He washed it down with three cups of coffee, abandoning the whiskey.

"Yes, of course I do. Care to make use of it?"

Devon leaned back in his chair, eying her for a moment. He ran a hand across his jaw. "Yeah. Might even shave, too."

"And lose that charming bearlike facade? Be careful. You might begin to look human again."

"Would that soften your blamed tongue?" he grumbled, but she saw the amusement lighting his eyes.

"It might. Then again, it might not. I like most animals better than I do most men."

"Good." He snagged her by the arm when she leaned over the table to pick up his empty plate. His gaze riveted her in place, hot and burning with lights she'd come to recognize. "You're safer that way, Maggie Malone."

She drew in a shaky breath. "Oh, I don't know about that. You're pretty dangerous stuff, Devon Conrad."

He drew her around the edge of the table and into his lap, holding her so close against him that she could feel the steady beat of his heart. His head bent and he nuzzled her neck, his beard rasping against her tender skin. She must have made a slight noise, because his head lifted.

"Rough, huh?"

She drew a hand over the dark bristle of beard, amazed to see her fingers shake slightly. "Rough," she agreed in a whisper.

He grimaced. "If you'll start heating me some water, I'll get rid of it. Along with this layer of dirt."

Maggie stood up, briskly smoothing her skirts to hide her sudden uncertainty. Devon ignited a quivering fire in her every time she was near him, despite any vows she made to keep her composure. She hoped he didn't notice, that it was not as obvious to him as it was to her.

"Drag in that tin tub off the back porch," she directed calmly, "and I'll start the water heating."

"Don't make it too hot." Devon's spurs rattled as he crossed to the back door. "And don't put any of that rose-smelling stuff in it. It smells good on you, but I'd hate for someone to make a smart-aleck comment to me about how sweet I smell."

She laughed and set the huge kettle atop the cast-iron stove to begin heating water. It took three kettles to fill the tub with enough water, and when it was full, Devon began unbuttoning his shirt. Maggie stood uncertainly. She'd already placed soap and towels on the table near the high-backed tub.

She cleared her throat. "I have to straighten up my office. I'll be in the next room."

Devon slanted her a glance as he peeled off his shirt. "Aren't you going to offer to scrub my back?"

"There's a long-handled bath brush there on the table by the soap. I think you can manage it."

"Yeah, but it'd be more fun if you'd do it."

Her throat tightened, and she bit her bottom lip. With his shirt off and his chest bare in the glow of lantern light and setting sun, he looked magnificently appealing. The thought of scrubbing Devon's back left her feeling oddly unsettled, and she shook her head.

"I have paperwork."

His glance was one of disbelief, but he didn't say anything else when she left the room. In her office, she found it singularly difficult to concentrate on any of the medical journals she'd been going through earlier, and even her efforts to tidy up the chaos of a full day were halfhearted at best. She kept fighting mental images of Devon in the kitchen, his lean-muscled body glistening with water, his eyes half-mocking and half-lidded with desire.

Her stomach knotted. She wished she could accept his sudden appearances in her life as casually as he seemed to make them. His emotions weren't involved and she knew it, yet she couldn't resist temptation. She should. She didn't need her brother to tell her that. It made her sick sometimes when she thought about it, but when Devon appeared she was lost. No wonder Johnny thought she was crazy. Instead of his level-headed, independent sister, he saw a calf-eyed woman in love. She moaned softly and buried her face in her palms.

The minutes ticked past, and she eyed the clock with growing irritation. He should be through by now. He'd had enough time to bathe twice, and she fought her rising impatience. What if someone came looking for him? Lawmen, or even bounty hunters? If they caught him off guard in a tub of water . . .

When a sudden noise sounded suspiciously like a loud *thump*, she was certain her fears were supported.

Heart pounding, Maggie raced for the kitchen. She halted in the door, eyes widening.

Devon had his back to her, muscles flexing as he scraped at his face with a razor. He was using a small piece of broken mirror that was propped up on the window sill; his pants hung loosely on his lean hips as he worked at shaving, and his feet were bare.

"Are you—" She paused, her voice embarrassingly squeaky, and started again. "Are you all right?"

Devon turned to look at her, wiping shaving soap off his clean-shaven jaw. His dark brow lifted as if to ask why she was looking at him so closely, and she flushed.

"I thought . . . I mean, I heard a noise."

"Sorry. Knocked over the chair." Water glittered in the brown hair on his chest, and he left the towel draped around his neck as he reached for the upended chair. Amusement flickered briefly on his features, and Maggie had the thought that with his beard gone, Devon could pass for an East Coast gentleman. His jaw was strong and square, with a cleft in the center that gave him a determined, indomitable look. A snowy smudge of shaving soap clung to a spot below his ear.

"You missed some."

His mouth quirked. "Can't see good in this pitiful excuse for a mirror." He held out the towel. "Come wipe it off for me."

"Oh no, I'm not falling for that trick. Johnny used to find it quite amusing to wipe shaving soap on me."

She leaned against the doorframe when he grinned and swiped it away with an accurate graze of the towel. He looked almost boyish, and she caught a glimpse of how he might have been a long time ago, before life had taught him grim lessons of survival.

"You're too smart for me, Maggie," he said, and she ignored the clenching of her heart and the silent *I wish I were too smart to fall in love with you.*

"You're right," she said instead, pushing away from the door. "Why don't you see if you can help me empty this tub?"

"I'll do it. You just open the back door." Devon stepped to the tub and reached for the handles to drag it out. When Maggie moved past to open the door, he moved in a swift, blinding motion that caught her by surprise and startled a squeal from her.

He lifted her into his arms. She struggled, but saw his intentions in the laughter in his eyes. "Don't you dare, Devon Conra—"

Her protest ended in a loud splash as he dumped her in the tub. Her skirts immediately billowed up, then quickly deflated as water soaked them, making her flounder helplessly in the cool water.

"Devil!" she choked out, caught between anger and amusement. "If I had my pistol, I'd shoot you."

"Are you a good shot?"

"Very." She glared at him, wiping at the water trickling down her face. He was grinning, and when she shot a spray of water at him with the flat of her palm, he dodged. It hit him in the chest, and he reached out and put a hand on her head to duck her.

But Maggie had grown up with Johnny and Lindsay, and she knew a few tricks of her own. With an agile twist, she grabbed his arm and yanked at the same time as she put an arm behind his neck and pulled. He gave a surprised grunt, and fell on top of her. More water geysered up and over the sides of the tub as Devon sprawled half in, half out.

"Now who's so smart?" Maggie asked in a choked voice, and burst into unrestrained laughter when he gave her a watery glare.

"It ain't me, that's for sure."

"I noticed."

He levered himself partway up. Soapy water drizzled down his face, and small bubbles clustered at one corner of his mouth. Maggie collapsed into hilarity at the sight, and Devon grimaced.

"I don't know what made me think I could get the best of you for even a minute. You've beat me at every turn since the first time you tried to knock me off the porch."

She wiggled so that more water sloshed over him. "And don't you forget it again."

His arms went around her, and he slid the rest of the way into the tub, pants and all. Maggie laughed again, even while she was protesting that there wasn't enough room, he was making a dreadful mess, and who was going to clean it all up?

"We'll make room, I don't care about the mess, and we can clean it up later." Devon plucked at the wet material of her blouse. "Take this off."

"I can hardly—Devon!"

"I'll buy you another one," he muttered as one of the buttons came off in his impatient hand. "I'll buy you a dozen. Just take this one off *now*."

Reckless with love and the residue of laughter, Maggie threw caution to the wind and slipped out of her blouse. In short order, Devon had her undressed and had wriggled out of his wet pants. Naked, they splashed in the cool water of the tub, play turning to passion.

Devon twisted so that he was on the bottom, and pulled Maggie astride him, smiling at the surprise in her eyes. "I think you might like this," he murmured, and showed her how to regulate the rhythm of their lovemaking.

She slid down slowly, breath catching in her throat as he slipped deep inside her. It was different than before, with her setting the pace, taking as much of him as she could, an inch at a time. Breathless from the luxurious slide of his body, the way he filled her slowly and completely, she shuddered. Her entire body tingled as he pulled her forward to press kisses on her damp flesh. She put her hands on his shoulders to brace herself, gasping a little when his mouth found her breast and drew the nipple slowly inside, sending tiny tremors racing through her. While Devon licked and suckled, she rocked her hips in a wild, unrestrained ride that soon had them both clutching at release. It was as if they had been sucked up into the tornado that had roared through Buffalo Gap, swept away on the winds of passion and left hurtling through space unimpeded.

One of them cried out; Maggie thought it might be her, but she wasn't certain. She was aware only of the slow shift from mind-numbing passion to a drugged drifting of mind and body.

Finally Devon pushed her to a sitting position, grimacing. "This tub ain't made for this."

Maggie smiled dreamily. "But I am."

He looked startled, then smiled, leaning forward to kiss her. "You sure are, honey. Come on. Let me dry you off. The water's cold."

Devon toweled her dry, insisting upon doing it for her, and grinned wickedly as he focused on certain areas of her body. Though it was still warm outside, Maggie shivered at the whisper of air on her bare skin and the rough feel of the towel whisking over her.

When Devon lifted her into his arms and carried her into the bedroom, she put her head against his shoulder and wished that the night would never end.

## Chapter 12

"What are you going to do about the murder charges?"

Devon started to shrug, then thought better of it. "Nothing right now."

"What do you think they'll do?"

Devon didn't answer for a moment. Maggie worked around him, her scissors making soft, snicking sounds as she trimmed his hair. He felt several snippets fall down his collar and sighed.

"I think I'm gonna feel like an itchy bear, is what I think."

She tapped him on the head sharply when he started to turn. "Be still. I've seen how Ira Howell butchers men's heads in what he calls a tonsorial parlor. He took lessons from Comanches on haircuts. You should be grateful I offered to cut your hair for you."

"I'm grateful. I just wish you'd catch the hair goin' down my collar."

"Whiner." Maggie tucked a towel more securely around his neck. "Well, do you think the law will come after you?"

Devon didn't want to tell her what he thought. The less she knew the better he liked it. Knowing too much could be dangerous at times, but he had no intention of telling her that.

"There's no telling what they'll do," he said evasively, but she wasn't put off.

"You must know something. I saw that Indian the other night."

"What are you talking about?"

"Don't try to pretend you don't know. I heard a sound like an owl, and then you had the sudden urge to visit the convenience out back. I saw him come out of the shadows, and you talked for a while."

"You're too nosy for your own good, woman."

"Maybe. And maybe I just like to know whether I should be laying in a fresh supply of bandages in case you decide to resist arrest."

"You don't have much confidence in me, do you?" Devon felt a surge of irritation, and it wasn't helped at all by the worry in Maggie's voice.

"I have confidence in you, but I don't trust our local sheriff or bounty hunters."

"I don't either."

"No, but your damn pride won't let you be as sneaky as someone like Ash Oliver. I'm afraid you'll be ambushed again."

Devon's mouth thinned, and he was glad when she finished cutting his hair in silence. He stood up and brushed away the loose hairs from his shirt. She cared too much. It was evident in everything she said, the way she looked at him. And it made him feel penned in, suffocated.

He'd alternated between misery and lust since coming back to Belle Plain, and if not for the fact that ferreting out information took a good portion of his time, he would have probably spent too much time with her.

Part of him wanted to be with her constantly. The other part—the more rational part—started to suffocate when he let himself think about her in terms other than physical. The only part that he truly understood was the blinding lust he felt for her when she touched him or smiled at him, or he caught the sweet scent of her perfume. That need made him want to run like hell, and his reluctance to leave made him want to lash out at something or someone.

Like now, when he was standing on her back porch in the fading daylight, in full view of anyone who might pass, and the gentle teasing of her perfume and soft hands had made him rise hot and uncomfortably hard. He felt feverish, swollen with desire for her. The impatience of his need made him angry with himself and her, and sick with indecision.

God, what was the matter with him? Why didn't he just finish what he had to do and ride away? He was tired of dealing with the turbulence of his conflicting emotions, tired of wanting a woman he didn't want to be involved with except on one level.

And knowing that she deserved more than he wanted to give left him ashamed.

"Devon?" she murmured, and he flashed her a glance. Her face was troubled. "What's wrong?"

"Nothing."

His flat, cold reply elicited a lifted brow from her, but that was all. She wouldn't whine or plead, he knew that much, and while he was grateful, he wondered sourly why she didn't act like other women. Damn these independent females who left a man so uncertain of where he stood.

It wasn't comforting to realize that within the space of a few heartbeats, he'd run the entire gamut of contradictory emotions. It left him feeling strangely vulnerable and irritable.

"I'm done," she said coolly, her tone clipped, and it jarred him that she could dismiss his bad mood so easily.

"Thanks." He stood awkwardly, and put up a hand to finger his shorn hair. "You give a good haircut."

"That's what Johnny always said." She'd taken a broom and begun sweeping his hair off the porch. Pale blond snips blended in with the brown dirt and scrub grass.

"So, have you seen your brother lately?"

She glanced at him. "Didn't know that you cared."

"I don't. Not about him." *Damn.* She was going to end up making him say something he shouldn't. His mouth thinned into a tight-lipped frown.

"I see. Well, no, as a matter of fact, I haven't seen or heard from Johnny since the day he brought me those news clippings and old posters. I guess he's waiting on Lindsay to get here next month before he comes into Belle Plain again."

"Lindsay?"

"An old friend. Actually, she was raised with us and is like a sister. Her father is the Double M foreman."

Devon remembered him, a grizzled man with the obstinate look of a bull and the competence of an executive. They'd met at the Brass Lady, and Devon had sensed the foreman's disapproval of him even before the introductions were over. He frowned. David Brawley had seemed to take great pleasure in introducing them, emphasizing the name Cimarrón so that Hank Mills had slowly turned and looked him up and down.

"What do you know about David Brawley?" he asked so abruptly that Maggie looked startled.

"Know about him? Not much, I suppose. He came into town the same day I did and owns stock in the hotel." She leaned on the broom, frowning slightly. "Why do you ask?"

"Just curious. I don't like him."

"I'm not surprised." Maggie gave him a wry smile. "He wasn't impressed with you either, that night we went onto the hotel roof to look at stars."

"For a man who's unimpressed, he's sure made it his business to stick as close to me as bark on a tree lately."

He'd surprised her again. Her brows lifted, eyes widening so that they made him think of shimmering gray pools. "Oh? How odd."

"Irritating better describes it." Devon reached for

his hat where it was lying on a wooden stool. "He asks too damn many questions."

"I'm certain you know how to avoid them."

A faint flicker of amusement made him smile. "Yeah, I reckon I do." He stepped down off the porch and jammed his hat on his head. Maggie didn't ask when he'd be back or even if he'd be back, but he felt her eyes on him as he went to the lean-to where Pardo was saddled and ready.

It wasn't until he was riding away from Maggie and Belle Plain that it hit him what was wrong.

Johnny Malone stood on the platform at the train depot in Baird, sweating nervously and swearing silently. What was he doing here? He should have forced Hank to come, but the foreman had shrugged and said he'd wait at the ranch for Lindsay. *Damn.* What if she took one look at Johnny and refused to go with him?

It was possible. They hadn't parted on the best of terms.

Puffs of steam rose in the distance, quickly drifting away on the wind. A whistle blew loudly, and within minutes the train was rattling to a shrieking stop. Johnny started to take off his hat, then left it on. He wasn't going to do anything he wouldn't do if it was anyone else getting off that damn train, by God.

But when Lindsay Mills stepped daintily down the metal rungs and her eyes met his, he felt the plummet of his heart and his good intentions. Hat in hand, he went forward to take her gloved hand and help her down the last rung.

"Lindsay." Was that his voice? Shaky and rusty?

"Johnny Malone, you have filled out! Look at you!"

Relief flooded him. She was smiling and looked genuinely glad to see him. He grinned, feeling foolish but unable to wipe it from his face.

"Guess I've grown a bit. So have you." He swallowed the "in all the right places" that trembled on the tip of his tongue, not wanting to see the coldly aloof stare she'd been famous for giving him before she left.

Lindsay put her hand lightly on his arm as he escorted her down the wooden platform, and he felt the interested gazes of some of the men focusing on her. She commanded male attention, from the top of her elegantly coiffed hair that was barely covered by some kind of hat that looked to be made of nothing but a few feathers and a wad of netting, to the tips of her shining, highly polished kid slippers. Her skirts were fitted to her curving hips in the front, but drawn up in the back to fall in graceful folds, and Johnny didn't dare let his eyes wander to the form-fitting bodice. He felt strangely short of breath and knew that if he didn't watch it, he'd find himself tied into knots again.

"I suppose Daddy is at the ranch," Lindsay was saying, and he paused in the shade of an overhang to smile down at her.

"Yeah. You know Hank. The farthest he goes from the Double M is into Belle Plain."

Lindsay smoothed one of her gloves, and he caught the sweet scent of perfume that wafted up. His belly clenched, and he gritted his teeth to keep from giving in to the temptation to kiss Lindsay's full, pouting mouth. Damn, but she had the sweetest lips that always looked ready to be kissed.

"Belle Plain was little more than a few buildings the last time I was there," Lindsay said. "Has it grown?"

"Yes and no."

Her head tilted to one side, her mouth curved into an amused smile as she gazed at him, and Johnny felt the searing burn of her green eyes. "That sounds like a good story."

"Boring. Has to do with cattle and trains." He

grinned. "Why don't I entertain you with a decent meal and a night on the town?"

"Town?" Her gaze swept over the wide rutted streets and bustling traffic. "Baird has certainly grown. Last time I saw it, it was barely a dot on the map."

"Yeah, well it's a lot more than just a railroad division point for the Texas and Pacific now. Some of the ranches are diversifying into crops."

Lindsay gave him a disbelieving stare, and he couldn't help laughing. "Sounds unlikely, don't it? Well, I grant you that only one or two have tried anything. It's mostly cattle as usual."

"And you? Have you thought of doing more than raising cows and tempers?"

It was a barbed question, and he saw from the sudden flicker in her eyes that his future depended on the right answer. No matter what she said, Lindsay still cared. She couldn't hide it, couldn't hide it no matter how hard she tried. Johnny fought an overwhelming surge of hope.

"I've thought a lot about things during the past few years." He paused, staring past Lindsay to the monster of iron belching steam on the tracks. "There are more important things than makin' money."

There was a little quiver in her voice when she said, "I think I could use a cup of hot tea right now. Maybe we can talk in one of the hotels."

Johnny arranged for her trunks to be sent over, then escorted Lindsay down Market Street to the hotel.

"Mr. Brawley." Maggie opened the door wider to admit him. "Come in. I certainly didn't expect you to be one of my patients."

A grin made him look boyish, and his hazel eyes were alight with humor. "Actually, I'm not here in a professional capacity, Miss—uh, Dr. Malone."

"No? Then why are you here?" Maggie smiled back at him, unable to resist his infectious good humor.

"Purely recreational. There's a dance at the school house tomorrow night. Thought I might talk you into going with me."

"A dance? My, aren't we getting festive. I hadn't heard about it."

David Brawley turned his hat in his hand, looking rather awkward and shy. "Is that a yes or a no?"

"Neither." Maggie gestured to the empty waiting room. Sunshine slanted through a thick windowpane, trailing dusty streamers of light that enveloped the pot of fading zinnias. "I need this time to catch up on paperwork, not dance."

"I've never yet met a person, man or woman, who didn't need some recreation." David smiled. "Your work will still be here. The music won't."

Caught by a sudden desire to forget work and revel in a few hours of gaiety, Maggie heard herself say, "I'll come, but by myself."

"What time?"

"Seven."

"I'll be waiting just outside the school-house door." He hesitated as if wanting to say more, then shrugged and left. Maggie watched him go. There was something different about David Brawley, and a small voice in the back of her mind whispered a warning she couldn't quite understand. It was as if someone had posed a riddle lately, and the answer hovered just out of reach. She knew there was something she was supposed to know, but it wasn't clear.

"I'm imagining things," she muttered to herself, and was startled at how loud her voice sounded in the thick silence of her empty house. Her cherished privacy now felt appallingly close to loneliness. Devon's absence was like a sharp ache inside her. He'd been gone over a month.

Frequently she found herself looking up expecting to see the muted gleam of his sun-tarnished hair as he read a book in a pool of lamplight, his body relaxed in the stuffed chair that stood near a small reading table. Devon, she had discovered, had an insatiable thirst for knowledge. During his convalescence, he had spent many hours poring over her small library. When she'd remarked upon it, his eyes had narrowed in faint mockery as if at some private inner joke, and he had made a light reply.

"Not much room for books in my saddlebags, so I catch up when I can."

There was more to it than that, and she sensed it but was afraid he would misunderstand her interest. He was much more complex than she'd ever thought, though she had sensed at their first meeting that he was not what he appeared to be on the surface. Now she was convinced of it.

She wondered, with a blend of impatience at her own weakness and reluctant yearning, if he would come back.

Fiddles twanged gaily, and the schoolhouse was lit by two dozen lanterns. Dressed in their Sunday best, town folks as well as nearby ranchers and their families crowded into the stone building, all eager to dance and socialize. Doors and windows were left open despite the chill breezes, and the elegant stone archways gave evidence of the thickness of the walls that kept the interior cooler on hot days, warmer in the winter.

Johnny Malone stood impatiently near a table covered with cakes, pies, and cookies, drinking punch from a cup while he watched Lindsay Mills greet old friends. He'd brought her to Belle Plain to visit Maggie, but Mrs. Lamb had said she had ridden out to help with a difficult delivery. Though reluctant to see Maggie again until she came to her senses, Johnny had been even more reluctant to leave Lindsay on her own at the hotel.

So here he was, standing glumly by, watching Lindsay charm everyone who came near her. She did it effortlessly, just as she'd done as a child, her light, tinkly laugh like bells sounding on a cool, clear night. His throat tightened and he wished desperately that he didn't care.

Lindsay, dressed in a gown that looked like an expensive concoction of pink lace and satin, glided among the crowd like a beautiful, exotic bird. Her blond hair was up high and held with ivory combs, framing her exquisite face, and though she didn't wear a lot of jewelry, she seemed to glitter as if bedecked with diamonds.

"She turned out to be a looker, didn't she?"

Ira Howell took an involuntary step back when Johnny turned to glare at him. "Yeah," he bit off, "she did."

Ira cleared his throat. "Yes. Well. Did you hear about Cimarrón?"

"You mean killin' those two men up in Abilene? Yeah, I heard. Much as I don't like him, it don't sound like somethin' he'd do."

Ira looked surprised, then nodded. "True enough. I also heard that Cimarrón caught some of the rustlers. Looks as if he's pretty good at finding other outlaws, wouldn't you say?"

Johnny answered in a growl, and Ira managed a smile. "I was there, you know," Ira said with the air of a man desperate for a neutral topic of conversation, "when Cimarrón shot Jenkins in the saloon. It wasn't pretty. Never seen a man so fast, though. Too bad Jenkins didn't listen when Cimarrón warned him to go away."

"Ira, ain't you got nothin' better to talk about than a two-bit desperado?" Johnny half-snarled, wishing the man would take the hint and leave. Instead, Howell nodded, eyes behind his thick spectacles sly and knowing.

"Yes, indeed. Where is your lovely sister tonight?"

It was another bad choice of subjects, and Ira seemed to decipher that from the look on Johnny's face. He paled and began to stammer, and Johnny wished savagely that he'd never come to the damn social.

"My sister ain't here. I don't know where she is, but if I find out, I'll tell you."

His bad mood sent Ira skittering to safety across the room, and Johnny watched him go without regret. He gulped down the last of his too-sweet punch and stepped outside for some fresh air. It was cool and crisp, and he went to stand beneath a spreading cottonwood and smoke.

Maybe he should go to the Brass Lady and have a drink instead of hover at the edges of Lindsay's admiring crowd, wishing he had her all to himself. It had been all he could do to keep his hands off her in Baird, and the short trip to Belle Plain had been torturous.

They'd talked in the hotel lobby, and it hadn't taken Lindsay long to discover that he hadn't changed into what she thought she wanted. Johnny burned at the memory of her lovely face going white with distress.

"You told me you thought about more important things than making money, John Malone!"

He hadn't been able to hide his own distress. "Dammit, Lindsay, you don't look like you're doin' without money. Why do you act like fancy dresses don't cost your daddy most of his hard-earned pay?"

Those remarkable green eyes could flare with a white-hot fury that he hadn't forgotten, but he was still amazed by how violently it could burn. "Don't you dare suggest that my father resents sending me money! And besides, my mother's family pays for the extra necessities—"

"Necessities? Like that stupid hat? I bet it'd cost Hank a month's wages to buy something that ain't no more than a clump of net and chicken feathers."

"Which shows how much you know about style."

"Right. I know more about land and cattle, and what it takes to buy feed and hay in the winter and enough food to last till spring. That's what I know about."

When she'd started to rise, he'd caught her hand and held her, unable to hold back the words. "Lindsay, a man just naturally wants to buy his woman things she likes, but survival has to come first. You should understand that."

"I understand that better than you do. Pretty clothes are not vital, but there are other things that are." Her mouth had trembled, and he'd had to hold hard to his self-control to keep from jerking her into his arms and kissing her. "This never was about *things,* Johnny. Our disagreement has always been about the intangibles."

She'd pulled away then and he'd let her go, and on the ride back to Belle Plain he'd never dredged up the nerve to rekindle the argument. Now they were here, and there were too many distractions even if he'd found the words he wanted to say. Damn. He wished he and Maggie were on speaking terms so he could ask her advice.

As if summoned up by the thought, he heard someone say, "Miss Malone!" and turned to see David Brawley greet Maggie at the schoolhouse door.

Maggie. Dressed in her best gown, the watered blue silk that made her eyes look like a blue-gray lake. And she was smiling prettily, her face lit with amusement as she allowed Brawley to escort her inside. Johnny frowned. Maybe he'd been wrong about her and Cimarrón after all, though he didn't think so. But no one in town had seen the gunman in a while, from what he'd heard, so it looked as if Maggie had decided to be sensible at last.

Johnny took a final drag off his cigarette and crushed it out on his bootheel, then went back inside. He paused in the doorway just as Maggie and Lindsay saw one another, and heard their exclamations.

"Lindsay!" Maggie broke away from Brawley's proprietary hand at her waist and flung herself toward Lindsay, who greeted her just as enthusiastically. Half-laughing, half-crying, the two women embraced, talking at the same time.

"Wait a minute," Lindsay finally said, pulling away with a smile. "We can't hear each other if we're both talking."

"When did you get here? Why didn't you come to my house to see me?"

"This afternoon and I did. You were gone."

Maggie laughed. "I forgot. Mrs. Darden had a difficult delivery."

"I can't believe you're a doctor."

"Did Johnny tell you?"

"Reluctantly." Lindsay glanced up and saw him in the doorway. Her eyes met his with a cool challenge that made him answer it immediately. He walked over to them.

"It's no secret how I feel about that, is it, Maggie?"

"I'm afraid not." She gave him a searching glance and apparently decided that he wasn't going to be nasty. "But I have to admit that he's tried to understand."

That surprised him. So she'd seen that? He hadn't thought she did, but he hadn't known how to make it clear. He could understand her being a doctor better than he could accept her with Cimarrón. Maybe the last had eclipsed the other in terms of being unbearable. He shrugged.

"Not always." His voice was gruffer than he wanted, and he cleared his throat, slightly embarrassed. "Come on, Lindsay. Dance with me. You and Maggie can talk later where it's more private."

He didn't give her the opportunity to refuse, but swept her away and into the steps of a Texas reel. It felt good to have his hands on her, even knowing that she was betrothed to some city dweller back in Georgia. Well, maybe he'd just change that before too long, by God, and show Lindsay that she belonged out here, not in a stifling city with a slick-talking dandy who had more money than sense.

When he had her laughing and breathless from the fast-paced dance, he whisked her across the room to stand out on the tiny back porch where it was quieter. She leaned back against the wood railing, staring at him in the muted light that came through the door. Johnny felt the familiar ache in him and wondered how he'd managed to stay away from her for the past four years.

"You belong here, Lindsay," he said, his voice guttural. She stared at him a moment, eyes as big as saucers.

"Why?"

" 'Cause this is real. The city's all right for some people, but not you. I'm surprised you didn't smother there. Did you ever think about me?"

"About coming back, you mean?" She paused, looking past him. "I'm here, aren't I?"

"Yeah," he growled, "but not for good if what Hank says is true." He grabbed her slender arms when she started to turn away. "Dammit, Lindsay, you know I want you here. You know I've been miserable since you left."

Her gaze was cool. "Do I? I don't recall your writing and asking me to come back."

He let go of her, staring at her with growing frustration. "I ain't much of a letter writer."

"How much writing does it take to pen the words,

'Dear Lindsay, I miss you. Come home. Love, Johnny.' "

"I'm sayin' it now."

"Now it's too late. I'm betrothed."

"He'll get over it."

"So will you, much quicker than Quincy, I think."

"*Quincy.*" He spat the word as if it was sour. "I can't believe you'd marry some milktoast named Quincy and live in Atlanta when you could be here with me. We were always together. Dammit, girl, I've been inside you. Or have you managed to forget that?"

Her face went white, then red, and her chin lifted. "I haven't forgotten," she said in a husky whisper. "But maybe it's more important to me than to you."

This time when he grabbed her, he pulled her into his arms and kissed her, his mouth hot and hard on hers, not giving her the chance to pull away. All the old passion was still there, hiding just below the surface, exploding now into a raging desire that he wasn't certain he could control. He had to release her to keep from embarrassing both of them on the tiny back porch of the schoolhouse.

Lindsay stared at him, eyes wide, lips wet and bruised-looking from his kiss. She reached up to touch them, her fingers lightly grazing her mouth.

"Well," she said with a shaky little laugh, "we always did have that between us."

"I know. We're older now, Lindsay. And smarter. This time we'll wait for the preacher."

She backed off a bit, her gaze searching. "Why do you want to marry me, Johnny? I'd make you miserable. You'd make me miserable. One of these days, your temper will get you killed, and then I'd be a widow. I told you a long time ago that I won't risk that."

"Dammit, you've put up all these fences between us. If I listen to you, I care more about the ranch than you, or my bad temper will get me killed, or money is more important than you. Why don't you just be honest and say that you're afraid to marry the man you love because you don't want to give up your goddamn independence? You want a puppet you can twist around your little finger, not a man."

Lindsay started to brush past him, anger shadowing her perfect, pure features, and he grabbed her arm again. "Oh no, you're not runnin' again. This time, you're gonna stay."

Her soft, rounded chin lifted, defiance firming it. "I hope you can think of a way to make me, John Clark Malone. Because if you can't—"

She ended the sentence abruptly, and he saw from the determined light in her eyes that she'd leave and he'd lose her. What the hell did she want from him? He wanted to shake her, then kiss her until they both ended up in a pile of hay or on a bed somewhere, and he could sate himself in the soft sweet velvet of her. That was the only thing that had kept him going sometimes, the memory of Lindsay beneath him, her body fit to his and her voice soft and loving in his ear. It was the only memory that had ever made him think she might come back to him.

"Why did you leave?" he couldn't help asking. "Why?"

"You know why."

He groaned. "You know I didn't mean half those things I said. I was just mad."

"And the next time you get mad? Will you say them again?" Her lovely eyes filled with tears that glittered like silver in the glancing light. "You hurt me. I won't give you that chance again."

Before he could say anything, she was gone, brushing past him to step back inside. He could hear someone call to her, heard Lindsay's bright, brittle reply that almost hid her distress. Damn. He was a bastard. He'd known then he would pay one day for losing his temper and taking it out on her, but he'd never dreamed it would cost him what he held most dear.

Miserable and feeling like he wanted to hit something, he stepped inside. And heard someone say in a shocked whisper, "Cimarrón is here!"

# CHAPTER 13

"Dance with me."

Maggie turned, a half smile curving her mouth, and her breath caught in the back of her throat. Devon. Here. And it was obvious from the whispers and stares that she was among the last to see him arrive at the dance.

He looked arrogant and faintly challenging, standing in a room crowded with disapproving citizens, a gunbelt low on his lean hips in blatant disregard for the rules. Silver streaked his tawny hair and made it gleam in the blaze of lamplight, and his eyes were shadowed by his thick lashes so that she couldn't quite read his expression. He was a hellion, a prairie pirate bent on self-destruction, yet she couldn't help admiring the controlled recklessness that had brought him here among so many enemies. Her heart thudded alarmingly.

A waltz quavered up from guitars and a harmonica. The touch of Devon's hand at her waist provoked an intense ache and made her mouth go dry when he took her into the middle of the schoolhouse floor without waiting for an acceptance or refusal. She should have sensed his arrival. He radiated a raw sensuality that ignited an immediate response in her. Every fiber of her body clamored a welcome, and the hot, hungry animal heat of him made her quiver inside.

Desks and tables had been pushed aside to make room for dancing, and Devon swept her around and

172

into his arms. Maggie was dimly aware of David Brawley giving an impotent protest, and of her brother's angry reaction. Johnny started forward with a blistering curse, but Lindsay grabbed him by the arm and held him. Maggie could hear her arguing with him.

"My brother will be here in a minute," she said softly, and saw Devon's mouth slant in a wry smile.

"Figured he would. Can't help it. I need to talk to you." His hand was warm against the small of her back, and he moved with an easy grace that didn't surprise her. Everything he did, he did well. "Step outside with me, Maggie."

"Why not? If there's anything left of my reputation, it's certainly shredded now."

Devon scowled. "I know. If there was another way to talk to you, I would have taken it. No one would give you my message with your brother in here."

She allowed him to dance her toward the back exit, well-aware of the curious, avid gazes following them. Johnny was a dark, glowering picture of fury, and David Brawley watched them narrowly. She caught a glimpse of Lindsay's thoughtful expression and knew that of all of them, only she might understand. No one seemed inclined to dispute Cimarrón's right to ask her for a dance, though it was obvious no one approved.

"What's so urgent?" she asked when he'd stopped in the doorway. He carefully positioned her with her back to the room. It should be apparent to anyone watching that he was not attempting to take liberties. He glanced down at her.

"I need your help. A friend of mine is hurt."

"Why didn't you say so? Good heavens, let me go get my bag and—"

"No." Devon's hand caught her by the arm when she began to turn away. "I don't want anyone to know about it."

Maggie studied his cool blue eyes and saw the flicker of concern. She nodded slowly. "All right. Then what do you suggest?"

"I'll come for you later. Try not to stay too long." His gaze moved past her to where David Brawley stood, and his dark brow lifted. "You're keeping bad company, Maggie."

She flushed. He must have seen David greet her and seen the way he'd hovered nearby all evening. "It's not like you think."

Devon's shoulders lifted in a brief shrug, but there was a burst of light in his eyes that betrayed his anger. "I don't have a stake rope on you. Do what you want."

"I usually do." Her tart reply seemed to take him back, and his mouth thinned into a grimace.

"Right. I knew that."

"Wait for me in my office. I'll get away from here as quickly as possible without arousing suspicion."

"Here comes your brother. I wondered how long he'd let that girl hold him before somebody put spark to his powder." Devon took a step away from her, and Maggie grew alarmed.

"No fighting! Especially not here in public . . ."

"Maggie." Johnny's tone was sharp as he came to a halt beside them. "This man bothering you?"

She turned. "No. He's just leaving. Would you please escort me to the punch bowl?" She put out her hand and saw her brother's hesitation. He glared at Cimarrón, then took her offered hand with reluctance.

"Leave my sister alone, Cimarrón," he growled. "Go on back to the Bar Z if you want to stay healthy."

"Anytime I need your advice, I'll come askin'. You go back to starin' at your pretty little friend and stay out of my business, cowboy."

Devon's eyes heated with amusement when Johnny made an automatic grab at his right side, obviously forgetting that weapons had been forfeited at the schoolhouse door. Maggie grabbed her brother's arm and hissed at him not to be stupid, and Devon took advantage of the distraction to step back off the porch and disappear into the night. She stared into the shadows where he'd gone, feeling strangely unsettled again.

"Dammit, Maggie," Johnny was saying as he jerked away from her, "don't ever do that again."

"Don't ever be stupid enough to draw an invisible gun on a man that has a real one," she shot back irritably. It was only vaguely gratifying to see Johnny flush.

"I forgot I wasn't wearin' it, but next time I will be. Who the hell let him in with his iron, anyway?"

"Who was going to take it away from him?"

Frustration thickened Johnny's voice. "I wish to hell that damn gunman would ride on. He ain't been nothin' but trouble since he got here."

"He's caught several of the rustlers, don't forget."

"You always gonna take up for him?" Johnny's eyes were a dark, stormy gray that made her think of thunderclouds. "I thought maybe you'd come to your senses by now."

"This is neither the time nor the place to discuss this, but if you insist, I'll talk to you about it later."

Johnny took a step back. "Naw. Guess I should have kept out of it. You're too blamed hardheaded to listen to me anyway."

Maggie stared after him when he pivoted on his heel and stalked across the floor, threading roughly through the dancers. Music made a lively counterpoint to the swirling couples who'd seemed to lose interest in Maggie once Cimarrón had left.

She sighed when David Brawley approached with a resigned expression. "Miss Maggie, would you care to dance?"

"Actually, Mr. Brawley, I'm feeling quite tired. Would you mind escorting me home?"

He seemed to expect it and nodded gravely. "Of course."

When they arrived at the house, David reached around her to open the front door. It creaked softly on its hinges. Maggie turned, feeling suddenly awkward. She put out a hand.

"Thank you for walking me home, Mr. Brawley."

"No problem." His smile gleamed in the soft light that came through the open door. "Anything for a beautiful woman. I admit to being one of your most ardent admirers."

Maggie felt his hand close around hers, and he showed no inclination of releasing it. A breeze tugged at her hair and shimmied the leaves on the cottonwood at the corner of the house, throwing eerie shadows across the porch. She was half-expecting it, but couldn't help a startled "Oh!" when David exerted pressure on her hand to draw her forward. His other hand came up to cup her chin as he bent to kiss her.

His mouth was warm and dry, lips softly brushing over hers in a light caress. It wasn't unpleasant but had none of the electrifying affect on her that Devon's kisses had, and Maggie took a step back. David stared down at her in the diffused light, eyes searching her face.

"I'm in love with you, you know," he said abruptly, and she flushed.

"You can't be serious."

"I am."

"You hardly know me."

"I know you well enough. I've watched you these past months, and seen how hard you work. You're a very intelligent, dedicated young woman. You deserve better than this town."

"I thought you came to Belle Plain on a note of hope and industry." She couldn't help the tart sarcasm in her tone and saw that he heard it as well.

"Yes, that's true, Maggie. May I call you Maggie?" He caressed her cheek, then dropped his hand to his side when she moved away. "I came here with the hope of revitalizing the town, bringing new jobs here. It all depended upon the railroad, however, but the cattlemen did not compromise, and I'm afraid that the original plans must be abandoned."

"Compromise?" Maggie stared at him. "What was expected of them?"

"Land rights. Water rights. Trains need land to lay rails, and water to make steam, you know."

"It seems to me that the Texas and Pacific made up its mind what it wanted when it built the roundhouse and repair shops in Baird instead of Belle Plain. I hardly think they would seriously consider building a spur here. In fact, you are the only one I've ever heard discuss it."

His brow lifted, and a faint smile curved his mouth. "I assure you that my information comes from good sources. But none of this is as important as your situation right now."

"My situation?"

David took her hand again, holding it tightly when she tried to pull away. "Yes. I know what some people are saying about you, but it doesn't matter. Not to me. Maggie, I've got a good position, not only as an investor in the hotel here, but as a division director for the T&P."

"So that's it." Her gaze locked with his. "That's how you know so much about the railroad's plans. Why haven't you made it known to everyone here?"

He shrugged. "It was better that I didn't at first. You know how people are. Everyone would present this argument and that, and not allow me to study the situation for myself. Fred Murphy sold me stock in his hotel for a small amount and agreed to keep my secret."

"And your decision?"

David looked away from her, his mouth thinning. "It is my opinion that nothing would be gained by building a spur here," he said at last, his tone regretful.

"I see."

"God, I hope you understand. Look at it this way, Maggie, you're not directly affected. Belle Plain wasn't even in existence until a few years ago, and this won't harm the Double M."

"What about the people who have invested time and money and hope in Belle Plain? Won't they be affected?"

"Yes." His hazel eyes were pleading. "But that can't be helped. Ultimately it was not my decision. Please understand."

She sighed. "I suppose I do. It's just that I hate to see the town die."

"The people won't die. Some are already moving to Baird and there are jobs there and in Abilene."

"Yes." She felt suddenly exhausted. "Yes, you're right. I should have realized what the eventual outcome would be."

"But it won't matter to you, Maggie. Or to your brother. You have the Double M, and it's one of the finest spreads in Texas."

"It could be if the rustlers leave any cattle behind." She felt a sharp ache behind her eyes and a rising urgency to go inside. "Mr. Brawley—"

"David."

"David. Please, I'm tired. It's been a long day."

"May I see you again?"

She fought a swelling impatience and nodded. "Yes, of course. I have no immediate plans to move."

"That's not what I meant."

She took a step away, toward the house, wishing he would take the hint and leave. "Certainly you may see me again."

When he left after pressing an ardent kiss to the back

of her hand, Maggie eased inside and shut the door behind her, unable to stop a sigh of relief. For a moment, she'd thought he meant to declare himself. It would have been exceedingly awkward. But he was gone, and now she had to prepare for a long night with Devon's injured friend.

She pushed away from the door and moved down the hall toward her office. From the shadows, a hand flashed out to grab her, and she had to stifle a sudden scream.

"You scared me!" Maggie's voice trembled when she jerked her arm from his grasp, and Devon shrugged.

"You told me to wait here."

"Well, I didn't mean for you to sneak up on me in the dark."

"Afraid I overheard Brawley's love-talk?"

The pool of light grew larger as Maggie turned up the lamp on her office desk, and he saw the splotches of color burning her cheeks when she said, "It was not love-talk."

"Sounded like it to me." Irritation knifed through him, and he tried to keep it from showing in his voice. "He ain't what he pretends to be, Maggie. Stay away from him."

She began jerking at a large leather bag, her face taut. "You aren't what you seem either. Should I stay away from you?"

"Definitely." He couldn't help the husky thread that he was afraid was too betraying when he added, "But I hope you don't."

She turned. Her eyes searched his face. "Devon. Why did you stay away so long and not get word to me?"

"I'll explain later. My friend needs your help, and I don't know how long he can last." He stepped back to let her move past him, and she paused in a rustle of silk.

"I need to change gowns and fetch my coat. Bring my bag, please."

Nights were cool now, with the hint of approaching winter in the brisk wind that blew down from the northwest. Devon felt Maggie's shiver as if she were seated in front of him, and he wished she were. Instead, she rode a rangy bay gelding that bared his teeth and rolled his eyes every time Devon rode too close. Damn. Even horses didn't want him close to her. When was he going to get smart enough to back off and leave her alone?

"It's not much farther," he said when she glanced at him questioningly. "A line shack just ahead."

Moonlight silvered the ground with a pristine glow that threw sharp shadows. A coyote howled somewhere close by, and the brisk fragrance of sage stung the air. A sense of urgency made him ride faster, until finally the line shack was just ahead. Smoke curled from a pipe in the roof and drifted on the wind, heralding its location as they crested a steep slope. Then the faint glimmer of light from a window stabbed the deep shadows, a hazy square in the night.

"There it is," Devon muttered, and felt his horse's increasing pace. Hoofbeats apparently alerted the men inside, and the door of the shack opened briefly, allowing a slice of light to escape.

*"Hola!"* Devon shouted, reining in and motioning for Maggie to do the same. Her face looked pinched and pale in the shimmery moonlight, and he cursed silently. He should not have brought her here, but he hadn't known what else to do. Latigo needed help.

A dull gleam flashed off a rifle barrel, and Danza stepped out of the shadows. "He grows worse, amigo."

Maggie was already moving her horse forward and sliding from the saddle. Devon dismounted to help her as she struggled with her black leather bag.

"A gunshot wound, I presume?" she asked, moving past Danza with barely a glance.

The Apache glanced over her head toward Devon, a faint smile tugging at the corners of his mouth. "You are as wise as you are beautiful, little one."

"It doesn't take a genius to figure out the reason for being brought here secretly at night." She pushed open the door and stepped into the rush of warm air in the shack.

Devon waited outside. He already knew what she'd find and hoped he'd been able to bring her in time. He looked at Danza. "If Latigo can be helped, she'll help him."

"*Sí*. I know that."

Silence fell, and they stood outside the shack in the cool, clear air that smelled of woodsmoke and sage and waited. Devon felt some of what Danza must be feeling, though he was not as close to the young man lying wounded on a hard cot. Latigo was Danza's cousin, a boy of only sixteen years, but with the necessary experience of a lifetime of hardship and struggle.

But it was Devon's fault that the boy lay with a bullet in him. Another mistake that weighed heavily on him.

"It was not your fault, amigo," Danza said after a moment, as if reading Devon's mind.

"No? He wouldn't have been shot if he hadn't been trying to cover my back."

"My cousin has the heart of a lion, but the rash temper of a small boy. He did not heed your advice. It is his own fault that he was shot."

"That should be a great comfort to his mother."

Danza sighed, and the wind whipped his long black hair over his face. "Do not take this guilt on you, amigo. It is not yours. If the blame is to be placed, it should be mine. I let the boy ride with me, though I knew he was too young."

"He was never shot when he was riding with you. Only with me."

"When a man chooses a path, he also chooses the risks on that path. Latigo is old enough to choose his own path and would not appreciate you taking blame or glory for his choice."

Devon raked the side of his boot across dirt and clumps of grama grass. "Oliver was my choice."

"He made himself mine also, when he chose the coward's way and attacked a man's back. Now he has made himself my enemy for certain. You may kill him, but I claim his scalp."

Their gazes met, and Devon nodded slowly.

By the time he was through with Ash Oliver, he didn't intend for there to be much more than his scalp left. Oliver had gotten in his way too many times, leaving nothing but death and misery behind. He was one of those men Devon hated most, a dispassionate killer, ruthless and brutal. Young Ralph Pace had not deserved to die as he had, alone and frightened and humiliated, but he had.

"Tell me, amigo," Danza said with that uncanny knack he had for reading Devon's mind, "what did the young caballero who was killed mean to you?"

Devon stared grimly over the moon-washed slopes and gullies. "He was a reminder," he said at last, softly, and was thankful that Danza seemed to understand what he meant without further explanation. Ralph had been young and forced by circumstances into a life he didn't want, much as Devon had been so long ago. At first, Devon had assumed that the boy wanted to either make a name for himself by riding with Cimarrón or by shooting him; then he had realized that he was only afraid.

It had taken him aback at first, made him remember how afraid he'd been a long time ago, when he was very young and orphaned, with only Kate beside him. Then he'd had to keep up his own courage to comfort his sister, and it had been a lonely, terrifying ordeal. That was before he and Kate had found others to ride with, grown old enough to form a plan of vengeance that had set them on a spiral of robberies before ending in tragedy.

Tragedy for him, anyway, and he'd recognized in Ralph Pace's pleading blue eyes the same need he'd once felt to be comforted. Orphaned and alone, Ralph followed Devon like an unwanted puppy he couldn't shake until finally he'd given up trying to run Pace off and let him ride with him.

It had been a mistake, as he'd known it would be. Getting close to someone brought inevitable loss, but Ralph had managed to get under his skin with his eager efforts to please. Devon had even started to enjoy his company. Until last Christmas Eve. He'd left Ralph outside El Paso and returned to their camp late, anticipating the boy's surprise at the gift he'd impulsively purchased for him. It wasn't much—a new pair of spurs to replace old ones, but he'd seen Ralph eyeing his and knew the boy would like them. Hell, it had been so little to do, and he was half-embarrassed at the impulse to buy a Christmas gift when he'd never even received one before, but he hadn't been able to keep from it.

Then he'd seen the dead fire and the body sprawled on new snow turned to red slush with fresh blood. The iciness had gone bone-deep then. It wasn't until after he'd buried the boy in the frozen ground that the ice inside him had begun to thaw into a red-hot lust for vengeance.

For the next six months he'd followed any lead he could find; the killer was riding a horse making crescent-moon tracks. He knew those tracks, because they belonged to the horse stolen by Ralph's murderers. No horseshoe could disguise the print. It was as distinctive as a particular brand. It was what had eventually led him to Callahan County and Zeke Rogan. What he hadn't expected was that Ralph's murderer and Rogan were old acquaintances.

The chain of circumstances was too strong to ignore, and he puzzled over the seemingly unconnected facts he'd managed to gather. There was a lot more to this than just a few stolen cattle and the promise of a railroad depot to a dying town, but he didn't know what. It hovered at the back of his mind, nudging him to figure it out, and frustration battled with worry over Latigo.

When the door to the shack opened and Maggie finally stepped out, Devon turned sharply. She looked weary, but she managed a faintly reassuring smile.

"He'll live, I think. He's awake if you want to go in."

Danza nodded gravely and moved past her to go inside. Devon stood silently, watching Maggie. Faint bluish circles bruised the thin skin under her eyes, and her shoulders slumped with weariness.

"Are you all right?" His voice sounded overloud in the still air, and he saw her jump slightly.

"Tired. Heartsick. Oh—Devon."

He saw her face crumple, and he reached out to catch her when she stumbled toward him. His arms went around her, and she pressed her face into his chest and shuddered. He held her tightly, one hand stroking her hair, the other arm around her back in protective comfort. He hadn't expected this reaction and wondered if Latigo was worse than she wanted to admit.

"Maggie, is it the boy?"

She shook her head, her long hair coming loose from its pins and escaping down her back and over his arm.

He lifted a silky strand in his hand, rubbing it between his fingers as he waited for her to recover enough to talk to him.

Finally she said, her words muffled by his thick flannel shirt and vest, "It's me. I can't stand the waste."

Devon's throat tightened. "Waste?"

Her head tilted back and she gazed up at him; tear-tracks shone on her cheeks, and her lower lip quivered slightly. "Yes. It's a waste of strength and blood for a boy to have to suffer what that young man is suffering."

"I know what he's going through, and I agree."

Maggie's wet gaze held his, and he saw the shadows of condemnation in her eyes. "He was with you."

"Yes." Nothing she could say would be worse than what he'd said to himself.

"You were looking for Ash Oliver."

Again: "Yes."

"Damn you, Devon! Are you so set on proving yourself the fastest that you'd risk a boy like that?"

His mouth tightened, and he curled his hands around her wrists and set her back from him. She looked angry and very tired and very hurt. "Maggie, it wasn't quite like that."

"Oh no, I'm sure it wasn't. I'm just as sure that you never meant for that boy to be hurt, but the end result is the same. He's lucky to be alive, and as it is, he may not be able to walk again without a limp. *If* he manages by some miracle to keep his leg."

He stared down at her. That was unexpected. A flash of memory tortured him, of Latigo running and laughing with all the exuberance of youth, flinging his athletic body over a fence and daring Devon to follow. *Damn.*

It felt as if the breath was slowly being squeezed from his chest. She was looking at him with grief and scorn, and he felt the sting of her censure as if it were a

whip. She believed in what she'd said; he could see
that plainly, but he couldn't stop the question.

"Do you believe that I'd do that? That I'd risk a boy
just to see if I'm faster than Oliver?" he asked carefully.

"It doesn't matter what I believe. The facts stand for
themselves."

"I see." Devon took a step back. She could have shot
him and the pain wouldn't have been worse. It burned
white-hot in his throat and chest and belly, and the
worst of it was that he suspected she was right. The
facts stood alone, and Latigo lay on a cot and might
never walk straight again. He had been careless, if not
deliberately so.

Maggie leaned back against the outer wall of the
shack. She shivered at the cold, and he realized that
she didn't have on a coat.

"Go inside, Maggie. It's getting colder."

She gave him a bleak look. When she opened the
door and stepped into the shack, Devon reached for
Pardo's reins and swung into his saddle.

"Where did he go?" Maggie stared around the flat,
empty land surrounding the line shack, but there was
no sign of Devon or his dun. She turned back to look at
the long-haired Apache still in the doorway. He met
her gaze with flat black eyes that sent a shiver of apprehension through her.

"He did not say his farewells before leaving."

There was a note of reproof in his tone that made her
flush. Had he heard what she'd said to Devon? She
cleared her throat.

"I see. Am I to ride back alone, then?"

"If you insist." The Apache did not look away from
her but seemed to study her for a reaction. Maggie
lifted her chin in angry defiance.

"Very well. I'm quite capable of doing so."

"I am certain of that." He turned and said something to one of the men behind him, using a mixture of what sounded like Spanish and Apache. A man stepped forward, and the Apache looked back at Maggie. "But you will be gracious enough to accept this man's escort. He will see you safely back to your home."

Maggie couldn't help a sweep of relief, though she would have sewn her lips shut before admitting it to the Apache. She nodded. "If you insist."

A faint glimmer of humor lit the black eyes for an instant, and his well-cut mouth moved in a faint smile. "I do. Cimarrón would not forgive me for allowing something to happen to his woman."

"I am not his woman!" Her quick retort was too fast, too emphatic, and she saw the Apache's brow quirk upward in mocking disbelief.

"No?"

"*No.* I'm my own woman. I belong to no one but myself."

"Even you do not seem to believe that."

Maggie drew in a shaky breath and reached for her black bag. The first rays of sunlight were coming over the eastern horizon, shimmering on flat-topped ridges and making black lace of staggered groves of mesquite trees. "I'm ready now. Be certain Latigo takes all the medicine in the brown bottle I left, and it is best if he is not moved for three or four days."

"If the leg swells with poison?"

Maggie paused, then said, "I have shown one of your men what to look for, the red streaks and tight skin. If that happens—remove the leg. Bring him to me if you wish, and I will perform the amputation. "

She did not add that it would probably be necessary. Very rarely did an injury like the one Latigo had received heal well enough without amputation. Even with it, the patient frequently died. With great luck, he might be able to keep his leg and walk again, though almost undoubtedly with a limp. Helpless tears stung her eyes, blurring her vision as she thought of the young boy lying on the cot.

"Ma'am?"

Maggie turned blindly and accepted the help of the man who was to be her escort. He held her horse still while she tied the black bag to the back of the saddle and mounted.

They rode silently for a time, while the sun slowly rose and painted the world with rose-colored light. Jackrabbits were startled out of the brush, and a young deer grazed on the tender shoots of grama grass near a stream. What had seemed lonely and forbidding the night before, now teemed with visible life. She thought she knew where they were when she saw the distant curl of smoke that rose above a smudged line of hills.

"That's the Bar Z."

Her escort slanted her a quick glance, then shrugged. *"No comprende, señorita."*

"Rubbish. I heard you speak English earlier." Maggie met his slightly sheepish gaze with a cool stare. "You don't have to commit yourself to an answer. It doesn't matter where we are. I have no intention of telling anyone about last night."

He grinned and looked more youthful. "Reckon you won't tell, but it pays to be careful when the law's always on the other side."

His accent was pure Texas, and Maggie couldn't help an answering smile. Though he had obvious Indian heritage, his green eyes and the streaks of red in his black hair spoke of Anglo ancestors.

"Have you known Devon long?" she asked after several more minutes of riding.

"Devon? Oh. You mean Cimarrón. Yeah, long enough, I guess. We've run into each other a time or two."

"Well, tell me, Mr.—"

She paused to let him finish, and noticed his hesitation before he said, "Frayser. Roe Frayser."

"Frayser. That explains the red in your hair. Tell me, please, if he was successful in dispatching Ash Oliver."

"Reckon you mean did he kill him. Naw. Not this time either. Someone's tippin' Oliver off, is what I think. Must be, otherwise he wouldn't always know when Cimarrón is close to him. Danza thinks so, too."

"Danza? Oh, you must mean the—the—"

"Apache. Yep. Latigo's gettin' hisself hurt like that was a pure mistake on Oliver's part. Havin' Cimarrón after you is bad enough, 'cause he don't quit till you're got. But when you get Danza after you, too, might as well shoot yourself in the head and get it over with."

"I understand that Danza must be angry, but after all, it was Devon who started it."

Roe Frayser shot her a frowning glance. "Don't know what you mean by that, ma'am."

"Well, you know, wanting to prove who's the fastest. If Danza gets involved, then nothing will be proved."

She had the distinct impression that she'd startled Roe Frayser into silence, because he gave her an odd look before shaking his head. "One of us is mixed up. I think it's you."

"Isn't that what this is about? Devon wanting to prove he's faster than Ash Oliver?"

"I never heard tell that Cimarrón had to prove anything like that to anyone. He's about the fastest there is around here, but he goes out of his way to keep from braggin' about it. It don't figure that he'd change just for Ash Oliver."

"Whether he challenged Oliver or not," Maggie said with a slow frown, "it was Devon who's responsible for Latigo's being shot. He should give up this mad-ness and leave Oliver alone. Let the law handle him as it certainly will one day."

"Ma'am," Frayser said after a moment, reining his horse in to stare at her with his clear green eyes, "I think you need to start askin' yourself some questions instead of just gallopin' off to the wrong conclusions. Now, I'm not one to stick my nose into someone else's business, and this is between you and Cimarrón, but I got to tell you that you're dead wrong."

"Wrong? How?" Maggie halted her bay and stared back at him. "How am I wrong?"

"In the first place, Cimarrón told Latigo to go back and wait with Danza, but Latigo bein' a hardheaded kid, he didn't. And he didn't think about who might be behind him when he waited around that corner to shoot Oliver, either. And finally, he didn't think about how blamed mad Cimarrón would have been if he'd managed to shoot Oliver first. It was Cimarrón's fight, no one else's. Latigo is young and hotheaded, and he brought this on himself."

Maggie sat silently. Her bay shook his head impatiently, noisily rattling the bit and curb chains. A cool wind tugged at the open flap of her coat, chilling her. Even with the excuse of being exhausted and soul-sick, she'd lashed out at Devon unfairly. She should not have accused him of being responsible for young Latigo's injury without at least giving him a chance to explain. But knowing Devon, he would not have offered an explanation. No, he'd just looked at her with those cool blue eyes and said nothing in defense. Why?

She looked at Roe Frayser. "Why didn't he tell me?"

"You'd have to ask Cimarrón that, ma'am. Like I said, I don't pry into his business."

"I wish he'd stop this pursuit of Ash Oliver," she said in a whisper. "What does it matter who's the fastest if he's dead?"

Roe Frayser just looked at her silently, and when

Maggie finally nudged her horse into a trot, he followed at a close distance. He didn't speak to her again until they were on the rise overlooking Belle Plain, and he reined in his mount.

"Ma'am," he said softly, "if I was you, I'd listen to what your heart tells you instead of your ears."

Surprised, Maggie stared at him. "What do you mean by that?"

"Some folks might say things that aren't true. But your heart is always honest if you take the time to listen."

"A prairie philosopher," Maggie said with a faint smile. She saw from Roe's answering smile that he wasn't offended by her remark. "Well, Mr. Frayser, I'll try to do that."

He left her there on the hill, letting her ride the rest of the way in alone. While she took care of her horse, unsaddling and brushing, then feeding the bay, she thought about his cryptic advice. Was he trying to tell her that Devon wasn't as harsh as he seemed? She wanted to believe it, hoped it was true, but everything she'd seen and heard disproved it. Oh, she knew that Devon wasn't the cold, ruthless killer she'd heard him called, but there was a side of him she'd glimpsed that was frightening. She'd seen the icy ferocity in his eyes at times, the way he had of looking at a man that could make him back away. And she knew there was good reason for men to fear him. His reputation was not completely unearned.

*"I never heard tell that Cimarrón had to prove anything like that to anyone . . ."* Was that true? Roe Frayser said it convincingly enough. And if she thought about it, all the times that Devon had been given ample opportunity to draw his pistol and add another notch . . . Yet if she listened to David Brawley and some of the town folk, Cimarrón was every bit as ruthless as Ash Oliver.

Maggie shut the door to the lean-to and hefted her

bag under her arm as she walked to the house. Her steps were loud on the porch, and she fumbled at the door before getting it open. She was chilled to the bone despite the sun and shivered as she set her bag down on a chair and began peeling away her gloves and coat.

It was while she was boiling water for tea that it occurred to her that Devon and Cimarrón were a contradiction in terms. Devon had a depth of humanity that came through even his best effort to project a tough veneer while Cimarrón was a counterfeit image created by those who wanted a genuine desperado. Her spoon clattered loudly against the edge of the teacup, and she stared across the kitchen without really seeing it.

That was what Roe Frayser had meant by advising her to listen to her heart. She should have been viewing Devon with the love and understanding of her heart, instead of the fear and prejudice of others.

"God," she whispered. "I've been so blind!"

# CHAPTER 14

A cold wind whipped down the middle of the wide street of Brackettville with a low, mournful whine. Stray bits of paper fluttered in a brief show, then disappeared. A shutter banged somewhere, and there was an air of tension that was even more desolate than the howling wind the Mexicans called Ráfaga. Silent men gathered on boardwalks in small clusters, watching. Soldiers from nearby Fort Clark lounged against walls and in alleyways, but no one moved to interfere.

Two men faced one another at fifteen paces. Long cattleman coats flapped around their legs, molding to taut muscles, snapping loudly in the wind. Both waited for that imperceptible moment when something would signal the end. For Cimarrón, it was in Ash Oliver's eyes, that faint flicker that was the only indication of a man's intent.

It came like a streak of lightning, quick and hot and deadly, and Cimarrón responded. His hand flashed down, and a pistol filled his fist as if magical, spurting flame and death. He felt the hot blur of a bullet near his cheek and recoiled as Oliver's shot went wild. He watched with grim detachment as the gunman slowly crumpled to the ground in a pinwheel of abruptly limp arms and legs.

Dust funneled up around him as the wind caught it and carried it in the air, peppering his back and bare skin, and Devon slowly straightened. He walked to where Oliver lay in the street, grunting in pain. Devon crouched beside him and reached to take the smoking pistol from his faltering hand.

Sprawled on his side, Oliver glared up at him. Air rattled his lungs. "Reckon you done kilt me this time, Cimarrón."

Devon saw that his bullet had punched a hole in Oliver's left side. It was mortal, and both men knew it. He nodded.

"Yeah, looks like I have, Oliver."

Ash Oliver wheezed noisily, and there was a watery sound to his breathing. "Lung shot," he muttered in disgust. "If your aim was better, you'da kilt me outright."

Blood smeared the hand he held up, and Oliver glanced from it past Devon. "Where's that damned Apache?"

"Waiting."

A faint smile curled Oliver's mouth. "Yeah, I guess he is. Well, lucky for him I still got a full head of hair to hang in his lodge." Another cough rattled him, and he gasped for air for a minute. "Damn . . . Cimarrón, tell me somethin'."

"What?"

"What got you . . . set on my trail?"

Devon stood up, uncurling his body to gaze down at the dying man. "A kid named Ralph Pace." When Oliver stared up at him with incomprehension, Devon added softly, "A grulla gelding and two dollars in a camp outside El Paso last Christmas."

Understanding finally clouded Ash Oliver's eyes, and he gave a snarl of disgust that was the last sound he'd ever make. Slowly he fell facedown into the thick dust and shuddered as blood bubbled from his mouth and he died.

Devon stared down at him without moving for a moment, even when Danza came up behind him, cat-quick and light on his feet. There was the quick slice of a knife, and when the Apache rose to his feet, he held up Oliver's scalp. None of the men gathered on wooden boardwalks watching seemed inclined to dispute Danza's right to take Oliver's scalp, not with a full cadre of armed bandidos standing guard.

"It is done," Danza said softly, but Devon shook his head.

"No. It has just begun."

He pivoted on his heels and walked back up the street to his horse. No one spoke as he swung into the saddle, though he could feel their eyes on him and knew what would be said. Another victim to Cimarrón's bullet, another death to lay at his door. No matter that it was well-deserved, that it was an eye for an eye. It would be part of the myth, part of the legacy of murder that he'd never wanted but didn't know how to escape.

"What is this man called Cimarrón to you, Maggie?"

For a moment, Maggie didn't reply. Lindsay idly stirred her cup of tea with a spoon, dissolving the liberal chunk of sugar she always used.

"What makes you think he's anything to me?" she finally replied, and saw Lindsay's eyebrows lift.

"Johnny may have a rotten temper and leap to a lot of conclusions, but he was truly upset at the dance. I've seen him angry before, but he really wanted to kill Cimarrón."

"That's not so unusual. He wants to kill Sheriff Whittaker, too, but he hasn't."

"Maybe, but not with the same intensity." Lindsay's pretty mouth turned down in a frown. "I came to see you the night of the dance, but no one was home."

Maggie sighed. Lindsay was far too perceptive anyway, but she'd hoped she wouldn't have to explain, especially when she wasn't certain what she felt.

"Cimarrón needed me to help a friend. I went with him."

"There's more to it than that." Lindsay took a sip of tea, and when Maggie didn't respond, she said, "I know you. I've always been able to tell when you've got a secret. And you have a secret."

"Oh, bother!" Maggie fought a wave of irritation mixed with affection. "Must you know everything?"

"Yes. I'm nosy. I've always been nosy. And I hate secrets that I don't know."

"One of your major character flaws, I must tell you."

"Admitted. Humor me. One of the Malones might as well."

Maggie eyed her for a moment. "All right. A secret in trade for a secret. Deal?"

She saw the quick flicker in Lindsay's eyes, then she nodded slowly. "A deal."

Maggie raked a hand through her hair, scattering pins without caring. "Cimarrón is really Devon Conrad. He . . . he's different, Lindsay. He's not all they say. I think he had a good reason for hunting Ash Oliver, though I don't know what it could be."

"You believe in him." Lindsay said it softly, and Maggie realized that it was true.

"Yes. I do. Perhaps he's ruthless at times, but there is usually a reason for it." She sighed. "With the latest news, I'm afraid people will believe him much more ruthless and dangerous."

"You mean Ash Oliver?"

Maggie nodded. "Yes. Killing him was bad enough, but to scalp him . . ." She shuddered, and tried to visualize Devon doing that, but couldn't. "I don't think he did that. I think it was someone else. A friend of his."

Lindsay made a face. "Wonderful choice of friends."

"Well, we don't always make the best choices." She saw that Lindsay understood what she meant, and looked away. "I think I'm in love with him."

"Cimarrón?" There was a potent silence, then Lindsay said softly, "I thought as much. There was something in the way you looked at him that night, and something in the way he looked at you . . ."

"I didn't say he was in love with me." Maggie's mouth twisted wryly. "I said I was in love with him. There's a big difference in the two."

"Maybe not as much as you might think."

"Lindsay, Devon may want to take me to bed, but he has never given the least indication that he's in love with me." She drew in a shaky breath. "I think he's still in love with his dead wife."

There was a short, shocked silence, then Lindsay reached out to cover Maggie's clenched hands with one of her own. "Oh honey—are you sure?"

Maggie nodded mutely. She felt the sympathy in Lindsay's grip, saw the compassion shining in her forest green eyes, and managed a trembling smile.

"He hasn't made any promises to me, if that's what you're thinking. He's been as honest as he can, but that didn't stop me from making a complete fool of myself. Now with Oliver dead and his reason for being in Belle Plain gone, I suppose he'll just ride away."

"But the cattle rustling hasn't stopped. Johnny has even organized some riders to capture or shoot any man they find trespassing the Double M without good reason." Lindsay's eyes were troubled and grim. "Daddy hates it, but he's going along with it because they're losing so many cattle. It's almost as if the rustlers know where the men are going to be. Johnny has stopped telling his plans to anyone but Daddy."

"I know. It's the same way with some of the other ranchers. Even Zeke Rogan's army of gunfighters hasn't stopped them."

"But Cimarrón did kill some of them, is that right?"

"Yes, but it obviously hasn't deterred whoever is

doing this. I thought since Devon killed Ash Oliver, it would stop. It hasn't. Don't you find that odd?"

Lindsay nodded. "Yes."

They sat quietly for a moment, then Maggie leaned forward and prompted, "Your turn."

Lindsay looked startled. A faint flush crept up her neck to stain her cheeks, and she bit her bottom lip. "I was hoping you'd forget."

"Fat chance. And you know what secret I want to hear."

"No. Tell me."

"All right—what happened between you and Johnny? Before you left for Atlanta, I thought you two planned on getting married. It's always been obvious you love each other."

"Obvious to whom?" Lindsay toyed with her half-empty teacup for a moment, frowning. "Not to Johnny. He loves the ranch. And making money. That's more important to him than a mere woman."

"I think you're wrong."

At Maggie's soft protest, Lindsay looked up, her eyes shimmering with unshed tears. "I wish I was, Maggie. But he told me straight out that I came second. And he was mad as a whole nest of hornets that I couldn't understand why."

"I know Johnny can be bullheaded and ornery, but I never thought he was that stupid. He really told you that?"

Lindsay nodded miserably. "Why do you think I left like I did? Maybe if . . . if he hadn't said it at the time he did, I wouldn't have been so hurt, but he did."

Maggie was silent for a moment. There was a female awareness in Lindsay's eyes that telegraphed the situation much more loudly than her words, and she felt a surge of anger toward her brother. The idiot. To have said something like that to Lindsay was provocation enough, but it was obvious he'd done more than just talk. She sighed.

"Johnny's stupid. But he's a man. Men have a different way of looking at things, I've discovered. Even the most articulate man cannot talk to a woman without verbally cutting his own throat. I think it's bred into them through long years of conceit and arrogance. In my opinion, if a man even suspects that a woman might want to be the most important thing in his life, he goes out of his way to show her how unimportant she is, then is amazed when she leaves him."

Lindsay chuckled. "You've described your brother's reaction perfectly. He still doesn't understand why I left. And of course, I was so angry that I said anything I could think of that would make him feel as low as he made me feel. I'm not certain I want to take any of it back, either."

"What about your betrothed?"

"Quincy? Oh, he's pleasant enough, I suppose." She leaned forward, lowering her voice. "I haven't really accepted his proposal yet. I guess I wanted to see if I still loved Johnny before I did."

"And do you?"

Lindsay sat back in her chair. "Yes. I can't imagine why. He's pigheaded and vain. He thinks cows smell good." Her eyes grew slightly dreamy. "But when he touches me or kisses me, I forget everything but how much I love him. I think I must be hopelessly insane."

"Yes. You are." Maggie smiled at her startled glance. "So am I."

Johnny paced the parlor floor impatiently. He hated to wait. Lindsay knew he hated to wait. So why was she keeping him waiting? He exchanged a frustrated glance with Hank, who had the good sense not to defend his daughter.

"Have another drink," the older man said instead,

but Johnny shook his head. One more drink and he'd be on the raw edge of drunk, and he sure didn't want to try and talk to Lindsay when he wasn't in full control.

It was almost an hour before she sailed down the stairs to join them, smiling and giving pretty apologies for making them wait. "You know how it is, getting used to a new place. I couldn't find a thing."

"What were you looking for that took so blamed long?" Johnny snapped, then wished he hadn't. Lindsay turned, her brow lifting in that elegant, condescending tilt that made him hover halfway between rage and embarrassment.

"This." She put a hand to her throat, and her slim fingers caressed a strand of matched pearls that glowed with a gentle luster against her tawny skin. "It was a gift."

Johnny glared at her. He wasn't about to ask who had given her such an expensive gift. It was apparent that was what she wanted him to do. He stalked to the sideboard.

"I'll have that drink now," he growled, and Hank seemed to understand.

"Daddy," Lindsay said, gliding toward her father and tucking her hand into the bend of his arm, "won't you at least consider coming back to Atlanta with me? I'd love for you to meet Quincy. He's very knowledgeable about a lot of things."

Johnny glowered and swallowed a huge gulp of whiskey. That was an obvious dig at him. He'd only gone halfway through school before his parents had died and he'd quit to take charge of the ranch. It was a deficiency that he felt keenly at times, and this was one of those times. Maggie was supposed to have made up for the Malones' lack of education, but she'd gone and studied medicine instead of the classics. He wondered what Lindsay thought of that. She hadn't said, but he suspected she approved. Women. Always doing the unexpected.

Hank was clearing his throat and shaking his head. "No, I don't want to go to Atlanta. I like it here."

"But you've never been there. How do you know you won't like it?"

"Don't. Do know I like it here, though. Don't see any reason to waste my time somewhere else."

Lindsay laughed and squeezed his arm. "Why do you make sense when you shouldn't? Atlanta is so busy nowadays with people starting new businesses and rebuilding old. Quincy's family is fairly new there. They came down from Massachusetts after the war ended and started a thriving mercantile store. It's very profitable now."

"Damn carpetbaggers, huh," Johnny muttered. He met her slightly narrowed eyes with growing hostility. "Made their livin' offa misfortune. Probably charged ten times more for a pair of socks than they were worth back then."

"Is that something like charging ten times more for a cow than it's worth?" Lindsay asked sweetly, and he slammed his empty glass on the sideboard.

"I've never done that."

"Rubbish. Do you think I don't know how cattlemen make their money?"

Johnny ignored the frown on Hank's face as he took a step closer to Lindsay. "No, I don't think you know anything at all about ranchin'. Or makin' money. All you know how to do is spend it."

"Since I'm not spending yours, I can't see that it's any of your business."

Her eyes were green frost, and her mouth was still curved into that damned superior smile that made him want to crush her against him and kiss her until neither one of them could breathe.

"Don't push your luck, Lindsay."

"Are you threatening me, John Malone?"

He sucked in a deep breath. "No. Givin' you some advice. Do us both a favor and take it."

The evening went downhill from there, with Lindsay taking verbal shots at him through dinner and Hank just gazing at her with a troubled look that made Johnny wish he'd say something, even if it was insulting. Finally it was over, and the Mexican cook cleared the table with a swiftness that made it obvious he'd overheard the dinner conversation. More like warfare, as far as Johnny was concerned.

Disgruntled and edgy, he gave a vague excuse and went outside to lean on the corral fence and watch the stars come out. Damn. Nothing was the same. It hadn't been like this before. Before, Lindsay may have gotten angry at him, but she never would have sniped at him all night. She'd have blown up, said what bothered her, and he'd have had the chance to shout back. Then it would have been over and they could have made up.

He slid his hands over the rough-cut pole of the top rail and leaned his head against the wood, wondering bitterly what had gone so wrong. Rustlers. Maggie. Cimarrón. Now Lindsay. His world was careening crazily out of control, and he couldn't seem to do a damn thing about it.

A door slammed behind him, and he knew from the soft crunch of footsteps that it was Lindsay. She was looking for him. He straightened and turned, resigned to another argument.

"I was looking for you," she said, then gave a half-shrug in recognition of the trite comment.

"What for? Need bait for wolfin'?" He fumbled in his vest pocket for his tobacco pouch, found it, and pulled it out. It gave him something to do with his hands instead of reach for her.

"No respectable wolf would have you." She smiled, a faint replica of the smile that once would have had him at her feet. Damn. Who was he fooling? It still did. He rolled his cigarette deftly and stuck it in his mouth.

"Never met a respectable wolf," he said when he'd lit the cigarette and put out the match between his fingers. The slight burn gave him something to focus on.

"Four-legged or two-legged?"

He sighed. "Lindsay, what do you want? I came out here to give my brain a rest. And my ears."

She came to lean against the corral fence, and he caught a whiff of her perfume. It was light and powdery and made his stomach clench with sweet agony.

"Do I tax you?"

"Just my patience." He looked away from her and took another drag of the cigarette. Smoke curled in front of him. He blew a ring and watched it slowly dissipate in the rising breeze.

"Johnny."

"Yeah?" He shifted uncomfortably and risked another glance at her. She was staring at him, eyes huge and shadowed in the soft moonlight.

"I owe you an apology for being so insulting and rude tonight."

"Did Hank make you say that?"

A faint smile curved her pretty mouth. "Well, he did strongly suggest it."

He grunted irritably. "Don't want no second-hand sorries."

It was a holdover from their childhood, a phrase they had used as children, and it made her laugh. The sound hit him with the force of a brick, though it was light and soft and musical. It seeped inside him and left him wishing he were someone else. He couldn't bear being near Lindsay and not having her, knowing that she was going back to Atlanta to marry someone else. Someone with money.

He threw down the cigarette and caught her hand.

She didn't resist but stared at him with a fading smile when he pulled her toward him.

"Lindsay girl, don't you ever think about us?" The words came out harsher than he meant them to, but she didn't recoil.

"Sometimes. No—a lot. Of course I do. You meant more than anything to me at one time, Johnny."

*At one time.*

"And now?"

"Now I don't know."

He let go of her abruptly. That was answer enough, he guessed. Hell. He ground his boot down on the still-smoldering cigarette he'd thrown in the dirt.

"So you intend to marry this merchant?"

"He expects me to."

Johnny's head snapped up, and he stared at her with narrowed eyes. "That ain't no answer."

"It's the only one you're liable to get right now."

A sudden flare of hope burned him. Without pausing to think about it, he reached for her again and pulled her into his arms. His mouth came down over hers with a fierce urgency he couldn't disguise, couldn't deny, and he could hear her faint moan.

That soft, sighing sound erased the last of his control in a flash of blinding heat and need that had been pent-up too long. He kissed her mouth, her cheek, her closed eyelids, and then her mouth again. She tasted slightly of face powder and perfume, delicious and tempting and painful all at the same time. He held her and felt the rapid thud of her heart against his chest. She was breathing raggedly, too, as affected by his kisses as he was. He wanted her, God, he wanted her so badly he was shaking with hunger, but he didn't want to destroy their fragile new beginning.

"Lindsay?"

She lifted her face blindly to be kissed, and he bent his head to brush his mouth over her half-parted lips.

Long lashes shadowed her cheeks like silk lace, and there was a faint flush that darkened her tawny skin to a dusky glow that looked almost gold in the moonlight. He leaned back against the fence, pulling her with him so that her body was pressed to his from chest to knees. She was shivering.

"Cold?" he muttered against her cheek, and felt her shake her head.

"No."

She was shaking with tension, the same as he was, and he pressed his mouth to her forehead before setting her back and away from him.

"Lindsay, let's get married. Now. Tonight."

Her eyes widened. "Why?"

The soft question took him back. "Why? Damn, ain't it obvious?"

"Because you want to make love to me? Or because you want me with you for the rest of your life? Which is it?"

"Both. Hell, you're making me crazy. I can't eat and I can't sleep, and all I can think about is you. I'm miserable as hell."

Her mouth quivered, and she reached up to touch his drawn-down brows with one finger. Moonlight glittered in her eyes, and there was an odd note in her voice that he couldn't interpret.

"But is that all?"

"What else is there?" He fought a wave of crushing frustration at the cooling lights in her eyes. "Dammit, don't back off from me again. You want me, Lindsay, I know you do. You love me."

"Is that enough?"

"It's enough for me, yes."

"But not for me." She took a deep breath and stepped back, untangling herself from his clinging hands. "It's not enough for me, Johnny."

"*Christ!* What the hell do you want from me?" The words were torn from him, raw and painful.

"More than you can give, it seems."

He watched her go back to the house, helpless to fight the surge of pain and rage that filled him.

Mrs. Lamb removed a pan of cookies from the oven and set it on the table near Maggie. Her face was flushed from the scorching heat of the big stove, her eyes bright.

"Might as well eat some, dear. We'll pack the rest in tins for later. Cookies make nice gifts."

"I'm really not very hungry, though they smell delicious." Maggie fought a sweep of restlessness. There were too many hours in the day now, too much time to think. She wished Lindsay would come back into town for a visit, though Mrs. Lamb was a welcome respite from boredom.

"Well, you ought not to brood. I know that time hangs heavy, but it does for a lot of people these days. Everyone in Belle Plain is either moving or talking about moving." A frown knit her brow. "Going to Baird, where the railroad is, I suppose. Most of them hate moving, but when you live in a town and the town moves, why I guess you just have to go along."

Maggie leaned back in her chair. It was true. Every day more people moved. Belle Plain was dying by slow degrees, and it was evident in some of the abandoned buildings with empty windows and doors left open to sway in the wind. Soon, she would have to make a decision as to her future.

Her throat tightened. Not too long ago, she would have had no doubts as to what to do. Now, since Devon, she was filled with uncertainty and she hated it. She hated the way she waited for him, even when she didn't think about it, always listening for his steps in the night, for the shadow in the dark that would be him coming to her. She didn't want to be dependent upon anyone or to have her peace of mind dependent upon anyone but herself. It was galling to be so vulnerable, to be in love.

But she couldn't help it.

Devon was a contradiction that she couldn't explain, a mystery she couldn't solve, an affliction she couldn't cure.

And she ached for him so badly it was almost crippling.

She was only vaguely aware of Mrs. Lamb's cheerful chatter as she finished the baking and cleaning. When the widow went to get her coat, Maggie rose to fetch her money. She paid her wages with a distraction that didn't escape notice.

Mrs. Lamb held her hand as the money was pressed into her palm, forcing Maggie to look at her. "Here now, dear, don't be sad. Things will get better. You'll see."

Maggie blinked and managed a returning smile. "I'm certain they will."

Mrs. Lamb gave her an affectionate pat on the cheek. "I promise they will. Change may be unsettling at times, but it's not always bad."

"You're right, of course. I guess I'm just disappointed at the way things are happening." Maggie squeezed her hand. "You'd best hurry before it gets too dark. With the sun down, nights are cold now."

When Mrs. Lamb had gone, Maggie went to her office to try to balance her accounts. Money was dwindling fast. She really didn't have the funds to keep paying Mrs. Lamb, but she didn't have the heart to stop. The widow needed the money as much as anyone else, and she knew it.

Finally she put down her pen, staring dismally at the neat ledgers. The lamp flickered, then steadied again, and Maggie reached out to turn it down a bit. Might as well conserve oil.

It had gotten late without her realizing it, and she gave a weary sigh and pushed her chair back from the desk. The office was quiet and neat, with no sign that she had treated patients. Tomorrow, she would send out letters of inquiry to see what towns were in need of a physician. There was no point in staying where there were no patients.

# CHAPTER 15

It was late. The wind was cold and biting and smelled like snow. Devon dismounted and led Pardo into the lean-to. His spurs rattled slightly in the still night air, sounding much too loud in the silence. He paused, listening, but heard no alarm raised. Not even a dog barked. There was no moon, and the night was dark and blanketing.

When he approached the house, he saw that a window had been left open. It was only half-open, but that was all he needed. His steps were silent on the frozen ground as Danza had taught him. Straws stuck into the rowels of his spurs muffled any rattle, and he moved quickly and stealthily to the low window.

It lifted noiselessly, and he heaved himself into the dark opening, then swung a leg over the sill. Nothing moved inside, and he eased his body in and dropped to the floor. A faint patch of light glimmered in a room down the hall.

It came from Maggie's bedroom. He frowned. It was late for her to be awake. For the first time, he wondered if she might have company. David Brawley's ardent attentions had remained in his memory the past month, sometimes making him feel like hitting something. Had Maggie succumbed to his sweet words?

A knot formed in his belly. Damn. He hated coming to her like this, hated having to sneak around to protect her reputation when a man like Brawley could openly visit. Maybe she hated it, too. Maybe she'd decided that she didn't want to wait on him to drop in. She'd said that once, frustration in her voice, her eyes dark with pain.

"I never know when—or if—you're coming. You just drop in when you feel like it and expect me to be here."

She was right. He did. He didn't know why he couldn't stay away from her, why he didn't take his own good advice and leave Texas behind. It wasn't as if he had business here anymore. Oliver was dead. He didn't give a brass nickel about the rustlers or Zeke Rogan, or even the murder charges against him. Maggie was all that kept him close. And she probably hated him now. He hadn't forgotten the look in her eyes, the condemnation in her voice when she'd blamed him for Latigo. He was certain she'd heard about Oliver by now, certain she still thought he'd only gone after him for the notoriety.

But it didn't matter. He moved down the hallway, drawn by an invisible thread that he couldn't sever, drawn by the need to see and hear her.

She was sitting in bed, head bent over a book, the lamp on her bedside table burning low. He paused in the doorway and watched her for a minute. She was wearing a high-necked flannel gown, white with tiny blue flowers, and her hair was caught at the nape of her neck with a wide ribbon, gleaming black and silky in the light. It framed the sweet ivory oval of her face; with her head bent to read, she looked to him like an angelic child.

He started to back away, suddenly ashamed to have come creeping into her house like a thief in the night, but she looked up and saw him. Her eyes widened, and there was an instantaneous flash of warmth and joy in her tremulous smile that kept him rooted to the floor.

"Devon . . ."

He made an awkward motion. "It's late."

"You must be half-frozen." She slipped from the bed and came toward him, her face more guarded now, but with the light still in her eyes. "Are you hungry?"

"I didn't come for food." He winced. That was blunt, too blunt, and he hadn't meant it the way it sounded. He cleared his throat, embarrassed. "I ate on the trail."

"Let me guess—beans?"

He grinned. "Cold beans and jerky. How'd you know?"

"I have had some experience with the availability of food on the trail." She shrugged into her robe and found some slippers for her feet, slanting him half-shy glances from time to time. "Come to the kitchen. Even if you've eaten, you might enjoy a piece of Mrs. Lamb's pie and some of her cookies."

"You know the way to a man's heart, Maggie," he said as he followed her, peeling off his gloves, and she turned to look at him.

"Heart or stomach?"

"They're connected. Didn't medical school teach you that?"

"Hmm. I must have been absent that day."

It was warmer in the kitchen. The stove radiated a heat that drew him, and he stood by it watching as Maggie began to take food out of pie safes and cupboards. She moved with spare elegance and grace, and he was grateful that she hadn't thrown him out yet. He liked just watching her, drinking in her sweet beauty with a thirst that he could never ease. It was an ache that never ended.

In short order, she had pie, cookies, and a glass of milk on the table. Devon shrugged out of his coat and draped it over a chair, then sat down, still feeling awkward.

"Aren't you going to eat?"

She shook her head. "No. I'm getting fat. Too many of Mrs. Lamb's sweets lately."

Devon smiled, eying her. "I don't see any fat."

"You're just being polite until you've eaten."

He grinned. "Hedging my bets, so to speak."

"So to speak." She pushed the plate toward him. "Eat."

He did, doing justice to the dried apple pie and plate of sugar cookies. Maggie chatted easily, telling him what had been going on in Belle Plain: how the rustlers were still working and the railroad had reneged on a promise that shouldn't have been made.

Devon grunted. "That wasn't the railroad's promise. It was Brawley's."

She lifted a brow. "How do you know?"

"Did some checking of my own." He looked up from his second piece of pie and met her gaze. "Brawley and your brother aren't the only ones who can send telegraph wires."

"You make that sound like an accusation."

"It's not. Just fact."

Maggie colored slightly, and he knew she was thinking about the last time he'd seen her, the night she'd tended Latigo's injury. She'd accused him of certain *facts* then, and he wondered if she still believed them.

"Devon . . ."

She paused and looked down at her hands. They were tightly clenched on the table, and he felt a spurt of dread for what she might say. He put down his fork. "Yeah?"

"I have . . . have a confession to make."

His stomach knotted, and the pie sat heavily. He gave a short nod. "All right. I'm listening."

"I was wrong. About you, about Latigo—about Oliver shooting him. I'm sorry. I was cruel and unfeeling, and I said things I should never have said."

He stared at her. He hadn't expected that. Relief shot

through him. "It's all right. You didn't know the truth."

"But I didn't bother to ask, either." Tears shimmered in her clear gray eyes, silvering them. She blinked, and a dewy drop fell from her lashes to her cheek. "I'm so sorry."

He reached out to brush the tear from her cheek with his thumb. "You don't have anything to be sorry for, Maggie. I haven't exactly given you a lot of reason to believe in me."

"Oh, but that's just it—I *do* believe in you. I did then, but I was afraid."

"Afraid?"

She nodded. "Afraid of losing you. Afraid you'd go after Ash Oliver and he'd kill you. I was almost crazy with it. And then, when that boy was hurt and I knew that you were not going to give up looking for Oliver, I said those things to you."

Devon stared at her. He knew he was treading on dangerous ground here. She cared too deeply, and her love was drawing him into a net he may never escape. Could he risk it? Could he take the chance that she might be snatched from him like everything else in his life had been?

"Maggie." His voice was hoarse. "Maggie, don't ever worry about me. It's a waste of time and energy." *Damn.* She was staring at him with wide gray eyes like saucers. He felt the familiar throbbing of his conscience. He owed her honesty, at least.

"Why did you come back tonight?" she whispered, and he shook his head.

"I don't know. I only know that I can't stop thinking about you." He drew in a deep breath. "But it won't work between us, you know. It's not your fault. It's mine. I lost something so long ago that I don't think I'll ever find it again. Maybe I never had it, I don't know."

"You're talking about Molly."

He flinched. "Yes, in a way. But she was only a result, really, just another bit of proof that I was trying to
hold something that wasn't mine. She wasn't meant to
be mine, but I was too hardheaded, too selfish to realize that then. I know better now."

"Devon, you don't know what you're saying. You
wouldn't keep coming here if there wasn't a part of
you that knows what you're missing and what you
need."

"Don't count on that."

Maggie's chair made a harsh, grating sound as she
stood up. "I refuse to accept that. You need me."

He was standing, too, but didn't remember getting
up. His eyes burned into her, and there was an answering response from her that vibrated in the air between
them like heat waves. He was lost and he knew it, and
he groaned as he reached out for her.

Maggie came into his arms in a rush of muttered
words and kisses, and he swept her from her feet and
carried her into her bedroom, kicking the door shut behind him. There would be no room for doubt and self-
denial tonight, no room for anything but sweet passion.

Feverish and hasty, they undressed one another
with an impatience they didn't bother to hide. Devon
ripped her gown as he pulled it over her head, and a
small ribbon came loose in his hand. It fluttered to the
floor atop his shirt, boots and trousers, and he lifted
her into his arms and fell onto the bed with her. The
book she'd been reading earlier thudded to the floor
unnoticed.

He lost himself in her body, in the soft creamy skin
and firm, ripe breasts that drew him again and again to
their tempting sweetness. He held her face and kissed
her until she was breathless and he was hard and hurting with need for her, then tortured himself by taking
his time and stroking her in slow, luxurious caresses.

ZEBRA HOME SUBSCRIPTION
SERVICE, INC.
120 BRIGHTON ROAD
P.O. Box 5214
CLIFTON, NEW JERSEY 07015-5214

GET
FOUR
FREE
BOOKS
(AN $18.00 VALUE)

When he brought her again and again to a sobbing, clutching release, he finally stopped denying himself his own.

Slowly, holding her arms out to her sides as he stared down into her glazed eyes, he entered her in a silky glide. He felt the heat of her around him, clenching him in small convulsions as he stroked back and forth, the tension growing tighter and tighter until Maggie cried out and arched upward in a shattering move that exploded his control and sent him over the edge. He shuddered with pleasure, his breath coming in great, ragged gulps for air as he gave a final thrust and went still.

For Devon, there was no retreat. He'd fought and lost, and now he'd have to face whatever came next. He'd tried, God knew, he'd tried, but he knew with a dim despair that if he ever lost Maggie, he'd lose everything.

"Tell me about her." Maggie felt him move restlessly and held her breath. Maybe it was too soon, but she had to know.

"About Kate?" Devon finally asked, and she shook her head.

"No. Molly. Kate, too, but Molly first." There was an awkward pause, and Devon tugged at the quilt over them with a quick, impatient motion. "Devon, I know she was a very special woman," Maggie said softly, and felt his glance of wary surprise.

"Yes. She was. Not much more than a girl in years, but in other ways, very much a woman." He paused, tone altering, and Maggie waited. Then he began to talk, words pouring out of him as if flood waters over a dam. He talked about how he'd met Molly in Leadville and how she'd fallen in love with him despite the fact that he was a hunted outlaw.

By the time he'd finished telling how she'd died in a

hail of bullets meant for outlaws, Maggie was sobbing quietly. She should be comforting Devon, but instead, he was comforting her. Tears drenched the sheet over her, and she wiped her eyes and sat up.

"And Kate? Did you ever go back to see her?"

He shook his head, eyes distant. "No. I was too bitter at first. Then, later, when I was glad that she had someone to love her, it just never seemed like the right time. I've kept up with her. She's got the mine, so she doesn't have to worry about her own money, doesn't have to be anywhere she doesn't want to be."

"The mine your parents left you?"

"Yeah. You know, Maggie, having that mine didn't seem important after . . ."

He jerked to an abrupt halt, and Maggie sighed softly. She recognized the bitter light in his eyes. "Devon, don't you think Kate's worried about you? That she wonders if you're dead or alive, and where you are?"

He shrugged. "She can read. I make the papers on occasion, and even on a remote Colorado ranch, they get the current news."

"But Devon, that's not the same thing."

His arms went around her, and he pulled her to lie atop him. When she protested, he kissed her silent. He rested his forehead against hers finally.

"Maggie, I'm not ready. Her life is settled, and if she's forgotten about me or resigned herself to the fact that I'm not coming back, that's for the best."

"You're a selfish beast."

He scowled. "What the hell do you mean by that?"

She pulled away to stare into his eyes. "If it was my brother and I knew that he'd been devastated by grief, I would move heaven and earth to find him and let him know that I loved him."

"You're not Kate."

His voice was tight, guarded, and Maggie heard the

warning in it but couldn't give up yet. Her fingers curled into the thick mat of hair on his chest.

"And you're not Johnny. He would never let me worry like that."

Devon swore horribly, and she winced. He rolled her off him and swung his legs over the side of the bed, and Maggie thought for an instant that she'd pushed him too far. Then he shot her a frowning glance and sighed.

"I'll send her a telegram. Will that do?"

"For now." She patted the bed beside her. "Come back before it gets too cold under the covers."

He grinned, and her pulses leaped. "I'll get it warm for you quick enough . . ."

She opened her arms, and he came to her. Maggie felt the rise of hope. Even with everything else that seemed to be against them, there was a link between them now that was binding and reassuring.

That reassurance did not, however, transfer to her brother.

He stormed into the small house one afternoon when Devon was gone, and Maggie whirled around to see Johnny filling the doorway and looking like a thundercloud. He stepped into the kitchen and slammed the door, stomping snow from his boots.

"What's this I hear about Cimarrón stayin' here? Have you lost your mind as well as your morals?"

Maggie straightened sharply and snapped shut the oven door. Alarm shot through her. "How did you know?"

"Hank recognized his horse." Johnny's mouth thinned into a grim line. "Don't worry. I didn't tell Whittaker, though I probably should."

"Devon didn't kill those men in Abilene."

"If I didn't believe that, he'd already be swingin' from a tree. It ain't his style, backshootin'. But dammit, girl, it ain't your style to spread yourself for a two-bit outlaw, either!''

Maggie stiffened with outrage. ''If you cannot be civil in my house, then you may leave.''

''If I leave, I'm takin' you with me!'' Johnny kicked at a chair, and it teetered for a moment. ''Dammit, Maggie. What the hell has gotten into you?''

''Apparently, I'm in love. So are you. Have you managed to convince Lindsay to marry you yet, or are you both still in your miserable state of limbo?''

He darkened with fury. ''That's not the issue here. At least I care enough about Lindsay not to flaunt her as my whore.''

Maggie's breath caught at the insult, and she put one hand on the table to steady herself. ''But you don't care enough about her not to treat her like one.''

It was a low blow, and it was obvious that it hit him below the belt. He rocked back on his heels, and his mouth went thin and white. ''What are you talkin' about?''

''I think you know.''

''Did she . . . did she tell you that?''

''No, Lindsay told me nothing except that you don't love her enough.''

''Damn—I've done everything but stand on my head and gargle goat meat to show her how much I care! What the hell does she want from me?''

''Obviously, more than you are capable of giving.''

Johnny stood there uncertainly, his rage fading into an expression of confusion. Maggie almost felt sorry for him and would have been kind enough to tell him what Lindsay needed to hear if he hadn't been so blamed insulting about Devon. And if she didn't know that he needed to figure it out himself or it would never mean as much. She sighed.

''Johnny, I know you love me. I'm grateful. I'm also happy. Go home. Talk to Lindsay. *Listen* to Lindsay.

And then hurry up and figure out what she needs before she goes back to Atlanta and marries a man she doesn't love."

He scowled. "I won't let her leave here. I'll tie her to the kitchen table first."

"You'd better have a good supply of strong rope if you choose to do it that way, because if I remember Lindsay's stubborn determination, you'll need it."

An unwilling smile flickered for a moment, then he shook his head in disgust. "I never will figure out you blamed females. One of you won't accept a decent marriage proposal, and the other won't ever get one, and you both think you're right." He snorted. "Contrary, that's what you are, ornery as two mules."

Maggie smiled. "If we weren't, you men would run over us. Now go back home and convince Lindsay to marry you."

Johnny stood uncertainly for a moment, conflicting emotions on his face, then he sighed. "Damn, girl. I just hope you know what you're doing."

She waited until he'd gone to whisper, "So do I."


"Do I treat you like a whore?" Johnny saw the flash of surprise on Lindsay's face, then her anger. He wasn't as surprised by that reaction as he would have been in the past. Everything he said lately made her mad.

"Damn you, John Clark Malone! How dare you ask me a question like that?"

"Because Maggie said I did." He caught her arm when she stepped back and saw the Mexican cook sidle out of the kitchen with the dexterity of a fleeing snake. Good thing. He'd forgotten Diego was in there.

Lindsay's palm crashed across his cheek, and he grabbed her other arm before she could repeat the action. Now he had both arms and brought her up against him. He briefly wished he wasn't wearing his coat, then focused on the furious girl in his arms.

"Listen to me. I want to know what it is I'm supposed to say that will convince you to marry me."

Lindsay gave a muffled shriek of rage, and he waited it out, his patience thinning when she sputtered incoherent threats and recriminations. He gave her a slight shake.

"Lindsay, I've got enough money for us now. Hell, I've done—damn. I won't let you go back to Atlanta and marry Queasy, and you—"

"*Quincy!*" she spat, glaring at him. Her heel came down on his instep, and he gave a grunt of pain and lifted her off the floor.

"All right, Quincy then. Forget him. I'll write the letter if I have to, but you ain't goin' back to marry him."

"That's right!" She was shaking in his grasp, and her body twisted as she tried to get away. "Write Quincy. Go ahead. You'll write a complete stranger, but you never sent me so much as a note in all those long years! Nothing!"

The last word came out in another shriek, and his eyes narrowed. "That what's got you so mad? Hell, I'll write love notes in cow patties if you want. Just simmer down and say you'll marry me."

"Love notes? What would you know about love, you pigheaded buffoon!"

He scowled, anger overriding common sense. "What do you mean by that? Dammit, girl, I love you, don't I? I've loved you since you were six years old with skinned knees, teeth too big for your mouth, and eyes as big as your ass. I could write a damned book about love, so don't be stupid."

Lindsay stared at him, going so still that he thought for a moment she was hurt. He was about to ask if she could breathe when she whispered, "Say that again."

"Don't be stupid?"

"No, you jackass, the other."

Frustration edged out his anger, and he dropped her back to the floor and snatched off his hat, tossing it on the kitchen table with total disregard for the plates already placed at each chair. He raked a hand through his hair, feeling wild.

"What?" he almost shouted. "What is it you want to hear now?"

When Lindsay stared at him, eyes wide and shimmering with a light he hadn't thought he'd ever see again, Johnny felt an odd clench in his chest. And suddenly he knew what she wanted to hear. It wasn't about money. It was about love. His voice came out hoarse, all wrong, but he couldn't help it.

"Lindsay, sugar, I love you. I've always loved you more than anything. Don't you know that?"

"How could I? You never said."

"But didn't I show you? Didn't I bring you things and take care of you and . . . and try to please you?"

She nodded. A noise sounded behind him, and he saw her gaze flicker away then back to his face. "Yes," she said softly, "but that isn't always enough. Sometimes, a woman just wants to hear that she's loved. Words are important, Johnny. Words are—" She paused, obviously searching, then said, "Words are like the mortar that holds bricks in place. Bricks aren't strong alone, but held together with mortar, they can build palaces."

"Damn." He stared at her. "That's mighty fanciful for a man like me. Hope you don't expect me to say pretty things like that to you all the time."

"No, just the other. That's all I need. But I need it a lot."

"Sounds good to me. I love you. Now will you marry me?"

"Yes!" She flung herself at him, and his arms went around her automatically.

He grinned. "Damn. 'Bout time you came to your senses."

" 'Bout damn time you figured out what to say," he heard Hank Mills mutter, and turned with Lindsay in his arms to see his foreman and the first shift of ranch hands that had come to eat. He flushed, heat burning his face.

"Did you hear all of that?"

"Enough to know you better write good ole Queasy a letter." Hank moved past Johnny to pick his hat up off the table and drop it on the floor. "Where's dinner?"

# Chapter 16

Devon was gone again. Off doing whatever it was he found to do, leaving Maggie alone and restless without him nearby. She felt oddly disgruntled when he disappeared like he did, riding off without telling her where he was going, then coming back at night to sweep her into his arms and smother any questions she might have with kisses that made her forget everything but being with him.

There had been no more confessions, no more shared pain and confidences, but Maggie sensed his growing trust. It was there, still shrouded behind his barriers but shining more brightly every day. Soon, she hoped, soon the barriers would be gone and Devon would realize he could fully trust her not to disappear. At times, she caught a certain wistfulness in his eyes that he couldn't hide, a brief glimmer of longing that seemed to embarrass him.

She suspected that he'd begun to love her, even if he didn't want to admit it to himself just yet. The knowledge was a precious secret that she held closely to her heart.

"Dear," Mrs. Lamb said, coming flushed from the kitchen with a steaming bowl, "do try this. It's a new recipe."

Caught in her daydreams, Maggie stood quickly from behind her desk, half-embarrassed. "What is it?"

"Stew."

Her brow rose. "Stew? That's not new."

"This is." Mrs. Lamb gazed at her with a twinkle in her eyes and lowered her voice. "A secret ingredient."

Maggie laughed. "Ah. A secret ingredient. What do I get if I guess what it is?"

"An entire bowlful." Mrs. Lamb held up the bowl and spoon enticingly. "Come now—see if you can guess."

There was a distinctive aroma that curled up on waves of steam, teasing Maggie with a familiar hint. She smiled and dipped the spoon into the bowl and lifted it closer. It was then that a wave of nausea so strong it was almost overwhelming hit her, and she released the spoon with a startled gasp. It splashed into the bowl, sending up a geyser of stew that stained her gown.

Maggie thrust the bowl back at Mrs. Lamb and clapped a hand over her mouth, then raced for the porcelain bowl on a nearby cabinet. She barely made it, and bent, gasping and retching, over the bowl as she emptied the contents of her stomach.

"Well, my word," Mrs. Lamb said, coming to her with a wet cloth for her face. "I've never had a new recipe affect anyone like that before."

Maggie managed a weak smile. "I didn't even taste it. I think I must be coming down with something. I've felt queasy for several days now, and . . . and just the smell of the stew must have been enough to prompt this reaction. I'm sorry."

Mrs. Lamb remained quiet for a moment, dabbing at Maggie's forehead with the cloth as the young woman sagged weakly in a chair. "There's no need to apologize, dear. Being sick is hardly something one can help."

Maggie frowned. "I should have paid more attention when I first began feeling ill. I know better, but things have been so . . . well, so hectic in some ways lately, that it was easier not to notice."

For a long moment, Mrs. Lamb was silent. She continued to dab at Maggie's face with the cloth, her movements soft and gentle. "Dear," she said at last, "I think perhaps that you should treat yourself like a patient."

"Oh, there's no need to go to bed. I'll take some elixir and I'll be fine."

"I don't think elixir will cure what ails you now."

Maggie gave her a surprised glance. Mrs. Lamb looked very serious, her brown eyes kind and thoughtful. A warning thrum fluttered in her stomach, and Maggie swallowed.

"What do you mean?"

Mrs. Lamb sighed. "I mean, dear, that there seems to be times when even a physician can be blind to what her own body is doing."

She grew still; somewhere deep in the recesses of her mind, she'd known. Yet she hadn't wanted to acknowledge it, hadn't wanted it to be true. There were too many obstacles, too many unanswered questions for her to risk her fragile relationship with Devon by being pregnant.

She inhaled deeply and met Mrs. Lamb's steady gaze. "I suppose you're right. Maybe I just didn't want it to be true."

"But you love your young man. I know you do."

"Yes." Maggie's hand trembled as she reached for the wet cloth to press to her mouth. "Yes, I love him. But that's not always enough."

"Dear." Mrs. Lamb put a hand over Maggie's and drew her gaze. "Dear, I believe he loves you. And now you've created a child between you. This baby is an innocent life and will know nothing of your doubts and fears. Trust Devon enough to allow him to do the right thing. Didn't you tell me that his wife is dead?"

Maggie nodded miserably. "Yes. But he hasn't let go of her yet. I can't force him into a decision before he's

ready, or I'll never know if he truly cares about me or
only did the right thing. No. I can't. I just can't."

Distraught, Mrs. Lamb stood up, staring down at
Maggie and twisting her hands. "You must. Child, you
cannot bear this baby unmarried and alone. It's difficult enough when you have a man by you, but to go
through an entire pregnancy without a husband
would be devastating. Please, tell him."

"No." Maggie shivered. "Not now. I can't tell
Devon I'm pregnant, I just can't."

A scuffling sound at the door of her office drew her
attention, and she turned, freezing when she saw
Johnny in the open doorway. He was pale beneath his
dark tan, and his eyes were burning with a dark, fierce
glitter.

"Maybe you can't tell Cimarrón," he grated
hoarsely, "but *I* damn sure can!"

Maggie surged to her feet, sudden terror sending a
burst of adrenalin through her. "No. Johnny—don't!"

"God, Maggie—*God*."

Pain shattered his voice, pain and rage, and she saw
it in his tortured expression. She was barely aware of
Mrs. Lamb leaving the office and shutting the door behind her; her gaze fixed on her brother.

"Johnny, please understand. This is not your decision to make. It's mine. It's my life, my body—"

"And his bastard." The words were harsh, grating.
"No, I ain't gonna let him get away with it. Damn. I
should have shot him months ago. I don't know why I
didn't." He shook his head with the baffled rage of an
animal, slicing her a glance that made her quail inside.
"I woulda shot a thievin' coyote quick enough, but I
was too damn soft to shoot a bastard like Cimarrón
when I knew he needed it. Jesus." He slammed his
hands flat on the surface of her desk, making the lamp
rattle and Maggie jump.

She held her breath. She'd seen him like this before,

filled with anger and grief, yet this time there was a steely purpose that terrified her. His dark head bent, and he said grimly, "Cimarrón will marry you, by God, or I'll kill him. Hell. I'll kill him anyway."

"If you shoot him now," she said calmly, though she was quivering with apprehension inside, "then I'll still be in the same husbandless condition."

Johnny turned to glare at her. Maggie spoke quickly, her tone reasonable.

"Give him a chance to come to the decision himself. I don't want him marrying me because he thinks he has to. No, I mean it, Johnny," she said when he gave an impatient shake of his head. "If you even mention the baby to Devon, I'll never forgive you. He loves me. I know he does. He just has to realize it himself."

"Dammit, girl, what if he don't realize it till you've whelped the brat?"

Maggie paled at his snarling insult but kept her voice calm. "Johnny, I believe that Mother Nature will reveal my condition long before then. Devon is fairly observant, after all. This is not a secret that can be kept forever."

Johnny raked a hand over his face and muttered under his breath. Then he straightened and came to stand in front of her. Maggie wanted to flinch from the accusation in his dark eyes, the searing rage and raw pain. She forced herself to hold his gaze.

"Maggie, looks like I ain't done right by you. I listened to you when I should have done what I knew was best. I ain't gonna make that mistake again."

"Johnny—"

He held up a warning hand. "No. I'll wait. But I won't wait long. And he better decide pretty damn quick that he wants to make this right, or so help me, I'll decide for him."

"If you so much as breathe a word about the baby to Devon, John Clark Malone, I promise you that I'll leave

Belle Plain and Texas and you'll never hear from me again. I'll do it. You know I'll do it."

Johnny stared at her for a long moment, and whatever was in her face seemed to convince him. He looked away, his jaw tightening. "All right. I understand."

Her throat tensed, and she put out a hand, but he jerked his arm away. She let her hand fall to her side. "Johnny, I hope you do understand. Please. Trust me enough to let me do what I think is right."

He glanced back at her, then shrugged and stepped away. "I've already seen what your idea of right is, Maggie. I don't think much of it."

That stung. "I suppose you've never let love make you act unwisely?"

He flushed and shot her a quick, angry glance. "Yeah, you know I have. But at least I was tryin' to get her to marry me." He cleared his throat. "That's what I came to tell you. We're gettin' married next week. I don't think Lindsay would mind if it was a double weddin'."

"Johnny . . ." Maggie paused, fighting a sudden wave of nausea, then said softly, "I'm glad for you. I know you're happy."

"Was till I got here."

Maggie flinched. "I'm sorry you overheard. I would never have hurt you."

His mouth twisted bitterly. "I mean it, Maggie. Cimarrón will marry you. I don't care if he stays after the vows are said, but by God, he better make this right."

"If he asks me to marry him, it will be right. I know that."

Johnny gave her a last, baffled stare, then turned on his heel and slammed out of her office. Weak with relief and racked with guilt and grief as well, Maggie sank slowly back in a chair and stared into space. She was barely aware of Mrs. Lamb returning, of her soft, whispered words of comfort and reassurance. Like a miserable child, she allowed Mrs. Lamb to put her to bed.

It would be all right. She knew it would. It had to be. Devon loved her. Didn't he?

"My brother's getting married."

Devon glanced up at Maggie. "To the pretty blond at the dance?"

"Yes. Lindsay." Maggie sat beside him to watch him clean his pistol. "She's loved Johnny since they were kids. It's about time he figured out how to get her to marry him."

"Sure she's not making a mistake? Your brother is pretty hot-tempered."

"Lindsay's no frail flower herself. She can manage it." Maggie watched him in silence for a moment, then said, "Are you planning something I should know about?"

He grimaced. "I'm just cleaning my weapons."

"Um-hmm." Maggie gazed pointedly at the array spread out on the kitchen table. "That's quite an arsenal, Mr. Conrad."

"I like to be prepared."

"So I see." Another heartbeat, and he was expecting it when she repeated, "Are you planning on trouble?"

Devon snapped the cylinder back into his .45 and spun it, then set it down. "Maggie, there's something I've been meaning to tell you." He felt her tension and wished there was another way to put it. "I think I know who's behind the rustling, but I've got to catch them at it."

She paled, and he saw the rush of questions that trembled on her tongue. "But why?" was the first one out, soft and plaintive. "Let the law handle it."

"In the first place, Ben Whittaker is not much use as a lawman. In the second, he wouldn't believe me if he was. I'm not, you may have noticed, the most respectable of sources. No," he forestalled the next question, "listen to me. There's more at stake than just a few hundred head of cattle being rustled. And one of the men responsible was the one who shot Latigo."

She frowned. "I thought Ash Oliver did that."

Devon shook his head. "No. Remember? Latigo was shot from behind while I was flushing out Oliver. He couldn't be two places at once."

"But what does the rustling have to do with you?"

"I've been asking myself that same question." His mouth twisted wryly. "Maybe I just don't like to see some folks get away with murder."

"Murder? You mean—"

He stood up, suddenly unwilling to answer her questions when he wasn't certain he was right. "Maggie, it's just a feeling I have."

She searched his eyes, and he saw the flash of comprehension. "It's about the murders you were charged with. You know who really did it, don't you?"

"Yeah. Pretty sure I do. No, don't ask me any more because I won't tell you. I've already told you more than I should, but you've got a way of figuring things out too damn quick."

"It's the company I keep."

He pulled her to him, rubbing his jaw over the top of her head. "Yeah, outlaws and desperadoes. That should teach you to close your windows at night."

"Then you couldn't get in." Her muffled words made him smile, and when she tilted back her head, he kissed her, then set her back.

"I need to leave as soon as it's dark."

"Devon, if the rustlers managed to get you charged with murders you didn't do, then they won't stop at killing you to keep you from catching them."

"I know."

Her lower lip quivered slightly, but she didn't offer another protest. "Are you riding with anyone?"

"Yeah." He didn't elaborate, and she sighed an acceptance of his reluctance. The less she knew about Danza, the better it was for all of them.

He studied her a moment. She looked pale, with the faint bruises under her eyes that were always the first sign of worry and exhaustion. He cupped her chin in his palm and held her face up for his kiss.

"Maggie, don't worry. I can handle this. I'll be back before you know it."

He felt her tremble, and frowned. She'd been so quiet lately, so withdrawn and distant. He hesitated. Maybe he should tell her whom he suspected, but something inside him still clung to the wary reticence that had saved his life more than once. Not that he didn't trust Maggie. He trusted her with his life as well as his heart. But she was strong-willed and hardheaded, and he had terrifying visions of her storming off to his rescue and ending up as Molly had, limp and bloody in his arms. No, he wouldn't take that risk again.

His kiss was gentle and loving, and he finally set her back from him with reluctance. She stared up at him with great, solemn eyes.

"Devon, I know I shouldn't ask this, but did you send that telegram to your sister?"

His mouth twisted wryly. "Afraid I'll get killed without settling our differences?"

She smiled. "Something like that."

"Yeah, I sent it."

Maggie took a deep breath and reached up to straighten his collar, a simple loving gesture that made him feel suddenly soft inside. Damn. Maybe it was time he did something with this feeling he had, this warmth that she sparked in him even when he resisted.

"Maggie—"

She lifted her brows when he jerked to a halt, and he swallowed the words he'd been about to say. It wasn't the right time, not with him riding off and risking the possibility he wouldn't be back. No, once it was over, he'd say what he was feeling and hope that she still wanted to hear it.

"Keep my place in bed warm," he finished lamely, and looked away from the flash of disappointment in her eyes. He knew she longed to hear him tell her he loved her, but it just wasn't the right time.

Still, when he saddled Pardo to ride away from Belle Plain that night, he couldn't help remembering the stricken look in her eyes. It bothered him, and he considered turning back but didn't.

"Here he comes." A cold wind ruffled the fur collar of Johnny's coat, but he didn't even feel it. His attention was fixed on Cimarrón. Moonlight brightened the clear night sky with radiant intensity, shedding enough light to make it easy for a man to follow the road. The outlaw's dun picked its way over the brittle ruts in the road, past frozen blades of grama grass coated with ice and frost. It was slow going for a horse and rider when the ground was like that, but perfect for what he wanted.

"You sure about this, Johnny?"

He flashed a frowning glance at Hank. "Yeah. Damn sure. He can't do that to Maggie and get away with it. She's soft in the head, but I ain't. The bastard is gonna do right by her or wear a rope collar." He fingered the rough hemp that was coiled on his saddle, then slowly shook out a loop.

Six men waited just beyond the ridge on one side, he and Hank on the other. Cimarrón had to ride between them, and with only the moon for light, he wouldn't see them until it was too late. He'd be boxed in and trapped before he had a chance to draw a gun, if it went according to plan.

Frost formed a cloud in front of Johnny's face, and his body went taut when Cimarrón reached the point in the road where it closed in on both sides. This was it. He'd waited nearly a week for him to ride out on this road, and now he was here.

"Now!" he said, putting spurs to horse. His huge black lunged forward, and he had the loop of rope sailing through the air toward Cimarrón with the swiftness of a striking snake. He saw Cimarrón turn, saw his gloved hand flash down in a blur that was startling, and at the same time, the rope dropped down over his head and shoulders. Johnny's well-trained cutting horse immediately braced, putting tension on the rope that tightened the noose.

The clatter of hooves on frozen ground and the panting breath and grunts of men and animals filled the night. Then it was still, with only faint rasps and hazy breath-clouds that floated on the air.

Johnny eyed Cimarrón and saw the wary glitter in those cold blue eyes as well as the deadly bore of the pistol in one hand. He smiled to hide his surprise.

"Well, Cimarrón, looks like we got a Mexican standoff here. I got my rope on you, and you got your gun on me."

Cimarrón flicked a glance toward Hank, who'd ridden down at the same time, his rifle lifted menacingly. Then his gaze moved toward the six riders fanning out on the other slope, and he shrugged.

"Looks more like an ambush than a standoff."

Johnny grinned. "Naw. I wouldn't ambush nobody. Never minded gettin' the drop on a man when it was called for, though." His black edged backward some, keeping the rope taut when Cimarrón's dun snorted nervously and began to prance.

"So I see."

The gun in Cimarrón's hand didn't waver; it remained fixed on Johnny's chest with a deadly certainty that could get unnerving if he let it.

"Drop your weapon, Cimarrón."

"Why should I?"

" 'Cause if you don't, my boys will fill you full of lead before they hang you."

"All the more reason to take you with me."

"Maggie would like that."

He saw Cimarrón's mouth tighten, the moonlight giving his face a silver luminosity that made him look even more dangerous. Johnny shifted uneasily at the flicker of promise in the outlaw's eyes, and glanced at Hank.

"If he moves so much as an eyelash, shoot him."

He slid from the saddle, his gaze a challenge as he kept the black stretching the rope tight around Cimarrón. It was taking a big chance, but he counted on the bastard being unwilling to shoot him because of Maggie.

"All right, Cimarrón, I got something to talk to you about."

"I'm listening."

"I want to make sure I got your attention, 'cause this is pretty important." Johnny took another step forward and saw the Colt follow his movement. "Look, you ain't got the chance of a snowball in hell if you shoot me. I got you by the short hairs right now, so you might as well settle down and hear me out."

"Like I said—I'm listening."

Johnny stalled for time, waiting for the chance to disarm him. He took another slow step forward, arms held out to his sides to indicate that he didn't intend to draw. Cimarrón ignored the gesture, and the Colt never wavered in tracking him. Damn. The bastard was faster than he thought. No man should have been able to draw that fast, not under those circumstances. Maybe he'd underestimated him. His mouth thinned.

He saw a flicker of movement behind Cimarrón and realized that one of his men was circling around to catch him off guard. Ordinarily it would work, but Cimarrón was so damn fast he could probably put a bullet in Johnny, and Hank, too, before he went down. Johnny held up one hand.

"Get down off your horse and let's talk."

"I'm fine here."

Johnny shrugged. He braced his feet to keep from sliding on the frozen ruts of the road and put out a hand as if to catch his balance. His fingers grazed his black's bridle, and he gave it a sharp yank. Snorting and rearing, the horse jerked backward, snapping the rope around Cimarrón's shoulders so tight it pulled him from the saddle.

There was the loud crack of a gunshot, and he felt something burn his arm. He spun halfway around, grabbing at his left arm. When he looked back, he saw Cimarrón on the ground and Hank Mills standing over him, the rifle barrel nudging against the side of his face. Johnny smiled and walked over to where the outlaw sprawled on his back.

"You ain't bad, Cimarrón, but you ain't quite good enough." He bent and picked up the pistol lying near the outlaw, then motioned for Hank to step back. He crouched down beside Cimarrón, holding that icy blue gaze for a moment. "I wasn't lyin' when I said I want to talk. Whether you get up off the ground or get dragged off with a rope is up to you. You can let me know which it is when I'm through talkin' to you."

"Never met a man before who liked talking so damn much. What makes you think I want to hear what you've got to say?"

Anger exploded inside him, and Johnny drew back his right arm and backhanded Cimarrón across the face. It snapped his head back, and there was the instant reflex action of his body tightening, muscles tensing to strike back. Only the warning prod of Hank's rifle stopped him. Johnny met Cimarrón's gaze for a moment. He saw the flare of murderous rage in his eyes, that white-hot flash of pure fury that matched his own.

"You'll listen, damn you. If it wasn't for Maggie, I'd just as soon shoot you. But she wants you alive."

Cimarrón's eyes narrowed slightly. "What's she got to do with this?"

"Do you think I don't know? You've been humpin' my sister for four months. I'd of killed you before, but she's old enough to make her own choices, bad as they may be. Only now it's different."

Cimarrón's icy stare was infuriating enough; the slow smile that curled his bloodied mouth pushed Johnny to the brink so that he barely heard the drawled, "Thought maybe you were trying to collect the bounty on my head."

Johnny caught two fistfuls of Cimarrón's coat front, ignoring the pain in his left arm as he hauled him to his feet. "Smart-ass bastard," he snarled, and plowed a fist into his stomach, driving it upward so that Cimarrón doubled over. He brought up his knee, smashing it into the outlaw's face and snapping him backward. The rope around his neck dangled loosely, trailing on the ground to tangle in his legs.

Cimarrón half-fell and managed to catch himself; he was panting for breath, eyes ablaze with fury. Johnny heard the clicks of rifles being cocked. It was obvious Cimarrón heard it, too. He remained in a crouch, mouth bloody and grim.

"Don't you want to call in your help, Malone?"

"Don't need to. Only takes one man to kick a coyote."

Cimarrón rose slowly to his feet. They faced each

other like two dogs, wary and ready, hackles raised. Johnny could hear the crunch of boots on frozen ground, the jangle of tack on the horses, and the rasping breathing from himself as well as Cimarrón.

"What do you want, Malone?"

"You're gonna marry my sister."

Johnny saw the surprise in Cimarrón's eyes. Then his mouth tightened into a mocking line, and he laughed.

"What makes you think she wants to marry an outlaw? Hell, Malone, I've got a price on my head."

"I know that. If I had my way, I'd be collectin' the reward tomorrow. But Maggie don't want that." He took a step closer and saw Cimarrón tense again. "You ruined her, damn you, and you'll marry her. It don't matter whether you want to or not, or even if you stick around after, but you'll do it up nice and legal and quick, or you'll be swingin' from that tree over there."

Cimarrón glared back at him. "I don't like threats, and I don't like men who make them."

"Draw down on him, Hank."

Hank Mills pumped the lever on the Winchester he held and lifted it to his shoulder. Cimarrón didn't back down. He didn't even flick an eyelash, but kept his cold, opaque gaze riveted on Johnny. Tension vibrated between them, choking the air.

"Shoot and be damned," Cimarrón said softly, but Johnny knew that Hank would never do it. He wasn't sure he could shoot an unarmed man, either, even the man who'd ruined his sister and her life. Hatred almost choked him, and he felt the rising need to hurt something, to deal out punishment in an effort to ease his own pain.

Despite the cold and the hot pain in his arm, Johnny let his fury rage into action. He was only vaguely aware that two of his men had stepped up behind Cimarrón to grab his arms and hold him, while a third tightened the rope around the outlaw's neck as insurance. All he was aware of was the sense of satisfaction he felt each time he pounded a fist into Cimarrón and heard his grunt of pain. The months of frustration and worry fueled him with enough energy to beat Cimarrón into a bloody mess, and when he felt Hank Mills reach out to grab his arm, he jerked away.

"Leave me alone. I'll kill the bastard."

"Not like this, Johnny. This ain't what you set out to do."

Johnny staggered slightly. He was panting for breath and wheezing; he felt the cold slice of freezing air chill his lungs. Oddly, it did nothing to cool his flushed face or his temper. Hank was looking at him with a grim frown, and Johnny slowly straightened. He looked down at Cimarrón where he half-sprawled on the ground, held up by the rope and one of the men.

"Damn. Looks like hell, don't he?"

Hank knelt to examine him; moonlight glittered from blood that looked almost black in the pale dusting of snow on the ground. When Hank stood up, he said wearily, "He'll live, but you got him pretty good."

Cimarrón groaned when they lifted him to his feet, and his legs buckled when he tried to stand, boots sliding over the slick ground. Johnny reached out and grabbed a fistful of blond hair, jerking his head back.

"Listen up, Cimarrón. You can marry Maggie or hang. I don't care which."

The words came out in a painful rasp, but Cimarrón got his feet under him as he said, "Think she'll . . . thank you for this?"

Johnny stared at him. No, Maggie wouldn't thank him. She'd be furious. Even though he hadn't told Cimarrón about the baby and didn't intend to, especially not with his men anywhere near, he knew that Maggie might just be mad enough to shoot him for hurting Cimarrón. But that didn't matter. He had listened to enough, and seeing her hurt and teary and unwilling to make the outlaw own up to what he'd done had only raked across his sore temper like a dull blade.

But he had no intention of letting this bastard think for a minute that Maggie was so lacking as to let him get away with what he'd done to her, either.

"Hell, Cimarrón, who do you think sent me after you?" he snarled.

He saw that his taunt had hit the mark when Cimarrón grew still, his cold blue eyes chilling to ice.

"You're lying, Malone."

"No, I ain't. And you know it. I can see by the look on your face." Johnny spat on the frozen ground. "She sent me after you, all right. My sister ain't no fool. Think she don't know about that damn bounty on your head?"

"What do you mean by that?"

"Hell, you've been playin' without payin'. That's gotta change. Maggie got tired of waitin' on you to be man enough to own up to what's right."

"You're not only wrong, you're lying, Malone. Maggie wouldn't send you after me."

Johnny laughed harshly. "Why shouldn't she? If she ain't your wife and you've been hanged for murderin' those two men in Abilene, somebody might as well get the bounty on your head."

There was a long moment of silence. He could see the flicker of reaction in Cimarrón's eyes, a brief flare that was quickly extinguished to leave them icy and opaque again.

"And you think a shotgun marriage is legal."

"I do. Maggie hopes you're smart enough to see reason." His gaze narrowed slightly. He didn't like the glitter in Cimarrón's eyes when he stared at him; even with one eye puffy and swollen, there was a menace and danger that would have been warning enough to any man. His jaw clenched. He was damned if he intended to let a two-bit desperado back him down.

"So what's it gonna be, Cimarrón? A weddin' or a hangin'?"

# CHAPTER 17

"Come out here, Maggie."

She sat up in bed, her heart racing until she realized that it was Johnny. He stood in the open doorway of her bedroom, a lamp in one hand. It cast half his face in light, the other in shadow.

"Johnny—what's the matter?"

"Get dressed." His voice was rough. "And hurry. I ain't got all night."

She pushed her loose hair from her eyes and tried to focus on her brother, confusion racking her brain. She slept so much lately, and it felt as if she were trying to move through deep water, her every motion a wearying drag of energy.

"But I don't—"

"Dammit, Maggie, do what I say," Johnny snarled, and stepped into her room with the lamp. He tracked snow and mud on the floor, and she shivered at the chill breeze that came with him. He went to the small armoire against the far wall and yanked open the door, holding the lamp up high as he reached inside and jerked out one of her wool gowns. "This will do. Put it on."

Some of her lethargy dissolved into the beginning of anger, and Maggie pushed impatiently at the hair in her eyes as he threw the gown on the bed.

"I won't move until I know why you're here. Is someone ill?"

"Yeah. Come out here and cure him."

241

Maggie slid from under the covers. Her bare toes curled at the chill on the floor as she reached for the rose wool dress. To save time, she slid it over her head, not bothering with proper undergarments. It buttoned up the front from waist to throat, and the long sleeves were full enough to fit over her nightgown.

"Who's sick?" she asked, bending to retrieve her shoes from under a chair. She sat down to pull on her stockings, and when Johnny didn't answer, glanced up at him.

He was staring down at her, face grim, the lamp still in his hand. "You'll find out soon enough. Hurry up."

"I am hurrying. I don't usually wear my nightrail as an undergarment, you know." She shoved her foot into her shoes and left them half-unbuttoned in her haste, then stood up. "All right. Is the patient in my office?"

"The *patient* is in the kitchen."

"The kitchen! Good lord, you don't have a lick of sense, Johnny." She hurried down the hallway, buttoning the cuffs of her sleeves as she went. "Is he able to walk?"

"A little."

Something in his tone made her pause and turn around, and he halted abruptly, almost running into her. The lamp wavered in his hand. "What is it, Johnny?"

His hand clamped down on her shoulder and spun her around. "You'll see quick enough."

Maggie's throat tightened at the grim promise in his tone, and she had the swift, horrible thought that something had happened to Devon. But when she hesitated in the kitchen door, blinking at the bright glow of lamps and knot of men, she knew it was something else. Another disaster had befallen, and she saw it in the eyes that couldn't meet hers, the quickly averted gazes of men she'd known half her life. Why were so many Double M ranch hands here?

Johnny's hand in the small of her back pushed her forward, and as she stumbled, he caught her and held her.

"Over here."

Maggie turned blindly, confused, and then saw Devon. He was sagging against the wall by the door, held up by Hank Mills and another man; his bright hair was dark with mud and what looked like blood. Her heart lurched.

"Devon. Are you all right?"

He lifted his head, and she gasped. One eye was swollen shut, and his mouth was puffy and bloody. A bright purple bruise marred his right cheek, and she could see the irregular rasp of his efforts to breathe without pain.

"My God—" She started forward, but Johnny caught her by the arm.

"Not yet. Business first."

Maggie tried to wrench free, but Johnny's grip was hard and steely. She turned to glare up at him.

"What business? What's the matter with you?"

"Nothin'. Just stay quiet until it's time for you to say the words."

"Johnny—"

But he was pulling her with him, and she had no choice but to follow. Confusion dulled her reaction, and even when she saw Reverend Puckett standing nervously by the kitchen table with a Bible clutched in his hands, she didn't quite comprehend what was happening. It was all a blur; only Devon stood out clearly and sharply in her mind, his battered face generating an urgent need to help him.

Johnny shoved her forward, and two of the Double M ranch hands dragged the kitchen table aside. For the first time she noticed that the Double M hands wore guns. Most of them rarely did, but they were now. It came to Maggie with a jolt what was intended, and she began to shake with fury as her haze of confusion dissipated.

Her brother grabbed her arm in a painful vise when she whirled on him. His voice was low and threatening. "You do what you're told, by God, or so help me, come mornin' you can visit Cimarrón in jail. I'll turn him in, Maggie. I mean it. He'll hang, and you know it."

Angry words caught in her throat, and she saw from the grim look in her brother's eyes that he meant what he said. He'd do it. He'd turn Devon in to the sheriff for those murders and there would be nothing she could do to help him.

"What do you want me to do?" she asked tightly.

"Act agreeable. It don't matter if you are, just so long as Cimarrón and the reverend think you are. If you tell either of 'em any different, Cimarrón will be swingin' from a rope before you can blink."

"All right," she said in an anguished whisper. "I'll do it for Devon."

"That's smart. He don't deserve you, but he's gonna get you anyway." Johnny looked over at Hank Mills and nodded.

Hank shoved Devon to Maggie's side to stand in front of the reverend. The dull gleam of a cocked rifle prodded into his back, and Devon muttered a hoarse oath. Then he looked down at her, his mouth twisting slightly.

"Did you send him after me, Maggie?" he asked in that husky, painful whisper, and she felt her world shatter. There would be no reprieve for him if she didn't say what Johnny wanted her to say, but God, it was so hard when she knew what Devon would think.

Choked with anger and pain, Maggie nodded stiffly. "Yes. I did."

"If I don't marry you, he says I'll hang. That right?"

Maggie wanted to die at the look in his eyes, but she forced herself to nod again. "That's right. Marry me or hang."

Devon seemed to freeze, turning to ice. He didn't move or change expression, but just looked at her. Pain clouded her vision, but she could see shadows fill and darken the blue of his eyes until the unhurt eye looked as black as the other. She vaguely heard Reverend Puckett's quavering voice begin the marriage vows. A rushing sound filled her ears, growing louder and louder until she could hear only the sound of blood like the roar of the ocean.

When Johnny prodded her, she repeated what was asked of her, and her own voice sounded foreign. Devon's was a rusty grating, barely recognizable. Then Reverend Puckett pronounced them man and wife, and Johnny put her hand on Devon's arm. She felt his muscles tighten beneath her fingers, and she gave him an agonized glance.

He still wouldn't look at her; his jaw was taut, and there were bruises on his face and a red, raw rope burn around his neck. It was obvious what had happened, and she wanted to burst into agonized tears. She drew in a deep breath to steady herself. She'd explain to him later that it was not her doing, that Johnny had acted on his own. He'd listen to her, and he'd understand. All she had to do was explain.

"May I offer my best wishes, Mrs. Conrad?"

Maggie blinked and realized that Reverend Puckett was speaking to her, his face worried and kind at the same time. "Th . . . thank you," she managed to say. She felt Devon shift and reached for him blindly, but he stepped just out of reach.

"Happy, Malone?" he grated in that rusty, painful voice, and Johnny stared at him coolly.

"Satisfied, Cimarrón."

"Good." Devon's icy glance swept over Maggie, then he was moving away from her again, ignoring the hand she held out to stop him. Before she could protest, he'd reached the door and opened it to a chilling blast of wind that made the lamps dance erratically.

"Devon!" Maggie started after him, but Johnny grabbed her arm.

"Let him go. He ain't worth it."

She pulled free, shooting her brother a scathing look that should have frozen him on the spot, and ran to the door. Devon had moved more swiftly than she thought him capable of doing, and reached the dun tied to the corner post of the back porch.

"Devon! Devon, wait! I can explain—"

He didn't even glance at her, but clumsily pulled himself into his saddle and reined the dun around. Maggie cried out and stumbled after him, slipping on the icy planks of the porch. She grabbed a post to keep her balance, skirts whipping around her legs in the tug of wind.

"Devon! Oh God—Deeevooon!"

The wind carried her words away, losing them in the brittle clatter of hooves on frozen ground, and her cry was like the wordless wail of a coyote in the night. It seemed to echo around her as she collapsed, sobbing.


"Your bruises are almost gone, amigo."

Devon tossed down another drink as he met Danza's steady gaze. "Yeah."

The Apache studied him for a moment, then shrugged. A warm breeze filtered over them and stirred the branches of a tree growing in the middle of the small patio. Red-tiled roofs gleamed in the sun, and a dark-eyed señorita smiled prettily as she passed. Danza gave her an interested glance.

"We have been in Mexico a month," he said when the girl had gone into the cantina. "While I like the sunshine, I find myself growing impatient to finish what we began."

"As far as I'm concerned, it's over." Devon felt Danza turn to look at him, but the gunslinger wouldn't meet his gaze. He didn't give a damn anymore. The price on his head didn't matter. He couldn't think of much that did matter, except maybe more sunshine and an occasional bottle of rye.

"It's not over for me," Danza said after a moment. "I have not forgotten the man who shot Latigo."

"Heck Raines. That's who did it." Devon poured more rye into a glass. "Rode with Ash Oliver a while. I heard he's been seen out at the Bar Z a time or two."

"So you were right about Rogan being involved with Oliver."

Devon shrugged. "Seem to be. Don't know what Rogan got out of it, though. Except some stolen cattle."

"Men have been known to turn on one another like snakes, amigo. Perhaps Oliver saw the opportunity to strike at Rogan without consequence to himself."

"Maybe. Don't seem likely." It was getting almost hot under the benevolent sun that beamed down on the small Mexican village. Devon took off his hat and raked his sleeve over his face.

Across the street, just outside the small adobe church, he saw a group of children laughing and playing. A brightly colored piñata swung from a cord attached to the beam of a latticed porch roof, and the children were taking turns batting at it with a sturdy stick. When a blindfolded child would swing and miss, he would be sent to the end of the line to try again, and the next child would don the cloth over their eyes and take up the stick. A robed priest was conducting the festivity, and Devon smiled faintly at the sounds of their merriment.

He rose to his feet and crossed to the arched stone walkway that led to the patio, leaning against it to gaze at the children. "What's today, Danza?" he asked after a few minutes had passed.

"Today? Why, amigo?"

Devon pointed. "It looks like they're having some kind of celebration over there."

"Ah." There was the sound of a chair being pushed back, then Danza came to stand beside him. He crossed his arms over his chest, resting one shoulder against the stone support as he watched Devon. "Today is Christmas Day, amigo. When they have broken the piñata and given out the sweets and gifts inside, they will go into the church and light many candles. If the pipe organ is working, Father Garcia will direct some of the children in singing, and their parents will smile and listen and think how fortunate they are to have enough to eat this day."

Devon rubbed a hand across his jaw. His beard was growing out again. He stared moodily across the street and was about to turn to go back to the table and his bottle of rye when he saw a familiar, limping figure approach the children and the still-dangling piñata. His throat tightened.

Though he couldn't hear what was said, it was obvious that Latigo had asked to join in. After a moment, the priest blindfolded him and put the stick into his hands. The boy moved clumsily, half-dragging his bad leg, and took a mighty swing at the piñata and missed. The force of his swing unbalanced him, and he crashed to the stone floor.

"Damn." Devon pushed away from the wall and started to step off the patio, but Danza caught his arm.

"No. Do not help him."

"Damn, Danza, didn't you see him fall?"

"*Sí.* And I will see him get up."

Frustrated, Devon glanced back and saw that Latigo was indeed pushing himself off the ground. He was laughing, unfazed by his miss or his fall. He took a step back to take his second swing, and this time the stick connected with the donkey-shaped piñata and shattered it. Candy and small gifts showered down on the squealing children, and they scrambled for them while Latigo pulled off his blindfold and grinned.

"You see, amigo," Danza said quietly, "my cousin is only crippled in body, not in spirit."

Devon stiffened. "Is there supposed to be a lesson in that for me?"

"Only if you find one."

Outrage battled with grudging agreement. Devon looked back across the street and saw Latigo lift a child into his wiry arms. They were both laughing, and none of the children gathered around him seemed to notice Latigo's halting step as they followed him to a stone bench with the prizes from the piñata.

"Point well taken," Devon said finally, his voice a low growl that made Danza smile.

"Will you ride with us, amigo?" Danza asked when they were seated at the table again.

Devon frowned, pushing idly at his empty glass. "No. I like riding alone. I know that you will take care of Raines. I don't care about the others."

"You mean the rustlers."

"Yeah. I intend to be smart enough to mind my own business from now on." His mouth twisted. "I feel like a damn fool for ever thinking I could make a difference anyway. If those ranchers get tired enough of losing beef, they can do their own fighting."

"*Sí,* if they know who to fight."

Devon shrugged. "Let 'em find out the same way I

did. I don't have any more interest in shooting at shadows."

"Or ghosts?"

His head snapped up, and his eyes narrowed. "There are limits, my friend," he said softly, but Danza only nodded.

"*Sí*, amigo. I hope you learn to stretch yours."

Devon's mouth tightened. "What did you do, wake up this morning and decide to spend the day lecturing me with Apache philosophy? Forget it. I don't give a damn anymore. I don't have any ghosts, and I don't care if all the cattle in Texas end up in New York."

"And the price on your head? The two thousand dollar bounty for killing two men you never met? Do you not care about that either, amigo?"

"Not in the least." Devon stared at him coolly. "There is a fine line between friendship and interference, Danza. I never knew you to cross it before."

"Perhaps I have grown weary of watching you suffer when there is no reason for it."

"No reason?" Devon choked back a string of curses. "If I was suffering—which I'm not—I sure as hell wouldn't tell you about it."

The black eyes watching him didn't flicker, but Devon saw the disbelief in Danza's gaze as if he'd spelled it out in large letters. He looked away, wishing he'd followed his first instincts and stayed to himself instead of meeting Danza in Baird that night. He'd barely made it there before falling from his horse, and the rest of the night had been a blur. The only sharp memory was Maggie and her betrayal.

Devon shoved back his chair. "I'm riding out in the morning." He didn't wait for a reply but strode from the cantina without looking back. The bitter mood of controlled fury that he'd held in since leaving Belle Plain still waited like a hungry beast, watching for the slightest slip that would allow it to run free. He had no intention of loosing it on Danza. No, the dark side of him grew more vicious with every passing day, and that he was saving for someone else. He was saving it for the person who had caused it.

# CHAPTER 18

"How are you feeling today?" Lindsay smiled brightly at Maggie. Late winter sunshine coming through the kitchen window made a hazy halo around her head, leaving her face in shadow.

"Fat." Maggie managed an answering smile, and saw the way Lindsay's gaze dropped to the swell of her abdomen. Her gown hung loosely but couldn't disguise her pregnancy. At least the early morning nausea had stopped, so that she didn't bolt at the sight, smell, or suggestion of food. She reached for one of Mrs. Lamb's cookies.

Lindsay stirred another chip of sugar into her tea and sighed. "Well, you don't look very fat. Not like I've seen other women look."

"The baby isn't due until late May or early June. Give me time."

A worried look creased Lindsay's face. "But are you sure you feel all right? I mean, here by yourself and all."

"I'm not by myself. Mrs. Lamb is staying with me now."

"She is?" Lindsay looked relieved. "Oh good. I didn't know that. I had hoped you'd come stay—"

"I wouldn't. And I won't." Maggie looked away from Lindsay's distressed face. "I told you that."

"But Maggie, how long can you stay so angry at Johnny? He's sorry he hurt you, but he only did what he thought was right." When Maggie didn't reply but sat stiffly silent, Lindsay blurted, "I know he was wrong! What he did was terrible, and I think he realizes that now. But please try to understand how he felt, how upset he was when he found out about . . . about the baby."

"That does not excuse what he did. Nothing can excuse it. I don't know if I'll ever be able to forget it." Maggie put down the rest of her cookie. It tasted like sawdust in her mouth, and she reached for her tea with a shaking hand.

"Maggie, please forgive him. He's miserable."

"I forgave him. Didn't he tell you?"

Lindsay sighed. "Yes. He told me you looked at the wall and gave him forgiveness, but you wouldn't look at him."

"If I had looked at Johnny, I don't think I could have forgiven him. I keep seeing Devon that night, his face all bruised and battered, and the look in his eyes—" She choked to a halt and took a deep breath. "There was a look in his eyes that I'll never forget. He thinks I betrayed him. Maybe if he'd known that was a lie, he would have cared about the baby . . ."

"Maggie, that was four months ago. He's gone. You have to go on with your life. Can't you talk to Johnny now?"

Maggie shook her head. "No. I lost something very precious to me that night. I don't want a reminder of it."

"Does that mean you want me to stop talking about it?"

"Yes. Please." Her hands shook only slightly when she lifted her teacup, and her eyes met Lindsay's worried green gaze calmly. "How's Hank?"

But when Lindsay had gone and she was alone and sitting in her empty office, Maggie couldn't help think-

ing about it. The memories were still sharp and painful, almost unbearable at times. She'd thought they
would ease with the passing of the days into weeks
and months, but they hadn't. There was still that vivid
ache that Devon had left behind.

She thought about him so much and wondered if he
was alive, or hurt, or even thinking about her at all.
Her only comfort was the child she carried, the ener-
getic life that was a reminder of what she'd almost
had. Everything around her had changed; the only
constant was the promise of a spring miracle.

*Devon's child.* How could she ever have thought she
wouldn't want a child? She should have believed Mrs.
Lamb.

"When the right man comes along, you'll want to
have his children," she'd said.

She was right. Devon had been the right man, and
even if he was gone, she wanted this child. It wasn't
the baby's fault that its father had abandoned them.
Her first sharp grief at her loss had turned into anger
when Johnny confessed that he'd told Devon about the
baby. That had been a shock. He'd known and had still
not wanted to marry her. Somehow, it made her unwilling betrayal less important. It also snapped her out
of her grief and gave her the necessary anger and
strength to go on.

If Devon Conrad had not cared enough about her or
their child to stay despite the bad beginning, then she
didn't need him. She'd do it on her own. Already, she
had two replies to her inquiries about positions in distant towns needing a physician. Once the baby was
born, she'd accept one of them as soon as feasible.
She'd make a new life for herself and a good life for her
child. And she wouldn't look back.

"She won't even discuss it." Lindsay sagged wearily
into a parlor chair, and Johnny nodded.

"I didn't think she would. Don't hurt to try, I guess." He moved to stand at the window and stare out over the pens and buildings scattered in a neat pattern. His hands were shoved deep in his pockets, his shoulders hunched. "Did she say . . . say anything else?"

"Nothing important. Oh. Mrs. Lamb is staying with her now. She's not alone."

"Damn."

"Johnny?"

He turned in a savage motion that betrayed the anger simmering inside him. "Dammit! She's so blamed hardheaded and stubborn. What the hell did she expect me to do—let that bastard get her pregnant and ride off without a thought? I couldn't do that. Anymore than I could do that to you."

Lindsay gazed at him with sympathetic green eyes that did nothing to ease his conscience. He kept seeing Maggie's accusing gaze, her ravaged face when Cimarrón had ridden away and not looked back. And he kept hearing her heartbroken sobs when he'd finally had to drag her back into the house. He'd have gone after Cimarrón then, but Hank Mills had stopped him.

"Reckon you done enough damage tonight, Mr. Malone. Let it be."

*Mr. Malone.* After fifteen years of camaraderie that had been unaffected by any hardships, Hank Mills had looked at him as if he were a stranger. He still did, despite the fact that his daughter was married to him now.

"Johnny." He looked down and saw Lindsay standing in front of him. "You never meant to hurt her," she whispered. "She'll realize that one day."

"Sometimes," he said heavily, "I think it's the careless acts of kindness that can hurt the most."

Lindsay put her arms around him and drew his

head down for a kiss. When she finally drew away, he managed a smile.

"Let's go to bed."

He put his arm around her, and together they went up the stairs to their bedroom. It was only later, when their passion had died and Lindsay lay sleeping in his arms, that he thought of Cimarrón again.

No one had heard anything about him since he'd left Belle Plain in November. There had been a rumor that he was the one responsible for the latest rash of rustling, but that had not been proven. Zeke Rogan had added to the reward offered for Cimarrón, saying that the outlaw had killed two of his men. One of them he declined to name, but the other had been a drifter and casual gunman by the name of Heck Raines. Raines had been discovered by a line rider, his body staked out on the prairie as if left there by Comanches. Ben Whittaker had said it looked more like the work of Apaches than Comanches, but most folks believed that Cimarrón had done it. A news clipping about the killing of Ash Oliver down in Brackettville had been found pinned to the bare chest, as if to explain the reason for the death. Like Oliver, Raines had lost his scalp.

It was a warning, some said, not to cross Cimarrón.

Cimarrón. Johnny groaned and pressed the heels of his palms against his eyes. Damn him. Why hadn't the bastard just gone on? Why had he stayed around Belle Plain so long? Everyone knew he was a loner, a restless drifter who never stayed in one place long. He would have left sooner or later anyway, and Maggie would have been shattered. Hadn't he just taken matters into his own hands by forcing Cimarrón to marry her? It was the only thing he could have done. He was just trying to protect his sister.

It had nothing to do with rustlers and guilt. Nothing at all.

\* \* \*

A late spring snow blanketed the mountains, shining with a rosy glow as the setting sun was reflected. Devon reined in his horse and sat there for a moment, staring at the high, jagged peaks he hadn't seen in over four years.

Colorado.

It looked just as it had in his elusive dreams, the brief pictorial impressions that sometimes visited him at night in a hazy collage of landscapes and vast empty spaces. He'd spent most of his life here, yet nothing looked as he remembered it. There were more settlements, more settlers, fewer miles between towns. One day, Colorado might even be civilized. It made him feel strangely restless.

He nudged Pardo into a brisk trot down the shadowed slope toward the scattering of buildings below. Smoke rose in a thin curl above the main house, and split rail fences crisscrossed the ground like a patchwork quilt. It was obviously a prosperous ranch, and he was looking forward to a warm bed and a hot meal.

Dogs barked as he rode close, and he saw several men step out of a long, low building to watch his approach. He slowed Pardo to a walk, keeping an eye on them. Two held rifles loosely, barrels pointed down in a guarded welcome. He knew how quickly those rifles could be brought up if trouble started.

One of the men stepped off the low porch and crossed the yard to meet him. "Afternoon, stranger."

Devon reined in. He nodded. "Afternoon."

"Lookin' for a place to sleep?"

"Maybe."

The man nodded, sizing Devon up and apparently reserving judgment. "Might oblige you if you're willin' to do a little honest work."

There was the sound of boots scuffing wood, and another man stepped off the porch. He laughed loudly.

"Honest? Hell, not him. Don't you know who that is, Shorty?"

The man named Shorty frowned, glancing back at the man before looking at Devon again. "No. Who is he?"

A faint smile curled Devon's mouth, and he pushed his hat to the back of his head as he recognized the second man. "You old bushwhacker. What the hell are you doing here?"

Doug Morton grinned widely. "Playin' cards, mostly. A little work when they can get me int'rested in it." He turned to Shorty, jabbing his thumb in Devon's direction. "This is Devon Conrad."

"So?" Shorty looked from Doug to Devon, then his eyes widened with sudden recognition. *"That* Devon Conrad?"

Devon met his gaze, uncertain how he meant it. When Shorty relaxed his grip on the rifle, his welcome was assured. Doug was grinning from ear to ear, and as Devon dismounted and suffered an enthusiastic back-slapping welcome, Morton began a running history of everything that had happened since he'd last seen him. The history lasted through dinner.

"And so I came out here to work for Kate," Morton ended finally. He shoved another cup of coffee across the table toward Devon and indicated the bunkhouse with an expansive wave of one arm. "Like it pretty good."

"How do you like working for Lassiter?" Devon sopped up the last of the beef gravy with his fourth biscuit and chewed it slowly. It beat beans and jerky all to hell, he decided.

Morton scratched his head, obviously considering how to answer Devon's question. "Well," he said slowly, "Lassiter ain't so bad. Guess I done got used to him after three years of workin' here. Hell, I like him pretty good."

Devon leaned back in his chair. "I can remember a time when you didn't."

Doug grunted. "Neither did you."

"No. Sure didn't." Devon paused, then asked the question he'd been wanting to ask since riding in. "How's Kate?"

"Busy." Devon's brow lifted, and Doug laughed. "You'll see what I mean quick enough."

His throat tightened. "Has she—changed?"

"Yep. Gotten meaner. Takes her half as long as it used to to send Jake Lassiter outta that house wantin' to eat live grizzly and gunpowder."

Devon couldn't help a grin at the image that provoked. From what he remembered of Jake Lassiter, the man could hold his own well enough with Kate. He wasn't too sure about himself, though. Maybe after a good night's sleep and clean clothes, he'd be ready to face her.

Hat in hand, Devon stood in the front parlor of the low, rambling ranch house and looked around. He felt damned uncomfortable and didn't know why. It was a comfortable room, with stuffed couches that showed evidence of wear, hooked rugs, a few green plants scattered here and there in front of high, wide windows, and a huge stone fireplace with a cheery blaze burning at the far end. A comfortable room. A room that looked welcoming and lived in.

And he felt like an intruder.

He could hear sounds from upstairs, the scuffling of feet and laughter, and waited impatiently for Kate to come down. The woman who had answered his knock had hesitated for a long moment before agreeing to fetch her mistress, until Devon had begun to wonder if Kate had left orders he wasn't to be allowed in.

"Who shall I say is askin'?" she'd finally snapped, eying him up and down.

"An old friend."

It was all he'd tell her, and finally the woman had jerked around and gone up the wide staircase that angled to the second floor. Devon was left to stand awkwardly in the parlor and wait, and he began to think he'd made a mistake by coming here.

A flurry of sound came from the direction of the stairs, and Devon half-turned, brows lifting when he saw the three children. They halted in a shaft of sunlight streaming through a window, and he knew they had to be Kate's. He wondered how she'd managed three kids in four years but acknowledged that with Kate, anything was possible. The two youngest looked like twins. Red-gold curls shimmered around small, piquant faces with Kate's wide eyes, and the two little girls put hands over their mouths and giggled, annoying the older boy.

"Stop that," the child said firmly. His dark hair was streaked with hints of red, and dark, solemn eyes regarded Devon as suspiciously as Jake Lassiter had once done. Devon smiled wryly.

"Who are you?" the boy asked.

What did he say? Your uncle? Devon wasn't sure Kate would appreciate that. Or Jake. He settled for something safe.

"A friend."

"I don't know you."

Direct and to the point, wasn't he. Devon shrugged. "Your mother does."

There was a flash of something in the boy's eyes that could have been interpreted as protective if he hadn't been so young, and Devon was startled by it. It was almost adult, but the boy couldn't be much more than three.

"How old are you?" he couldn't help asking, and after a brief hesitation the boy replied, "Four next month."

Four. Damn. It had been longer than he'd thought. Was it closer to five years since he'd seen Kate? Since he'd lost Molly?

Molly. Thinking about her didn't give him the same, sharp pain it once had. She was still a sweet memory, but oddly enough, her face was blurred. The image he saw most clearly was Maggie's, a flash of silky black hair and wide gray eyes, with the faint fragrance of roses that he'd always associate with both women. Maggie. He resolutely tore his thoughts from her and turned back toward the front door. He shouldn't have come here.

"Oh my God—"

Devon looked up. Kate was poised on the landing, one hand resting lightly on the balustrade, her eyes wide with shock. His throat tightened. Damn. Caitlin had grown into a beautiful, poised young woman. It was hard to reconcile this self-assured beauty with the Kate he had known, wild hair tumbling in a russet tangle around her face, pants fitting snugly on slender hips swathed in gunbelts.

"Devon." Her voice shook slightly, and she came down the last steps in a rushing glide. He didn't realize he'd moved toward her until he had his arms around her, crushing her to him in a vise.

"Kate." His voice choked to a halt. He couldn't get anything else past the thickening in his throat.

She was laughing and crying at the same time, kissing any part of him she could reach, the bottom of his jaw, his neck, his chest. His collar was damp from tears and kisses, and he drew back a little to look down at her again.

A sudden, sharp pain in his ankle directed his immediate attention downward, and he wasn't too surprised to see the boy kicking the hell out of him. He put out a hand to stop him, but the boy deftly evaded it.

"Thomas Clay Lassiter," Kate said sternly, "You stop that this moment."

The boy stopped, though the look he gave Devon was hot and fierce and protective. "He grabbed you."

Kate moved to him and knelt, taking both his shoulders in her hands. "This is my brother. He was hugging me. There is a difference, but I'm glad you are brave enough to protect me."

Devon rubbed at his ankle. He was glad his boots were thick enough to protect him. "Rough rascal, ain't he," he muttered, and heard Kate laugh.

"Rough enough," she agreed. Her eyes were still wet with tears, and she stood up to tuck her hand between his arm and side, grasping him firmly. "Come with me. I have no intention of letting you get away again until you tell me just where the devil you've been for so long."

"Didn't you get my wire?"

"Oh yes. 'Kate. Am alive and well. Devon.'" She glared at him. "Very comforting and informative."

His brow lifted. "Didn't know you expected a book."

"Don't be an ass." She smiled sweetly, then turned to the three listening children. "Go and tell Mrs. Baker to give you a treat, and when you're through, come into the parlor to get acquainted with your uncle."

One of the girls stared up at Devon, a finger stuck in her mouth, her eyes as wide as a baby owl's and just as solemn. Her brother scowled.

"Stop suckin' your finger, Molly."

That jolted Devon, and he tensed. Kate tightened her fingers on his arm, said something soft to the children, and they scampered away like puppies. She turned and gazed up into his eyes earnestly.

"Melissa and Molly. I hope you don't mind."

He shrugged. "Why should I?"

"Well, I just thought . . . Devon, don't look so remote. It reminds me of the last time I saw you. Haven't you—aren't things better?"

A surge of impatience made him wish he'd avoided this. He didn't need to think about Maggie. "Where's Jake?" he asked abruptly, and saw her eyes darken.

She smiled shakily and pulled him into the parlor to push him down into a huge, stuffed chair near the fire. She took his hat and tossed it to a nearby table, then dragged a pillow over to sit at his feet. "Jake's gone down to the mine to check on things. He goes twice a month, just to be certain things are running smoothly."

"Quite a businessman now, huh."

"Don't sound so bitter. Yes, I suppose he is." She gave him a searching look. "You could have stayed, you know. The mine is half yours."

"I told you—"

"I know. You don't want it. Too bad. Half of it has been put into a bank account in Denver in your name for the past four and a half years, and has probably earned a great deal of interest by now. You're probably richer than you've got a right to be."

His mouth tightened in grim surprise. He hadn't known, but apparently Maggie had. The brief memory of a pile of newspaper clippings flashed into his mind. Some of the puzzle pieces fell into place, but it wasn't very comforting. He shook his head.

"Dammit, Kate, don't you ever listen to me?"

"Not when you're being stupid. Oh Devon, don't look at me like that. You were so wild with grief when I last saw you, but I always thought you'd get over it and come back. Do you really think I'd spend your inheritance?"

He shifted restlessly. "No. Guess not. You should have. A ranch like this doesn't run on wishes."

"No, but Jake has plenty of money of his own. His grandfather, remember."

"Yeah, the millionaire merchant of Philadelphia, or something like that."

"Jacob is a fine man. And a doting great-grandfather. He comes often to visit."

"Unlike your brother," Devon drawled, catching the faint hint of censure in her tone. "Didn't think you'd want your low-class family hangin' around with swells like him."

"You sound contemptuous."

That startled him. "Do I? I don't mean to."

"Devon . . ." She rose to her knees in a rustle of skirts and took his hands in her own. "Devon, I know what happened was horrible. It was for me, too. But it's over. It's in the past."

"Not for me." He saw the flash of protest in her eyes and shook his head. "Kate, I know you're trying to help, but don't. I wanted to see you again. Don't make me sorry I came."

She sank back onto the pillow and stared up at him with wide, miserable eyes. He shouldn't have come. Everything he touched in his life he hurt somehow. Why had he ever thought he could see Kate and not feel the old rage, the old pain? He couldn't. And it was rubbing off on her.

"You don't mean that, Devon," she said at last. "Haven't you missed me? Aren't you glad to see me?"

That pierced something inside him, and he felt a surge of protective love for his sister that he'd almost forgotten he could feel. The years of loss and loneliness were suddenly unbearable.

"Yes." His voice was husky with emotion. "God, yes. I've missed you, Kate . . ."

"Then don't shut me out now."

Tears filled her eyes and overflowed, and he sighed as he reached out to wipe them away. Before today, he could recall only one other time he'd seen her weep.

That had been in the cave when she'd been recovering from bullet wounds and had awoke to find gentle Molly dead and her brother empty of emotion. It hadn't touched him then, though he'd felt a detached sense of pity that she was so distraught. Now it seared him to the bone to see her tears, but he couldn't allow himself to show it.

"Don't cry, Kate. I hate to see you cry. My collar's still wet from the last time."

She fumbled in her skirt pocket for a handkerchief, drew it out, wiped her face, then blew her nose. He couldn't help a faint smile at the sniffling sounds she made.

"Don't laugh," she muttered, words muffled by the scrap of cotton and lace. "I'm always emotional when I'm pregnant. I'm like a waterfall."

"Another baby?" His brow lifted again. "Haven't you figured out yet what causes that?"

She glared at him over the handkerchief, but he saw the tugging of a smile at her lips and in her eyes. "Don't be crude."

"I seem to recall you not always bein' quite so dainty, Colorado Kate."

"And I seem to recall you not always being quite so grim, Cimarrón."

Shock was quickly replaced with amusement. "You know more about me than you pretend."

"I keep up. I can read, you know."

He glanced across the hall to the large room filled with floor-to-ceiling shelves crammed with books. "So I see. Anything besides novellas?"

"A few things. Jake hired a tutor for me. It opened up an entirely new world."

"I'm sure it did." He brushed a finger over the tip of her nose and grinned. "You've conquered all the other worlds, it seems. Wife. Mother. Socialite."

"Outlaw," she reminded, eyes lighting a little and losing some of their shadows at his teasing.

"Ever miss it?"

"Miss what? Lonely nights punctuated by stark fear? Not me, Devon Conrad. I'm not a complete fool. I like having someone to love and having someone love me. I spent too many years without it not to appreciate what I have now."

"Yeah." He looked away. "I can imagine."

She took his hand. "No love in your life, Devon? Do you think Molly would want to know that she'd ruined you this way?"

He snatched his hand away and stood up. Kate shifted back to watch when he stalked to the long window that looked out over snow-capped mountain peaks. It took him a moment before he could say calmly, "Molly didn't ruin me. I ruined myself."

"Well. At last. Something we can agree on."

He turned to look at her. "Don't feel like you have to sugarcoat anything for me, Kate. Be blunt."

"Thank you." She rose to her feet and smoothed her skirts with one hand, a dainty feminine gesture that seemed alien to the way he remembered her. "While I'm being blunt, dear brother, why don't I remind you that you can't take the guilt of the world on your shoulders."

"I don't know what you're talking about."

"Bull dust."

"Ever delicate Kate," he mocked, and saw the flush rise to stain her cheeks. This was a Kate he was more familiar with, not the prim and proper young matron that had made him feel more distanced than ever before. She was glaring at him, hands curled into fists on hips covered by an expensive dress, her green eyes blazing with fury.

"Damn you, Devon Conrad!" Her foot slammed against the floor with an angry thump. "You're trying to distract me with insults. It won't work. I won't let you. If no one else cares enough about you to tell you that you're ruining your life, I will."

"How kind and noble. I'll remember that at least until I get to the Colorado border."

She caught him before he reached the door, and jerked him around by the arm. "Don't you do this again, Devon. Are you going to be a coward all your life?"

That stung. "I'm no coward."

"Aren't you? Afraid to look back, afraid to look forward, afraid to be loved, afraid *to* love—I call that cowardly. What do they call it down in Texas?"

"Sensible."

She stepped close, rising to her toes and shoving her nose in his face. "Don't you mean stupid?"

He was caught between rage and grudging amusement. Kate never had done things by half. He shook his head.

"Do you talk to Jake this way?"

"If he needs it." She stepped back, and some of the anger faded from her face, though the flush remained to make her eyes look even brighter and greener. "I never thought I'd feel sorry for Lassiter until now. I don't know how he puts up with you."

"He manages."

Devon lifted his shoulders in a helpless shrug. "What do you want from me, Kate?"

"First, I want you to stay a while. Don't run off yet. Meet my children. Talk to Jake. Let yourself relax a bit."

He blew out a heavy breath and let her lead him back into the parlor. He'd forgotten his hat anyway, he told himself. No point in leaving a good hat behind just because of an irritating female.

# CHAPTER 19

Spring was rapidly easing into early summer. It was already hot, and Maggie straightened slowly, pressing a hand to the small of her back. The ache had returned, sharper this time, and steadier.

She put the small trowel she'd been using to spade the soft dirt of a vegetable bed into a bucket, then started toward the house. When she was near the back porch, she felt the sudden gushing of moisture between her legs. It wet her skirts and frightened her, even though she knew what it was.

"Mrs. Lamb!" Her voice came out a terrified croak, but it was loud enough.

Mrs. Lamb appeared in the open door of the kitchen and sized up the situation at once. "So. It's your time. I must say, I've been expecting this for over a week. You may be early, but you've had all the signs, dear."

Maggie leaned on the older woman gratefully, glad she was there and that she'd borne nine children of her own. The logical part of her brain told her that this was done every day by women all over the world; the irrational, frightened part of her brain offered the argument that it had never been done by her.

While Mrs. Lamb bustled about making all the necessary preparations, assisting Maggie into a clean nightgown and placing towels and cotton pads on her bed, then gathering the instruments from her office, Maggie briefly allowed herself to think of Devon.

He should be here. Damn him. He should be at the

birth of his first child. There had been no word from him, and very little about him. For the past few months, not a hint of a rumor about Cimarrón had been heard. It looked as if he had disappeared.

A pain clamped down on her, and for a moment she could think only of what her body was doing. Then Mrs. Lamb was there, murmuring soothing words and patting her face with a cool, wet cloth.

For the next twelve hours, it became a rhythm. The pain and the cool cloth and soft words, then an easing, until finally the pains rolled atop one another in a continuous swell that made her groan with effort.

"You're doing wonderful, dear," Mrs. Lamb said again and again. "It's almost over now. Almost over."

Maggie convulsed, body arching. Her nightgown was damp with perspiration; a cool breeze came in the open window Mrs. Lamb had forgotten to close, and she could smell the brisk, strong scent of sage. Lamps burned brightly in her bedroom, and she saw the weariness etched into the widow's face as she placed a steaming bowl of water near a pile of clean towels.

"Is everything ready?" Maggie gasped out between the pains, and Mrs. Lamb nodded.

"Of course, dear. I'm the doctor now. You just relax."

Never again, Maggie thought wildly, would she tell a laboring woman to relax. It was impossible. The demands of the body contradicted every effort she made.

But when, at last, the baby slid into the waiting hands of Mrs. Lamb and Maggie heard the thin, wailing cry of her new son, she understood why women followed the biological instinct to be mothers. There was a clutching joy in holding the mewling infant to her chest and watching his small face screw up in a lusty howl that would put any coyote to shame.

Until Mrs. Lamb wiped her face with a dry towel, Maggie didn't realize that she was weeping.

"He's strong and healthy, dear," Mrs. Lamb said as she took the baby to clean him up. "Look at him protest."

"Lungs like leather," Maggie said fondly. "You didn't even have to start him crying."

"No, he came into the world mad as blazes, didn't he?"

Maggie lay back on her pillow, exhausted. She closed her eyes and smiled, listening to her son scream his displeasure with the world and Mrs. Lamb's placating efforts. Devon would have been very proud of his son.

Lindsay Malone rocked gently on the porch with the baby. The rhythmic squeak of the chair going back and forth added to the night sounds of nocturnal creatures in the dusk beyond the house.

"Aren't you going to miss Belle Plain, Maggie?" she asked once, and Maggie turned to look at her.

"There's nothing left to miss. A few people, and those leaving soon. No, I can't say I will."

Lindsay was quiet. The baby made a soft gurgling sound that drew her attention momentarily, then she looked up at her sister-in-law again. "It'd be nice if you'd tell Johnny goodbye."

Silence greeted that comment. Maggie turned to look past Lindsay, staring up the road toward the empty stone buildings that only a year before had held businesses and families. Had it been only a year? Her entire world had been turned upside down in that time. She'd been so full of eager ideals when she'd gotten off the stage in Belle Plain, so naive and foolish.

Well, she'd learned some bitter lessons. And it had made her much stronger.

"I'll tell Johnny goodbye if it will make you happy, Lindsay," she said softly.

Lindsay stopped rocking, and the baby began to

squirm and fret. She stared at Maggie for a moment, then smiled and began rocking again.

"It will make me very happy. Thank you. Can he come tomorrow?"

She hesitated, then nodded.

Maggie thought she was prepared to see her brother again, but the sight of him dismounting from his horse at her back door brought back the sharp, painful memory of the last night she'd seen Devon. She reached out blindly for the support of the kitchen table, grazing her hand on boxes packed and ready to be stowed into the buckboard.

When Johnny stood hesitantly in the open door, hat in his hand and his dark eyes searching her face, Maggie saw his uncertainty. She inhaled deeply and realized that whatever he had done, he'd done it for reasons he thought right.

"Maggie . . ." His voice cracked, and he cleared his throat and tried again. "Lindsay said you're leavin' Belle Plain in the mornin'."

She nodded. "Yes. I've taken a position in Belton. It's a fairly large town and even has a women's college. They are more—progressive—than many Texas towns in that the citizens do not summarily dismiss females as primarily wives and mothers."

Johnny flushed and looked down at his feet. When he heard the baby cry, his head lifted. There was a strange expression in his eyes. Not once had he expressed any interest in seeing Cimarrón's child. It was as if the baby did not exist for him, though Lindsay made frequent visits and a lot of fuss over Joshua. He cleared his throat again.

"That the baby?" he asked gruffly. Maggie nodded but did not offer to get Joshua. Johnny shifted uncomfortably. "I wish you wouldn't go. Not so far, anyway."

Maggie shrugged. "It's not that far. I need a clean start, anyway. And there's nothing for me here."

Johnny's dark gaze was pleading. "Hell, Maggie, I wish I could do things over. I can't. I never meant to hurt you like I did."

"I know. It's over and done with. There's nothing that can be done to change it, and we must go forward. I have a child now. I can't spend my life wishing it were different. I have to make it different, make it the best I can."

He blew out his breath in a heavy sigh. "You're right. I always have admired your backbone. Reckon you can put most men to shame when it comes to gettin' things done." He paused, then asked, "Have you ever heard from him?"

She knew who he meant. "No. I don't expect I shall. It was too much for him before he was ready. I knew he wasn't quite ready for marriage, but I certainly didn't think he would abandon a pregnant wife on her wedding night. People are always surprising me." She steadied her voice and added softly, "I just thought Devon was different."

Johnny twisted his hat in his large, work-roughened hands. "Maggie, there's something I gotta tell you. It . . . it concerns that night and Cimarrón. See, maybe you should know that . . . that. . . ."

She waited, and when he didn't continue, prompted, "Yes?"

He crossed to her and seemed to be searching for words, but before he could say anything, Mrs. Lamb stepped into the kitchen with the baby.

"Oh. I didn't know you had company, dear." She smiled. "Mr. Malone, hasn't your nephew grown like a weed?" She went to him and held up the baby for inspection like a proud mother.

It was an awkward moment, and Maggie saw the internal struggle reflected on Johnny's face as he dragged his eyes toward the baby. Joshua's small fist filled his mouth, and he chewed it solemnly as he returned his uncle's stare. Wide blue eyes that reminded Maggie of Devon focused on the silver concho at Johnny's throat, and he reached for it. Johnny looked startled, then embarrassed when the baby began to howl at being unable to touch it.

"Here." Johnny pulled the concho from the string tie around his neck and held it out to the baby, awkwardly, looking faintly sheepish. It went immediately into Joshua's mouth, and Mrs. Lamb was properly horrified.

"Oh dear, I must wash it first. Do you think it's too big for him to swallow, Maggie?"

"Much too big to swallow, but not too big to choke him. See if you can distract him, please, and I'll give it back to Johnny."

"He can have it." Johnny flushed. "Save it until he's big enough."

While Mrs. Lamb skillfully interested Joshua in a new object that was more acceptable, Maggie and Johnny walked out onto the porch. His spurs jangled, and he turned with an awkward smile to stare down at her.

"Reckon I won't see you again for a while."

"Probably not." On impulse, she moved to hug him, and his big arms went around her in a tight embrace that was almost painful. She felt him shudder, then he relaxed his grip and stepped back. His dark eyes were damp, and his mouth thinned into a grimace.

"Feel like a damn fool."

"That's not incurable, you know." She smiled when he shrugged. "We both made mistakes. And you probably did me a favor, though it certainly didn't seem like it." Because she felt the hot press of tears stinging her eyes and didn't want to cry, she asked, "Have you had any more trouble with rustlers?"

"Not lately. Rogan sold most of his cattle to a big Eastern firm. Guess the rustlers figure there ain't much left to steal out here."

"Is there? Johnny, is the Double M in trouble?"

He raked a hand through his hair, then pulled his hat down to shade his eyes. "I had to sell off some of the land on the north end to pay for feed for this past winter. Hell, it wasn't much more than sand and gullies anyway."

"Who bought it?"

"David Brawley found me a buyer."

"David Brawley?" Maggie's brow lifted. "I thought he went back East."

"Did for a while. He's back in Baird now. Since he'd spent some time out here, the railroad sent him back. He's supervising the hold lots for cattle waitin' to be shipped out of Abilene, too."

"Do you trust him?"

Johnny looked startled. "Yeah. Reckon I do. Why?"

"I don't know. Devon never did."

"Oh." Johnny looked away. He frowned again and shifted from one foot to the other. "Maggie, I was gonna tell you—"

"I'll be staying with Mrs. Lamb tonight while I finish packing," she said quickly. "Once the wagon is loaded, we'll be on our way. I want to be settled in before winter. I'll write."

He looked at her for a moment, then nodded. "All right. I hope you'll be happy there. If you ever want to come back, all you have to do is let me know. There will always be a place for you at the Double M."

"Not once you and Lindsay start filling up that nursery. She's anxious to start a family, and I can tell from the way she holds Joshua that she'll be a wonderful mother."

He grinned. "I ain't too sure I'll be a good father, but I'll sure try."

"You'll be a good father, Johnny. I think we've both done a lot of growing up this past year."

When he'd gone, Maggie leaned against the porch post and thought of Devon. Every time she looked at their son, with his bright, sky blue eyes and tawny hair, she couldn't help but be reminded of him. She wondered if Devon would have been a good father and why he hadn't wanted to stay and try.

Jake Lassiter slid down into the cushions of the sofa and eyed Devon for a long moment. His voice was as rough as Devon had remembered, and he was still blunt.

"You're making Caitlin unhappy."

Devon lifted a brow. "I can leave anytime."

"That will make her more unhappy."

"So what are you suggesting, Lassiter?"

"Agree to stay a while."

"I've been here a while." Devon frowned. "Too long. She keeps prying into my privacy like a damn possum. Thought you would have trained her better by now."

Lassiter laughed. "Train Caitlin? Teaching cows to fly would be easier than getting her to do anything she doesn't want to do. You ought to know that."

Devon stood up and crossed to the window. He'd been back in Colorado almost six months. During that time, Kate had introduced him to every available female in the entire state at least once. She'd poked and prodded into his life with the persistence of a hungry grizzly, and with the same finesse. He was almost crazy from it.

Worse, he couldn't sleep at night without dreaming about Maggie Malone. Every dark-haired woman he saw made his heart leap and his belly knot, and if he didn't do something with this restless feeling inside, he'd end up shooting something or somebody. Maybe Doug was right. He wasn't civilized.

"Hell, Dev," Morton had drawled one night when they'd had too much to drink, "you know what yore trouble is?"

"No," Devon had said, too drunk to resist listening to Doug's opinion. "What's my trouble?"

"You ain't civilized."

"You just figurin' that out?"

"Naw. But you are. Trouble is, you been ridin' that wild hoss too long to know how to get off. I can see it in yore eyes sometimes, when Miss Kate has got you pinned up in a corner with some sweet-smellin' female. Reminds me of an ole hound I had one time." He'd leaned forward to gaze blearily at Devon. "Know what you need? A dog."

"A dog?" Devon had grimaced. "What the hell do I need a dog for?"

"So you'll have somebody that loves you."

Drunk, it had been funny. Sober, he wondered if Doug was right. He needed somebody to love him.

Devon turned away from the window and looked at Jake Lassiter. "Know any lawmen down in Texas, Jake?" He saw the surprise on his brother-in-law's face.

"One or two. Why? Do you think I'll turn you in?"

"If you'd wanted to do that, I'd already be sittin' in jail somewhere." Devon's mouth twisted in a wry smile. "I might be doing that soon anyway."

After a moment, Jake said, "Do you remember Roger Hartman?"

"The U.S. marshal in Colorado? Yeah. I remember him."

"I can put you in touch with him. He's still a marshal. He's not limited to Colorado, you know." There was a pause, then Jake said, "Devon, Kate wants you to stay here."

"I can't stay."

Jake nodded. "Kinda figured you were going to say that. You look like a man who's just remembered something important." He paused. "But you're gonna be the one to tell Caitlin."

It was a lot harder than Devon had thought it would be. Kate stared at him with wide green eyes filled with hurt, and he sighed.

"Kate, I can't stay."

"Why? Dammit, Devon, you can't keep running all your life."

"I know."

"Then why—?"

He took her hands, holding them when she tried to twist away. "Listen to me. I left some unfinished business in Texas. I need to go back."

She succeeded in wrenching her hands away and stared up at him with bitter frustration. "When are you going to find out that you can't single-handedly save the world, Devon? If Texas has managed to stay on the map without you these past six months, it will still be there six months from now. What's so important that you have to go back and risk your life?"

He looked away from her, muscles bunching in his jaw. Kate watched him for a moment, silent and still. Then she asked softly, "Is it a woman?"

"No." That was a lie, partially anyway, and when she reached out to turn him to face her, he saw that she knew it. He sighed. "I have a bounty on my head, Kate. For two murders I didn't do. It's time I took care of that."

"Was it over a woman?"

He laughed. "No. Don't start coming up with crazy ideas like that. I wasn't anywhere near when those men were killed. Actually, at the time, I was taking care of other business."

She shivered. "You never used to talk about killing men so casually."

"I never used to kill men so casually." His mouth thinned into a tight line. "I still don't. You've probably heard all the rumors about Cimarrón, but half of them are pure fiction."

"I know how it is, Devon. We used that to our advantage, remember." She bit her lower lip, fighting a smile. "Even Jake was surprised to find out we'd never killed anyone in any of our robberies. People who only read the papers are even more shocked to find out the truth. I guess it's more exciting to believe the worst instead of the best."

Devon thought of the clippings Maggie had read. It still rankled that she'd known so much about his past. He should have been more careful. He should have read more. It would have saved him a lot of trouble.

"Right," he said, "but it's not so exciting to wonder when a bounty hunter is going to end up at the door."

"Bounty hunter?" She looked startled.

"Yeah. If it wasn't for Jake being an ex-lawman, I'd probably be wearing chains and bruises right now."

"No one knows you're here."

"Kate," he said with a sigh, "everyone in this part of Colorado knows I'm here. You haven't kept it a secret. And you've made damn sure I've met every single female you could talk into coming near me."

"That was the easy part. Getting you to go near them was damn near impossible." Her eyes narrowed, lashes casting long shadows on her cheeks and making her look like a curious cat. "It *is* a woman, isn't it? There's a woman in Texas. Tell me about her."

He shrugged. "Not much to tell. She's probably counting her blessings that I'm gone."

"Don't be stupid. I hate it when you say dumb

things. If she's got any sense at all, she's probably crying into her pillow every night."

Devon's mouth twisted. "I don't think so. Not Maggie. She's not the type to cry." He paused, recalling her wild sobbing when he'd ridden away. Her cry had echoed in his ears and mind and heart for longer than he wanted to think about. Sometimes he thought he could still hear it, especially when the wind was blowing through the pines or aspens and making that soft, sighing sound that was so mournful.

"Devon?" Kate came to put her hand on his arm. She was frowning. "Devon, what is it?"

"Hell, Kate, I ruin everything I touch." He gave her a bitter look. "My life is one long example of that. First our parents were killed while I hid in a damn well and listened. Then Molly was cut down by bullets meant for me, and so were you. It's a damn miracle you're still alive." He couldn't help the raw pain that vibrated in his voice, the words that wouldn't stop coming. "And Ralph Pace—he was just a scared, lonely kid who made me think of how I always felt inside. Jesus, even killing his murderer didn't make things better. And then Latigo was crippled because of me, and even those men in Abilene were killed because someone wanted people to think I did it. God." He raked a hand through his hair, giving in to the bitterness. "And Maggie. She's the worst of all, I think."

"Maggie." Kate's voice trembled. He heard it but didn't know how to ease her. "Did she die, Devon? Is that what has you so wracked with guilt and remorse?"

Devon turned to look at her. "No. I thought she . . . loved me. I was wrong."

"What makes you think she doesn't?"

He didn't answer. Nothing could induce him to try to put that night into words. He sighed, suddenly weary.

"Just let it go, Kate."

"Let it go? No, dammit, I have no intention of letting anything go." Anger threaded her voice, and he lifted a brow when she grabbed the front of his shirt as if to shake him. "Don't be so damn noble! Do you honestly think you're responsible for all those deaths? I was hiding in that well, too, remember. Am I supposed to lie awake at night and tear myself apart with guilt for not dying, too? I won't. And I won't let you. Durant killed Molly. It was his bullet and his greed that did it. Oh Devon, I don't know the others, but somehow I think they managed to get killed on their own. You weren't responsible."

"Responsible enough."

"God, Devon, what's wrong? It can't be just guilt for things beyond your control. You . . . you don't even look the same. Your eyes are so cold now, and even when you laugh or smile, there's this sense of danger around you. As if you could break into violence at any moment."

"That's the way I feel most of the time, Kate." He blew out an exasperated breath. "Leave it alone, will you?"

She shook her head, bright coppery strands coming loose from a neat braid to tangle on her neck. "No. I won't. You're my brother. I love you. I'll always love you. I know what they say about you, that you can kill a man and not blink an eye, but I don't believe it."

"Believe it. If it's the right man, I can do it and not think twice about it."

She searched his face a moment and apparently saw something there to convince her. Her lower lip trembled until she caught it between her teeth to steady it. "Maybe you can. But I know you well enough to know that you're not as cold as you want to think."

"Christ, Kate, will you drop this?" He stepped away

and ran a hand through his hair, wishing he'd just left in the middle of the night and avoided this.

"Devon—if you love this Maggie, then you need to go back to Texas and marry her."

Devon couldn't help the harsh burst of laughter that made Kate's eyes widen. "Marry her, Kate? You're too late with that suggestion. I already did."

# CHAPTER 20

A brisk wind blew a cloud of thick dust across the road. It hung there for a moment, almost as if suspended, then drifted into streamers. Devon reined in his horse. He'd pulled his bandanna up over his nose and mouth to keep out the blowing dust, and now he slowly pulled it down as if it would help clear his vision.

Weeds choked empty streets. A loose shutter banged loudly in the wind. Stones were tumbled in small piles, and some of the wooden boardwalks had been ripped up and carried away. Clumps of cactus had begun sprouting in the middle of Texas Street. Belle Plain had become a ghost town.

Even with this evidence, he couldn't help turning his horse toward the small house on the other edge of town. It was as if he was drawn there by an unseen cord, a strong pull that he couldn't resist.

It was empty, of course. He'd known it would be. He stood in the vacant kitchen and listened to the wind whispering around the corners. A broken window pane allowed a dry, brown leaf to flutter in and drift to the floor that was littered with dust and the careless scatterings of small animals. The stove was gone, and so was the icebox Maggie had been so proud of. No curtains hung at the windows, and the back door sagged drunkenly from a broken hinge.

Drawn by an urge he couldn't explain, Devon went from room to room as if to verify that nothing remained. There was no hint of who had lived here or that anyone had ever cared about the house.

When he reached the room that had been her office, he found it empty save for a clay pot of dead flowers. It sat in the middle of the floor as if forgotten, brittle stalks sticking forlornly into the air.

Devon sank to the floor beside it and remembered seeing the bright blossoms that Maggie had once tended so carefully. He didn't know why he felt so bad, so abandoned. He'd come back to Belle Plain with the intent of confronting her with his anger at her betrayal, but now he felt strangely defused. There was only this sense of loss, as if he'd hoped for something else when he saw her again.

He didn't know how long he sat there. When he finally got up, he was stiff with cold. His spurs rattled loudly as he walked back down the echoing hallway and went outside. Pardo was grazing on tufts of grama grass that had smothered the pretty Texas roses he'd seen growing wild by the back door last summer. Funny thing about Texas roses—most wild roses were red or pink. Texas roses were a deep purple.

Devon swung into his saddle and reined Pardo around, still feeling a sense of unreality at the quiet desertion around him. He walked the dun to the front of the house and saw the dangling chain that had once held a sign.

*Dr. Margaret Anne Malone, M.D.*

He sat there a moment, picturing the shingle and the day he'd stopped to talk to her.

*"So you're the new lady doctor in town?"* he'd said with a feeling of astonishment blending with amusement at the way she was staring up at him. Her response had been prompt and pert.

*"I am. I take it you're the new Rogan gunman in town?"*

He hadn't been able to help grinning at her. *"You don't mince words, Miss Maggie Malone."*

*"Not usually. Unless I have a reason to do so. Care to have a seat and enjoy a cool breeze?"*

She'd looked so poised and beautiful, sitting there in a chair on her front porch and almost daring him to fall in love with her. Well, he had, despite all the good reasons not to. He deserved what he'd gotten.

So why was he going after her now? It just didn't make sense, but he turned his horse toward the Double M.

"Johnny."

There was an odd quiver in Lindsay's voice that made him look up from the ledgers on his desk. He frowned. "Yeah?"

"We . . . we have a visitor."

"Damn, Lindsay, I'm tryin' to balance these books. Can't Hank or—"

"No." She slipped into the room. "No, he wants to see you. Johnny—it's Cimarrón."

Shock rendered him speechless for a moment, and he saw from the fine white lines curving around her mouth that Lindsay was afraid of his reaction. He was, too. Cimarrón. Here, at the Double M. He didn't have to ask why. He knew, with a swift, sick feeling, why he'd come.

Maybe he should have told Maggie what he'd done, how he'd kept the knowledge of the baby from Cimarrón, but he had been too big a coward. God, Maggie would have looked at him with those wide gray eyes so full of hurt and disbelief, and after all that had happened to her, he just hadn't been able to get up the courage to tell her that her brother was the cause of most of her pain.

Now Cimarrón was here and retribution was at hand. But he had no intention of letting him hurt Maggie anymore than had already been done. *Christ.*

He was standing but didn't remember getting up, and was at the door before Lindsay caught his arm.

"Promise me you won't start anything. He's not wearing a gun."

He stopped at that and turned around. "I don't believe that for a minute. He may not be wearin' it where you can see it, but I've never known any gunman not to have at least three more weapons somewhere on him."

"Johnny—I think he wants to find Maggie."

That wasn't unexpected. He nodded. "I'll bet he does."

"Will you tell him?"

His hand tightened on the doorknob. He could still see Maggie's face that night, her eyes wide and hurt, and hear her anguished cries. That had been his fault. He'd interfered when he shouldn't, and he knew that now. Could he do so again?

"I don't know."

Lindsay must have heard the misery in his voice, because she came to him and put her arms around him. "She loves him, Johnny. I know she does. Maybe he had a reason that we don't know about for leaving her when she was pregnant."

The now-familiar flush of shame burned into his throat. He should tell Lindsay. He should have told Maggie. He just hadn't been able to do it. He stroked Lindsay's hair with an awkward motion.

"Hell, Lindsay. He didn't know she was pregnant. I only told him that she sent me after him, that she'd collect the bounty on his head if he didn't cooperate. He didn't *know*."

He wished he could recall the words as soon as they were out. Lindsay slowly moved away from him, her eyes wide and green and accusing. "Why?"

How could he answer that? He shook his head. "I don't know. I was crazy mad. Hurt. Convinced he'd hurt her more if I didn't do something. So, I did the wrong thing."

"But you told Maggie that he knew about the baby."

His throat tightened painfully. "Yeah. I know. I had to tell her something that would make her mad enough to stop hurtin' so bad. It worked, but . . . but it wasn't true."

"John Clark Malone, I never thought I would be ashamed of you, but I am now. It was bad enough, beating that man and then forcing him into a shotgun marriage when Maggie asked you to let them work it out alone, but now, to hear that you lied to both of them—is that why Daddy avoids you?"

He nodded miserably. "Yeah."

"I wondered. He wouldn't say." Lindsay drew in a deep breath. "Well, there's only one thing you can do to make some kind of amends."

"Don't say it. I won't tell him that. It wouldn't help, and it's too late anyway."

"That's not your decision to make. You have to tell the truth. Johnny, you have to."

He pulled open the door and stepped out into the hall. Weak sunlight made grayish patches on the floor under the windows, and he saw the faint flicker of a shadow. Cimarrón. Damn. After eleven months, he'd thought he'd never see him again. He sucked in a deep breath and walked down the hallway to the parlor.

Cimarrón stood near the piano, running his hand idly over the smooth wood. He turned when Johnny stood in the doorway.

"Malone."

"Cimarrón." When silence fell, Johnny cleared his throat. "My wife tells me you want to talk to me."

"Yeah. I do." Cimarrón lifted his arms away from his body. An empty holster was tied to his thigh. "I'm not wearing a gun. I just want some answers."

"I don't know if I can help you until I hear the question." He walked to the sideboard flanking the door. "Do you want a drink?"

"No. Just some answers."

Johnny shrugged and poured himself a drink. When he turned to look at him, Cimarrón was still standing by the piano on the other side of the door. There was a quiet intensity in his gaze that was unnerving. Johnny tossed down the drink and set his empty glass on the sideboard.

"What's your question?"

"Still got rustlers?"

That was unexpected. Johnny's mouth curled in a slight smile. "Do you care?"

"Not for the reason you might think."

That was almost as unnerving as the stare from those cold, opaque eyes that held no hint of life or emotion. No mercy, no pity was evident in that hard, ruthless face, and Johnny saw now more than ever before why some men turned and ran rather than endure Cimarrón's scrutiny. It seemed to reach inside him, search out all his secrets, and bring them out into the light for closer observation.

He wanted another drink. He reached for the glass and decanter again, and felt Cimarrón watching him narrowly. His hand hovered, fingers brushing the cut-glass design, then curled into a fist. Damn him.

"No rustlers. Not here, anyway." He turned back to look at him. "You'd have to ask the other ranchers. I don't keep up with what they're doin'."

"You still shipping out your cattle on the T&P?"

"Damn. You workin' for the railroad now?"

"No. I work alone. I always did."

Johnny bristled. There was an implied threat in that if he cared to look below the surface of the words. He almost wished Cimarrón was wearing a gun; then the memory of that icy night when he'd drawn his pistol with blurring speed despite the rope around him quickly dissipated the half-formed thought.

Spurs rattled as Cimarrón shifted position, running a bare hand over the gleaming wood of the piano. "You know, Malone, Zeke Rogan hired me to find the rustlers that were stealing his cattle. I don't think he really wanted me to actually do it, though." He glanced up, catching Johnny off guard. "What I think he wanted was someone to get rid of some folks who'd gotten inconvenient."

Johnny's mouth twisted. "I ain't never met a rustler yet that was convenient. 'Less it was to another rustler."

"Or to the men who bought stolen beef."

"Damn you. Are you tryin' to say that I bought—"

"No. But I think you know who did."

Johnny blinked. Cimarrón didn't. There didn't seem to be a speck of color in his eyes, though he knew full well that there was. The clear shimmer surrounded black pupils that made him think of the steady stare of a snake, and he shook his head to dispel the image. Apparently Cimarrón took it to mean that he disagreed with him.

"Think about it, Malone. Maybe the men you're trying to protect wouldn't like the thought of you talking to me. It's a dangerous situation." His mouth curled into a mocking smile. "But since we're family, I know I can count on your discretion. Right?"

Johnny's jaw tightened. "Why is it everything you say sounds like a threat, Cimarrón?"

"I don't make threats. I don't like them. Remember?"

He remembered. *I don't like threats, and I don't like the men who make them,* he'd said that night.

"Are you through askin' questions, Cimarrón?"

"One last one. Where's Maggie?"

"She's *your* wife. Can't you keep up with her?"

"Let's not play that game. Where is she?"

He hesitated. If Maggie had wanted him to know where she was, wouldn't she have left word? Damn, he'd made so many mistakes already, he sure as hell didn't want to make another one. And Cimarrón didn't exactly look like he was in the mood for a happy reunion.

"She left town. That's all I can tell you."

"I don't believe you."

Anger narrowed his eyes and shortened his temper. "I don't give a damn if you do or don't. If Maggie wanted you to know where she was, she'd have told me. She didn't. Maybe she wants to forget she's married to a man like you."

Cimarrón grew still. He didn't seem to even breathe for a moment. Then some of the tension left him and he lifted his brow.

"If she wanted that, she shouldn't have sent you after me that night. Gotta be careful about that kinda stuff, you know. Sometimes you find out that what you thought you wanted ain't too good for you."

Now was the time to tell him the truth, when he was unarmed and fairly reasonable, but Johnny didn't. Maybe he *had* wronged him, but he'd done it for the right reasons, dammit. Lindsay was wrong. She just didn't see it the way it was. All she saw was that Maggie had loved him and he'd left her behind, not knowing she was pregnant with his child. She didn't understand that a man like Cimarrón would never be able to make Maggie happy. Hell, he'd be killed before another year was out. Gunmen never lived long.

"I don't know where she is," he repeated.

"*I do.*"

Johnny groaned silently, and both men turned to see Lindsay in the doorway. She wouldn't look at him but went to Cimarrón and held out a scrap of paper.

"This is her address. I think you should go and talk to her, Mr. Conrad. It would do you both good."

Cimarrón took the paper, glanced at it, then folded it and put it in his inside vest pocket. "Thank you, ma'am. Is she all right?"

Lindsay hesitated, and Johnny thought for a moment she intended to blurt out the entire truth. But she didn't, only nodded and said, "Yes, she was doing fine the last time I saw her."

"I'm grateful for your help." He started toward the door, then paused to look at Johnny. "Yours too, Malone."

"What did he mean by that?" Lindsay asked when he'd gone and the front door had shut behind him.

"Nothin'." Johnny stared at the empty space where Cimarrón had been. "Nothin' at all."

It had been a full day. Maggie had stitched up cuts and set two broken bones and dug a bullet out of a rowdy cowboy who'd drank too much and shot himself in the foot. She hoped that this night was quiet, because the last three hadn't been.

Belton was on a portion of the Chisholm Trail, and herds of longhorns were still driven up the trail to a shipping point to send to market. Liquored-up cowhands looked forward to a rest stop in the town, and that, of course, meant brawls and bullets.

"You need to get some rest, dear," Mrs. Lamb said when Maggie dragged herself from her office into the small parlor across the hall. "Joshua is asleep, and I will tend to any but the most critical patients. You've not been getting your rest lately."

"You know, I may take you up on that suggestion." Maggie looked at the stuffed chair and footstool next to the reading table and knew that if she sat down, she would end up spending the night in that chair. She'd done it before, too weary to get up and go to bed.

"Take the lamp on the hall table. It has fresh oil in it," Mrs. Lamb said, and turned her attention back to the mending.

Maggie smiled. If not for Amelia Lamb, she would have been mired in household tasks too numerous to name, not to mention the constant care for the baby. It would have been impossible to perform her medical duties. It was easy to see why many women had to surrender their ambitions in the face of a daily routine, unless they had help.

She'd met some of them, downtrodden, defeated women who suffered abuse from their husbands or even fathers, and had no recourse but to accept it. A woman had no rights, no vote, not even her own property. Upon marriage, all that she owned went to her husband, while he kept what was his. He could even take away a woman's children if she left him.

It didn't seem fair, and Professor Goodwin at the Mary Hardin-Baylor College that had been established in 1845 frequently invited speakers from the Woman's Suffrage Movement to lecture. Maggie had attended a few of those meetings and found herself eager and enthralled. Unfortunately the demands of her life left little time to focus on them.

This house was a bit larger than the one in Belle Plain and had been one of those houses that one could order from a catalog. There were a lot of those types of houses in Belton, and Maggie had been quite amused to see the graceful lines and sometimes too-ornate curlicues that looked as if they had been pressed out with a cookie cutter. But it was progress, just like the advances that were being made with women's rights.

She picked up the lamp and started down the hallway, pausing to look in on Joshua before she continued to her bedroom at the very back of the house. He was a good baby, though an active one. Poor Mrs. Lamb looked quite frazzled at times from caring for him. Her bed was near his, so that if he woke in the night, he wouldn't have to cry for attention.

A cool breeze lifted the curtains over her window, and Maggie set the lamp down on a table across the room. She should probably use the gas lamps, but she hated the hissing sound and the smell that went with the convenience. Oil lamps provided light when and where it was needed.

Her clean nightgown lay across the bed, and Mrs. Lamb had already turned down the quilt. Pillows were plumped in an invitation that made Maggie quickly unbutton her dress and pull it off to hang on a hook behind the door. She washed her face and hands and took the pins from her hair, letting it fall free around her shoulders.

Her heavy, silver-backed hairbrush and hand mirror lay on the chest of drawers, a gift from her parents on her twelfth birthday. She could remember her mother brushing out her hair for her, lovingly dragging the brush through the length as they talked at night. It was still a familiar, comforting ritual, to brush her hair and slowly relax. When she had brushed it just enough to remove the tangles, she slipped out of her undergarments and into her gown.

The floor was cool, and she curled her bare toes up as she buttoned her gown. A gust of wind caught the curtains again, bringing the smell of rain into the room. She went to close the window, and the lamp guttered and died, plunging the room into darkness. Maggie paused.

It could have been the wind, of course, but she had put the lamp across the room. The skin on the back of her neck grew taut, and she was suddenly aware of someone in the room with her. She didn't move. It was dark. Maybe they couldn't see her. Was her pistol still in the drawer of her bedside table? She couldn't remember. Joshua got into so much, his busy little hands pulling open drawers and doors and creating a mess, and it was all they could do to keep things out of his reach since he'd started crawling.

She finally edged toward her bed, moving cautiously and holding her breath, trying to pinpoint the location of whoever was trespassing in her room. She'd heard no sound, no indication other than the sudden dousing of the lamp and the fact that her instincts told her she wasn't alone.

Her toes grazed the leg of the bedside table, and she slowly slid her hand up to find the drawer handle. Her heart was thumping furiously, and she had the distracted thought that anyone else in the room could probably hear it. There was only a slight, grating sound as the drawer slid open, and she slipped her hand inside to fumble for the pistol.

A loud *snick* came from only a few inches away, and she gasped when she heard a low, rasping voice drawl, "Looking for this?" There was a solid metallic click, as if a hammer striking on an empty chamber.

Maggie could hardly breathe. It wasn't the unmistakable click of the gun that terrified her. It was the voice. She knew that voice.

Before she could force her paralyzed muscles to respond to her brain's frantic urging to move, a hard, warm hand closed around her wrist and gripped it in a crushing vice. She felt a movement at her side, heard the bedsprings creak a protest, then she was being pulled downward. She sank with a sudden plop onto the mattress. Her legs were too weak to hold her upright now anyway. Reaction made her shiver, and when she heard the sound of a striking match and saw the brief, bright ellipse of light illuminate his face, she closed her eyes.

*Devon.*

And he had looked distinctly hostile. God, he still blamed her for that night, still hated her for being a part of something she'd had no control over. When her muscles stopped quivering and she thought she could speak without degenerating into stuttering gasps, she'd tell him what had happened. And then she would tell him to leave.

"You can open your eyes now, Maggie."

His cold voice held no hint of welcome, no hint that he would be agreeable to hearing an explanation. A spurt of anger momentarily drowned out her smothering fear. How dare *he* be angry at *her?*

Her eyes snapped open. The lamp had been lit again, and she realized that he must have been hiding in the shadows of the corner. She flushed. He'd watched her undress and get ready for bed. Somehow, it was embarrassing, even with what had been between them before.

"What are you doing here, Devon?"

"I've come to visit my wife. Aren't you happy to see me?"

"I see you haven't lost your penchant for sneaking into open windows," she returned coldly, ignoring his question.

"I meet a lot of interesting people that way."

"No doubt." She glared at him. He didn't look in the least bit uncomfortable. He was sprawled on her bed as if he belonged there, his lean frame as predatory and dangerous as it had always been. A cattleman coat was open and loose, tangling around his long legs. Corduroy pants fit him snugly, and the ever-present gun and holster was tied to his thigh by a leather thong. Lamplight gleamed in his bright hair with silvery glints that made her think of Joshua. Did Devon think about his son? The thought scared her.

"Your muddy boots are making smears on my quilt," she said to hide her fear, but he only lifted a dark brow and didn't seem about to budge.

Devon still held her wrist, his fingers biting into the

tender skin in a painful grip. "Don't be shy, Maggie. Say anything that comes to mind."

"Please leave."

"Ah." His grip tightened and she winced. "Anything but that."

"Devon, what are you doing here?"

"I told you."

"No, I mean—"

"How did I find you? Maybe I'll tell you that later. For now, just relax. You look as if you think I intend to do something terrible."

"Don't you?"

"Poor, guilty Maggie. Conscience burning?"

She tried to jerk away, glaring at him. "No, if you must know, my conscience is enjoying excellent health. How's yours?"

"Ah, if I had one—which I don't—it would probably be as smooth as new-fallen snow."

Maggie frowned. He sounded different. Hard, yes, but he'd always sounded that way. It was the way he was talking, as if he wanted her to say something specific. She felt a wave of nausea. She wished he'd go away. She'd not been prepared for this, not thought he would even bother to look for her, much less show up in her bedroom. Maybe old habits died hard.

"What do you want from me?"

He smiled at her curt question and reached out a hand to toy with the loose hair hanging over her shoulder. The backs of his fingers brushed against her breast, and she couldn't help a shiver. Her eyes were on his, and she saw the quick explosion of light in them at her reaction, then it was gone. He clenched his fist in her hair to pull her slowly toward him.

"Oh Maggie, my sweet little fraud, I don't think you are ready to hear what I want from you."

"Devon—"

"No. Don't say anything. I'm not sure I could keep from hurting you."

His hand shifted, fingers spreading to curve around her throat in a light, threatening clasp. They tightened briefly, constricting the air in her throat, then relaxed. She drew in a shuddering breath and wasn't at all reassured by his cold smile. His hand dropped away and he coiled his body away from the bed in a smooth motion that made her think of the sudden strike of a rattlesnake.

"Get up, Maggie. Put your clothes back on."

"Why?"

"Don't ask questions." He jerked her up, one hand curling in her hair to tug her head back sharply so that she had to look up at him. His face was only inches from hers, and she wanted to flee from the hot condemnation she saw in his eyes. "Get dressed, Maggie."

When he released her and reached for the dress hanging on a hook behind the door, she backed away, hands behind her as she searched frantically for something to use as a weapon. This wasn't the Devon she remembered. This was an angry, determined desperado who had vengeance on his mind, and she was suddenly quite terrified of him.

She bumped into the chest of drawers, and her fingers grazed the hand mirror. She clutched at it, staring at Devon when he turned back with her dress in his hand. He looked so intimidating that any lingering hope she'd held that he might be persuaded to listen was extinguished. This Devon would not listen.

He held out the dress. "Are you going to put it on, or do you want me to do it for you? I'm not real handy with all those female hooks and buttons, so you might end up a bit uncomfortable if I have to do it."

"I seem to recall your being more handy with removing my clothes, it's true." She didn't move, stalling for time as he eyed her coldly. The impatient snap of his voice told her that he knew what she was doing.

"Dammit, put the dress on."

Maggie pushed away from the chest of drawers and moved toward him slowly. She clutched the mirror in one hand and reached for the dress with the other, her gaze never leaving his face. She couldn't let him do this to her. It was obvious he had no intention of listening to any explanation, and she had the terrifying thought that he was angry enough to do anything, even take Joshua from her.

Devon's grip was firmly on the dress, and Maggie gave it a sudden jerk that snapped him forward. She brought up the mirror in a slashing swing toward his head. He ducked, swearing, and caught her arm with his free hand, forcing it up and behind her back.

"Let go of it," he snarled. His fingers tightened around her wrist until she gasped with pain, and he held her so tightly against his chest that the press of his belt buckle against her stomach was hard and sharp. "Drop it!"

She didn't want to, but the pressure of his thumb into the tendons of her wrist forced her fingers into a numbing release, and she heard the mirror crash to the floor and break. A faint sob of fury escaped her. She could barely breathe. His muscles were taut and steely, and she felt him slowly relax them enough to allow her to drag in a tortured breath of air.

"If you try anything like that again," he said between clenched teeth, "I'll blister your ass. You got that?"

"How primitive." Her words would have been more effective if her voice had been steadier, but she saw the faint flash in his eyes that told her it had some effect. He gave her a slight shove away from him, still holding her wrist.

"Maggie, you have no idea just how primitive I can be."

"Oh, I think I'm finding out."

His smile was as cold as his eyes. "Not yet. But you will."

She considered screaming for Mrs. Lamb. Terror was slowly squeezing the breath from her lungs, terror and a choking sadness. It shouldn't be like this. None of this should be happening. She didn't understand what had gone so wrong and how the Devon she had known and fallen in love with had evolved into this snarling, dangerous predator. Even with his fierce reputation as a killer, there had been a soft, sweet sensitivity to him that had contradicted what others said. Now she wondered how she could have been so wrong and so foolish.

Devon backed her over to the bed, not taking his eyes from her. He wedged her between the mattress and his hard body, and began to pull the dress down over her head and her nightgown. He was rough, and Maggie struggled furiously but ineffectively. Her hair caught painfully in one of the buttons, bringing tears to her eyes when he jerked it loose. Her elbow came up in reaction, jabbing into his throat.

He grabbed her wrist, breathing hard, eyes flinty and cold. "Stop wiggling, dammit."

"Let go of me or I'll scream my head off."

"Do that, and I'll take Mrs. Lamb with us." His smile was nasty. "Where we're going, she'd get plenty of attention from some of the men."

Maggie had brief visions of being held captive in a camp filled with armed, dangerous outlaws. Her heart thudded alarmingly. He meant to take her somewhere and hold her, and she had no idea why. Her first inclination was to scream for help, but she knew he'd do what he threatened. Devon wasn't the kind of man who made idle threats. Her head pounded. What did he want? God, if he wanted to hurt her, this was an excellent way.

A paralyzing thought exploded in her brain. He had not mentioned the baby. If he thought about it, he'd know that that would be the way to hurt her most. She had to get him away from the house before Joshua woke up and cried. She had no intention of risking her son when Devon was in such an unpredictable, dangerous mood.

"All right," she whispered thickly. "I'll go with you."

She saw the quick narrowing of his eyes in suspicion, but he only nodded.

Maggie finished dressing in shaking silence, and when she was ready, Devon pulled her with him out the window and into the cold night air. The horses were already saddled, and he put her on her gelding and tied her hands tightly. Hoofbeats were muffled by mud, and there wasn't a sign of a witness to her abduction as they rode slowly out of town.

A light drizzle changed to a driving rain, obliterating their tracks and making Maggie thoroughly miserable. She wondered what he intended to do with her.

# CHAPTER 21

"Where are you taking me?"

Devon ignored her question. Light was beginning to glow on the eastern horizon, a soft, chill promise of dawn. The rain had quit hours before. Black humps of rock jutted up from the ground in hulking shapes that looked almost human at times, keeping him edgy. No one had seemed to notice when he'd taken Maggie from town, but he never trusted the obvious.

Later in the day it would get warmer this far south; now it was cold, and glancing at Maggie, he saw her shiver again. She looked miserable. He wondered if she felt half the misery he did. He hated this. He hated the contradiction of wanting her and resenting her at the same time. Danza would say he was crazy for taking her. He held to the rationalization that it was hardly kidnapping for a man to take his own wife.

Any feelings he might have had for her had vanished when she'd sent her brother after him. It had been replaced with the familiar, icy knot of indifference that had kept him from feeling anything for more years than he could count. Maggie had brought this on herself by caring more for what she thought he was worth than for him. He still didn't understand why, or how he'd been so blind not to see it coming. He'd begun to believe she loved him. *Christ*. He'd begun to believe he loved her. He should have known better. Like he'd told Kate, love wasn't in the cards for a man like him. It never had been.

"Devon."

He looked at her finally. She was slumping in the saddle. Lines of exhaustion marked her face, and her loose, dark hair was whipping into her eyes. He had to hand it to her—she hadn't complained since he'd put her on her gelding and taken up the reins, and he'd set a hard pace. It certainly didn't absolve what she'd done, but it left him feeling a grudging admiration for her fortitude. His mouth set.

"Complainin' already, Maggie?"

Her eyes flashed, and he saw her chin tilt stubbornly. "No. You'll know when I start complaining. I have to relieve myself. Do you want to stop, or do I just—"

"No. I'll stop. Don't get any cute ideas, though. I ain't in the mood to wrestle with you."

"The thought chills me."

He reined in and dismounted to hold her horse. She struggled for a moment, trying to manage her bunched skirts and stiff legs. It was hard with her hands tied in front of her, but he didn't intend to take any chances. Maggie was full of unpleasant little surprises.

She slid down and leaned briefly against the gelding. He could see the resentment in her eyes when she shook back her hair and looked up at him.

"Do I try this with my hands tied, or will you be civilized and allow me to have some freedom? And privacy?"

"I have it on excellent authority that I'm uncivilized. I'm also in a hurry. If you want to waste your time arguin' instead of—"

"Never mind. I get your point." She straightened and jerked around to step to the nearest clump of scrub. He kept his eye on her and wondered with a flash of amusement how a woman physician could be so prim about her own needs when she had absolutely no qualms about discussing his bodily functions.

When she returned, her face a faint pink in the glow of the rising sun, he silently lifted her back atop the bay gelding. It was more unnerving than it should have been to hold her against him, however briefly, and he bitterly cursed the fact that his body hadn't yet seemed to get the message his brain had been forced to accept. Just handling her this casually had him so hard it hurt.

God. When he'd stood in the dark corner of her bedroom and waited, he'd been paralyzed when she began undressing. The heat that had flashed through him caught him off guard, as if he'd never seen her slender white body and lush curves before. There was so much he'd forgotten about her, and he'd remembered her as more slender than she was now. Now she had the full, ripe curves of a woman instead of the coltish grace of a girl. No, he hadn't been at all prepared for the glimpse of her or the need it had ignited in him.

"Keep up," he said roughly to hide the direction of his thoughts, "or I'll drag you along."

There was no need for him to tell her that; she'd kept up well. But the urge to say something harsh and cutting was undeniable and strong. Damn her. She just looked at him, her eyes clear and contemptuous.

"I'll keep up."

She did. He stopped only twice more that day, both times to rest the horses instead of himself or her. He was used to this kind of pace. It was telling on her. He could see it, but the need to put miles between them and Johnny Malone and the Double M riders was imperative.

When the sky began to darken and the sun took warmth with it as it sank behind a ridge of low, chewed hills, Devon found a small cave notched into rock. It wasn't that big, but big enough to hide the horses as well as them.

Maggie fell when she dismounted, her legs going out from under her in a graceless sprawl. He tamped down the immediate urge to help her and watched as she struggled back to her feet. She swayed slightly but followed him into the cave.

It was pitch black near the rear, but the low-ceilinged front still held faint shimmers of light that would be quickly extinguished once the sun went completely down. Devon built a fire while she crouched motionless and silent on a flat shelf of rock. He tossed her a canteen, then rose to tend the two horses. It took him several minutes to get them unsaddled and cooled down; he gave them some water in a shallow pan, then a few handfuls of grain from his saddlebags.

While he took care of the horses, he kept glancing back at Maggie. She didn't seem to have moved but huddled by the fire and stared into the low, leaping flames as if mesmerized. Or on the verge of exhaustion. Devon's mouth tightened. Too bad. She'd asked for this. Just like her brother had asked for what would happen to him.

When he'd stood in the parlor of the comfortable ranch house where Maggie had grown up, it had come to him in a quick flash of comprehension just how easy it would be to put Johnny Malone right where he wanted him. He had the weapon at hand; all he'd had to do was use it. It was almost too easy.

Before, he'd had some half-baked notion of finding Maggie and making her regret what she'd done, then moving on. Divorces were easy enough to get. And he still had those damn murder charges hanging over his head that he needed to get cleared. But it had come to him when Malone had sneered the information that Maggie didn't want to see him, that he could solve all his problems at the same time and with one potent weapon: Maggie.

It was so simple. He should have thought of it months ago, but he'd been too busy burying himself in anger and unanswerable questions to think beyond that. Danza wouldn't agree, and he knew the Apache would offer a mild protest when he saw Maggie, but he'd go along with it. It was the quickest, safest way for Devon to get the men who had framed him for two murders.

He didn't want to think beyond that right now. After it was over with, he'd do what had to be done about Maggie. Now he just acted on instinct and vengeance, powered by it like wind powered the huge windmills that drew up water from the ground.

Maggie was still huddled silently by the fire when he finished with the horses and returned to her, seeming to have withdrawn into herself. It made him as suspicious as it did wary. He didn't remember her having ever been so quiet before unless she was up to something.

"You awake?" he asked roughly, and she glanced up at him.

"Unless this is a nightmare, yes."

He didn't know what to say to that, so let it pass. He guessed it would be a nightmare to have to face up to what she'd done. Hell, he ought to know that. Hadn't he been living in a nightmare for longer than he could remember?

Devon jerked irritably at his saddlebags to drag them closer. He reached inside and took out a couple of flat, hard biscuits and gave them to her. Maggie allowed him to press them into her bound hands, but just stared at them dully.

"Eat, dammit. It's all you're liable to get."

"I'm not hungry."

"You will be by this time tomorrow."

She looked up at him. "Does that mean we won't stop again until then?"

"Probably."

"Devon, where are you taking me?"

Anger jolted him. He bit into a biscuit and chewed it for a minute, then washed it down with water from the canteen. "You don't need to know that."

"But why are you doing this?"

The soft question raked across his already raw temper and made him look at her coldly. "I think you know the answer to that question. If you want to pretend you don't, I can refresh your memory quick enough."

She dropped her gaze, fingers closing around the hard biscuits. "No. No, that's all right."

Somehow, that didn't help his temper either. He ate two more biscuits that he didn't really want and drank sparingly of the water, then rolled out blankets on the floor.

Maggie eyed them for a long moment, and he could almost read her thoughts. "Don't worry," he said nastily, "the only thing I want right now is sleep."

She flushed, and that made him feel better. Still, when he'd stretched out on the cave floor and forced her to lie next to him, he couldn't help remembering how good she'd always felt in his arms. A faint, sweet fragrance teased him, and he tensed. *Roses.* Damn. He was beginning to hate the smell. It reminded him of too many things he should forget.

That night was the longest he'd spent in recent memory, and he stared up at the ceiling of the cave until the fire died down to just faint, glowering embers. Maggie had fallen asleep quickly, and he was alone with his thoughts and his doubts.

"Ride that hoss!"

Men shouted encouragement, waving their hats from safe perches atop the fence rails while a Double

M hand attempted to stay on a wildly bucking horse. Johnny cupped his hands to his mouth. "Don't let him toss you, Blue!"

Dust stung the crisp air. The sweaty smell of horse and rider was pungent and familiar. This was something he enjoyed, the struggle between man and beast. It was almost as much fun to watch as to attempt.

"You gonna try him, Johnny?" Hank asked, leaning on the top rail when Joey Blue ended up in a groaning heap on the ground.

Johnny eyed the snorting stallion prancing in triumph around the corral while hands tried to catch him. "Think I will, Hank."

Some of the tension between them had eased, and he was grateful for it. Though Hank still avoided him most of the time, at least he'd gone back to calling him by his first name instead of the remote, cold "Mr. Malone."

Hank nodded. "Well, be careful. Blue won't be workin' for a few days, maybe a week, looks like."

The stallion had bucked forward, kicking up its hind legs so high that Blue had landed on the hard cantle of the saddle. A groin injury usually had a man down for a while, which was why Johnny preferred buying horses that were already rideable instead of these wild mustangs. But this one had been caught the week before, and the men needed an outlet for the tension that had been riding them hard. Breaking in a bronc had seemed a good way to do it.

Johnny leaped down from the top rail and started toward the middle of the corral. He needed an outlet himself.

"Johnny!"

He paused and turned to see Lindsay running toward the corral, her skirts tossing up as high as her knees. He scowled and moved back to the fence, intending to tell her not to be showing off her legs like that when the men were around. They were respectful of her; hell, half of them had watched her grow up, but there were always the drifters and trail trash who never stayed long that might want to see how well they could do with a pretty woman.

"Lindsay, dammit," he began when he'd climbed over the fence and she'd reached him, but she grabbed his shirt front with a grip that conveyed her distress. "What is it?"

She gulped in air; her voice was wheezy. "Maggie."

"What do you mean?"

Lindsay held up a crumpled piece of paper. "A telegram. Bull Richards brought it from Baird . . . Mrs. Lamb . . . An open window . . . broken mirror . . . Oh, Johnny, this is awful . . ."

He snatched the paper from her hand and smoothed it out, brows dipping into a scowl as he read it. Then he looked up at Lindsay. He knew, but he had to ask.

"Do they know who took her?"

"It had to be him . . . Cimarrón. Oh Johnny, I sent Maggie a telegram warning her he was coming to see her, but I guess he got there before I could get into Baird and send it. So help me, I never thought he'd abduct her like that . . ."

"He's gone too far now, by God. I will kill him for this, and no man can blame me."

"He's her husband, Johnny." Tears rolled down Lindsay's cheeks. "Who's to blame for that?"

Frustration made him want to put back his head and howl his rage into the air. Instead, he snarled, "You should never have told him where she was, dammit."

Lindsay paled. "I was only trying to help. I thought he loved her. I *know* she loves him. With the baby, it seemed right for them to be together."

He gave a harsh laugh. "Well, they're damn sure together now."

Maggie woke slowly. If not for the stinging cuts from the cactus and mesquite branches they'd ridden through, she might have thought she had died during the night. As it was, she ached all over. No, she was in too much discomfort to be anything but alive.

She bit her lip to stifle a groan and turned her head on aching neck muscles. Devon lay beside her, his hard, lean frame stretched out in a casual sprawl that tempted her to give him a sharp jab. It wasn't fair that he should look so peaceful and rested when she was throbbing in places she never remembered having. Not even the trip in the uncomfortable, rocking buckboard all the way from Belle Plain to Belton had been as bad as this. The grueling ride had tested muscles in every part of her body.

Devon's cold fury had tested her soul.

She shivered and let her gaze travel up his body to his face. He was clean-shaven again, with only a night's growth of beard darkening his strong jaw. She wasn't sure if she liked him better with his beard or without, then had the bitter thought that her preference couldn't matter in the least. Why did she even bother considering it? She'd put him out of her mind and heart when he'd callously ridden away and left her behind, pregnant and weeping. It had taken too long for her to accept the finality of his defection to take the risk of getting soft now. No, she'd not allow him to hurt her like that again.

A pale shimmer of light at the mouth of the cave widened a little, and Maggie could see the silhouette of the horses grow sharper and more defined. It would be dawn soon. He would force her to ride again, until she was so far away from anywhere she knew that she'd be totally lost.

It was obvious Devon didn't care about their child. He had not mentioned it once, even to ask if it had survived birth. She was Joshua's only hope. If she were to get away and return to the baby, she had to try to escape even if it meant taking the chance of being caught.

She looked at him again. He was still asleep, his chest rising and falling in an even rhythm. She lifted her right arm slowly, to test the depth of his sleep, but he didn't stir. His weapons were lying just off the blankets, within his easy reach, but where she'd have to cross him to get to them. Except for the heavy pistol in the holster on his thigh.

Maggie eased her hand downward; Devon still slept. The growing light gradually defined the silky brush of his eyelashes and the faint lines that fanned from the corners of his eyes. His lips were slightly parted, breath coming softly between them. Her hand inched closer until her fingers grazed the smooth handle. It was a Colt, one of the heavy models with a short-barrel, double action and accurate at twenty paces. Nothing fancy for Cimarrón, she noted. The butt was a plain brown, and there was no scrolling or any kind of decoration on the very businesslike barrel. And no notches. She almost smiled at that. If anyone could have cut notches into their pistol, it would be the man they called Cimarrón.

When Devon stirred slightly, Maggie froze. She didn't dare move until his muscles had relaxed again. He'd brought up one leg, bent at the knee. She waited, her heart pounding furiously, then curled her fingers around the butt of the Colt and paused. Still no indication that he was awake. Her arm shook slightly, and she tightened her grip on the Colt.

It slid easily enough from the holster, a smooth, slick glide that gave her an instant's hope.

"What the hell do you think you're doing?" Devon growled; his fingers clamped down on her wrist before she could bring up the Colt.

The glitter of fury in his eyes was hot and wide-awake. Did he come awake so instantly, or had he been aware of what she was doing? Her own temper flared.

"I'm trying to shoot a snake. Let go of my arm."

"Let go of my gun."

They stared at each other, but Maggie knew she'd lost. Without the element of surprise, she didn't have a prayer. He was too big, too strong for her to succeed in a physical confrontation. Only stubborn pride and temper kept her from immediately releasing the pistol.

"If my finger twitches, you'll have a bullet in the leg," she said calmly. His eyes narrowed.

"If I do, it better be fatal. You won't like what happens next."

"I don't like what's happening now."

"This ain't the worst I could do, and you know it."

That was indisputable. She attacked from another direction. "Let me go and I won't tell anyone about this."

"If I take you with me, you won't tell anyone about this."

"Does that mean you intend to keep me forever? How cozy. I didn't realize you cared so deeply."

That got him. She saw it in the sunburst of light that exploded in his eyes, the quick, fierce reaction he couldn't hide. Then he dug his thumb into the tendons of her wrist in a savage move that made her cry out and release the butt of the Colt.

Devon palmed the Colt in his right hand and reached for her with his left. Maggie tried to scoot back and away, but he coiled forward so swiftly that she couldn't avoid his harsh, hurting grasp. His hand tangled in her hair, and he pulled her across his legs, dragging her up so that she lay half across him, her face only inches away from his.

The pressure of his grip made her scalp burn, and she glared at him with frightened defiance. There was no mercy or pity in those cold blue eyes, only a ruthless determination that cooled her temper and made her quake inside. This couldn't be Devon, yet it was. She couldn't help a shudder of apprehension.

"You wake up too damn frisky in the mornings," he said softly. "Maybe I was too easy on you yesterday."

Maggie remained silent. There was little to be gained in prodding this loosed tiger much more. She'd tried and failed at escape; enraging him would only earn her a reaction she didn't want to consider.

He studied her for a moment, then rose to his feet, pulling her up with him. "I don't have the time or patience for this, Maggie. If you want trouble, I can give you trouble. Or you can go easy on yourself and I'll go easy on you. It's your choice, but tell me now. Next time, I'll do what suits me best."

Pride nudged her to fling his damn choice back in his face, but common sense and the aching throb of her sore muscles begged her to be sensible. She looked away from him, but he pulled her head back so that she had to stare into his eyes.

"Which will it be?" he demanded harshly.

"I won't be any more trouble."

The words were torn from her, and she hated the way her voice quivered slightly on the last syllable. For a long moment he held her that way, his hand gripping her hair to hold her head still, then he seemed satisfied with whatever he was looking for in her face.

"Good." He released her abruptly, and she put up a hand to rub her throbbing scalp. "There's some tins and an opener in my saddlebags. Dump something in a skillet and heat it while I tend the horses."

Maggie shot him a sullen glare, but he had already turned away and was scooping up his weapons from the floor of the cave. She stirred up the fire and had beans and salted meat hot and ready when he came back to kneel next to her. They ate silently; when they were through, he allowed her a few minutes of privacy in a tangle of bushes outside the mouth of the cave, then they began riding again.

With every mile covered by the steady pace of the horses, Maggie's resentment grew higher and hotter. Devon seemed completely unaffected by the grueling pace. He was like an extension of the heavy-muscled horse he rode, a graceful centaur that she began to hate with each passing mile. The only time he spoke to her was when she slowed him down. She didn't mind that nearly as much as her own thoughts.

At the back of her mind was the nagging fear that she would never see her child again. Thank God, Mrs. Lamb was with Joshua. She didn't know what she would have done if she and her son were alone. Reminded Devon of his existence possibly, preferring the risk of his wanting Joshua to the risk of leaving the baby by himself. It rankled that Devon hadn't even asked about his child, but at least she hadn't been faced with that decision.

And at least Joshua was old enough to drink his milk from a cup, something that had been forced upon him when her milk had dried up over a month ago. Overwork, Mrs. Lamb had said. Sometimes it happened like that. But she'd been able to nurse her son for almost six months before that happened.

Dear God, would she ever see him again? Sweet,

funny Joshua, with his thatch of pale hair and those bright blue eyes that were so much like his father's.

The knot of pain in her chest grew, almost choking her. Whatever Devon thought she'd done to him, she didn't deserve this.

# CHAPTER 22

They'd ridden south, and it was warmer. The sun beat down so fiercely during the day that Devon stopped in a small village and bought her a hat to keep her face from being too badly burned. It was a wide-brimmed sombrero, used and stained, but better than the alternative. Stalks of aloe plant eased the slight sting of sunburn already suffered, but she fussed that it was gooey and sticky.

"Don't complain," he said shortly, and she glared at him.

"I wasn't."

"Good." Damn. She made him feel like the ruthless bastard he'd provoked her into calling him earlier. She was teetering on the edge of collapse; he could see it in her eyes. Maggie was traveling on raw courage and temper alone.

Devon hesitated. They were in a tiny village that was mostly Mexicans. He didn't even know the name of it. But it had a hotel, or what passed for one in this hind end of creation. It was two stories—impressive if he considered the other buildings—and he could barely make out the name painted over the front door in sun-bleached letters that had once been red: Casa de Felicidad. A little ambitious, but at least it wasn't a bordello like the one in Tucson that bore the same name and a host of sporting girls.

He kicked Pardo into a walk, and Maggie was forced to follow at the same pace. A Mexican in a sombrero dozed on a bench in front of the hotel, only waking when Devon rode his horse close enough to nudge him. After a brief discussion and the eventual lowering of his rates for room and livery, Devon motioned for Maggie to dismount. She stared at him until he scowled.

"We'll stay here tonight." He didn't miss the relief in her eyes, but she remained stubbornly silent as he helped her down and through the door into the cool interior of the hotel. Her silence suited him well enough, especially after the argument that had ended with him so blamed mad he'd come close to knocking her off her horse.

That had alarmed him. He shouldn't let anyone push him that far, and certainly not a woman. The days of riding and running had taken their toll on him, too, and if the truth were known, he was stopping as much for himself as for her. But he'd be damned if he'd admit it.

Tables and a few chairs were scattered at the far end of the hotel's lobby, evidently meant to be a dining area. A long door opened onto a small patio shaded by beams covered with trailing vines and sweet-blooming flowers. Devon steered Maggie in that direction; in a few minutes they were seated at a table, and a man in the loose-fitting white calzones of the peasant brought them steaming bowls of rice and chicken as well as a bottle of dark red wine.

Maggie picked at her food and drank none of the wine, and Devon ignored her as he did justice to the meal. It was better than the food they would have gotten at one of the shabby cantinas he'd seen, and he was glad to get it. She'd learn quick enough not to be too choosy about getting hot meals on the trail. When he was through, he sat back in his chair and poured another glass of wine, preferring not to look too closely at the chaff in his glass.

"No wine?" he mocked, but Maggie wouldn't look at him. She sat quietly, her dark hair framing her face in a silky fall that obscured her features. If she was trying to make him feel bad with her sulking, it wasn't working. He didn't give a damn if she didn't like where she was or who she was with. As long as she kept her mouth shut about it.

Devon finished the bottle of wine and bought another one, taking it with them up the short flight of stairs to the room. He reached around her to unlock the door, careful to keep her wedged where she couldn't decide to run. She was behaving so oddly that he didn't quite trust her.

The key turned with a grating sound, and he shoved open the door and pushed Maggie inside. He followed and shut the door, locking it before he slung his saddlebags to the floor. Maggie had gone immediately to the opposite side of the room, away from him, skittish as a colt. He ignored her and looked around the room.

A double bed sagged invitingly. It had an iron bedstead and a quilt that looked frayed but clean. A single pillow was at the head. A bureau with a cracked mirror and a lamp was against one wall, and a washstand with a chipped china pitcher and bowl was against the other. Light from the open window overlooking the street slanted into the room through gauzy curtains.

Maggie sidled closer to the window.

Devon leaned back against the door and crossed his arms over his chest. She looked nervous. For a moment he wondered why, then saw the way she glanced from him to the bed and back, and knew. His mouth tightened against a flash of irritation. He pushed away from the door.

"How do you like our honeymoon suite, Mrs. Conrad?" He saw the flicker of alarm in her eyes, and it made him even madder. He indicated the bed with a wave of his arm. "This ought to do, don't you think?"

"Do for what?" Her voice was a thin croak.

"Well, we've had the wedding but not the wedding night. It's been about a year, and I think I've been patient long enough."

*Damn her.* She was looking at him as if he'd threatened to kill her, and he couldn't help remembering those nights in her bed in Belle Plain when she'd clung to him and taken him in her arms and body and whispered her love in his ear. Lies. It had all been lies, and for God only knew what reason.

Her wide gaze had darkened to a slate gray, and her eyes were focused on him with a strange intensity. He held her gaze, compelled by some deep emotion he couldn't ignore and didn't want to acknowledge, and began to unbutton his shirt.

"Come on, Maggie sweet. We're alone, we have a bed, and I'm sure you want to show your husband how much you love him." He peeled his shirt over his head and tossed it to the floor, then began to unbuckle his gunbelt. Maggie watched him in silent, rapt attention. He rolled the gunbelt with the holster on top, and set it on the bureau next to the bottle of wine.

He walked toward her, and she pressed back against the wall as if trying to vanish through it. Then she twisted in a quick, agile motion and flung herself at the open window. Devon leaped forward and barely caught her. He swung her around; he was furious that she would try something like that, inexplicably hurt that she hated him so badly.

"Damn you," he snarled, shaking her until her hair was in her eyes like a sable curtain. He flung her down on the bed and pinned her there with his hands and knees when she began to struggle. He sat back, panting slightly, while she bucked and heaved beneath his weight. His knees were locked around her squirming hips while his hands pinned her to the mattress by her shoulders.

It was startling; she looked as frantic as any virgin. What the hell did she think he'd do to her that he hadn't already done? Had she really managed to forget those nights in her bed? On her kitchen table? Hell, in her brass tub?

"Settle down, hellcat," he muttered, determined to remind her that she hadn't always looked at him with such loathing in her eyes. It shouldn't matter, but somehow it did.

He only meant to prove something to her at first; then, as he held her head still and forced her to accept his kiss and touch, he felt the high, hot sweep of desire that had been rekindled the night he'd watched her get ready for bed. He'd been raw and edgy since then, and it occurred to him that he didn't need to deny himself. This was Maggie. He had married her, and despite the reason for it, she was his wife. He had a legal right to her body.

"Easy," he said again, talking to her as if she were a fractious mare he was trying to gentle. He caught her arms when she tried to hit him, curling one hand around her wrists to draw them over her head. His other hand moved to caress the soft skin of her throat. "Easy now. I won't hurt you, Maggie. God. I'd forgotten how soft you are there."

Blood pounded through him, coalescing in his groin, making him throb painfully. Her struggles and soft, fierce protests went ignored. He couldn't think about anything but possessing her again; the need to slide into her heated warmth and ease himself was so strong he could barely think. Nothing mattered but Maggie, and the driving urgency he felt to be inside her.

His breath came in ragged pants for air, and he was vaguely aware of some of what she was saying as he pulled away her clothes with total disregard for seams and buttons.

"Devon . . . don't do this to me. . . . I'll never forgive you if you force me . . ."

None of it registered, though he understood the words. It was the content that escaped him, dissolving somewhere in that red haze of need that was consuming him. No other woman had ever made him feel so taut and driven, as if he were sliding down a hill toward a precipice with no way to stop.

Just the feel of her soft, satiny skin under his hands, the weight of her breasts in his palms, the taste of her against his mouth and tongue, made him oblivious to everything but having her. She was naked and quivering, her thighs closing convulsively against him.

"Spread your legs for me, Maggie," he whispered, his voice sounding hoarse and unrecognizable to him. One hand moved to brush against the tight curls there while his other still held her wrists together and locked over her head. Her breasts were pale, with a delicate tracery of blue veins, the nipples a deep, tempting rose. He abandoned her hot, protesting mouth and moved lower to her breasts, his tongue wetting the swollen nipples into a hard little knot. She shuddered, and he felt as if he were about to burst.

Almost feverishly, he moved to unbutton his pants, unable to bear the aching pressure another moment. When he freed himself, he groaned at the brief respite, then moved his hand back to her tightly clenched thighs.

He couldn't understand why she wasn't opening for him. It wasn't until he glanced up at her face that he knew with a sudden flash of clarity.

A small pulse fluttered rapidly in the hollow of her throat, and she was breathing in short, panting little drags for air. Her eyes were wide pools of fear. He'd seen that look before on a woman up in Indian Territory, that dread anticipation of what was about to happen. It hadn't been directed at him, and he hadn't allowed the man to continue, but he'd never forgotten it, either. He had never thought some woman would look at him that way one day, and especially not his wife.

*Rape.* It was an ugly word for an ugly act. Yet for a brief moment, he was tempted to give in to the driving instinct to possess her, willing or not. A dozen different justifications flitted through his mind in the space of that moment, then were gone.

His hand opened, releasing her wrists, and he rolled to the bed beside her, driving his fist into the mattress in savage frustration. A string of vicious curses provided his only relief, hoarse and guttural in the quiet of the room. He felt Maggie beside him, could smell the warm female smell of her, and it only kept him hard and aching. He wanted to hit something again, something much more solid than feathers and ticking.

Instead he lay face down beside her, tense and swearing in a repetitious litany of Spanish and English. When he felt Maggie touch his shoulder, he lifted his head to stare at her.

"If you touch me or try to get off this bed," he said in a tautly controlled voice, "I won't be responsible for my actions. I swear it, Maggie."

She paled but nodded silently and curled her hands into the quilt. He put his head down into the crook of his arm again, and it was some time before he felt able to lift it.

A hot breeze belled out the gauzy curtains but didn't ease the stifling heat in the room. Maggie stirred and felt Devon's hand tighten on her wrist. He held her as if he knew she would escape at the first opportunity.

And she would. Oh yes, she would flee him as quickly as possible given half a chance.

The sheets were damp beneath her, the remnants of her garments draped over the edge of the bed. At some point during the night, she'd managed to shrug into Devon's cast-off shirt, half-buttoning it.

Devon still slept, eyes closed, lashes shadowing beard-stubbled cheeks. She stared at him for a long moment. She should hate him. She did hate him. He'd changed more than she'd thought possible. Where was the gentle man that she'd often glimpsed beneath his gruff exterior? Had she been so blind that she'd believed in an illusion? This Devon would never give her a chance, would never care that they had created a precious child.

Tremors of desperation shook her. She had to get away. When he remembered that they had a child, he might use him against her. She knew it.

Several minutes passed. A fly buzzed annoyingly near, and she heard the sound of horses and men outside. The voices below their window grew louder, waking Devon. He rolled to one side, releasing her wrist, and swung his legs over the edge of the bed and got up.

"Damn," he muttered softly, peering out the window. The curtain fluttered against the side of his face, and he held it with one hand. "Just what I need."

"Who is it?"

He turned and flicked her a mocking smile. "Rangers."

Her heart thumped. "Texas Rangers?"

"Don't get any big ideas, sweetheart. I know one of them. I just don't need to run into him right now."

Maggie stared at him. He was a darker silhouette against the pale curtains and light, his muscled body taut, unbuttoned pants hanging low on his lean hips. She could never best him in a contest of strength, but perhaps there was a way to beat him after all.

A faint smile curved her mouth, and she lay back against the thin pillows and crossed her arms behind her head. "Did I say anything?"

"No. You don't need to. Your eyes tell it all. I can see how much you'd like to run down there and tell those Rangers I'm some escaped felon."

"Well—aren't you?"

His mouth tightened, eyes narrowing. "Technically. But you and I know better."

"Maybe you know better. I can't believe that abducting a woman from her home is condoned by the Rangers, however." When Devon just glared at her, she closed her eyes. It was easier not looking at him, not seeing the transformation that bothered her so much.

"All right," he said after a moment of taut silence, "I guess you have a point. Would you have come with me willingly?"

"What do you think?" she asked blindly, keeping her eyes shut.

"I think it doesn't matter. You're here, and that's all that matters."

Her eyes opened. He'd moved away from the window and was by the bed again, thumbs tucked into his drooping belt loops, his eyes narrowed and hard. She swallowed heavily. He looked so fierce, so intimidating.

"Devon," she whispered, "let me go."

"No."

She hadn't expected him to agree, but couldn't help a spurt of disappointment. Her heart lurched, and before she could change her mind, she opened her mouth and let out a piercing scream.

Devon looked shocked, then sprang forward to silence her, but not before she managed to scream again, calling for help. His hand clamped down over her mouth, muffling her.

"Damn you," he snarled. "I hope you know what you've done . . . "

She did. She heard the voices outside lifted in alarm and, in the space of a few moments, heard heavy boots on the stairs leading to the second floor. Loud knocks could be heard on some of the doors. In a matter of seconds, they would be outside this door. She saw fury and grim admiration in Devon's eyes as he released her and reached for his gun.

"I know what I've done," she said softly. "You're caught. There's no way out."

Devon stepped to the window and looked out, muttering a curse before turning back to her.

"I hope you're happy about the results you're gonna get in the next few minutes," he drawled, spinning the cylinder on his pistol before shoving it back into the holster. A loud thump sounded on the door, rattling it on its hinges.

"You in there!" someone shouted. "Open up!"

"Just a minute," Devon said, eyes never leaving Maggie as he buttoned his pants and buckled his holster.

"Now!" the voice commanded.

Maggie held Devon's gaze. "Hurry," she called, and saw his mouth tighten at the corners with mocking amusement. The door shook heavily; someone was attempting to break it down.

"I don't know whether to shoot you or the first man who walks in that door," he said calmly, and before she could do more than squeak with alarm, he jerked her up and held her in front of him.

"Devon! I . . . I'm not dressed—"

"You shoulda thought of that before screaming." The cold barrel of his pistol pressed against her cheek, and his forearm tightened under her breasts. The tails of his shirt only reached halfway down her thighs. She tugged at it frantically as the door shuddered again, then burst open.

A man stood framed in the opening; the sagging door swung slowly, creaking on torn hinges. For a moment, Maggie thought he intended to shoot them both.

There was purpose in the cold green eyes staring at them from beneath a lowered brow.

"Cimarrón," he said grudgingly. His voice was a harsh rasp, like the sound of grating metal.

Maggie squirmed. "Please—no shooting."

Both men ignored her, facing each other with grim intent and curiosity. It was Devon who said, "She'll get the first bullet, you know."

"Looks that way," the Ranger acknowledged. "Is that what you want?"

"What I want won't matter much to her then, will it?"

"Then let her go."

"I will." Devon paused. "Once I get away from here."

Maggie twisted. "No!" She felt Devon's arm tighten under her breasts, cutting off her air. She gasped, then went still. The pressure eased a bit.

The Ranger snorted. "If I was dumb enough to let you go, I'd have no guarantees you'd release her, now would I?"

"You've got no guarantees I won't shoot her, either." Devon thumbed back the hammer of his Colt. "Or that you won't shoot her tryin' to get me. Ever shot a woman, McRae?"

McRae's eyes narrowed even more. "Not willingly."

"Seems like I heard different." Devon chuckled softly, apparently enjoying the Ranger's mounting fury. "But then again, you Rangers make your own laws. Reckon if you was to shoot this little lady, no one would say a word about it. It would all be in the line of duty, right?"

"Cimarrón, ain't you got enough troubles without adding to 'em?" McRae gestured with his drawn pistol. "If she got shot, it would be you who was charged with her murder, not me. I ain't the one hiding behind a woman."

"This time, anyway." Devon took a step to one side. "I see only two ways this can end, McRae. One, you can have enough sense to let me get out of town with my sweet little wife here, or two—we can shoot it out and maybe kill her as well as each other."

Frustration creased McRae's face. Maggie's heart was beating so hard she was certain the Ranger could hear it. She knew before he finally nodded what he would say and was half-ashamed to hear herself whimper.

"No, please don't let him take me," she pleaded when McRae said he'd give Cimarrón a half-hour's start on him. "I don't want to go with him!"

McRae gazed at her a moment. "Is he really your husband, ma'am?"

Maggie wanted to deny it, but was afraid to take the chance. She nodded. "Yes."

"Then you'd best go with him." His mouth hardened. "He won't stay free long, I can promise you that. He's a wanted man, with posters out all over Texas. Rangers don't give up when they're on a man's trail."

"No," Devon cut in, "you hound a man till he's tired of runnin' and turns to fight."

"Make your stand here, Cimarrón." McRae's eyes burned hot and green. "Quit hidin' behind a woman and fight."

"I would, McRae, but I've got some unfinished business to tend to first. Hate to disappoint you." Devon backed slowly to the bed and snatched up Maggie's skirt, shoving it in her hand. Numbly she clenched her fingers around it as he reached for his boots, keeping a tight grip on her. "Now back off, McRae," he said, when his boots were on.

McRae backed away a few steps, and Maggie caught a glimpse of several faces in the hallway. "Devon—let me put on my skirt."

"Not a chance." His arm tightened around her. "Not until we're clear of town."

Face flaming, she had no choice but to go with him as he half-walked, half-dragged her out of the room and into the hallway. Despite the heat, her bare legs prickled with chill bumps as he forced her past the line of men, down the narrow steps, and into the hotel lobby.

"Let 'em go," McRae ordered when one of the Rangers muttered a threat. "We'll get him soon enough."

"Don't bet too much on that, McRae." Devon backed to the front door, keeping Maggie close, his bare chest burning against her shoulder blades. When the door was shoved open, a hot shaft of bright sunlight shot across the lobby. Sparks of light glinted from gunbarrels and spurs.

Devon eased out, boots scraping across the stone steps. Maggie whimpered again, and he felt a moment's repentance for terrorizing her like this. Not that she hadn't brought it on herself, but he had to admit a certain grudging admiration for her quick wit and courage.

"Be still," he growled when she made a sudden movement, and she flung back her head to glare up at him.

"Half the town has seen my bare legs, and if you don't mind—or even if you do—I'd like to cover them."

"Not now. Your legs are an excellent distraction at the moment. Maybe those Rangers will forget why they're after me."

"I doubt it."

Devon dragged her with him into the shadows of the hotel livery. Pardo whickered a greeting in the dusty gloom.

"I doubt it, too," he said to Maggie, "but it's worth a try."

"I hate you, Devon Conrad."

He reached for his saddle with one hand, still holding her with the other. He let the sting of her words pass before he turned to look at her. She was staring at him in the deep shadows; chaff hazed the air, and there was the sharp scent of new hay. He dragged in a deep breath.

"Maggie, it doesn't matter what you feel about me. You might as well accept the fact that you're going with me for now. I'll let you go when I don't have a need for you any longer. Maybe."

"The Rangers will never give up looking for you."

"They might if I leave Texas." He hefted his saddle to Pardo's back and motioned for her to cinch the girth. She did, bending her head to reach under the horse's belly. A shaft of dusty light fell across her, and when her hair slid to one side, exposing the nape of her neck, he felt a wave of unexpected tenderness. She looked so vulnerable, despite her defiance and hatred, and he wished suddenly that things had turned out differently for them.

Then he shoved that thought aside. Useless to wish for what was not, even more useless to waste valuable time thinking about Maggie when he should be thinking about escaping the Rangers. Maggie was right. They wouldn't give up looking for him.

After all, he was Cimarrón, the man accused of murdering two innocent men in Abilene. And now they knew he was back in Texas, and they knew he'd abducted Maggie Malone. If he wasn't careful, he'd be breaking in a new rope in the near future.

"Saddle your horse," he said tersely when Maggie straightened to look at him. "And don't make any sudden moves. I may need you as a hostage, but it won't matter how bruised you are."

"How chivalrous," Maggie said with a sneer. She stalked to her horse and began saddling it, not even

looking at him. When she was done, Devon tied her
hands in front of her and put her on his horse, ignoring
her glare.

He mounted behind her and tied her horse's lead
rope to his saddle horn. Her bare legs shone softly in
the gloom, and he reached for her skirt and pulled it
over her head, letting it settle over her thighs. Then he
put the barrel of his pistol against her ear and kicked
Pardo into a walk. Not even McRae would risk Maggie
now.

"Why don't you just let me go?" Maggie's hands
tightened on the saddle horn as the horses picked their
way down a steep slope. Rocks bounced erratically.

Devon shot her a fierce glance, and she refused to
look away. "Because I damn well don't want to, Maggie. Now stop asking me."

"I can't be of any use to you, Devon. I'm only slow-
ing you down. You've pointed that out to me on several occasions today."

"If you don't stop badgerin' me, I swear I'll stuff a
sock in your mouth. We'll be stopping soon, and I'll
find someone else for you to annoy. Until then—shut
up."

When they finally reached the cluster of rough
buildings nestled in the shade of a towering peak,
Maggie was almost reeling with weariness. She suspected that Devon had led her in circles a time or two
just in case she might be paying attention, but wasn't
certain. Not that she could have found this place on
her own. She had no idea where they were or even if
they were still in Texas.

Smoke from several fires drifted on the air, and a
few dogs barked a welcome as they rode in slowly.
Maggie was all too aware that their arrival had been
heralded some time earlier by guards posted at strate-
gic intervals. Bright bursts of light had flashed, like

sunlight reflected from a mirror, and she assumed it was some kind of signal.

A man ducked out of a low doorway and straightened as Devon rode toward him. Maggie recognized the man called Danza. His black gaze flicked toward her, then moved to Devon when they reined their horses to a halt in front of him. He said something to Devon in a language she didn't recognize, and she was startled to hear Devon respond in kind. It wasn't Spanish, but was more guttural and choppy. Apache, probably, she thought.

After a few minutes, and what seemed to be a sharp disagreement, Devon dismounted and came to pull her down from her horse. She didn't resist. Even had she wanted to, she couldn't have summoned the energy.

She expected to go with him, but to her dismay, he gave her into the care of a stolid woman who spoke no English. A mocking smile curved his mouth at her questioning glance.

"Don't bother Concha with questions or demands, Maggie. She doesn't understand English. She'll give you food and a bed. Even bring you a bath."

"And just how do I tell her if I want a bath?" she snapped back.

"Don't worry. When she gets close enough to you, she'll think of that on her own."

Maggie turned away angrily, flushing at Danza's soft laugh. She hated both of them. Especially Devon.

He *had* changed. He was harder, more ruthless, every bit the dangerous outlaw he was said to be. She knew that now. Any hope she'd had that the changes were superficial had quickly faded after the confrontation with the Rangers. If Ranger McRae had fired at them, she believed that Devon would have used her as a shield. It was a shocking fact to have to face.

When the Mexican woman reached to take her by

the arm, Maggie jerked away, her chin lifting in haughty defiance.

"I am quite capable of walking on my own, thank you."

The woman stared at her impassively and allowed her to walk without being held. It was a small triumph, but better than complete defeat.

Later—fed, bathed in a crude wooden tub with tepid water and strong soap of debatable quality—Maggie sat in a chair at a tiny table and dried her hair in front of the fire. Devon still hadn't made an appearance, though someone had brought his saddlebags earlier. Concha sat guard at the door, the only entrance or exit into the rough shack that passed for a dwelling. The fireplace was stone and blackened from many fires, and there was a rope bed across the room as well as the table and two chairs. That was the extent of the furnishings.

Days of exhaustion and tension finally took their toll, and Maggie felt her eyelids drooping as she huddled in a rough blanket in front of the fire. When she barely caught herself from falling out of the chair for the third time, she stood up and walked to the bed. Not even the threat of sharing it with Devon could bother her this night.

"Malone is riding after you." Danza's eyes narrowed as he stared at Devon over the campfire.

Devon stared into the flames. Danza had not liked him bringing Maggie here, as he'd expected, but had finally shrugged acceptance. Though it was not Danza's fight, he saw the advantage in having her as bait and insurance at the same time, as Devon intended.

"Hoped he would. I'll meet him away from your camp."

Danza's shoulders lifted in another shrug. "That is not necessary."

"But this fight is mine. I won't involve anyone else."

"If you like." Danza grew quiet again, then said, "It will take several days for them to follow the trail you left for them."

"I've waited a year already. A little more time won't make much difference, I guess."

"The woman's brother is coming for her. And if he is involved with the rustlers as you say, he will bring many armed men with him. We will fight with you."

"That's not necessary. I'll handle it."

"*Yínká duuda*," Danza said roughly in Apache. "You cannot ride alone every time, amigo. I know you like it that way. So do I. But I have learned the value of those who wish to help me."

"I won't risk anyone else."

"It will not be your risk. It will be theirs. No man will be forced to fight who does not want to."

"No. I can handle it," Devon repeated.

"I know you mean well, but do not ask me to suffer what you are suffering, amigo."

Startled, Devon stared at him narrowly. "I don't know what you mean."

"You would allow me to sit safely in the hills while you ride to face many men with weapons. And when you are dead, will I say to myself, 'My friend wanted it this way, so I will not feel bad that he died needlessly?' Or will I say to myself, 'If I had not listened to him, I would be able to smoke the pipe with him again before we meet in another life.' You do not want it for yourself, but you do not mind it for me. That is not friendship."

"Don't twist things to suit you," Devon said shortly. "I hate your Apache philosophy."

"Ah, the philosophy of *bélu* is so much better, heh?

The white man says whatever he wishes to do, then changes it later.''

"Dammit, this could get pretty hot. Look—back in the last town we stopped in, I ran into some Rangers. One of them recognized me, and if I know McRae, he'll be on my trail until he finds me. Do you want to fight someone else's battle?''

"No. But I will fight yours.''

Devon stared at him. He'd not thought Danza would get involved. He didn't want to think about anyone else's safety but his own. Yet if he let himself think past a certain point, it definitely would ensure that Johnny Malone got what was coming to him.

"All right,'' he said grudgingly. "Anyone who wishes to fight may go.''

"Then we need a new plan. This brother—how involved is he with the rustlers, amigo?''

Devon shrugged. "I'm not sure how deep he's in it. He's in it, though, that much I know. Before I left Texas last year, I saw him meet David Brawley. There was an exchange of money. I can't think of any reason for it but one, especially knowing what I do about Brawley.''

"Does your woman know?''

"My woman?'' Devon gave him a startled glance, then realized he meant Maggie. He scowled. He never thought of her that way, not anymore. Not since last year. Especially not since he'd almost raped her in a shabby hotel room.

"No,'' he said roughly, "she doesn't know. But I intend for her to know before too much longer.''

"Ah. I see.''

"What do you mean by that?''

Danza shrugged, his impassive face making Devon think of a wooden statue. "I meant nothing, amigo. It was only a sign of acknowledgement.''

"Sometimes you sound pure Apache, and at others you sound as if you went to some fancy college. I wish to hell you'd stick to one or the other." Devon stood up irritably. Flames leaped at a gust of wind, and a log collapsed in a shower of sparks that spiraled upward like tiny red stars. He felt foolish suddenly and regretted betraying his emotions. Danza would know what was behind his bad temper, and it certainly didn't ease it.

" *'Iíyá?'* " Danza stood up, too, facing him across the low fire. "Perhaps I have a wish also. Perhaps I wish that my friend would be honest with himself."

Devon didn't have to ask what he meant. He knew. And it didn't help to suspect that he was right. If he didn't come to terms with the contradictions he felt about Maggie, he'd end up doing something else stupid. It wasn't a pleasant prospect.

If Danza had remained, he might have admitted to uncertainty, but the Apache turned and left in a silent glide like a shadow. Devon jammed his hands into his coat pockets and stared into the flames for a long time, lost in thought and wrestling with his conscience.

None of his questions were resolved when he finally went to the small, dark shack where Maggie lay asleep on a cot. He held the door open, and Concha moved sleepily past him into the night. He closed the door behind her. A low fire flickered, shedding barely more light than the fuzzy glow of the lantern on the table.

His boots sounded loud on the planked floor, and his spurs rattled slightly when he crossed to the cot to stare down at Maggie. She looked exhausted; one hand was flung back to rest in the tangled dark hair on the pillow, and the other lay across her chest. There was a sweet innocence to her pale face that drew him into wondering how she had changed so much. The past year had given her a steeliness beneath that soft exterior that he hadn't expected.

Hell, he didn't know quite what he *had* expected from her. Explanations? Tears? Regret? Well, he'd gotten none of those, that was for certain. Resistance, yes. Anger, yes. A contempt that he didn't feel he deserved, and that made him want to hurt her like she had him. Damn. He'd been traveling on impulse and anger since leaving the Double M.

Why stop now?

Irritated with himself for dwelling on a subject that had no easy answers, and maybe not even any hard ones, Devon turned and stalked to the chair by the table. He sat down, not bothering to be quiet, and tugged at his boots. He dropped them to the floor one by one, with loud thuds and a brittle jangle of his spurs.

That worked. Maggie stirred, and he saw the glisten of her eyes when they opened and struggled to focus. Then she grew very still, and he knew she'd seen him.

"Didn't wake you, did I?"

His nasty drawl seemed to penetrate her drowsiness like a flash of lightning. She sat up abruptly, glaring at him.

"I'm certain it was an accident."

"Of course." He leaned back in the chair, tilting it to rest on the two rear legs. "Now that you're awake, maybe we can finish our earlier discussion."

"I'm tired. Finish it yourself."

She lay back down and rolled over, pulling the blanket up to her chin. Devon's chair slammed down, and he vaulted forward to snatch the blanket off, furious that she could so easily dismiss him.

"Maybe I just want company," he said when she rolled back to stare up at him with wide, wary eyes. "Humor me."

"You certainly didn't want to hear anything I had to say earlier. Why now?"

"Because now I want answers to some questions." There was a brief flare of something that resembled panic in her eyes, but it was gone so quickly he wasn't certain he'd seen correctly. He tossed the blanket on the floor and raked his gaze over her. Apparently someone had found her some clean clothes that belonged to a much larger woman. The blouse slid from her shoulders on one side, and the skirt was tied at the waist with a rope. His brow lifted.

"New clothes, Maggie?"

"Is that what you woke me to ask?" She pushed at the hair in her eyes with one hand, and he fought the temptation to bury his face in its shining length.

"No." He stepped back and motioned for her to get up. She did so grudgingly and came to sit in the chair he pulled out for her. When she was seated, wide gray eyes gazing at him solemnly, he asked, "How badly does your brother need money?"

For a moment she only stared at him. Then she asked warily, "What are you talking about?"

"Rustling. Murder. And honest John." His mocking words drew an instant reaction.

"Don't you dare insinuate that my brother was a party to any of those things!"

"I don't have to. He is. I just want to know how deeply he's in it."

She shot to her feet, quivering with anger, hands curled into tight fists at her sides. "If you think that accusing Johnny of doing rotten things like that excuses you from what you did, Devon Conrad, you're very much mistaken. I don't think there's any reason in the world good enough to absolve you from blame for what you've become. You've lived in such a criminal, murderous world for so long, you think everyone is like you are." She lifted her head, shaking the hair from her eyes, each word like the sharp lash of a whip. "You're not what I once thought you were, Devon. You are just what everyone told me you were—a lawless, corrupt killer with no morals and no conscience. I despise what you are and who you are."

For a moment there was nothing but silence broken
only by the soft hissing and popping of the fire. Devon
stared at her as if he'd never seen her before. Or maybe
he'd just never seen himself through her eyes before.

She was right in some ways, he supposed. He'd
become the kind of man he'd always hated, a cool
killer with no remorse for causing the deaths of human
beings. Maybe he didn't go around killing just anyone,
but that didn't excuse it. He was just a particular assas-
sin. Picky, Doug Morton would say. A long time ago,
he'd recognized that he'd die a violent death one day,
and he'd accepted it. It wasn't that he was afraid, or
even that he was a quitter, but survival simply wasn't
the most important thing to him.

Until Maggie. Until he'd been stupid enough to get
emotionally entangled with a woman who hated him
for some deep, dark reason he couldn't fathom. He'd
thought losing Molly was the worst thing that could
have befallen him. He was learning how naive he'd
been.

And it didn't improve his mood or lessen his pain to
realize that all the words Maggie flung at him were
based on false assumptions. If anything, it only sharpened it.

He barely recognized his own voice when he rasped,
"I don't think I'd be flinging around blame so quick if I
were you, Maggie. You're not exactly lily-white yourself."

"Oh, of course you'd say that. What else could you
say? 'Yes, Maggie, you're right—I'm the savage killer
everyone says I am?' Not likely. You'll go on pretend-
ing you have some noble reason for doing the things
you do and that you are just misunderstood, but I
know better."

He'd risen to his feet without realizing it and stared
down at her, fighting the urge to grab her and shake
her until she stopped pouring out all those venomous,

painful words. He grated through clenched teeth, "Shut up," and hoped she'd listen. He didn't want to hurt her, but God, if she kept lashing out like that, he didn't know if he could stop himself from doing something he would end up regretting.

"What's the matter, Devon?" Her head tilted to one side, dark, silky hair sliding over her shoulder and face and half-hiding her contemptuous expression. "Don't you like hearing the truth?"

He didn't know he'd moved until he had her by the shoulders, his fingers biting into her tender white skin and startling a cry from her. He shook her, and her hair lashed about her face and across his cheek like a stinging silk whip.

"Damn you, shut up!"

Her hands came up in tightly curled balls between them, and she shoved at his chest, then began striking him when he only held her more tightly. The blows weren't painful, though stronger than he'd thought she could be, but her anger and insults had pushed him to the limits. His own anger and exhaustion and months of mental torment exploded. He'd been walking the tightrope of denial for too long, and his sexual frustration did nothing to ease it. He needed a release, needed to work off his mood on something or someone, and Maggie had unwittingly provided him with the perfect opportunity.

He wasn't sure, but he thought she cried out his name when he shoved her back toward the cot. She struggled frantically, kicking at him with her bare feet, scratching his face with her fingers curled like talons. He ignored it all, ignored everything but the driving urge to make her take back those damning, hurting words.

In a swift motion, he had her on her back on the cot, pinning her down with rough hands that shook with restrained fury. She fought him like a wild tigress, panting and swearing words he hadn't known she knew, doing her best to heave him off her. If he hadn't been pushed so far, he would have found her efforts amusing. She looked so small and fragile most of the time that it was like a fly trying to swat a lion. He handled her easily, not really hurting her, but he knew there would be bruises on her arms and shoulders from his harsh grip.

When she finally wore herself out with her struggles and paused for a moment, panting, he asked coolly, "Think you can behave?" Her knee jerked up to hit him in the small of the back, and he grimaced. "Guess not."

"Bastard!" She dug her heels into the thin mattress and tried again to buck him off, but he only settled his weight on her more heavily, his knees on each side of her while he held her hands out to her sides and pinned down. Her head thrashed from side to side, and the words were torn from her. "Damn you, I won't let you do this, Devon!"

He studied her for a moment, her flushed face and eyes as dark as storm clouds with fury. It always came back to this. He wanted her, damn her knowing female soul, and nothing he said or did could change that. She was an ache inside him that he couldn't ease, a hunger he couldn't appease, an emptiness he couldn't fill. And he hated it almost as much as he hated her knowing it.

The black rage he'd felt at her words melded into another emotion, and he saw from the flicker of her eyelashes as he bent his head that she was aware of it. She twisted her head to one side to avoid him, so he kissed the slender arch of her throat instead. She tasted of strong soap and warm female, and he felt the familiar rise of need that she always provoked in him. His mouth brushed over her skin in a slow, lingering caress, then moved lower to the swell of her breasts. The thin blouse barely covered them. The low, scooped neck had come down to expose her to the nipples, and he couldn't resist that sweet, beaded temptation.

Maggie gave a half-sob, shuddering. He ignored it as his lips closed around the peak, drawing it into his mouth.

"Devon . . . God, please stop. Don't do this. I'll . . . I'll tell you anything you want to hear . . ."

His head lifted. He was aching and throbbing, tempted to forget everything but his need and the body in his arms. He'd thought of her even when he didn't want to, and now she was here and he could take her. No one would stop him. No one would come to investigate if she screamed the shack down around their ears.

But he couldn't do it now anymore than he could have back in that damn hotel room, and he knew that about himself, too. He wondered with aching bitterness why he kept torturing himself. He should take her and be damned. At least then he'd have some kind of relief, instead of this constant throbbing torment no other woman could ease.

He rocked his hips forward a bit, letting her feel the hard nudge of his erection against her where her skirts had ridden up. The flash of apprehension in her eyes was only vaguely gratifying. He smiled nastily.

"So—tell me."

She turned her head to the side, avoiding his gaze. Her words were muffled by her hair. "What do you want to know?"

"As much as you can tell me about your brother's recent activities."

Still not looking at him, she retorted, "How am I supposed to know anything when I live over a hundred miles away?"

"You haven't lived there that long. And your memory can't be so bad you've forgotten what he's been doing the past year."

She laughed bitterly. "You're wrong about that, as well as a lot of other things. But I don't guess you want to hear it."

"Probably not. What I want to hear is the answer to my question." He lowered his weight a bit, his hand tangling in her hair to drag her head around to face him. "Does Malone still swing a wide loop?"

For a moment she remained still, eyes widening to absorb light from the lantern. Her pupils looked like black pools as she stared up at him. "Why do you think Johnny is one of the rustlers?"

"I'm asking the questions. You're answering them. Try to keep that straight, Maggie." When she struggled furiously again, he tightened his grip on her hair, holding her. It was hard to keep his attention on what he was supposed to be angry about when she was wriggling under him and turning his body to fire. His physical reaction was annoying and increasingly difficult to ignore. He damned her and himself impartially, not knowing which he resented more at the moment.

"I can't breathe," Maggie said in a gasping wheeze. "You're too heavy."

He eyed her a moment. Her face was red, but that could be from her struggles. Though he wasn't certain he trusted her not to launch another attack on him, he eased his grip slightly and put more weight on his knees.

"All right, Maggie. Tell me, damn it. How long has your brother been in with the rustlers? And don't bother telling me he's not. I know better."

She glared at him. "If you already know everything, why are you asking me? You obviously know more than I do. After all, my brother and I haven't exactly been on speaking terms for the past year."

"You haven't been gone from Belle Plain that long. Don't bother with the lies."

"Lies." She laughed harshly, the sharp sound

slightly shocking him. "You don't know anything, Devon. God, you go on so blindly, believing yourself omnipotent, when you have no idea what has really happened."

"Suppose you tell me, then. I'm asking for answers, aren't I? Give me some, Maggie. Try telling me the truth. I want to understand. *Tell me.*"

He hadn't meant to sound so pleading, but the last two words were almost ragged. God, he needed to understand what had happened, not just with Johnny and the rustlers, but with Maggie. Why had she betrayed him that way? Despite his anger and pain at her betrayal, he knew it wasn't for the bounty like her brother had said. What he didn't understand was why she'd sent Johnny after him like that. He'd thought they had an understanding. She'd said she loved him. But if she had, she would have given him a chance. She would have given *them* a chance.

"Tell me," he said again. His eyes were locked with hers and he could see the confusion in them, the hesitation. Damn, did it take so much thought to tell him the simple truth? Or was she only trying to think of how much to tell and what to leave out?

"Never mind," he said when she opened her mouth. "I don't think I'm liable to get the truth from you. I should never have wasted my time asking. You and your brother don't seem to have much use for the truth." Her mouth closed again and she glared at him silently. That was as irritating as if she'd tried to defend herself. But what the hell had he expected from the woman who'd forced him into marriage?

It was then, staring down at her furious face, that he realized why she must have done it. He'd told her he knew who the rustlers were, who had framed him for murder. And he'd told her he was going after them. God, he'd been so stupid and blind. Did Maggie really think that if he married her he wouldn't go after her brother? Apparently he answered his own question, and it had worked.

"Damn you," he breathed softly. His fingers tightened and he fought a wave of fury. "Damn you for a lying, plotting little bitch. It worked, didn't it."

"I don't know what—Devon, you're hurting me . . ."

He didn't release his grip. The cold knot in his belly grew colder and tighter, and he felt it rise up into his throat as well. "Why didn't I see it? I didn't. So help me, Maggie, you had me fooled. After the neat little trick you and your brother played on me, I left Belle Plain. I might never have come back to Texas, and you counted on that, didn't you? Knowing what you knew—Jesus, I should have seen it then."

She squirmed, gasping a little at the pain of his hands biting into her shoulders. "I didn't . . . play a trick . . ."

"Oh yes, you did, Maggie. Was Johnny just waiting for you to tell him when I left? You knew I was going after him, didn't you. You knew I wouldn't stop until I got the men who framed me for those murders, the rustlers who wanted me dead. I kept after Ash Oliver, and you knew I'd keep after your brother unless you managed to stop me somehow." He gave her a rough shake when she tried to twist away, and pressed her down harder into the thin mattress. "Too bad that I don't think the same way you do. I don't give a damn if Johnny's your brother. And I don't give a damn if you're my wife. I can take care of both those problems without much trouble."

She managed to wrench a hand free and aimed a wild blow at him that he barely avoided. Even as he caught her arm and held it, she was spitting fury and denials at him.

"You're as wrong as you are hardheaded, Devon Conrad! My brother is not mixed up with rustlers, and I didn't send him after you . . ."

"Right." He lowered his weight on her again, this time pulling her arms up and behind her so that her own weight held them pinioned to the bed. It freed one hand so that he could grasp her chin and hold her head still. His fingers dug into her soft skin, forcing her to look at him. "Which lie is the truth? If you think I'll believe anything you've got to say now, you can forget it. You already proved to me how reliable and truthful you are, and I ain't likely to forget it."

"Go ahead—you can take your damn threats and choke on them, Devon Conrad."

"I don't make threats, Maggie. You should know that by now. I intend to remind your brother of that as soon as he comes runnin' to save his precious sister."

The words took a moment to sink in, then he saw the flare of fright and fury in her eyes. A low hiss of rage escaped her, and she brought up her knee to drum it into his back again, both legs flailing with a strength that took him by surprise. He grunted with pain and dropped his full weight on her again to stem the furious rain of kicks and blows she was inflicting. Damn. It was like trying to straddle a rattlesnake. Maggie twisted and fought, and when he shifted to push her legs down to trap them, she got a hand free and slapped him. It snapped his head back and made him see stars for a moment.

Swearing, he trapped her arms again, breathing hard from their struggle as she glared up at him like an infuriated cat. He wanted to hit something. His face felt on fire from where her nails had scratched him, and he narrowed his eyes at her. There was another way to release his anger—and make her more cautious about backing him into a corner. If she wanted to scratch and kick and slap, he'd convince her that it would be more uncomfortable for her than for him.

Devon uncoiled from atop Maggie in a smooth motion, bringing her with him, his hands hard on her wrists. She half-stumbled, shoulder digging into his chest, and he caught her and spun her around.

"I'm gettin' tired of you hittin' me whenever you feel like it," he drawled. One arm went around her waist to hold her next to him, and the other half-lifted her from her feet as he backed to the cot and sat down, dragging her across his thighs. "You remember what I promised you you'd get if you hit me again, Maggie?"

She tensed and grew still, her resistance stopped for the moment. "You wouldn't."

"I told you I would. I just waited too damn long to keep my promise."

Maggie pushed at his thighs in an effort to get up, but he held her easily. Her long hair brushed over his legs and the floor as she twisted, and hid her face from him. He was almost glad of that. His hand closed in a fold of her skirt to draw it up, but he paused. He didn't know if he would be able to keep his mind on what he intended if he saw her round, tempting behind, and he sure didn't need to look to know that she wasn't wearing anything under her skirt.

"Devon—don't."

Her voice shook slightly, and he ignored a quick thrust of indecision. She'd asked for this, and he was damned if he was going to let her make him soft-headed again. His grip tightened, but he left her skirt draped over her bottom and legs.

"I'd use my belt, but I ain't too sure I want any stripes on your pretty little ass. Not yet, anyway."

She began to struggle then, furious, frantic attempts to hit him and twist away that hardened his purpose. He held her down and brought the flat of his palm down on her bottom in several brisk blows. After her first choking cry, she clenched her hands into fists and didn't make a sound.

Somehow, instead of releasing his anger, it left Devon feeling more tense inside when he finally stopped. His palm was stinging, and he knew if he looked, he'd find red marks on her soft, creamy flesh. She lay limply over his thighs, her body quaking slightly with what he knew were swallowed sobs. Damn. How did she make him feel like such a bastard without even trying? He never did the right thing where she was concerned, it seemed.

Angry and disgusted with himself, Devon pushed her from his knees to the floor and watched silently as she knelt there without looking at him. Her slender shoulders were shaking. He wanted to comfort her, to tell her he was sorry, but didn't. It wouldn't matter to her anyway. And it was hardly worse than what he intended to do when Johnny Malone came after her. No, apologies wouldn't help anything. They never had.

# Chapter 23

It was still dark. The fire had long since died, and Devon had turned out the lantern before rolling up in his blankets on the floor. Maggie lay stiffly on the bed, envisioning Devon in various degrees of discomfort. Or even torment. She hoped his face hurt where she'd scratched him. She wanted to hurt him, to make him as miserable as he'd made her.

Sore muscles screamed a protest at her every movement, and she stifled a groan. For a short time, she'd lost all control of herself. It had been frightening to know she should be able to remain calm, yet feel it slipping away so fast she couldn't grasp it. All she'd felt was the need to lash out, to release the pent-up tension and fear and anger that she'd not been able to free. Not even the growing ferocity she'd seen in Devon's face had deterred her until her anger had catapulted her into provoking him to retaliation. But she wasn't sorry. Despite her aching muscles and the bruises she knew she'd have, she wasn't sorry she had lashed out. For that brief span of time, she had at least been able to force him to acknowledge her resistance, as well as her existence.

Then he'd retreated into himself again, into that cold, hard-eyed man who was nothing like the Devon she'd known and loved. This hostile stranger was like a desert mirage, shimmering heat with no substance once she looked closely enough, an empty facade.

In the past days her anger had grown, though she'd

thought she had no feelings left concerning Devon. But now he had awakened that anger, and with it, the need to see him writhe with guilt. He'd not believed in her, had believed that she would betray him, and she found that as hard to forgive as the way he'd abandoned her.

She'd loved him, given herself to him heart and body, and he had thrown it away. Maybe if she hadn't loved him so much she would never have felt that piercing pain at his lack of faith in her. But she had, God help her, and he'd almost destroyed her.

The only thing worse than her thoughts at this moment was the quaking knowledge that her brother would be riding into a trap when he came to her rescue. And she knew without a doubt that Johnny would come for her. He hated Cimarrón anyway, and knowing that the outlaw had abducted his sister would send him into a murderous rage.

There had to be a way to warn him. She may not like how he'd interfered in her life, but she didn't want Johnny's death on her conscience. He was impulsive and hot-tempered, and he had hated Devon on sight. Any man would have come under Johnny's close scrutiny and suspicion when he tried to court her, but for a dangerous desperado like Cimarrón to do so had only generated more trouble.

The past week of anxiety had grown almost unbearable at times, and her worry about Joshua was a constant pressure. On a rational level, she knew the baby was all right. On a purely emotional level, she fretted that he missed her, that he had gotten sick, or even that he'd forget her. She ached to hold him in her arms and bury her nose into the sweet baby flesh of his neck. At times, the ache was so sharp and painful it was like a knife thrust in her heart, drowning out even the cruel things Devon could say or do.

It amazed her at times that Devon could have fathered such a sweet child, but then she'd recall why she'd fallen in love with him and sigh. What had happened to the gentle emotions she'd glimpsed in him? She'd known he was trying to bury any hint of vulnerability, to hide the pain he'd suffered over something he couldn't help, yet that had only made her more determined to get past all that and find the man inside.

It was devastating to discover that the man she'd thought was there didn't exist.

In the place of that former wary vulnerability, a hard, implacable indifference had formed. There was no hint of the man she'd fallen in love with now, and it was as if another man stared at her from those ice blue eyes she'd once loved so much. That was a pain she couldn't bridge.

A rooster crowed, sounding thready and sleepy, and she realized it must be close to daylight. What would Devon do next? God, how could she look at him without wanting to cry for what they'd both lost?

Fortunately—though, perversely, it irritated her— she didn't have to look at Devon for a while. When the sun had risen high enough to poke fingers of light into the shack, she was startled to find him gone. He'd slipped out so quietly in the shadows that she hadn't seen or heard him.

Concha was back, as stolid and silent as before. Her broad features revealed nothing, but she somehow managed to convey whatever message she was trying to get across by gestures and a few grunts. Maggie burned with irritation.

At Concha's prodding, she found herself cooking enough beans, biscuits, and bacon for the entire camp. The men moved past politely for the most part, though a few paused to make an admiring comment that could in no way be taken amiss. It was as if they'd been warned not to approach her.

She was reminded of the times she'd had to help

with the cooking during branding, or when the men had gone out on the trail and she went along in a hard-bottomed wagon with food and necessities. She hadn't had to do that but on three occasions, and it had been quite an experience for a young girl, one that she'd never forgotten and never wanted to repeat.

This was the same basic routine. Cooking breakfast for the men, then cleaning up after. Then almost immediately beginning the preparations for lunch. A few hours of clean-up and a few minutes of rest, and the evening meal needed to be prepared. There were approximately fifty men, Maggie guessed, and not all of them came in at the same time, nor did they all file past her cooking shed. Some had small shacks of their own, scattered at random among the dry hills and gullies.

That night she spent alone, with a strange man standing guard outside the shack while she tried to sleep on the rope bed. Despite her wakeful night and exhaustion, she still found it hard to sleep. And when she did sleep, it seemed that it was only a few minutes before Concha was shaking her awake again.

Maggie was accustomed to hard work and long hours. As a physician, she'd often find herself sleeping in only spare snatches. Yet this was different. This left her bone-tired in body and spirit.

"Hey, Doc, do you remember me?" a voice asked hesitantly, and she looked up from the steaming kettle of venison stew to gaze at a familiar face.

"Of course I do." She ladled a portion of stew into his tin plate. "You're Roe Frayser."

He grinned. "Yes, ma'am. Didn't know if you'd remember me that good."

She eyed him for a moment. His green eyes were clear and friendly, and she couldn't help returning his smile. "I didn't expect to see you again."

"Well, I've been out of camp for a while. Back now, though."

"How's Latigo?"

"Meaner than ten skunks. Smells about as good, too. You can ask him yourself later. He ought to be wanderin' through here sometime soon. If he's through— hey!" Roe turned to shove at the man behind him who'd obviously grown impatient with the delay. "Watch your manners, Dusty, or I'll let you wear that stew 'stead of eat it." He turned back to Maggie with an innocent smile. "Sorry, ma'am. Some of these men ain't too mannerly. Danza warned 'em 'bout it, but looks like they can't pay attention when they should. Now, what was I—? Oh yeah, Latigo. Runnin' like a blamed deer. You did a great job, ma'am, and that's a fact."

Maggie felt a rush of pleasure. "That's wonderful. I was so worried about his leg."

"Wish you'd done something about his mouth while you had that needle and thread out, though. He's awful cocky. Well, reckon I better move on before Dusty curls up his toes and drops dead from hunger. He'd probably make a better lookin' corpse than he does a rider, but that ain't sayin' much."

Maggie stared after him with a smile, and to make it up to poor, hungry-looking Dusty, she ladled an extra large portion onto his tin plate. He smiled his thanks for her generosity, and she was reminded of the cowboys she'd grown up with. These looked the same, from dusty chaps and boots, bandannas around their throats and an assortment of serviceable shirts, to the distinctive, individual hats they wore.

It was hard associating these courteous men with the ranch hands from the Double M. They should look more like depraved outlaws instead of weary cowboys. Perhaps the major difference between these men and other cowhands was the way they wore their guns—low and competently. The average cowboy carried a rifle on his saddle, or if he wore a pistol at all, he wore it tied high around his waist. Pistols weren't that practical on horseback for a working range rider. They got in the way of the rope and necessary tasks. Rifles had better range and more force, and were used mainly for protection against four-legged predators.

These men were obviously prepared to defend themselves against the two-legged variety.

It was a disturbing thought and led back to her fears for her brother. If Johnny tried to take her from this camp, he would be killed. These men may not look like killers, but if they were here at all, they were here because they were not welcome in respectable towns.

No upright man lived out in an armed camp like this, with men posted as guards atop high ridges as well as men who would hold a woman prisoner. These men had to be wanted by the law for various reasons, and thus were inherently dangerous.

Later that afternoon, before she had to help Concha and another woman begin the evening meal, Maggie was allowed to sit in the shade of a huge cottonwood. It was the first opportunity she'd had for rest all day, and she was glad for it. She'd been in camp for three days and, since that first night, had not caught even a glimpse of Devon. She didn't know if she was relieved or simply unsettled at his absence. It was obvious that he'd left instructions that she was not to be bothered and just as obvious that she was not to be left alone.

She nodded quietly when Danza approached her and asked politely if he minded if he sat in the shade with her.

"I don't really have a choice anyway," she couldn't resist adding when the Apache sat down on the wide mat across from her. He looked at her gravely, black eyes focusing on her face until she flushed and looked away.

"One always has a choice, señora. When Cimarrón brought you here, did you not make a choice?"

She stared at him. "I was brought here against my will. I had no choice at all."

"Ah, but perhaps you did. He has not told me just how it came about that you are with him, but I know. And I know that Cimarrón does not know about the child you left behind in Belton."

Maggie felt the blood drain from her face. For a moment she couldn't speak, couldn't move. It felt as if all the air had been sucked from her lungs, leaving her light-headed and dizzy.

Danza shrugged. "You do not need to tell me I am right. I know this. But I will tell you, since your face is the color of new snow, that Cimarrón did not know you were carrying his son."

"Not—but of course he does. Johnny told him that I was pregnant that night."

"No, *chica*. That is not so. Cimarrón does not know that he has a child."

There was something so convincing in his soft denial, that Maggie suddenly believed him. Comprehension exploded in a painful flash of self-accusations as well as anger. Her hands curled into fists, and she sat silently for a long moment while Danza just watched her. It made sense. He'd not even asked. Even the most callous of men would at least be curious as to the sex of the child. Devon had not mentioned it at all. Yet if he did know, what would he do? He would never believe that she had thought he'd known, and he might still take Joshua from her.

"Don't . . ." She faltered, then said in a husky whisper, "Please don't tell him yet."

"It is not my place to interfere. That is between you. I would advise you, though, not to keep it from him for too long. To know would ease his heart. And his anger."

"No. No, you don't understand. He's so angry at me

now, and he won't listen to anything I say. He would take my baby from me to hurt me."

Danza stared at her without blinking, his night-dark eyes fathomless and yet somehow conveying sympathy. "He is very angry, *sí*. It is the anger that comes from pain that pushes him now, and until he can ease it, he will not allow himself to listen. You can help him ease that pain."

"I can't take that risk." Maggie shook her head, her eyes pleading with Danza to understand. "Joshua is all that I have left of something very precious, and I love him. He is *my* child, and I will not allow anyone to take him away from me."

Danza looked away for a moment, his gaze distant. Then a faint smile flickered on his lips, and he looked back at Maggie. "The *élchiné* are truly wondrous gifts but are never given to just one person. Children are not possessions. They are for all to love and cherish. You are being selfish, and you do not allow yourself to see into the heart of the man you love."

"I don't love him. I thought I did once, but that was only an illusion. He's not the man I thought he was."

"Perhaps it is because you are looking at him through the eyes of someone else. There is a saying: One must walk in another man's moccasins to understand his heart."

"This must be a popular lecture," Maggie said bitterly. "I heard it from Roe Frayser last year."

Black lights danced in Danza's eyes, but his mouth remained in a solemn line. "Perhaps you did not trust it. For some, answers are not believable unless they are hard. I beg your pardon. I mistook you for someone else, señora."

"I know what you're trying to do. It's not working. And you're lecturing the wrong person. Talk to Devon. He's the one who looks at me with murder in his eyes."

"My friend does not wish to hear, either." Danza sighed. "I had hoped one of you would be sensible. I see that I might as well bay at the moon like a coyote."

Maggie reached out a hand when he rose to his feet. "You . . . you won't tell Devon about the baby?"

"I am a man of my word." Danza looked affronted, and she bit her lower lip when he gazed at her icily.

"I apologize. I meant no offense."

"See how easy that was, señora? A sincere apology need not draw blood if one is careful."

She stared after him as he walked away in an easy, graceful glide. "What a peculiar man," she murmured. It didn't help her state of mind to find out he knew about the baby and Devon didn't, though she sensed that he would not tell Devon. Her throat tightened with anxiety. If Danza knew about Joshua, then Devon would find out one day.

Devon. God, he hadn't known all this time. All this time she'd thought he'd abandoned her without a thought as to her or his child; yet he'd believed himself betrayed for no reason. No wonder he was so bitter and angry.

She closed her eyes and sat there for a long time. A hundred different excuses occurred to her, but none of them would make up for what had been lost to both of them. A year had gone by, a year in which Devon could have begun to know his son. She shivered suddenly and opened her eyes to focus on a flat-topped ridge in the distance.

What would Devon do when he found out about his son?

"Amigo."

Devon turned to stare into the shadows. Danza moved out into the light from a campfire, nodding when Devon motioned for him to sit down.

"Did you find what you were looking for?" Danza asked as he sat on the rounded curve of a sturdy log.

"Depends on how easy I am to please."

"Ah." Danza held out an uncorked bottle. Devon took it and upended it, swallowing a long, burning gulp before he handed it back.

"Thanks."

Danza nodded silently. After a moment Devon stretched out one leg toward the fire, rubbing absently at his thigh. He could feel Danza watching him and knew he was probably aware of what had happened. His scouts would have made sure of that. Devon shrugged.

"Malone's got twenty riders with him, as I'm sure you know. I ran into one of his scouts early today." His mouth tightened. "Maybe I should have said nineteen riders, as they're down one now. Rogan is with him."

"Has your wound been tended?" Danza asked after a moment had passed, and Devon smiled ruefully.

"You know it hasn't."

"Then we are fortunate to have a doctor among us."

Devon's eyes narrowed slightly. "I'd rather take my chances with gangrene. It'd be kinder than letting Maggie get revenge."

"Ah, does she seek vengeance for your taking her from her home, amigo?"

"Among other things." Devon looked away from Danza's knowing black gaze. It was one of the things about the Apache that annoyed him most, that all-seeing, interfering attitude.

"I saw her bruises. I've never known you to harm a woman before."

"For a man who professes to allow other people to go their own way," he commented, "you sure do mess around in my life a lot." He paused, then leveled a cold stare at Danza. "Just what bruises are you talking about?"

The suggestion of a smile hovered on the Apache's lips as he met Devon's stare. "Are there bruises that only her husband would see? I find it insulting that you would even ask such a question. Which ones do you think, amigo?"

Devon looked away, irritated with himself. He knew better. He didn't know why he'd been prompted to ask, except that Maggie made him crazier than any woman ever had in his life. She made him do things he never thought he'd do, feel things he never thought he'd feel. He groaned softly.

"Hell, Danza. Maybe that bullet took more than just a little hide off me. Where's Roe? He can tend this burn."

"Are you afraid to face her?"

"Dammit, you're pushin'," Devon growled. "Has she got to you? What'd she say that turned you into this one-man crusade for reconciling our differences?"

"She has said nothing but that you are not the man she once thought you were."

Devon felt a white-hot flash of fury rip through him. "I don't suppose she mentioned what a betraying little bitch she is, while she was at it. I thought not. Women never do. There's only one side in a disagreement— theirs."

Danza took another pull from the bottle, eyeing Devon for a long moment. "That is so with some women. Do you think your woman is one of those?"

"She's not my woman."

"Ah, we've had this conversation before, I think. But soon, her fate must be decided." Danza stood up and held out the bottle. "It is getting late. I think I'll find my blankets."

After a short hesitation, Devon took the bottle. "I don't know what to do about her. It seems—" He jerked to a halt, swearing softly. Damn. He must be getting edgy to even bring up this subject with anyone.

Especially Danza, who seemed to always know what he was thinking.

Danza paused and looked back at Devon. "I don't allow myself to think about women in that way, amigo. It is too exhausting. I have noticed that some men lose their ability to reason when a woman is involved. For myself, I do not care to be miserable."

"You're smarter than you act most of the time." Devon met Danza's slightly startled black gaze and grinned. "No offense meant, of course."

"Of course." A faint smile tugged at Danza's eyes and mouth again, then he left the campfire and Devon behind.

Devon sat back down and wasn't too surprised when Roe Frayser appeared at his side a few minutes later.

" 'Lo, Cimarrón. Hear tell you took a piece of hot lead acrost the leg."

"You heard right." Devon propped his leg up on a rock. A portion of his pants leg was charred and stiff with dried blood. "Just a burn. What have you got to put on it?"

"Hell, not much." Roe shrugged and gave a sheepish grin when Devon glanced up at him. "I ain't no doctor, Cimarrón. You know that."

"Then why the hell did Danza send you over here?"

Roe met his gaze with lifted brows. "Damned if I know. I thought you asked for me."

Devon swore again and winced when he put his leg down to stand up. "I thought you knew something about bullet wounds, seeing as how you're always the one hanging around when a man comes in shot up."

"Ah, that." Roe reached into his vest pocket and brought out a small flask. "I'm just the one who brings the painkiller. Good whiskey makes a man forget what hurts."

"So does bad whiskey. For a while, anyway."

"Yeah. But don't worry. I got something better than whiskey this time."

Devon took a limping step. "What? Tequila?"

"Naw." Roe turned around, then said in a tone that brought up Devon's head, "A real doctor."

Devon didn't move, just watched as Maggie came toward them. She moved so gracefully, she made him think of a small doe stepping delicately through high grass. His muscles grew taut, and he flashed Roe a searing glance that was met with a slight shrug and a backward step.

"Uh, didn't think you'd mind, Cimarrón."

"You thought wrong."

Maggie stopped a few feet away, head up, eyes wide as she watched them. Devon swore silently. If he sent her away, he'd only look foolish. He could feel Roe's interested gaze on him and knew that he was aware of his reaction.

"Well come on," he said roughly, and propped his leg back up on the rock. "I need a doctor and I guess you're it."

"I don't know what anyone expects me to do without my bag and supplies," Maggie said as she stepped forward. Her touch was cool, and she motioned for Roe to hand her the knife he always kept at his belt. Devon caught her hand when she held the naked blade over his thigh. His tone was rough.

"If you intend to amputate, discuss it with me first." He saw a quick flare of anger in her expression but didn't release her wrist.

A tiny quiver threaded her voice. "I'm not at all certain that this little wound deserves so much fuss, but I'll certainly discuss any major decisions with you."

Devon finally released her and watched as she slid the point of the knife under the torn material to slice it away. A long, red, raw burn oozed on his thigh. Bits of material clung to it, and his breath sucked in with a hiss as she pulled some of it away. She didn't even glance at him but handed the knife back to Roe.

"I need hot water, clean cloths, and some ointment. Is there any here, Roe?"

"Hot water, maybe. If you give me a few minutes."

Devon swore aloud this time. "Damn. I'll do it myself. You two sound helpless."

Maggie stepped back to glance at him. Her wide, clear gaze was faintly contemptuous, and he hoped he didn't look as uncomfortable as he felt. Memory flashed of how he'd hurt her the last time he'd seen her. It was the reason he had ridden out to do his own scouting, because he didn't trust himself to be near her without doing something else equally stupid. And shaming.

"Suit yourself, Devon," she said in the same flat tone that grated on his nerves.

"Hey, Cimarrón," Roe protested, "ain't no need to get in such a hurry. I can find what she needs. Just give me a little time, is all."

Devon took several steps away, moving closer to the light from the fire. The burn had begun to throb with dull heat, and he swore softly under his breath.

Maggie came up behind him. "Bring me one egg, Roe," she said, and when Devon turned to look at her, she was looking at Roe. "I can ease the sting with that. If I had some plantain leaves, I could do a better job, but egg will do."

"Egg," Devon muttered. But he found that when Roe came back with an egg, a bowl, and a spoon and Maggie spread the mashed mixture over the cleaned burn, it did ease the pain. He gave a half-grudging shrug. "Thanks."

"Oh, do call on me anytime, Cimarrón."

Devon glanced up quickly, his eyes narrowing at her sarcasm. She was picking up the rags she'd used to clean the burn, not even looking at him. Damn. She hadn't really *looked* at him since he'd come back, as if she couldn't bear the sight of him. He wanted to shake her, to make her look at him as she once had.

Instead, he drawled, "I always do call on you when I feel like it, don't I?"

Now he had her attention. Her hands stilled, and he saw her draw in a quick, angry breath. "It seems that way."

Still motivated by a burning, inexplicable need to have her look at him, Devon said softly, "Like tonight, for instance."

"To—tonight?"

"Yeah. I thought maybe you'd missed me while I was gone."

"Like a festering sore."

He stepped closer and saw her tremble slightly. "You always did have a way with words, Maggie."

Now he had her complete attention. She half-turned, an abrupt movement like that of a frightened deer. Her eyes were wide and dark, pupils dilated and flickering with images of the campfire. She stared up at him finally, and he saw his reflection in her eyes.

"What do you want from me, Devon?"

Her voice was a husky whisper, a faint sound that he almost missed. He heard the fire pop, heard Roe mutter something about chickens, then they were standing alone.

The question made him pause. He knew what his body wanted from her, but there was more than that. There was something he needed, something only Maggie could give him, and yet he wasn't sure what it was. There had been a comfort in her presence a long time ago, and he'd felt its absence keenly. God, he wanted to shake her and demand to know why she had betrayed him, and he wanted to kiss her and not stop until they were both breathless and exhausted from making love. It was insane. He knew that. Yet he couldn't stop himself from wanting it.

"I don't know what I want from you." His voice was hard and thick, and he wondered if she could tell how much she affected him.

"Devon—" She put out a hand to touch him, fingers light against his chest, and he curved his hand around hers.

"Don't." He drew in a shaky breath. "Whatever there was between us a long time ago, it's over. It was over the night you sent your brother after me. But dammit, Maggie, I don't guess I'll ever understand your reasons."

"Did you ever stop to think that I might wonder why you left without looking back?"

He stared at her. "What the hell was I supposed to do? Wait around for the sheriff to measure me for a new rope? I may be slow at times, but I don't think I've ever been that damn slow."

"You could have waited to listen."

"To more lies?" He shook his head. "I wasn't in the mood for it that night. And I'm not in the mood for it tonight."

He let go of her hand, and she took a step back. Anger blazed in her eyes. "Do you know, I think you should listen to your friend. He makes much more sense than you do."

"What friend? Danza?" Impatience lent his voice a hard edge. "He likes to hear himself talk in riddles. If I were you, I'd ignore most of what he says."

"I'm sure you would." Maggie turned away, and he watched her walk back toward the small shack. A discreet shadow waited for her and went to stand guard by the door after she went inside.

Damn. Every encounter with Maggie left him feeling as if he'd lost something precious. She was his wife, no matter how it had come about, and part of him accepted that as much as he resented the reason for it.

A log in the fire popped, and he heard a woman's sultry laugh somewhere in the night. It made him think of Maggie and what they had once shared. Maybe he had expected too much from her. And himself. He should have taken what was given and not looked back.

But he hadn't. He'd wanted more, hoped for more, and lost it all. *Damn.*

Devon's hands curled into fists at his sides, and he stared long and hard at the small shack. He was suddenly filled with the driving need to make her his one more time, however he could, whatever it took.

# CHAPTER 24

Maggie whirled at the sound of the door slamming open, and her heart skipped a beat when she saw Devon pause in the doorway. Lantern light picked out the expression on his face and sent her heart plummeting to her toes. She took an instinctive step back but met the unyielding wall.

The door closed with a loud slam, and Devon moved toward her. Maggie thought of a wolf stalking its prey and knew suddenly how doomed creatures must feel at meeting such predators.

When Devon reached Maggie, his big hands flashed out to grab her by the shoulders, and she could only offer a choked protest before his mouth came down over hers. The kiss was rough and deep, devouring her as if he couldn't get enough. Maggie's hands pushed futilely at his broad chest, panic making her frantic.

"Devon—no," she managed to get out, but he was lifting her in his arms and moving toward the narrow rope bed against the far wall.

"Oh yes, Maggie." His voice was rough with restrained violence. "No more games. No more waiting. You're my wife and I want you in my bed."

She shoved at him with the heels of her hands and tried to slap him, but he easily controlled her movements, growling at her to stop. It wasn't fear that made her struggle against him, but an ingrained sense of justice. Devon hadn't known about the baby. He'd left her, yes, but because he thought she had betrayed him.

And he hadn't *known* about the baby. As badly as she'd felt over the past months of needing Devon and wanting him, she felt more betrayed by Johnny. Knowing how badly her brother hated Devon, she'd still let him manipulate her into making a mistake that had affected all of them. Especially a sweet, innocent baby who had never met his father.

Yet she couldn't allow Devon to override her wishes and take her without regard to her feelings despite all that had happened. Maggie pushed futilely at his hard chest.

"Devon . . . Devon, wait."

"No. No more waiting. You wanted me once, dammit. You still do. You're just too damn stubborn to admit it."

He dumped her on the bed, following her down with his body when she launched herself up again, his hands curling around her wrists to hold her. She managed to twist beneath him, bringing up her legs to wedge him slightly away.

"I thought . . . Devon listen to me—I thought you said it was over between us."

He shoved her legs back down and pinned them with his own, holding her wrists in one hand while he braced himself over her with the other. "It is. Everything but this." His weight shifted to her wrists while his free hand stroked down her face and throat.

She glared up at him. "No. You can find sex anywhere. I refuse to be just another easy woman for you."

"Easy?" His laugh was harsh. "If you think the hell you put me through this last year was easy, I hate to think what you might have planned for me next."

"I don't . . . have anything . . . planned." Her words were coming in short pants for air as his palm moved over her body in a lingering glide.

"That's an improvement." Devon's hand paused to

cup her breast, and he raked his thumb over the sensitive peak in an erotic swirl that made Maggie's senses leap. The loose cotton blouse was no hindrance to his touch, and she could feel the heat of his hand scorching her.

Maggie gave a futile little buck that only made his grip on her wrists tighten, then his hand shifted from her breast to the cord tying her skirt. There was no doubt in her mind that this time he wouldn't be stopped.

"Devon—we need to talk. I have to tell you . . ."

The cord came free, and he tugged the skirt down over her hips to tangle around her legs. Desperate now, she clenched her thighs on a fold of skirt, but he tugged it free with little effort. It slid down her bare legs in a cool glide, and she shivered.

"Devon, please listen to me."

He glanced up at her, and there was an unrelenting light in his eyes as he reached for the simple blouse she wore. It was intended to be pulled over her head, but he jerked it from her body, and she heard the ripping of seams.

"I don't want you to do this," she choked out.

"I think you're wrong." His head lowered, hair shining like gold in the muted light. "I think you want me to do this and this . . ."

Maggie's breath caught in her throat. He was right, but she wanted more than just this. She wanted what he'd felt for her before, that sweet tenderness he'd given her. There was no sign of it now, no hint of softer emotions in what he was doing.

But when his mouth covered hers in a deep, drugging kiss, she lost track of everything but Devon. She'd wanted him for so long, ached for him even when she wouldn't allow herself to think about it, that all her reservations and resolutions evaporated as if they had never been. Maybe he wasn't saying what she needed to hear, but his body was telegraphing clear messages about how he felt. All she had to do was absorb them.

It was obvious, in the tender-harsh touch of his hands on her, in the way he kissed her as if he'd never stop, his mouth moving from her lips to her closed eyes, then back. He sparked a blaze in her with his urgency, a throbbing heat that could not be ignored.

Maggie felt helpless under his weight, under the scalding heat of his body pressing into her stomach and thighs. Devon muttered something unintelligible, and because it had to be obvious that she no longer had the strength or will to resist, he released her hands.

There was a look of faint surprise in his astringent blue eyes when she put her hands on the back of his neck to draw his head closer, then a burst of light that was quickly eclipsed.

"Maggie . . . God . . . " The words came out thick and husky, then he was kissing her again, his tongue slipping inside to touch hers in a velvety, hot caress that made her breath catch and her heart thump erratically. Her fingers tangled in his hair, letting the silky strands slip through in a long glide when he left her mouth and began kissing her throat, then lower.

"Devon . . ."

His name was a throaty cry, sounding alien and yet so familiar, so achingly familiar. Another cry burst from her when his tongue traced a steamy damp path around her nipple, then sucked it gently into his mouth. The rough scrape of his beard against her sensitive skin was a sweet agony, and she felt the mounting heat inside. She arched upward, her hips lifting to feel him press hard between her legs. He was still wearing his clothes, and they were rough and rasping against her bare skin. It was oddly stimulating.

He lifted his head to look at her after a moment, and she felt his gaze sear into her. Her hands came up to hold his face, fingers brushing against the bristle of beard on his jaw. His hands spread into the mattress on both sides of her head, bracing him over her. She held his gaze with her own, and when her hands moved down over his broad chest and began flicking open the buttons, she saw the reaction deep in his eyes. Without taking her eyes from his, she unbuttoned his shirt and spread her fingers over the bare, taut muscles of his belly. They tightened. His breathing was ragged and fast, and he still stared at her as if at some wild creature he'd never seen before.

When she unbuckled his belt and began unbuttoning his pants, he bent his head to watch, not moving to help. His thighs were between her legs, holding them wide, and she felt his tension in the slight tremble of his muscles. Then he shuddered when her hand found him and closed around him, and she felt his immediate leap of response to her touch.

"Sweet Jesus," he muttered in a thick voice. His braced arms quivered slightly with strain, and when she began to stroke him as he'd once shown her, he groaned softly. It was a heady power, knowing that she could make him respond to her touch, to the gentle-fierce kneading of her hand on his body.

All her indecision, her resentment toward him, evaporated into nothing. She loved him. It had little to do with sex, and everything to do with the sweet intensity of emotions held in check for too long. The Devon she'd fallen in love with was still there, buried deeply inside a man who felt betrayed, but she knew she could find him again. It was evident despite everything he did to hide it.

"Devon," she half-sobbed when he grabbed her wrist to pull her hand away from him, but he quickly covered her lips and protest with his mouth, drowning out her words. He kissed her long and deep, shoving at his opened pants with one hand while his other braced him over her.

His breath came in harsh, fast pants, and she felt his urgency in the way he handled her, his hands hard against her as he pressed close. His head lifted, eyes hot with blue fire, the icy glint in them gone as he stared down at her. Then he flexed his lean hips in a swift movement and slid inside her in a hard thrust. Maggie gasped at the heated invasion.

The pressure and sense of fullness was almost unbearable at first. Maggie's body clenched around him as if to halt the intrusion of him inside her, and she heard his soft groan.

"Don't move," he muttered. He held her hips still with his hands when she gave an involuntary twist. Then he slowly pushed deeper, making Maggie gasp aloud with the increasing pressure. She could feel him deep inside, his heat and hardness filling her and sending small tremors of reaction to her nerve ends. It was an exquisite sensation that made her arch against him as if seeking all he could give her, and he seemed to know that. He withdrew slightly, then shoved forward in a rough thrust that made her cry out and hold him more closely. Her hands raked down his back, over smooth, damp skin that eluded her efforts to grip him.

"Am I hurting you?" he asked roughly, and she managed to shake her head.

"No. No. Oh Devon—"

There was no other chance to speak, because his movements increased in power and speed until she could do nothing but moan and clutch at him. Tension grew higher and hotter within her, coiling tighter and tighter until she couldn't control her own frantic movements. She was barely aware of Devon's muttered encouragement, the way he controlled her response with his body. When she heaved upward in a desperate reach for the ease to her tension, he slowed his thrusting until she calmed a bit, then slowly began to increase it until she'd reached that high plateau again. He repeated it several times until she was begging him for release in fragmented phrases.

"Easy, honey, easy," he whispered in a husky voice, then stopped her whimpers with his mouth. He kissed her to silence, then moved lower, his lips fastening on the hard peak of her breast.

Maggie felt as if she would explode with tension. "Devon, oh Devon please . . ."

In answer, he thrust forward, lifting her hips in his broad hands as he moved higher. When his fingers dug into her soft flesh, she arched upward and felt the blinding heat engulf her. It swept her away, into the widening chasm that awaited, and she heard her own voice crying out his name and her love for him as he took her beyond it.

Devon groaned hoarsely as he shoved deeply inside her, then grew still, his body shaking with the force of his release. Maggie felt the hot pulsing of him inside her, the exquisite shudder they both shared, and held him as close to her as she could.

His big body slowly relaxed, and he still held himself inside her, his bent arms holding up most of his weight as he buried his face in her hair spread out on the mattress. She felt his ragged breathing slowly return to normal, his chest warm and slick against her breasts, and her arms tightened around him.

Maybe it would be enough. For now. It was a beginning, a tentative search for what they'd once shared. Devon could lie to her and to himself, but he couldn't hide the depth of his feeling for her when they made love. It overrode everything else, his denials, his anger, his bitterness. If he'd cared only about himself, he would never have loved her so sweetly and tenderly, caressing her, comforting her, giving of himself as well as taking.

No, he couldn't hide the fact that he still felt something for her. She just hoped that she could force him

to recognize it before something irrevocable happened
to destroy them both.

Light from the oil lamp flickered erratically. Devon
held Maggie against him, refusing to allow her to shift
away. He liked the way she felt, her soft curves nestled
into his angles. Damn. She had him hard again, and it
hadn't been but a few minutes since the last time.

He lay on his side, holding Maggie into the angle of
his chest and thighs, his hand spread possessively on
her soft, rounded little belly. She'd matured a lot in the
past year. Her body was rounder, fuller, her curves
more lush than he remembered. Even her breasts had
changed, the color of the nipples deeper and darker
than before, blossoming larger on her creamy skin.

Maggie shifted slightly, and he rose to prop his head
in his palm, staring down at her. He wanted to say
something, but he didn't know what. Nothing seemed
right. The force of their passion had surprised him,
startled him into forgetting the angry questions he'd
wanted to ask before. Now he just wanted to taste her
again, to lick his way over her body in a slow, leisurely
exploration.

She looked up at him, gray eyes clear as rain, the
pupils expanding slightly when he just stared down at
her without speaking. He sensed her indecision and
waited.

"Devon." Her voice quavered slightly, and she
lifted a hand to touch him lightly on the jaw, running
her fingertips over the rough bristle of his beard.
"Devon, there's something I should tell you."

He tensed. He didn't want to hear it. Not an explanation, another denial of guilt or attempt to soften it. Not
now. Maybe later, when he'd thought things through
better and was more equipped to handle it.

"Save it," he said, and saw her eyes widen at his
rough tone. "Now's not the time for talking, Maggie."

"But you don't know something you should, and I—"

He couldn't help the swift, savage motion that startled a cry from her as his hand closed around her wrist in a bruising grip. "I said save it till later, dammit. I'm not in the mood for confessions right now."

Her eyes flashed resentment at him, and her voice was sullen. "What are you in the mood for, then?"

In reply, he brought her hand down to the hard thrust of his erection and saw her eyes widen. "This," he said in the same rough tone. He gave her no chance to refuse or even protest, but bent his head and kissed her. He ignored the tinge of desperation he felt that she might push him away, and focused instead on the only way he *knew* she wouldn't reject him.

Whatever else, they did have this between them. This wild, hot feeling that exploded despite the better judgment of more rational minds goaded them both into surrendering to it. It was crazy. Maggie's former resistance had somehow disappeared, and it was as if it had never existed. He didn't know the reason for it, but just accepted it. For now, this was enough.

He rolled her to her back, rising to his knees over her, gazing down at her with hungry attention. She'd never been more beautiful, with her dark, gleaming hair spread out on the pillow beneath her, her slender body glowing with an ivory sheen in the fitful light of a lantern. He slid one hand up a curved thigh, his fingers brushing against the dark, silky curls hiding her from him. He saw her breath quicken, her body tremble in response.

Devon used his knees as a wedge between her thighs, opening her for him, ignoring her incoherent protest and the way she moved her hands to cover herself. He gently pushed her hands away, watching her face as he explored her satiny folds with a probing finger. Maggie gasped. At his certain, intimate exploration, the gasp degenerated into a moan. Her nipples hardened, and he saw her breasts rise and fall in a rapid rhythm.

"You like that, don't you," he said softly, unable to hide his satisfaction at her response. Maggie's eyes were glazed and unfocused, and he saw her hands clench into the tangled rumple of thin sheets beneath her.

Devon bent his head to capture a nipple in his mouth, and she arched blindly toward him. Slowly he pushed inside her, his thumb grazing over her sensitive flesh while his fingers stroked and tested. He could tell when she was nearing her climax, heard with mounting satisfaction the quickened rasp of her breathing and the soft, erotic little cries she made. Her response made him even harder, made him ache with the effort of holding back until he was breathing as fast and hard as she was, tugging at the tight bud of her nipple with his mouth.

Maggie's hips rocked wildly, and her thighs closed convulsively around his hand. He felt her damp heat spread over him, heard her sob his name in a high, wild keening. When her internal muscles clenched around his two fingers and tremors vibrated so deeply it pushed him close to the brink of release himself, Devon withdrew his hand and replaced it with the aching need of his arousal. Maggie closed around him like a glove, still vibrating with the force of her climax, and it catapulted him over the edge almost immediately. A wash of release flooded him, and he felt as if he were deeper than he'd ever been before, reaching all the way to her womb. It was the most exhilarating intimacy he'd ever felt.

He groaned, and his voice was so guttural he almost didn't recognize it as his own.

"Maggie . . . sweetheart . . . my love . . ."

It was as close as he had come to admitting how he

felt even to himself, and as soon as the words were out, he regretted them. It was insanity to feel emotion. It was certain suicide to admit it.

Devon closed his eyes, his body still throbbing inside her. When she put her arms around him and stroked back the damp strands of hair from his forehead, he knew he'd have to distance himself from her if he wanted to escape with his soul intact. He couldn't let her shatter him again.

# CHAPTER 25

Danza eyed Devon closely for a moment. The morning fire burned hot and bright, and they were both crouched in front of it sipping coffee from tin mugs and waiting for the sun to rise.

Finally Danza said in the slow, mocking drawl that never failed to irritate Devon, "Was there a cat caught in your cabin last night, amigo? I heard strange noises."

"You're too goddam nosy." Devon swallowed a gulp of coffee that burned his throat, not looking at Danza.

"I prefer to think of it as curious," the Apache said after a second's silence.

"Dress it up any way you like. It's the same damn thing." Devon drained the last of his coffee and met Danza's steady gaze. He was certain the hostility he felt was evident, and saw Danza shrug.

"Perhaps you are right. I will not be so rude as to call you a liar."

Devon felt an instant's regret for his bad mood. Damn Maggie anyway, for making him feel guilty over something he shouldn't. How did she do it? She hadn't said a word, but just stared at him with hurt in her eyes when he'd risen from the ruined cot and told her abruptly that nothing had changed.

"You're damn good in bed, baby," he'd drawled, not flinching from the swift hurt in her eyes, "but that's all that's between us."

"Of course," she'd finally said, her voice husky and slightly shaky. He'd felt like a bastard, but had been driven by an emotion he couldn't quite define to keep her at bay. He couldn't let her in again, couldn't let her close enough to hurt him.

Aware that Danza was watching him with knowing eyes, Devon stifled a curse. One of the reasons he liked riding alone was so that he didn't have to constantly justify his actions. Too bad he hadn't remembered that before allowing Danza to become so embroiled in a situation that should have been left to him to settle. He stood up abruptly.

"I'm riding out."

Danza nodded. "Malone has reached the box canyon where your trail ends. He will wait on you to show yourself."

"I don't want him to wait so long he decides to go back home." Devon reached for a second gunbelt and draped it around his hips, buckling it. He bent slightly to tie the leather thong around his left thigh, then adjust the holster to an acceptable position. Bullets studded the leather belts in a single line. There would be few chances to reload, and he didn't intend to give Johnny Malone the opportunity to catch him out.

The mood of vicious frustration that had brought him from Colorado back to Texas had grown worse. Somehow, Maggie had managed to scrape his already raw temper to the bone. It didn't ease his mood any to know that she'd been able to do it so easily because she mattered to him.

Danza stood up. Rising sunlight made the ground shimmer with a soft, pearly glow that put everything else into stark silhouette. "My scouts tell me that both Rogan and Brawley are with Malone. They should all be at the canyon before noon, amigo. We will meet you there."

Devon nodded. He had a job to do, and he resolutely

put Maggie from his mind. He'd worry about her later, figure out just what he wanted to do about her. Now he intended to kill her brother and the men who had conspired with him to get him framed, thus ridding themselves of Cimarrón.

"I've got someone meeting us at the canyon, too. But keep in mind that this is my fight. I don't want any unnecessary interference."

Danza's gaze was bland. "How do you define unnecessary?"

"Same as always. Stay out of it unless they forget the rules."

"Ah, white man's rules? Or Apache?"

Devon shot him an amused glance. "You do so love to twist what I say, don't you. You'd make a damn good lawyer, Danza. Stick to the original plan. All I want is an even chance to take Malone down. Brawley and Rogan won't be a problem then."

"If you say so, amigo."

"Do you think differently?"

Danza shrugged. "I still cannot help but wonder if Malone is the man to have planned all this. There are facts that don't quite fit."

"I told you. Brawley made him an offer, and he threw in when he found out about Rogan's thriving business. Zeke Rogan's big mistake was in hiring me to find the rustlers when what he really wanted was a man to pin it on and draw suspicion from him. Rogan misjudged me, and I think he's got that figured out by now."

"He certainly did not expect you to catch any of the rustlers, it seems."

"No, and he didn't think anyone would care if a two-bit desperado got hung for throwing a wide loop, either. It might have worked."

"With another man." Danza smiled faintly. "You were not as careless or greedy as they hoped, amigo.

But I am still uncertain about Malone. He is hot-tempered, *sí*, but I never thought him so foolish."

"Hate makes a man do foolish things."

Devon's curt retort lifted Danza's brow. "I have noticed that. So does love."

"Don't start that shit again. I'm not in the mood for it."

"Last night with your woman did not improve your temper any, amigo. I am sorry for that."

Devon turned away without comment. He had no intention of letting Danza bait him about Maggie anymore. It was obvious the Apache had some misguided notion of helping him and just as obvious that he intended to ignore what Devon wanted. If he wasn't a good friend, they would have come to blows over Danza's notion of friendly interference by now.

His mood didn't lift on the long ride to the canyon where Johnny Malone waited. If anything, it grew worse, going from reckless indifference to barely restrained violence. He needed this confrontation, needed to loose his anger and frustration on someone, and Johnny Malone would be one of the first.

It was almost noon before he reached the canyon. Spare clumps of prickly pear and mesquite dotted the high, red bluffs that dropped sharply into deep canyons and ravines. It was an easy place to hide, an easy place to wait, and Devon didn't doubt that Malone and his bunch of riders were waiting on him behind the rocks. One of the reasons Devon had chosen this canyon was because of the pockets of rock that gave easy shelter. It was an asset as well as a drawback if a man wasn't familiar with the rabbit holes carved into rock by wind and time.

Fortunately he was more than familiar with all the different cubby holes and knew which one was large enough to accommodate more than two or three men at a time. The natural cave was on the north wall, ac-

cessible by a steep slope and half-hidden by cotton-
woods. It had a small seep in the cave to provide fresh
water and would be the logical position to choose if expecting trouble.

It also had another entrance, one that was not easily
seen nor widely known. And Devon was counting on
Malone not knowing about it.

His gray stumbled on loose rock and slid a bit going
down a slope. Scattered rock bounced down the hill in
a light patter. Snorting, the gelding braced on its haun-
ches before regaining footing, then leveled out on a flat
shelf of rock. The sound of rushing water was a distant
roar.

Devon reined in. From his vantage point, he could
see out over the canyon. Nothing seemed to be moving. Wind pushed at mesquite branches. Dust lay
thickly in the air. There was a sense of waiting that
made his muscles tense expectantly, but nothing else
to betray the presence of anyone else.

But they were there.

Devon knew it instinctively. There was a difference
in the air, a subtle shimmer as if someone was watching him. Long years of running and watching his back
had kept his senses honed, and he was rarely wrong
when he felt this way.

His hand grazed the saddle scabbard of the Winchester he always carried, and he shifted it slightly to a
more accessible position. Double gunbelts held loaded
.45s, and he had tucked a pistol into his boot. He was
as ready as he could possibly be and more than ready
for Johnny Malone to make his move.

Satisfied, Devon nudged the gelding forward again.
As he rounded a sharp outthrust of rock, he saw the
riders at the same moment as they saw him. There was
time only for a brief glimpse of several men before he
was upon them. His dun charged into the middle,
sending horses scattering and sliding for footing on

the rocky ground. Grunts and curses filled the air, and Devon managed to kick his horse into a lunge through the men, knocking aside a man he recognized as a Bar Z rider.

As he pushed through, he was pulling his pistol from the holster, drawing it in a swift, smooth motion and lashing out with it. The barrel caught the nearest rider just behind the ear, and he went down as if shot while his now-riderless horse panicked and half-reared. The distraction gave Devon enough time to get off a shot that took another man down, his gun discharging as he fell from his horse. In an instant, Devon had wheeled his horse back around and took aim at another armed rider who was trying to control his panicked mount. His shot was low but knocked the cocked pistol from the man's hand.

When he reined his dun into a turn, he saw Frank Jackson only a yard away, sighting down his drawn pistol and grinning. "You're dead, Cimarrón," Jackson drawled as his finger tightened on the trigger.

But Devon didn't stop in his forward movement, firing as he spurred the dun, the huge Colt bucking in his hand. He caught a brief glimpse of surprise on Jackson's face when he passed him, and felt the harmless buzz of a bullet pass over his head. Then he was turning in the saddle and firing again, and saw Jackson's surprise turn to pain. His pistol fired into the air in a reflex action, and Jackson sagged in the saddle, then dropped to the ground like a stone.

Another bullet whipped past Devon's cheek and he ducked, spurring Pardo into a dead run down the steep slope. A short spate of bullets followed him but passed harmlessly over his head.

Shooting stopped as soon as he was out of sight, but he knew it wasn't over. Those were Bar Z riders, and though he hadn't caught a glimpse of Rogan, he knew he was somewhere close by. More than likely, Brawley was with Johnny Malone.

Malone. That was who Devon wanted with a ferocity that he couldn't hide and didn't try to. He owed him a debt, and he intended to see it paid in full. The beating Malone had given him that cold winter night in Belle Plain had stuck in his memory for too long now, and he intended to erase it the only way he knew how.

All was still, dust rising in a thin cloud that hung just above the ground in hazy streamers. The crisp, cool air held a hint of the winter that was fast approaching. Bright sunshine was scattered now as clouds moved in, rolling over the sky in thickening patches.

Johnny Malone waited at the entrance to the small cave, smelling the dust and listening for danger. It had been two hours since the Bar Z riders had surprised Cimarrón on the trail, and nothing had been seen of him since. He felt Hank Mills stir just behind him and half-turned.

"Any sign?"

Hank shook his head, grizzled face grim. "None."

Johnny swore softly. "He couldn't have just disappeared into thin air."

A grunt was the only reply from Hank, and Johnny turned back to study the trail. He could see no more than thirty yards in one direction and maybe twenty in the other. Rock walls rose high and steep, and the grit and sand of the canyon shimmered in the fitful glare of the sun. Double M men were scattered at his back and to one side, stationed in the most accessible positions. Damn. They'd followed Cimarrón's trail to this canyon, as he'd obviously meant for them to do, and now they had to wait for his next move.

Water trickled somewhere close by, making him

thirsty. Johnny reached for his canteen and twisted off the top. The water tasted flat and metallic, but was wet and cool. When he put down the canteen, he shifted his rifle and studied the trail some more. He cursed Rogan for being so careless, but what was done was done. Cimarrón knew where they were now and was ready for them.

Hank leaned forward a bit. "What made you join up with Rogan and Brawley?"

Johnny shrugged. "More men we have, the better chance of getting Cimarrón. Rumor has it that he's started ridin' with that Apache killer who scalped Ash Oliver in full view of half the army in Brackettville."

"I heard that." Hank paused. "Still, never known you to cotton to the company of snakes before."

Johnny glared at him. "Rogan ain't my friend. He's here for the same reason I am."

"Do you believe that Cimarrón rustled all those cattle? And shot those men in Abilene?"

"No," Johnny said grudgingly, "but he's sure as hell done a lot of other killings. Don't forget that man named Jenkins, shot down in cold blood Cimarrón's first day in Belle Plain. Ask Brawley about it. He saw it."

"That's another thing. Brawley came into town on the same day as Maggie."

"Yeah. What about it?"

"Jenkins was shot the day before she got back home."

Johnny stared at Hank. He was right. Brawley couldn't have been there. He'd come in on the stage with Maggie the day after it happened. An uneasy feeling settled in the pit of his stomach. He couldn't be wrong about Cimarrón. Too many things had happened. He looked away from Hank.

"Don't matter if Brawley saw it or not. It happened."

"Where'd he go?"

"Said he was gonna wait on Cimarrón up in the rocks and fire a warning shot when he got here." Johnny shifted, a frown narrowing his eyes. Somehow, knowing Brawley had lied about seeing Jenkins shot down rankled, but he didn't want Hank to know he had doubts. Why would Brawley lie? Hell, it didn't make a nickel's worth of difference to him if he'd seen Jenkins go down, only that Cimarrón had done it. So why lie about it?

"Ever wonder why it takes so damn many men to catch just one man?" Hank drawled.

Johnny turned back. "What's that supposed to mean?"

Hank shrugged. "Just a thought." Several minutes passed in silence, then he spoke softly. "You thought about what you're gonna do with Cimarrón when you catch him?"

"Yeah." Johnny's tone was grim. "First, I'm gonna get Maggie back safely. Then I'm gonna beat the hell out of him again before we hang him."

Silence greeted his words, and he felt rather than heard Hank's disapproval. He turned to look at his foreman.

Hank was watching him from beneath the brim of his hat, a guarded expression in his eyes. Finally he said in a slow, measured voice, "Johnny, I've known you a long time. Watched you grow up, practically. I ain't never known you to be mean, but I have known you to be wrong. Think about what you're doin' here."

"What's that supposed to mean?"

"Well, we came after Miss Maggie 'cause she was taken against her will, and I ain't never held with a man doin' a woman wrong. But Cimarrón is her husband, and I think she loves him, no matter the bad beginnin'. It weren't her fault what happened that night, but she got stuck with the bitter endin' of it. Mebbe now is the time to clear things up and tell the truth."

Johnny felt a wave of incredulous fury. "You're taking up for Cimarrón? What the hell is the matter with you, Hank? He's a two-bit desperado who got Maggie pregnant, left her, then came back and took her off against her will."

"And I'm thinkin' that he didn't know she was pregnant or he wouldn't have left, no matter the bad blood between you two. That's what this is all about, Johnny. You and him. Miss Maggie just got caught in the middle."

It was the truth, and Johnny had to admit it to himself even if he didn't admit it to anyone else. He looked away from Hank, staring off over the rocky cliffs and gnarled humps of rock. A cluster of trees and stunted brush made short shadows on the hard ground. The sun was high overhead, and it looked to be a long day of waiting.

"There's only one way this can end, Hank," he said finally, and there was enough truth in that to keep the foreman silent.

Maggie stood in the shade of the cook tent and watched some of the men saddle their horses, and knew that something was about to happen. There was an air of taut excitement in the way they talked in low voices and checked their weapons. It had to do with Devon and Johnny, and she knew it.

She untied the long strings to the apron she wore over her clothes and pulled it off, shoving it into Concha's broad hands. "I'll be back."

"*Alto*," the woman began, but Maggie shoved past her so firmly that she staggered backward and had to catch herself. Concha called out sharply, and Maggie had gone no more than two yards before a man was at her side.

"Señora," he began as he blocked her progress, "you must not be foolish."

Maggie stepped around him. When he moved in front of her again, she jerked to a halt and glared up at him. "I want to see Danza. Take me to him. Now."

The man hesitated, but then shrugged and stepped back to let her precede him. "This way."

Danza was already mounted when Maggie reached him, and he stared down at her impassively as she broke into a spate of angry words.

"I know what's going on, and I demand to go with you. I refuse to just wait here in camp while Devon and Johnny do their best to kill one another. If you don't care about Devon, I do, and whether my brother is right or wrong, I care about him, too. Do you understand what I am saying, Danza? I demand to be taken to them, so that I can stop this ridiculous feud before it gets any worse."

The Apache had said nothing while she talked, merely gazed down at her quietly. Maggie felt her heart sink. He would take Devon's part, of course. Men never saw the futility in shooting at each other. It was left to the woman to weep over lost causes and dead bodies. She didn't know why she'd come to him, except that she felt a desperate need to try something, anything that would save lives and grief.

It was a surprise when Danza nodded. "You may come with me, Señora, but only if you will promise to abide by my orders."

"I promise, of course."

Danza's mouth curled in a faint smile. "We shall see how well you keep that promise." He held out a hand, and Maggie took it and was swung up behind him. She hardly dared believe it had been so easy.

It wasn't until they drew near the rocky slopes of the canyon and she heard the unmistakeable pop of gunfire that she began to wonder just how she'd be able to stop the inevitable.

# Chapter 26

Devon swore softly. His position was good, tucked into the folds of rock and brush, but not nearly as good as it should have been. Bar Z riders had rushed him, and he'd been caught short of his destination. But he had Malone where he wanted him, waiting at the mouth of the cave and watching for Cimarrón to make the first move or get careless. Devon grinned without real humor. Johnny Malone had a hell of a surprise in store for him.

Clouds obscured the sun now and made the light gray. A storm was promised in the growing whip of wind and dropping temperature. For some reason, Devon thought of the last time he'd been in a similar situation. That had been in the Lost Canyon, when G.K. Durant had managed to get past the guards and box them in. Only then it had been Devon on the defensive and Durant with all the odds on his side.

This time there were no surprises and Devon held the odds in his favor. Johnny Malone would suspect that Cimarrón would have help, but he wouldn't know how many. And he would not expect an ambush.

Devon's mouth thinned. It was time to finish this once and for all. Where the hell was Danza?

Maggie's arms ached from holding on as Danza urged his mount up the steep incline. More gunfire sounded, loud and brittle, echoing in the canyon and sounding as if it was all around them. She shivered.

Her skirt was hitched up almost to her knees, and her bare legs were chilled from the brisk bite of the wind. She should have worn pants. Danza had stopped at one point and given her a wool serape to wear, so she was warmer than she had been, but the weather had turned much cooler than before.

Roe Frayser said something in Spanish to Danza, and he answered in hard, clipped tones. Then the Apache was reining his horse to a halt in the shelter of a rocky overhang and reaching for Maggie.

"You will stay here," he said when she'd slid from the horse and was looking up at him. "Roe will be with you."

A protest formed, but before she could voice it, he shook his head. "No. You said you would abide by my orders. Do not argue. I do not tolerate disobedience from women."

Angry, Maggie burst out, "But how am I supposed to do anything if I can't get near enough to help?"

"That's not why you are here."

She glared at the Apache's impassive face. He was implacable, and she realized the futility of further discussion. Yet frustration made her say, "I did not come with you just to be left behind at the last moment."

Danza shrugged. "That is unfortunate. I did not bring you with me just to have you in danger. You will stay here."

Maggie stared after him when he wheeled his mount around and nudged it into a fast trot. The rest of the men followed him, leaving her alone with Roe. She gave the young man a quick, cursory glance and saw the sympathy in his green eyes.

He cleared his throat. "Cimarrón wouldn't like it, you know, if you was to get hurt."

"If he lives to feel anything at all."

Roe didn't say anything to that, and Maggie turned away to sit on a flat shelf of rock. Bushes lined the wall several yards away, stunted scrub that followed the line of the trail. The wind had picked up, and she could smell the promise of rain in the air. November could be raw in Texas, even as far south as she suspected they were. She pulled the serape more tightly around her and hunched against the wind.

After a few moments, Roe dismounted and came to stand beside her. He seemed uncomfortable and kept glancing at her and then away. He held the ends of his leather reins in one hand, popping them against his other palm in a flicking motion. It grew quiet, with no more gunfire, and nothing seeming to move except for the constant whip of Roe's reins against his palm. Finally Maggie couldn't stand it any longer.

"Will you stop that?"

He looked at her in surprise, then shrugged. "Sorry. I guess I'm wonderin' what's happenin', too."

"Well, I see no sense in us staying up here when we could be down there watching from a safe distance." Maggie saw the uncertainty in Roe's face and pressed home her point. "We wouldn't have to get too close, just near enough to be there in case we're needed."

Roe shook his head. "Danza said stay here."

"He just meant stay out of range."

"No. He meant stay here." Roe gave a half-shrug when she opened her mouth to argue some more. "He don't say what he don't mean, Miss Maggie."

"Do you always let him tell you what to do?" she couldn't help asking sharply.

"If I don't like what he says, I'm free to ride on."

"Does that hold true for me?"

Roe grinned. "Now, you know it don't."

Maggie's hand bunched into the folds of serape. Another shot sounded, and she swallowed her irritation and anxiety as she rose to her feet. Roe was looking up and past her, his gaze trained on the place where the ground dipped sharply away, then rose again into a narrow ledge.

"If you don't mind," she said, drawing his attention back to her, "I need a moment of privacy."

He frowned. "I don't know—"

"I'm certain Danza did not mean for you to follow me into the bushes," she cut in, her tone scathing and making his young face flush. "I assume that I am still allowed a certain privacy for some things?"

"Yeah, sure. I just—" He halted, then gave a helpless shrug. "All right. But don't go no farther than them bushes right there."

"I wouldn't dream of it."

Maggie followed the line of bushes for several yards before spotting the break where the trail cut through. She felt Roe watching her, and slid into the break and then turned to wave at him. He waved back, then averted his gaze as she had suspected he would.

She was nervous and could hear the rattle of gunfire again. Quickly she slipped the serape over her head and hung it on the bushes, certain that Roe would see it and think she was still there. A nervous laugh welled in her throat as she considered his thoughts when she remained in the bushes for so long. He'd probably think her ill and would eventually come closer to investigate. She could buy a few minutes at best, and she didn't waste any time in moving down the rocky trail toward the source of gunfire.

A crack of lightning flashed overhead, closely followed by a rolling boom of thunder. Devon sighted down his Winchester, squeezed the trigger, and heard the faint cry of pain from his target.

He pumped the lever and began a firestorm of bullets when he saw Danza on the far ridge. That should keep Malone and his men close to cover until Danza had a chance to get near enough, he thought grimly. It had taken him a while, but he'd finally maneuvered himself into a position where he had the distinct advantage.

Now the approaching rain might take it away, destroy his visibility, and make his situation hazardous. He swore softly, firing until Danza and the six men with him had reached the safety of the rocks.

" 'Bout time you got here," he commented when the Apache had circled around and joined him. "Been on a picnic?"

Danza grunted irritably. "The white man has a saying about not looking a gift horse in the mouth, I believe."

Devon squeezed off another shot, then turned with a grin. "This horse is a bit long in the tooth, I think, but a welcome sight."

Danza gestured to the mouth of the cave visible on the ridge below. "How many are there?"

"About ten or eleven. I've been keeping them penned in since I got up here. There are more men scattered through the canyon. Bar Z men, and I haven't seen Rogan yet, though I had a run-in with some of his riders."

Danza nodded. "I left five men behind me."

"Remember—Malone is mine. Did you tell them?"

"I told them."

Devon turned back and laid his rifle down to roll a smoke. He could smell rain in the air, and thunder rumbled in the distance. Damn the weather. It could complicate his plan.

When he'd finished his cigarette, he said, "Keep them busy while I circle around."

Danza stood up. "I'll go with you."

"No. This is my fight, remember? I just want Malone to myself."

When Danza nodded, Devon glanced back at the

mouth of the cave where Johnny Malone waited. He was ready for him.

"How the hell many are with him?" Johnny squinted into the gray light, counting. "I see six."

"Plus more up on the ridge," Hank said gruffly.

"Odds are about even then. Any sign of Rogan yet?"

"He's trapped in the brush on the north slope. He looks like he's tryin' to work his way around."

Johnny nodded with satisfaction. "He'll make it. With Rogan as backup, we've got Cimarrón almost where we want him. He's in those rocks just above that low ridge. We've got water and cover. If he wants us, he has to come and get us, and he'll get killed tryin' it."

"Wonder where Miss Maggie is."

"We'll find her." Johnny turned to look at Hank. "When this is over, we'll find her."

"He won't have her close by, I'm bettin'."

"And I'm bettin' we can beat it out of one of those men when we need to."

"Hope you're right."

Johnny looked back out the entrance of the cave. Rain threatened. Thunder growled in the distance, and the wind had risen sharply.

"I'm right," he said softly. "I have to be."

He was still gazing out the mouth of the cave when an explosion rocked the ground and sent a shower of rocks falling down like rain. The percussion knocked him to the ground and the breath from his lungs, and he scrambled back to his feet in a daze. A sharp, familiar odor hung in the air, as thick as smoke and unmistakeable.

"Damn them," he choked out. "The bastard used dynamite on us!"

Obviously rattled, Hank got to his feet more slowly. No one had been hurt, but the mouth to the cave was half-covered with a loose pile of rock. Other men were swearing and picking themselves up off the floor of the cave. A thin trickle of blood dribbled down Hank's face, and Johnny gave him a bandanna to wipe it away.

"If he thinks that will work," Johnny said grimly, "he is about to find out how wrong he is."

"Is that right, Malone?" a familiar, mocking voice rasped behind him, and Johnny turned slowly. Cimarrón stood on a low rock ledge, his rifle at the ready. Several Double M men swore, and Cimarrón gestured with the cocked rifle.

"I wouldn't try anything, boys, or Malone will be the first to go down. Tell 'em, Malone. It's me and you, just the two of us, one on one."

Johnny stared at Cimarrón for a long moment. "Where's Maggie?"

"Safe. What about it, Malone?"

Hatred welled high and hot, and Johnny nodded, his voice harsh. "You and me, Cimarrón."

Maggie stumbled, cutting her hand on the sharp edge of a rock. A shower of pebbles rolled from underfoot, and she skidded several feet down the trail. The gunfire had stopped after an awful, crashing explosion, and she was terrified. What had happened? Dear God, she couldn't bear it if Devon was hurt or—her mind wouldn't let her finish the thought. It was too much to contemplate.

Erosion had cut the ground into deep gullies, and she had to climb in and out of them as she worked her way down the canyon wall. A sense of urgency spurred her on, and she half-expected to find Roe Frayser behind her at any moment. If only she could reach Devon and Johnny before they got to each other.

But when Maggie finally reached the plateau, she saw that she was too late. Even from a distance, she would have recognized Devon. His gold hair glittered dully in the gray light of the day, and his lean frame looked dangerous and waiting. Johnny stood only a few feet from him, braced for trouble. Armed men were scattered behind them. She recognized some of the Double M riders, and even a Bar Z rider or two, as well as Danza's men.

Breathless and terrified that they were about to draw on one another, Maggie watched with wide eyes as she stumbled forward. When she lifted her arm and started to call out, she felt someone grab her wrist and was jerked around so quickly she had no time to do more than gasp.

"Don't you know any better than to distract men intent on shooting it out, Miss Malone?"

Maggie's protest stuck in her throat. David Brawley held her wrist in an iron grip, his hazel eyes cool and remote. "David," she said faintly. "What are you doing here?"

"I came to rescue you, of course. Only, the way I hear it, you don't exactly want to be rescued."

There was an insolent edge to his tone, and she drew her arm from his grasp. "I don't know what you mean."

David shrugged. "Sure you do. Cimarrón married you at the end of a rifle, but no one forced him into your bed."

Maggie flushed but lifted her chin proudly. "Don't be rude. It's none of your business what I do."

"No. It's not. Ah-ah," he said when she started to turn away, reaching for her, "you stay here with me."

"I will not. I intend to go down there and stop this before it goes any farther."

"You'll stay here, dammit." Brawley gripped her arm cruelly. "I won't let you ruin this after it's taken so long to get it this far."

She stared at him. "What are you talking about?"

"This." Brawley gestured to Devon and Johnny, who had unbuckled their gunbelts and obviously meant to fistfight. "When it's over, they'll both be dead."

Maggie tried to pull away, but he shoved her up against a sharp outcropping of rock. "Let me go," she began, and he twisted her arm up and behind her so hard and swiftly that she cried out with the pain.

"No. I told you, you're staying here."

"Have you gone crazy?" she gasped out. "What are you doing?"

"Protecting something that's taken me a year and a half to arrange, that's what I'm doing. No one is going to mess it up for me, no one." Brawley pulled her up the trail a few feet, keeping to the cover of the rocks. He forced her down into a tight crevice, then stood over her.

Frightened now as well as angry, Maggie looked up at him. "Why are you doing this?" She shifted slightly and gained a little more room in the snug position. She was bent almost double, so that her knees were just below chin level and her arms hooked on rough slabs of rock.

Brawley glanced down at her and gestured to where Devon and Johnny were situated. "If Cimarrón hadn't interfered, I would have managed things a lot quicker. Zeke Rogan is about as dumb as an anvil, and when he got the bright idea to hire a gunman like Cimarrón and pin the rustling on him, he didn't check with me first. It almost got us caught, if I hadn't been smart enough to figure a way out of it."

Still perplexed, Maggie shook her head. "Zeke Rogan is the rustler? But why would he rustle his own cattle?"

"Don't be stupid. It was to hide the fact that he was the only rancher in this area not suffering any losses. It was easy enough to cull the worst of his herd, take them along with the others, and sell them on the feed lot in Abilene."

Maggie suddenly understood. "All this time, you've been involved in the rustling. Your position with the Texas and Pacific Railroad made it easy for you to ship the stolen cattle, and the only ranchers to suffer any real losses were my brother and the others. Bar Z was never in trouble like Zeke claimed it was."

David Brawley smiled. "You're smarter than the rest of the folks around here. Even your brother still doesn't know the truth."

Anger rushed through her. "Do you think he won't figure it out quick enough? Or that I won't tell?"

"Ah, but he'll be dead, and you, my sweet, won't be able to tell anyone."

"You'll have to kill me."

"Maybe." Brawley knelt down, eyes fixed on her face. "Unless you're smart enough to see the advantages in all this. I meant it when I told you that I was in love with you." He reached out to lift a strand of her hair and let it slide through his fingers. "If your brother had been smart enough to sell out, I wouldn't have had to take drastic measures. But he wasn't. And I had Cimarrón to worry about getting out of the way as well. Malone almost took care of that problem for me, and when he sold me that land last winter, I almost had him where I wanted him. No bank would lend him any money to keep the ranch afloat without enough cattle to make it profitable, and I would have given him a decent enough price for it. Then as soon as Rogan was out of the way, I'd own most of Callahan County. I can still do it. Rogan's cunning, but he's no businessman. He signed a paper that virtually gives me the Bar Z." His voice lowered slightly. "With you as my wife, Maggie, we could do anything we wanted to do, go anywhere we wanted to go."

"You're mad!"

"No, just smart enough to get what I want. And I want you. I always have."

He wound his hand into her loose hair and tilted back her head, ignoring her angry protest as he bent to kiss her. Maggie tried to push him away but couldn't. He had all the advantage with her wedged into the splice between rocks. Desperately her hands flailed outward, and she grabbed a loose rock, bringing it up and down in a savage blow.

Brawley groaned, and she hit him again, then again. He sagged forward instead of sideways as she'd hoped, and she strained to push him away. He was heavy, and it took several tense minutes before she managed to push him aside, then more time to free herself from the rock. Brawley lay sprawled on a rock, breathing heavily, eyes closed.

Scratched and bleeding, Maggie staggered to her feet. She swayed slightly, then started down the slope. She saw Devon and Johnny, both of them slamming fists into the other. An involuntary cry burst from her, and she put a hand over her mouth. Brawley had been right. She shouldn't distract them. Rolling thunder growled overhead as she forced herself down the hill toward them.

Devon's right fist went high and hard, catching Malone on the chin and stopping his lunge. Johnny blinked, then shook his head and started forward again, swinging his fists. One of them caught Devon on the side of his head, making his ears ring while the other fist aimed for his belly. Devon managed to deflect the blow with his arm, then turned as Johnny smashed a fist into his shoulder.

When Malone swung back around, Devon smashed a left into his face, sending out a shower of blood. Johnny staggered but didn't fall, and came back with both hands moving steadily. There was the rusty taste of blood in Devon's mouth as he countered the blows. Then Malone jarred him with a right to the head and a short jab with his left fist. He recovered quickly, swinging low to butt Johnny in the chest and take him down.

Malone got up more slowly this time, swinging around to catch Devon's fist full in the face. Several short jabs took him to his knees again, and Devon stood wide-legged, pumping blows at Johnny Malone with fierce vengeance. His blood was running hot and high, and he stood toe to toe with Malone until finally he went down again and sprawled on the rock.

Devon was breathing hard and fast, and stood ready in case Malone got to his feet again. The big man just lay there for a while, out cold, and slowly, Devon relaxed. He looked up and saw men watching him. No one had moved to break it up. It had been a fair fight, which was more than Johnny Malone had given him on that cold winter night a year before.

Blood and sweat blurred his vision, and he barely felt the first drop of rain. Oddly, the hatred he'd felt for so long had dissipated. Now he just felt a cold weariness.

A crack of lightning split the air, closely followed by the rolling boom of thunder. Devon wiped the blood and sweat from his eyes with his shirt sleeve, and his gaze focused on Zeke Rogan.

"You want in this, Rogan?"

Rogan flushed and shook his head. "No. This is betwixt you two."

"Not all of it." Devon stood loosely, watching Rogan. Danza's men circled them and were just waiting for a signal to open fire. The Bar Z and Double M riders were boxed in and knew it. Devon didn't see Brawley, but he had Rogan where he wanted him and that was what mattered now.

"So, Rogan, which way do you want it?"

Clearing his throat, Rogan rasped, "What the hell do you mean?"

"I think you know what I mean. You can draw on me, or you can take your chances with a jury and a length of hemp."

"Hell, Cimarrón, this ain't my fight," Rogan protested. "Your beef is with Malone, not me."

"No, my beef is with both of you." Devon shifted slightly to keep Rogan in line when the big man began to shuffle away. "You hired me to find rustlers, only you didn't think I'd catch 'em. What you counted on was pinning it on me and watching me hang for what you were doing. You want to tell me that's a lie?"

Rogan glanced at Danza and his men, his expression growing faintly desperate. "Look, Cimarrón, it ain't quite like you think."

"No? Tell me how it is. I'm interested in hearing."

"Hell, we never thought you'd catch anybody. You were just supposed to be for looks, that's all. To keep anyone from suspecting." Rogan began to sweat despite the chill wind, beads standing out on his forehead. There was murder in some of the eyes staring at him, and he had to know it.

"Suspecting what? That you and Malone were partners in stealing half the cattle in Callahan County?"

"Malone?" Rogan looked startled. "Hell, he ain't got nothin' to do with it. He's just a dumb bastard like the others, makin' their plans and callin' meetin's, then sittin' back and watchin' their beeves disappear."

It was Devon's turn to be startled. He flicked a glance at Johnny Malone and saw him begin to stir, groaning. Could he be wrong about Malone? It didn't seem likely. He'd seen him take money from David Brawley, and there could only be one explanation for that. Unless—

"Who's in on it with you, Rogan?" When Zeke Rogan still hesitated, Devon drew his pistol, cocking back the hammer in the same smooth motion. Rogan turned an ugly shade of gray. "I asked you a question.

And when I get impatient, my hand shakes. When my hand shakes—"

"All right, all right." Rogan sucked in a deep breath and ignored some of the curses from his men as he muttered, "Brawley."

"Brawley? David Brawley?" It made sense all of a sudden. Only Brawley had complete access to shipping lots and buyers, and Brawley would know where and when to ship cattle without lot numbers. "Damn. I should have figured it would be Brawley. How'd you get hooked up with him?"

Rogan shrugged. "I needed money and he knew a way to get it."

By now Johnny Malone was sitting up, eyeing Latigo, who had a rifle trained on him. "Let me ask him a few questions, Cimarrón," he mumbled, the words mushy in his torn, bleeding mouth.

"You'll have your turn soon enough. I think there's some U.S. Marshals who might want to talk to him first." Devon holstered his pistol and turned away. A sudden sound made him turn back even before he heard Danza's sharp warning, and he was reaching for his gun as he completed the turn in a low crouch.

Rogan's gun was already in his hand, and he was thumbing back the hammer when Devon drew. The bullets fired simultaneously, and Rogan stumbled slightly. Devon fired again and saw the burly rancher take a sidestep and drop his pistol. Rogan seemed to hang in the air for a moment, then slowly collapsed to the ground with a harsh rattling sound in his throat. None of the Bar Z riders moved so much as an eyelash when Devon moved to Rogan and rolled him to his back.

Rogan's mouth moved soundlessly for a moment, then he shuddered and was still. Devon looked up at the silent men.

"Anyone feel like Rogan got a raw deal?"

No one spoke, then a Bar Z hand shrugged and said, "Reckon he shoulda kept his iron in leather."

"Reckon he should have," Devon agreed, and stood up. He felt suddenly weary. This was what he'd wanted, a showdown and some answers, but it left him feeling strangely unsettled. Maybe it was because he'd believed Malone responsible for so long, and it was hard to give up on vengeance.

"Amigo," the Apache said quietly, and pointed.

Devon half-turned and was startled to see Maggie coming down a steep slope, her hair flying behind her like dark ribbons. "Damn," he muttered, "what the hell is she doing here?"

Another crash of lightning smothered Danza's reply, and then Devon was walking away, moving toward Maggie. He'd gone no more than three steps when a burst of thunder sounded and he saw her fall. Then more thunder rolled, and he realized that the first had been gunfire. Moving more from instinct than anything else, he was running toward her.

Behind him, men shouted and shots rang out, but he didn't glance back. All his attention was focused on Maggie lying in the rocks. She hadn't moved since falling.

Then he saw David Brawley, saw him on a rock ledge just above, a pistol in his hand. Devon grabbed at his gun and rolled in the same movement, the Colt bucking in his palm as he fired. Brawley staggered and fired again, and Devon emptied his pistol, feeling helpless rage and a sense of panic that didn't ease even when he saw Brawley finally go down.

It couldn't be happening to him again. Unbelievably it looked as if Brawley had shot Maggie, but he couldn't have.

"God," he heard himself saying over and over again as he stumbled to his feet and ran toward Maggie. She lay on the ground, motionless, and he felt his heart in his throat. Just as he reached her, the clouds opened up and rain poured down with a vengeance.

Devon fell to his knees beside Maggie, choking with fear and grief. He put a trembling hand on her throat to feel for a pulse but couldn't find one. His hand shook, and he stared down at her in disbelief.

"Maggie, Maggie, oh Jesus not again, please God not again." He lifted her in his arms, and her head fell back limply, dark hair streaming over his arms. Blood stained her blouse, and he howled out his rage and anguish. Harsh sobs caught in his throat, and the tears he hadn't been able to shed for Molly so long ago flowed freely now. He loved Maggie, and God, he'd loved Molly, too, but this was different. He'd been able to put Molly to rest when he'd found Maggie, and though he'd never forget her, he'd known at last that he could go on with life and love again.

And now he'd lost the reason.

Rain mingled with the hot tears on his cheeks, streaming down his face and mixing with Maggie's blood.

"God," he choked out, burying his face against Maggie's neck and holding her close to him, "I never knew how I felt until it was too late. Oh Maggie, I never even told you I love you. I'm so sorry, damn, I'm so sorry."

His arms tightened, as if by holding her so closely he could bring her back to life. He was only vaguely aware of someone coming up behind him, of Johnny Malone kneeling in the mud and rock but not reaching for her, as if he knew that his sister belonged to Devon.

Devon looked up at last. His voice was raw, his throat tight with tears and pain. "I loved her, Malone."

Johnny nodded. "I know that now."

Something pushed at Devon's chest, a weak motion as if a small animal had been caught between him and Maggie, and he looked down. Maggie was staring up at him, her mouth turned down in a frown.

"About time . . . you said . . . that," she muttered, then moaned when Devon's grip tightened. "You're hurting me . . ."

"Damn, she's alive!" Devon surged to his feet, Maggie in his arms. He looked up wildly and saw the surprised relief in Malone's face. "Don't just stand there, dammit, let's get her to a doctor."

He felt Maggie stir and bent his head to hear her say weakly, "I have something . . . to tell you."

"Later, sweetheart. Right now, you're the most important thing on my mind."

Her lips curved in a faint, satisfied smile. "Glad to hear . . . that at . . . last."

"You're going to hear it a lot from now on," Devon said recklessly, and didn't even care that he was taking such a big chance. "I swear, you're going to hear it a lot."

She blinked against the rain as he carried her back up toward the cave, and just before she fainted, she whispered, "I love you."

Devon's throat tightened. "I love you, too," he said, but she didn't hear.

# CHAPTER 27

Maggie blinked against the bright press of sunlight. It came through the windows of the neat, comfortable cabin where they'd taken her to recuperate. It was the first sunlight she'd seen in days. Rain had scoured the countryside for almost a week, long gray days filled with pain and fever. Finally her fever had broken, much to the relief of Roe Frayser.

"I was beginnin' to worry, I don't mind tellin' you," he said cheerfully, when he brought her some hot soup. "I ain't a doctor like you."

Maggie managed a smile. She wanted to ask about Devon and her brother, but each time she brought up the subject, Roe changed it so swiftly she knew something was wrong. Had they killed one another? The last she recalled, Johnny had been with Devon at her bedside. She had only vague memories of them with her, but it seemed as if every time she opened her eyes, Devon had been there. She could remember the low rasp of his voice comforting her during the worst of the pain, then merciful oblivion.

Everything had blended together, become a blur of events with no beginning and no end, but Devon had been a constant. It was his face she saw when her eyes were open, and his face she saw when her eyes were closed. But she had not seen him for two days now, and no one would tell her where he was. She knew better than to ask.

But it was worrying her so badly she knew she had

to ask again, and she looked up at Roe. "Where's Devon? And my brother?"

Roe glanced behind him, then shrugged. "You'll have to ask Danza. I don't know."

"I want to see Danza."

"Well, he ain't here right now, and—"

"I want to see him, or I'll go find him myself!" Maggie said hotly, and reached to turn back the covers.

Alarmed, Roe stopped her. "All right, all right," he said hastily, "I'll find Danza for you."

He did, but Maggie quickly discovered that the Apache had no intention of telling her anything either.

"You must not worry. They are well. There is much business to take care of, señora, that is all."

Maggie glared up at him where he stood beside her bed, his face impassive again. She forced herself to speak calmly.

"Don't you know that if a patient is anxious it slows their recovery? Even if it's bad news, tell me. I can deal with that better than I can uncertainty."

"I agree with you, but I gave my word." Danza shrugged when she swore at him. "Your tongue is sharp, but it has not changed my mind."

"Don't you have any feelings at all? Can't you see how worried I am?"

"*Sí*, and I have told you that your brother and Cimarrón are well. You should not worry."

"But why aren't they here?"

Danza looked exasperated, a hint of it finally evident on his normally impassive face. He said something rough in a low growl, the language obviously Apache, then shook his head. "I have much sympathy for my amigo. I cannot answer your questions, though I sympathize with you. If you grow too agitated or too annoying, I will have you tied to the bed so you do not hurt yourself. Do you understand?"

"I understand," she said tightly, and watched him

pivot on the heel of his foot and leave the room. She sagged back into her pillows and stared up at the low ceiling.

Her shoulder ached, and her entire body felt as if she had been run over by a train. Yet her most pressing worry was the unknown. Where were Devon and Johnny?

Devon reined in his mount on the crest of the slope overlooking Danza's camp. Now that he was here, he wished he wasn't. He didn't know what he'd say when he saw her again. For the last hundred miles he'd turned it over in his mind again and again, and still wasn't any closer to the right words.

"You plannin' on sittin' on this hill long, Cimarrón?"

Devon shot Johnny Malone a narrowed glance. "Got any objections?"

Malone grunted an indistinct reply and shook his head. Devon looked past him to the guard perched atop a high rim watching them. They'd been watched for over an hour, and Danza would know they were back. He nudged his mount forward at last and heard Malone follow.

The tiny cabin where Maggie was recuperating was tucked in the middle of a grove of old oaks with spreading branches and massive trunks. The original owner had long been forgotten, but it was obvious the dwelling had been built with caring hands. It still stood strong and sturdy despite the wind and weather and neglect. When Danza had come to this remote canyon in the hills, the cabin had long since been abandoned. Until Maggie's recent occupation, the Apache had been the only occasional tenant.

Devon stepped up onto the low, planked porch and paused, still uncertain of his welcome. He'd hated to

leave before Maggie was awake enough to realize why
he had to go, but what was done was done.

"Cimarrón."

He turned and saw Malone right behind him. "Do
you have to follow me everywhere, dammit?"

"I'd like to see my sister." Malone's jaw thrust out
belligerently. "She's gonna want to see me, too."

Devon would have liked to argue the point but
didn't. He swung open the door and let Malone precede him, then stepped in and shut it behind him. Concha was there, her bulk cozily ensconced in a comfortable chair. From the main room, he could see through
the open door to where Maggie lay on a wide bed,
quilt drawn up to her chin.

"Is she all right?" he demanded, then remembered
that Concha didn't speak English. Before he could re-
phrase the question in Spanish, she rose from the chair
and nodded.

*"Santo y bueno."*

Johnny Malone was already walking into Maggie's
room, and Devon followed, feeling faintly foolish and
definitely awkward. What the hell could he say? That
he hadn't known he still cared? That he could forgive
and forget everything bad that had been between
them? It was true, all of it, but he didn't know if she'd
believe him. Hell, he wouldn't believe it if he didn't
know it was the truth.

He stopped just inside the door, watching when
Johnny went to stand beside the bed. Maggie's eyes
opened slowly, then widened, and she started to sit
up. Johnny pushed her gently back to the pillows and
cleared his throat.

"It's all right. I just . . . just wanted you to know I'm
here."

"Where the devil have you been?" she asked
crossly, then her gaze shifted to Devon. "And you as
well? Why weren't you here?"

"There was all-out war after you got shot, Maggie," Johnny said when Devon didn't reply. "Bar Z boys and Double M boys mixed it up pretty good for a while."

"I thought you were on the same side."

Johnny flushed. "So did I. But when Brawley shot you, I saw real quick which way the wind was blowin'."

Maggie stared at him incredulously. "David Brawley shot me?"

"You don't remember?"

Maggie's gaze moved back to Devon, and she frowned. "No, I just remember thinking I'd been struck by lightning, then Devon was holding me."

"That was a slug from a .45, not lightnin'," Johnny said grimly.

"I know that now. But why?" Maggie's gaze was bewildered. "I mean, I know he was behind the rustling, but why shoot me?"

"How did you know that?"

"He told me. Up in the rocks before I got away from him. He wanted the Double M and the Bar Z, and all this time he was plotting to get them." Her gaze held her brother's for a moment. "Did you know about it?"

"Not for a while. And when I found out some of it, I admit that I didn't tell anyone. I knew Brawley was tryin' to pin it all on Cimarrón, and that suited me fine." Johnny's mouth twisted into a grimace. "Reckon I should have gone to the sheriff with what I knew, but like I said, I wanted Cimarrón away from you."

Devon listened quietly. He'd already heard all this when Malone had given his statement to the U.S. marshal, but he knew how Maggie must feel at hearing it for the first time. Though Johnny had not actually taken part in the rustling, there was still the possibility that he might be charged with obstruction of justice for his part in everything that had happened.

"I found out about it," Malone was saying, "when I

sold Brawley that piece of land. I overheard him talking to Rogan, but I kept quiet. It was Brawley who shot those men in Abilene, and he was the witness who identified Cimarrón as the killer. He needed Cimarrón out of the way, and since he hadn't been able to pin the rustling on him yet, he tried another way. After Cimarrón killed Oliver, Brawley figured it would have to be the law who got him out of the way. But then—'' He paused and glanced at Devon. "Then I found out about you and him and decided to take care of him my own way. I'm sorry, Maggie."

Her voice was a low whisper. "So am I, Johnny." She glanced at Devon, and he felt his stomach muscles tighten. "Devon, do you mind if I talk to my brother privately for a moment?"

He shrugged. "I can come back later—"

"No. Just wait outside for a moment. I have something I want to tell you, but . . . but I have to talk to him first."

It shouldn't have made a difference, but somehow it did. Devon left the room and the cabin, and went to stand in the cold wind beneath an ancient oak. He saw Danza in the distance, his tall frame easily distinguishable from the men around him as he moved gracefully.

Danza came to stand beside him. "I am glad to see you safe, amigo."

"Did you think I wouldn't be?"

"No, I knew you would be back." Danza paused, then said softly, "What do you intend to do, amigo?"

Devon didn't say anything for a moment. "I don't know," he finally admitted. "I thought if I got my name cleared again I'd be satisfied, but I'm not. There's a lot of lost time, a lot of lies."

"Yet you have forgiven Malone."

"No, I've accepted it. There's a difference."

"That is true." Danza leaned against the broad trunk

of the oak, studying him. "It is not the truth that has you dissatisfied, amigo. It's the uncertainty."

"More Apache philosophy?"

"You could say that."

"Well, save it. I'm not in the mood."

"You never are." Danza shrugged when Devon shot him a quick glance. "Remember that the truth is not always easy to tell."

"Or hear."

Danza nodded. "That, too." A gust of wind blew his long hair across his face, and he shifted it away. "What will you do now, amigo?"

"That depends a lot on Maggie," Devon replied after a moment. "I did a lot of thinking on my way to Abilene and back."

"And what conclusions did you reach?"

A faint smile curled one side of Devon's mouth. "That I've been a fool, for one thing. For another, that if she doesn't want me anymore, I don't know where I'll go or what I'll do."

Danza's brow lifted. "You have been alone a long time, amigo. Why is it different now?"

"Because I know what I could have had, and what I'll miss if I lose her." Devon's throat tightened, and he felt more vulnerable than he could ever remember feeling. He'd never said these things aloud, and he wasn't certain why he was now, except that he knew Danza would understand. There was a depth to the Apache that he'd never wanted to see, but he knew it was there. Danza would not laugh or criticize.

Danza put out his hand, and Devon stared at it for an instant before taking it. A faint smile touched the corners of Danza's mouth.

"I am proud to call you my friend, amigo. I wish you well."

"Are you leaving here?"

"*Sí.* Some of us are moving on. It is time. Nothing stays the same, and that is good. I will see you again."

Devon nodded slowly. "*Hasta luego, amigo.*"

"I will say your farewells to Roe and Latigo. They are waiting ahead with fresh horses."

"Thanks."

"Do not be so dissatisfied, my friend," Danza said softly when Devon took a step back. "There is much to life that may yet surprise you."

When Danza walked away, Devon leaned against the oak and stared at the rock-rimmed horizon. He didn't understand why he wasn't satisfied with the way things had turned out. Roger Hartman had met him in Abilene and cleared his name, taking Malone's statement and some of the Bar Z riders' as well. There had been plenty of witnesses to Rogan's admission of guilt, and most had been eager to talk.

It should have left him feeling vindicated. This was different than the last time, when there had been no chance to bring Durant to justice. A bullet had been Durant's judge and jury as well as executioner, and though justice enough, it had left Devon feeling deflated. There must be something in the legal system to give a man the sense of having had his say and seen due process of law. Rogan and Brawley were dead the same as Durant, yet the men who had been involved in the scheme were in jail. It was justice of a sorts, and he should be content.

Devon rolled a smoke and had almost finished it before Johnny Malone joined him under the tree. For a minute nothing was said, then Malone sighed heavily. "I'm leavin'. Lindsay will be worried about me, and I need to get back to the ranch. Maggie wants to see you now, Cimarrón. Listen—" He stopped him with an outstretched hand. "I only did what I thought was right at the time."

Devon's eyes narrowed slightly. Malone looked

flustered, and he couldn't look up at him. Taking a step back, he eyed Johnny Malone and growled, "What the hell are you talking about?"

"You'll find out quick enough."

Maggie was sitting up in bed when Devon paused in the open doorway, looking uneasy and heartbreakingly handsome. She clutched her hands together nervously and prayed that he wouldn't be too angry to listen to everything she had to say. God, what if he was? What if he stopped listening and left? Johnny seemed to think she should wait, but enough time had passed. It was time Devon knew about Joshua.

She managed a smile and patted a spot on the mattress beside her. "Come sit by me, please."

Devon moved toward her warily, his eyes unreadable. She was struck, as she always was, by his careless grace and the way he moved so confidently. Nothing perturbed him, while she was tied up in knots inside.

"How are you feeling?" Devon asked when he'd sat down on the edge of the bed. The mattress dipped with his weight, and Maggie's thigh pressed against his.

"Much better. My shoulder hardly aches at all now." She paused, uncertain how to say what she must. "Devon—"

"Maggie—" they both said at the same time, then halted with an awkward laugh. "You first," he said.

She looked up at him, hoping that he would understand. Light caught in the thick strands of his pale hair, and she reached out to touch it where it curled over his collar in the back.

"Devon, you have a son."

She hadn't meant to be so blunt. She'd meant to preface it better, prepare him a bit more, but the words were out and she held her breath. He just looked at her, nothing registering in his eyes for a moment.

Then a sudden light flared, and his eyes narrowed. "What did you say?"

She inhaled deeply. "I said, we have a son. You and I. He . . . his name is Joshua, and he's seven months old."

"A son."

Silence fell while Devon stared at her narrowly. He seemed unable to absorb it, and she knew he must be mentally counting the days.

"He was born May 10th. He . . . he has your eyes and hair."

Devon rose slowly to his feet, and his hands opened and closed at his sides as he stared down at Maggie. "Damn you," he said at last, his voice a husky rasp. "Why didn't you tell me? Wasn't it important enough to let me know?"

"I . . . I thought you knew at first, that you'd just left me behind knowing I was pregnant. Then when you came after me, I thought you wanted to take him away. That's why I left with you so quietly. I was afraid you'd want him, and when I found out you didn't even know—"

"*Damn!*" Devon took a step back as if afraid to be too close to her. His eyes were ice-cold, and he ignored the hand she held out to him. "You must really think a lot of me, Maggie, to think I'd leave you when you were pregnant. I guess you don't know me at all."

"What was I supposed to think? And when was I supposed to tell you about him? I didn't want you to think you had to marry me. I wanted you to be with me because that was what you wanted more than anything, but when Johnny found out—"

"I knew I should have killed that bastard."

Devon started for the door, and Maggie flung herself from the bed with a terrified cry. "No! Devon, wait, he only did what he thought was right. Hasn't there been enough fighting now? Please wait . . ."

She stumbled and would have fallen if Devon hadn't turned and caught her. He held her to him for a minute, his body stiff with anger, and she began to cry.

Sobs tore at her throat, and finally she felt his taut muscles relax and he began to pat her clumsily on the back. "Don't cry, Maggie," he muttered. "Don't do this to me."

She couldn't help it. Grief and frustration welled so high that she couldn't control her tears any longer. Devon held her against him for another moment, then lifted her in his arms and carried her to the bed to lay her gently on the mattress. He pressed his bandanna into her hand after a few minutes, still patting her awkwardly.

"All right," he said finally, "I guess I understand. But dammit, Maggie, you could have trusted me enough to tell me about the baby."

She stared up at him through her tears. "How? You never said you loved me. How did I know you wouldn't resent being trapped into marriage?"

"Well, it would have been a hell of a lot better than the way we did get married," Devon growled.

"You could have trusted me enough to know I would never have done that to you. Did you really think I'd turn you into the sheriff for the bounty if you didn't marry me?"

"It was hard not to, with you looking up at me and saying it so loud and clear."

"I had to, or Johnny—" She jerked to a halt, unwilling to cause any more enmity between them.

"Yeah, I see that now. It wasn't so easy to see then." He blew out a deep breath, and his mouth curled wryly. "Guess neither one of us had much trust in the other."

"Guess not." Maggie looked down at the bandanna she was twisting in her hands. Her throat hurt, and her eyes felt hot and heavy. The sudden action of leaving her bed had made her shoulder begin to throb, but the fear that Devon would never forgive her overrode everything else. She dared a glance up at him after a moment. He was staring out the far window with a remote gaze that made her heart sink.

Well, she'd known it was a big risk, but one she had to take. Now she'd lost him forever. At least she'd heard him say "I love you" before she lost him. Tears blurred her vision and she stared back down at her hands.

"You . . . you don't have to stay," she said softly, and felt the mattress shift again.

"Is that what you want?"

She looked up. "No."

"Me either."

Maggie tried to ignore the sudden surge of hope in her heart. "What do you want?"

"Damned if I know. I thought—I thought maybe you and I would take it slow, see how we felt after a few months, then maybe give us a try. Now, I don't know."

Her heart fell, and she looked back down at his bandanna. "Oh."

He hooked a finger under her chin and lifted her face. A smile tugged at one corner of his mouth. "What I mean is, we might as well start off giving it a try, seeing as how we have a son I've never seen. I don't know if I'll be a good husband or a good father, but, Maggie, I swear I'll try my best if that's what you want."

"If that's what I want?" She inhaled deeply. "What do you want?"

"To try my damndest. To be with you the rest of my life. I . . . I don't want to be without you, Maggie."

For a moment she didn't speak, then she had to ask, had to hear the truth, even if it hurt. "What about Molly?"

"Molly?" He looked surprised. "What about her?"

"I know you loved her, and you may never love me as much, but will she always be between us?"

"Maggie, honey, she hasn't ever been between us. Oh, I loved Molly, and I guess I'll always feel responsible for her death, but life is for the living. She would be the first to tell me that, and I think she'd be the first to tell me to stop being stupid and hold on to you."

"Do you really?"

He pulled her close, and she could feel the strong thud of his heart beneath her palm. "Yes, I really do. Kate will tell you that much."

"Will your sister like me?"

"She'd better. I put up with that hard-ass husband of hers, and she damn well better like you."

Maggie smiled against his chest, and when he pushed her slightly away and bent to kiss her, she put her arms around his neck and held on. In between kisses, she said in a faintly breathless voice, "I . . . don't intend . . . to give up . . . my medical practice, you know."

"I didn't ask. I'll use my share of the money from the mine to invest in railroads. You keep what you make, if that's what you want. All right?" His mouth moved to the madly beating hollow of her throat, and his hand pushed aside the lace ruching of her nightgown. "You taste good."

Her hand curled into the length of his hair, holding his head still for a moment. "But will you mind?"

"I don't care if you wear pants and skin buffaloes for a living." He nipped lightly at her throat, and Maggie's head fell back, her hair trailing over his arm.

"Somehow—Devon, stop that."

"This?"

She moaned softly, and when he finally stopped kissing her and moved back with a regretful sigh, she reached for him. He caught her hands.

"When you're stronger. We've got the rest of our lives ahead of us, Maggie."

Her eyes widened, and she smiled. "Yes. We do, don't we? Let's not waste a minute of it."

"I don't intend to. I don't ever intend to waste time I could be spending with you. And our son. I'll be with you forever."

"Forever is a long time, Devon."

"I hope so." His tone was fervent. "God, I hope so."

Devon helped Maggie down from her horse, swinging her into his arms to hold her close to him. An icy wind rattled tree limbs and shook the small lean-to for the horses. He felt her shiver despite the heavy coat she wore, and decided to come back to care for the horses. Now, he had to get her inside.

He carried her across the yard despite her protest that she could walk, and stopped at the edge of the porch stretching across the front of the house. A sign hanging above the porch swung wildly, and he glanced up. It read *Dr. M.A. Malone.* Devon's brow lifted.

"Don't you like the name Conrad?"

She flushed. "I didn't feel entitled to it. After all, you didn't exactly want to marry me, you know."

"And you weren't exactly happy with me either, I imagine."

She snuggled closer to him and put her arms around his neck. "That too."

Devon set her on her feet and reached around her to open the door, fumbling with the knob and swearing softly under his breath. The wind was strong and smelled of snow. It was late December now, and a blue norther had swept across Texas the day before, turning the sky and ground that distinct shade of blue that promised bad weather. He'd been forced to push them harder in order to make it to Belton before the snow hit, and he was worried that he'd taxed Maggie's still frail strength.

—"Let me turn the knob the other way," she suggested, and the door swung open easily.

When they stepped inside, the aroma of fresh-baked bread filled the air, making Devon's stomach growl. The front parlor was neat and clean as a pin, though there was no sign of Mrs. Lamb.

He glanced around impatiently. "Where's the baby?"

"With Mrs. Lamb, I should think." Maggie hesitated, looking up at him with a searching gaze. "Devon, he may not come to you quickly. He doesn't know you."

"That's not my fault."

She drew in a deep breath. "No, it's not. But Joshua won't know that. Please—just be patient with him."

"I think I can manage that, if I ever get to see him." Something in her eyes made him realize how hard this was for her, and he tried to curb his impatience. "Maggie honey, I just want to see him. I'm not going to take him away or try to scare him, I promise."

"Oh, I know, it's just that . . ." She paused and gave him an uncertain smile. "I just want you to like him."

He stared at her in disbelief. "Like him? He's my son. I'll do more than *like* him, I'm sure."

"Just—oh, never mind. I'll find Mrs. Lamb. She's probably in the kitchen. If you don't mind giving me a moment or two with Joshua, then I'll bring him to you."

Devon couldn't refuse, though he wanted to insist on seeing the baby immediately. He'd thought about him, wondering what he looked like, if he had any teeth, if he'd want anything to do with a father he'd never met, and now that the moment was almost here, he wasn't certain what to do or say. Would there be a bond between them, or would the baby resent sharing his mother? God, if he'd known about Joshua, he would never have taken Maggie away like he had. Yes, he could certainly give her a few private moments with the child she'd had to leave behind.

"Take your time, honey. I'll wait."

He saw the instant gratitude in her eyes, and bent to kiss her. Maggie leaned into him, her face still pink from the rough wind, her eyes soft and a bright, clear gray. He couldn't help the sudden clutch of his heart or the brief moment of panic that something might still snatch her away from him. He'd come so close to losing her that he still couldn't quite believe that she was here and that she loved him.

"I'll be right back," she whispered when he'd kissed her until they were both breathing a little too hard. "Don't go away."

"You couldn't run me off with a stick."

Devon shrugged off his coat and tossed it over a chair that looked much too dainty to hold a decent-sized man. The room had roses on the wallpaper and pots of greenery that looked badly in need of a watering.

"I'll be right back," Maggie promised, and left him alone. He prowled the parlor as she moved toward the back of the house, and he could hear her opening doors and calling for Mrs. Lamb. He wished he didn't feel so damned awkward and uncertain, and smiled faintly at how Danza would laugh at seeing him nervous about meeting a baby. But this was *his* baby and his son, and he didn't want to scare him.

He ran a hand over his beard and had the rueful thought that he probably should have shaved. Maybe Joshua would be frightened by his beard.

A photograph in a heavy frame caught his eye, and he moved to the small table and lifted it. It was Maggie, and she was holding a tiny child in her arms that had to be his son. Maggie's dark hair was neatly parted in the middle and swept away from her face, showing her perfect features, and a serene smile curved her mouth. The baby, however, looked definitely disgruntled. He grinned. Fair hair crowned the infant's head in wisps that made Devon think of a rooster, and his big eyes stared solemnly at the photographer.

Devon studied the photograph for a long moment, and when he heard a sound behind him, he half-turned to tell Maggie that Joshua had her eyes. Something struck him between the shoulder blades with a solid *thwack*, and he let out a startled yelp as he grabbed at the weapon.

"Take that, you fiend!" a high-pitched voice shrilled, and another blow struck him much too close to the head.

His reflexes kicked in, and he grabbed at what seemed to be a heavy stick at the same time as he registered the fact that it was frail little Mrs. Lamb who was beating the hell out of him. "Hey!" he protested again when she lifted the stick. "What are you doing?"

The stick descended again, and he caught it this time before it could do too much damage, holding it while Mrs. Lamb did her best to wrest it free.

"You devil!" she cried. "How dare you abduct my Miss Maggie! I've called for the sheriff, I have, and you'll be in jail before the hour's up!"

"Wait a minute—ow!"

Mrs. Lamb gave him a solid kick in the shins, and not even his knee-high boots could keep it from hurting. He backed away, staring at her warily.

"Maggie!" he bellowed. "Maggie!"

Mrs. Lamb didn't seem to be in any mood to listen to anything he might say, and he was in danger of being beaten to a pulp by a little old lady if he didn't think of some way to defend himself.

"Oooh, don't you try and trick me," Mrs. Lamb said.

"I saw you drag her in here. What have you done with her?"

"She's looking for you," Devon began, but Mrs. Lamb had found a new weapon, brandishing a coal scuttle in his face.

"How dare you have the nerve to take her away like that, and don't deny that you did it. I'll do what I have to do to keep you from taking Joshua, I will, and you might as well sit down and wait on the sheriff."

"Mrs. Lamb—"

"Devil!"

"Maggie!" Devon narrowly avoided being bashed with the scuttle, and took two more steps back.

Maggie appeared in the doorway, and he felt a wave of relief. "What's going on?" she demanded, moving into the parlor. "Mrs. Lamb—are you all right?"

"Are you, child?" Mrs. Lamb slanted her a quick glance as if afraid to take her eyes off Devon for too long. "I saw him drag you in, and ran next door to send someone for the sheriff. He should be here any minute."

"But . . . but why? Didn't Johnny send you a telegram telling you that I was coming home?"

"I received a telegram, yes, but it said nothing about you returning home, only that you were well." Mrs. Lamb gave Devon a doubtful glance. "Do you mean that you're with him of your own free will?"

"Yes."

"Oh dear." Mrs. Lamb's face colored. "Oh dear me. I have behaved dreadfully. I'm so sorry."

Devon stared at her warily, not quite trusting her yet. Not until she lowered the coal scuttle, anyway. "Did you really send for the sheriff?" When Mrs. Lamb nodded, he muttered, "Damn."

"I'll tell him everything is all right, that it was only a misunderstanding," Mrs. Lamb offered, but Devon had had experience with sheriffs before and knew it would be a bit harder to explain than she thought.

"Where's Joshua?" Maggie asked, and Mrs. Lamb gave a small gasp.

"Oh dear. I hid him." The coal scuttle dropped to the rug on the floor unheeded, and she flew from the room with Maggie right behind her.

Devon stood his ground. He had no intention of getting in the way, not with Mrs. Lamb still unpredictable. In a moment, Maggie was back, and she moved straight to Devon.

"Are you all right?"

"I think so. Damn, for an old woman, she sure packs a mean wallop." He rubbed at the side of his face, and Maggie reached up to examine it.

"You're bleeding, but it's only a shallow cut. I'll tend to it in my office."

"No." Devon moved her hand, his patience gone. "I want to see my son. I've waited long enough."

A faint sound drew his attention, and he grew still. Mrs. Lamb walked toward him, holding a chubby-cheeked baby in her arms. Devon's throat tightened, and he stood like a stone statue, staring at the child. Blue eyes gazed back at him from beneath a fan of thick lashes that made him think of Maggie. Hair so blond it looked almost white covered Joshua's head, and it was long enough to fall against his tiny eyebrows. His fist was in his mouth and wet, and he wore what looked to Devon like a dress.

"Why have you got my son in skirts?" he demanded, and Maggie laughed.

"Because it's easier to change his napkin. Don't worry. He'll be wearing pants when he's old enough." She paused, then asked, "Do you want to hold him?"

Devon felt suddenly too big and awkward, and didn't know if he wanted to hold such a small human being. "What if I drop him?"

"He'll scream the house down, so don't." Maggie took the child from Mrs. Lamb and kissed him, then turned and held him out to Devon.

He was surprised to see his hands shake as he reached for him and was startled by how heavy he was. Joshua gave a small cry of distress and held his arms out to his mother, but she took a step back.

"Talk to him, Devon."

"God—what do I say?"

"Start with hello." She smiled shakily, and he could see that she was almost as nervous as he was. Almost.

Devon shifted the squirming, whining baby in his arms a bit, turning him awkwardly. His stomach knotted when Joshua looked up at him with a frown, tears making his eyes shine as his lower lip quivered slightly.

"Hey, little fella," he said huskily. Joshua's faint brows drew down in a frown, and his lower lip jutted out at an alarming angle. Devon felt panicky and looked up at Maggie. "He's going to cry."

"Maybe. *Talk* to him, Devon."

"What do I say?"

Maggie's smile was encouraging. "Anything that comes to mind. Tell him you're his father. Tell him he's got pretty eyes. He responds to the tone of your voice more than what you say, though he does know a few words."

Devon cleared his throat again. He felt foolish, and when Joshua began to whimper, he walked slowly to where a fire burned in the grate, jogging him up and down.

"Hey, Josh, your mama's back now. I'm your old man, and I hope you like me. I'm not so bad once you get used to me a bit."

Joshua's lower lip was still thrust out, but he was no longer whimpering. Instead, he stared up at Devon with a wide-eyed gaze that was both penetrating and assessing. Devon wished again that he'd shaved off his beard, but then Joshua was reaching up to brush his chubby hand over the bristles. He grinned suddenly, a wobbly grin that showed four shiny teeth. Devon tried not to wince when the baby tugged firmly at his beard, and reached up to loosen his grip a bit.

When Joshua's hand closed around his finger, he felt an odd loosening in his chest as if another piece of the wall he'd built so long ago had crumbled. He'd grown accustomed to loving Maggie, but had wondered how he'd feel about a child he didn't know, even if it was his. Now he felt an overwhelming emotion that was unfamiliar and vaguely frightening, while at the same time comforting.

Blinking, Devon was astonished to find his vision blurred. He looked up at Maggie and saw tears streaming down her face. He couldn't speak, couldn't swallow past the thick lump in his throat.

Maggie moved toward them and put her arms around him and the baby, sobbing softly. Devon wanted to tell her that he loved her, that everything was going to be all right, but he still couldn't force any words out.

It was left to Mrs. Lamb to say shakily, "It's Christmas. A time for love and family, and I'm happy to see that you've both come to your senses at last." She smiled broadly. "Well, I guess all's well that ends well."

# Epilogue

The hot summer sun blazed down, and Caitlin Lassiter gave a groan. "Is it always this hot in Texas?"

Maggie laughed. "Only in the summer. Don't try and tell me it doesn't get hot in Colorado."

"Not like this," Caitlin said fervently. She waved a fan, stirring up a breeze that shifted a long, coppery curl of hair over her face. "Do you know, somehow I knew I'd like you," she added suddenly. "Devon wouldn't fall in love with anyone who wasn't right for him, but still—I was nervous about meeting you."

Astonished, Maggie echoed, "Nervous about meeting me?"

"Yes." A faint smile curved Caitlin's mouth. "Devon's been alone so long, I was worried he might have fallen in love with the first woman he met who didn't work in a saloon."

"You underestimate your brother greatly," Maggie said dryly. "I had the devil of a time making him fall in love with me."

Caitlin's brows lifted. "Really? That's what he said about you . . ."

Footsteps sounded on the front porch, and both women turned to see Devon and Jake. Maggie's heart leaped. Every time she was away from him for even five minutes, the sight of him again made her pulses race and her heart swell with love.

Devon was sweeping off his hat and raking a hand through thick blond hair that was darkened with

427

sweat. "It's hot as blazes," he muttered, sinking down into the chair next to Maggie and taking the glass of lemonade she held out for him. "You two have the right idea, sitting out here on the porch where it's almost cool and drinking iced lemonade. Where are the babies?"

"Inside with Mrs. Lamb. She's put them down for a nap while it's so hot." Maggie tucked her hand into the crook of Devon's arm, watching as he gulped down the lemonade in two swallows. "Did you finish your business?"

Devon grinned. "Kinda. Old Jake here has some pretty good ideas at times."

Jake Lassiter's brows lifted. "*Old* Jake? I can tie you in knots without breaking a sweat, Conrad. Try and keep that in mind when you start handing out insults."

"I have the greatest respect for my elders, Lassiter. I wouldn't dream of letting you get tired trying it."

"Both of you be quiet." Caitlin tapped Jake on the arm with her folded fan. "Tell us what happened in Abilene. We're dying to know."

Jake stretched his long legs out in front of his chair and leaned back. "Your brother just became a major stockholder in the T&P. He had some innovative ideas and a lot of money, and they were pretty damn glad to see him at their board meeting. Of course, it's not quite that simple, but I don't feel like going into all of it now. David Brawley did a lot of damage to the company in Abilene, and Devon told them how to recoup some of their shipping losses without losing a great deal of their capital."

Maggie eyed Devon. "So you're going to become a railroad tycoon?"

"Hardly." He shrugged. "All those years of robbing trains did give me some practical experience, however, and my experience with Brawley's little scheme gives me knowledge of how to keep it from happening like that again."

"What do you intend to do?"

"Oh, I suggested they hire a few good men that I can recommend, then send them around checking up. I also gave them a good idea of what to check, since it's obvious to me that they would have lost money as long as Brawley could keep stealing from them."

Devon stood, pulling Maggie up with him. "I bought you something while I was in Abilene."

"What?"

"Come with me and find out."

Ignoring Jake's knowing grin and Caitlin's soft demands to see what he'd bought, Devon walked Maggie across the front porch and down the steps. A huge live oak spread heavy branches out like thick arms, and he stopped her under the shade. Maggie waited, watching his face as he reached into his vest pocket.

An errant breeze stirred his hair, brushing it over his brows and into his eyes, eyes that were no longer icy and cold, but warm and loving. In the past six months, she and Devon had managed to bridge most of the barriers between them, though at times there were still misunderstandings. He had finally seemed to accept the fact that she loved him, and she knew he loved her. It was evident in the gentle way he touched her and in the way he loved her night.

It occurred to her that she'd never known she could be so contented with life or that even when things went wrong, it would matter so little. Though she and Johnny would probably never have the same closeness they'd once had, she was able to think of him without resentment now. She even understood why her brother had felt driven to do the things he had. Maybe now, with Lindsay at his side, he would realize that he couldn't run anyone else's life. It had been a hard lesson for all of them.

"Here. I saw this, and—" Devon paused and gave her a faint smile. "I wanted you to have it."

Maggie took the small box from him and opened it. Her eyes widened, and she couldn't help a gasp. "Devon! It's beautiful! But why—?"

"You never got a wedding ring, honey. Until lately, I haven't had the money to get you a nice one. Let me put it on your finger."

Tears stung her eyes, and Maggie blinked down at the square-cut diamond glittering in a setting of twisted gold. It was lovely and delicate, with the gold wrapped in a heart shape around the diamond. Her hand shook when Devon lifted it and slid the ring onto her finger.

"It fits perfectly," she whispered, and couldn't help a small sob.

"Then why are you crying?"

"Because . . . I'm happy. And besides—" She leaned against his broad chest and slid her arms around him, laying her cheek against him. "I'm always emotional when I'm pregnant."

His arms tightened, and then he pushed her away a little and tilted her face up with a finger under her chin. "Are you sure?"

She laughed softly. "I'm a doctor. I'm fairly sure this time. Besides, it's not like we've been careful."

Devon grinned. "I'm not complainin'."

"But are you glad?"

"You bet. Josh needs a little sister to worry him. He's getting spoiled."

Maggie closed her eyes when he kissed her. All the bad memories were just that now—bad memories. Now there was this—Devon holding her, kissing her, loving her. And as long as she had him, nothing else mattered.

Kissing her, Devon had the same thought. He'd let go of the past at last, even his anger. Even Molly.

Somehow, he thought that Molly would have approved of Maggie, and that if she could see them, she'd be happy for him.

God, after all this time, all the long, lonely years when he'd given up on everything but harsh survival, to have found Maggie was nothing short of a miracle. He prayed that he would never let her down, never hurt her again. There had been enough of that. Now he had a family, and the life he'd once led was a fading memory.

Devon broke off the kiss and held her slightly away from him. "Where are the babies taking a nap?" he asked in a husky voice that made her eyes light with laughter.

"In our bedroom. Why do you ask?"

"Hell. There's no privacy around here anymore. Kate and Jake should go back to Colorado."

"What an ungracious host you are."

"Not ungracious. Just selfish. I want my wife, and I damn well don't want to wait."

Taking her by the hand, Devon started toward the small stable in the rear. Maggie laughed softly, and when they reached the hay-filled regions and he shut the door behind them, she began unbuttoning her blouse. Devon leaned back against the closed doors and watched with appreciation as she slowly discarded the thin cotton blouse and began to work on the buttons of her skirt.

"You're a complete hussy," he said in a voice that sounded strained and raspy even to his own ears. "Thank God."

He reached for her and drew her into his arms, and Maggie whispered as she began to unbutton his shirt, "I thank God every day for you, Devon Conrad."

Devon undressed her quickly and grew impatient when she lingered over his garments. He shed them without regard to buttons or rips, then carried her to a high pile of hay and tossed a blanket over it before placing her on the bed. He couldn't wait; he entered her slowly, her name a husky groan on his lips. "Maggie, my love . . ."

He held her close, relishing the feel of her under him in the hay, the soft little moans she made and the way she said his name. Everything that had brought them to this day, this moment, he'd do again. He'd do it all again for Maggie, for her love.

## TO MY READERS:

This is for all of you who read WILDFLOWER and wrote asking for Devon's story. I hope you enjoyed it as much as I enjoyed writing it. Devon touched my heart, too, and I was pleased to discover that so many of you felt the same way. I thank all of you who wrote to me and hope that you're pleased with WILDEST HEART.

As a point of interest, Belle Plain, Texas, was an actual town in the late 1870s and early 1880s until the county seat was moved to Baird where the railroad built a station. Though I used some fact and tried to remain true to the setting, none of the events in the story actually happened.

If you'd like to let me know how you felt about WILDEST HEART, you may write to me in care of:

ZEBRA BOOKS, 475 Park Avenue South, N.Y., N.Y. 10016.

Please send a self-addressed, stamped envelope for a reply.

Best wishes,

Virginia Brown

# DISCOVER DEANA JAMES!

**CAPTIVE ANGEL**                    (2524, $4.50/$5.50)
Abandoned, penniless, and suddenly responsible for the biggest
tobacco plantation in Colleton County, distraught Caroline Gil-
lard had no time to dissolve into tears. By day the willowy red-
head labored to exhaustion beside her slaves . . . but each night
left her restless with longing for her wayward husband. She'd
make the sea captain regret his betrayal until he begged her to
take him back!

**MASQUE OF SAPPHIRE**                    (2885, $4.50/$5.50)
Judith Talbot-Harrow left England with a heavy heart. She was
going to America to join a father she despised and a sister she
distrusted. She was certainly in no mood to put up with the insulting actions of the arrogant Yankee privateer who boarded her
ship, ransacked her things, then "apologized" with an indecent,
brazen kiss! She vowed that someday he'd pay dearly for the liberties he had taken and the desires he had awakened.

**SPEAK ONLY LOVE**                    (3439, $4.95/$5.95)
Long ago, the shock of her mother's death had robbed Vivian
Marleigh of the power of speech. Now she was being forced to
marry a bitter man with brandy on his breath. But she could not
say what was in her heart. It was up to the viscount to spark the
fires that would melt her icy reserve.

**WILD TEXAS HEART**                    (3205, $4.95/$5.95)
Fan Breckenridge was terrified when the stranger found her near-
naked and shivering beneath the Texas stars. Unable to remember
who she was or what had happened, all she had in the world was
the deed to a patch of land that might yield oil . . . and the fierce
loving of this wildcatter who called himself Irons.

*Available wherever paperbacks are sold, or order direct from the
Publisher. Send cover price plus 50¢ per copy for mailing and
handling to Penguin USA, P.O. Box 999, c/o Dept. 17109,
Bergenfield, NJ 07621. Residents of New York and Tennessee
must include sales tax. DO NOT SEND CASH.*

# FEEL THE FIRE IN CAROL FINCH'S ROMANCES!

**BELOVED BETRAYAL** (2346, $3.95)

Sabrina Spencer donned a gray wig and veiled hat before blackmailing rugged Ridge Tanner into guiding her to Fort Canby. But the costume soon became her prison—the beauty had fallen head over heels in love!

**LOVE'S HIDDEN TREASURE** (2980, $4.50)

Shandra d'Evereux felt her heart throb beneath the stolen map she'd hidden in her bodice when Nolan Elliot swept her out onto the veranda. It was hard to concentrate on her mission with that wily rogue around!

**MONTANA MOONFIRE** (3263, $4.95)

Just as debutante Victoria Flemming-Cassidy was about to marry an oh-so-suitable mate, the towering preacher, Dru Sullivan flung her over his shoulder and headed West! Suddenly, Tori realized she had been given the best present for a bride: a night of passion with a real man!

**THUNDER'S TENDER TOUCH** (2809, $4.50)

Refined Piper Malone needed bounty-hunter, Vince Logan to recover her swindled inheritance. She thought she could coolly dismiss him after he did the job, but she never counted on the hot flood of desire she felt whenever he was near!

*Available wherever paperbacks are sold, or order direct from the Publisher. Send cover price plus 50¢ per copy for mailing and handling to Penguin USA, P.O. Box 999, c/o Dept. 17109, Bergenfield, NJ 07621. Residents of New York and Tennessee must include sales tax. DO NOT SEND CASH.*